BEHAVING *Badly* IN VEGAS

BEHAVING Badly IN VEGAS

Sabrina Wagner

Stay Connected!

Want to be the first to learn book news, updates and more?
Sign up for my Newsletter.

https://www.subscribepage.com/sabrinawagnernewsletter

Want to know about my new releases and upcoming sales?
Stay connected on:

Facebook~Instagram~Twitter~TikTok
Goodreads~BookBub~Amazon

I'd love to hear from you.
Visit my website to connect with me.

www.SabrinaWagnerAuthor.com

Books by Sabrina Wagner

Hearts Trilogy
Hearts on Fire
Shattered Hearts
Reviving My Heart

Wild Hearts Trilogy
Wild Hearts
Secrets of the Heart
Eternal Hearts

Forever Inked Novels
Tattooed Hearts: Tattooed Duet #1
Tattooed Souls: Tattooed Duet #2
Smoke and Mirrors
Regret and Redemption
Sin and Salvation

Vegas Love Series
What Happens in Vegas
Billionaire Bachelor in Vegas
Behaving Badly in Vegas
Technically Yours in Vegas

Spotify Playlist

Notorious~ Adelitas Way
River~ Bishop Briggs
Legends Are Made~ Sam Tinnesz
Earned It~ The Weeknd
Eyes Closed~ Halsey
Own It~ Adelitas Way, New Medicine
Unstoppable~ Sia
What Was I Made For?~ Billie Eilish
Shatter Me~ Lindsey Stirling, Lzzy Hale
Bring Me To Life~ Evanescence

Listen and Enjoy!

Prologue
15 Months Ago

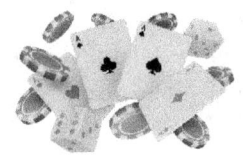

It's been said that power corrupts.

I disagreed.

It wasn't power that corrupted me. It was the pursuit of power.

My brother Trent and I were in competition with each other from the day we met.

He was the legitimate heir.

I was the bastard.

There was no love lost between us, only the desire to be the favored child and to reap the benefits of that title. The prize was Mystique, the Vegas resort and casino that was our legacy. One day, our father would retire, and the hotel would be handed down.

There would only be one CEO, and I'd do anything for it to be me.

Nice guys finished last, and I wasn't a loser. I'd cheat, steal, and lie to get what I wanted. I just never imagined Trent would make it so easy for me.

Sleeping with Gia, our new director of entertainment and events was a violation of company policy. He'd been warned.

I leaned against the wall in my father's office, waiting for my brother.

He walked in, finding not only my father, but me and his mother, Rose, as well. "What the hell is going on?"

"Shut the door," my father said.

"Family meeting? It's been a long time since we've had one of those." He nonchalantly sipped his coffee, not having a clue what was about to hit him.

My father leaned on his desk and folded his hands. "We got your email." When Trent didn't respond, he continued, "As a matter of fact, everyone on this floor got it."

"I didn't send an email. To anyone." He looked at the three of us, searching for answers. "What's going on?"

"You really should be more careful," I piped in.

My father turned his laptop toward Trent and pressed play on the attached video. I didn't need to see it to know what he was watching. The video I took of him and Gia fucking in his office wasn't the best quality, but there was no doubt who it was and what they were doing.

I could barely keep the smirk from my face. His secret escapade with Gia was over. I finally won.

His hand reached out and smacked the laptop closed. "Who's seen this?"

I chuckled from my perch by the door. "Everyone."

"I didn't send that. I didn't even make the tape! My office is supposed to be private!"

"It came from *your* email," I said.

He looked to our father and Rose for help. "I swear to God, I did not make that video, and I certainly wouldn't share it if I had."

Rose squeezed his hand. "We suspected you didn't."

What? I'd been careful. I snuck around for weeks, spying on him and collecting evidence. There wasn't a single thing that traced back to me.

"Then who did? Who would do something like this, not just to me, but to Gia?" Trent asked.

2

"I'm guessing the culprit is in this room." My father's gaze landed on me.

My brother jumped out of his chair and charged, taking me to the ground. "You fucking piece of shit!" He only got one good punch in before my father pulled him off. "Let me go!" Trent shook with rage.

"Sit down, son!" my father ordered. "We're going to get to the bottom of this." He pushed Trent into a chair against his will and turned to me. "Why?"

I straightened my lapels and wiped the blood from under my nose. "I knew there was something going on between them, but I had to prove it. Say goodbye to your job, Trent." He'd specifically been warned not to sleep with Gia and, as usual, he thought the rules didn't apply to him. My brother was a pompous asshole, and it was time he got put in his place. It was too bad the pretty redhead got caught in the crosshairs.

Trent dropped his head between his hands. "What about Gia? She's going to be humiliated."

"She put in her resignation this morning," Rose whispered.

That was a shame. I was going to miss the sexy little minx.

"You're fired," my dad said calmly.

I started to laugh until I realized my father's eyes were on me and not Trent. I pointed to my chest. "You're firing me? He's the one who broke company policy."

My father shook his head. "What you did goes so far beyond that, not to mention illegal. You've damaged the reputation of this hotel, violated the privacy of my employees, humiliated Gia, and cost me an event coordinator."

"Gia? That's what you're worried about?" I huffed. "Pretty pieces of ass are a dime a dozen. She's totally disposable."

"She's not disposable, you stupid fuck! I'm in love with her!" Trent shouted.

My father smiled—fucking smiled—at him. "Then you better go get her and bring her back."

"You're not firing him?" I asked incredulously. "That job is supposed to be mine!"

3

"You have thirty minutes to clean out your office before I call security to escort you out. You've burned your last bridge with this family." My father got up from his desk and opened the door.

"Fuck you! I don't need this family or this bullshit job!" I stormed down the hallway to my office where a box had already been placed on my desk. I opened the drawers and grabbed the few personal items I had, dumping them in the box. I ripped my Stanford diplomas from the wall and closed my laptop.

I should have known no matter how hard I worked, no matter how much I did for this company, I was never going to get the recognition I deserved. Trent always had been, and always would be, the golden child who could do no wrong.

I was the fuckup. The one who always had to prove himself. My best would never be good enough and I was done.

Done with this family.

Done with this job.

Done pretending to give a shit.

They didn't want me here? Then I was gone. I didn't need any of them.

Arrivederci. Sayonara. Adios.

There was only one place I wanted to be… The Sapphire Club. I'd get drunk, watch the strippers, and maybe get a blow job to round out the night. And I was going to do it all on the company credit card. One last *fuck you*. I was owed at least that much.

I'd worry about my lack of employment tomorrow. It wouldn't be hard to find a job. Any company would be lucky to hire the former CFO of Mystique.

Tonight, I was throwing myself the biggest pity party in history. One last hurrah before shit got real. I'd deal with the aftermath later.

4

Chapter 1
Hunter

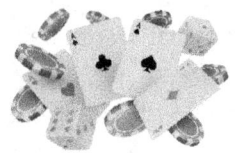

I was not a good man. I was born irredeemably bad. Unlovable. Even my own mother didn't want me.

She dropped me on my father's doorstep when I was only three. I didn't remember much about my mom, but I did remember running after her green car, chasing the taillights until I reached the bottom of the driveway. A strange man scooped me up as I screamed and flailed, carrying me back to a house I didn't know. A family that wasn't mine.

I never saw her again.

That memory hadn't surfaced in years, but the pink bundle sitting outside my apartment door brought it back like it happened yesterday. Almost thirty years in the past. I should have been over it, but some wounds were so deep they never fully healed. They scabbed, and all it took was an unintentional scrape for them to bleed all over again.

I didn't particularly like kids. They were noisy, dirty, and complete libido killers. I had no desire to be around them.

"Who the fuck are you?" I whispered as I reached for the envelope pinned to the fuzzy blanket covered in pink kittens. Running my fingers over the envelope, my stomach turned as the baby kicked her chubby legs and smiled up at me with eyes as cerulean blue as the ocean. Eyes that matched mine.

Not a good sign.

For a minute, I considered toeing the carrier in front of old Mrs. Hadley's door and shredding the unopened envelope. I could pretend I never saw it and walk away. That would be the easy thing to do, but not the right thing.

I'd never been big on doing the right thing. In fact, I went out of my way to do all the wrong things. It was expected. I was never going to fit into the perfect mold the Dorseys tried to shove me into. I wasn't one of them. Not really.

I was more of an annoying fire ant that showed up to destroy their perfect picnic.

Luckily for them, I'd extracted myself from their lives. We'd barely talked in well over a year. My job at the bank sucked, but I made it work. Admittedly, the stunt I pulled at Mystique was low, but I never expected my father to fire me. I should have known that even when my brother… correction, half brother… broke company policy, my father would take his side. We were practically Vegas royalty—Trent was the heir, and I was the surprise spare no one counted on.

Tossing the diaper bag over my shoulder, I picked up the carrier, took it inside my apartment, and set it on the coffee table. I dropped onto the couch and stared at the unexpected visitor. Having a baby in my apartment was a first.

There was no way this could be reality. It had to be some crazy dream my sick mind conjured from deep in my subconscious.

Abandonment issues.

That's what my therapist called it.

6

It was his explanation for me banging every available female in Vegas over the last ten years.

I honestly didn't see how the two were related.

I was a horny fucker. The explanation didn't get any simpler than that and now it caught up with me in the form of the *present* left at my door.

Running a hand over my jaw, I leaned forward, resting my elbows on my legs and stared at the tiny person on my coffee table. "Who the fuck is your mom? And why did she bring you here?"

Her eyes drifted closed, and her little lips sucked at the pacifier shoved in her mouth.

"You were the last thing I expected today," I whispered.

I turned the envelope over and over in my hands. It wasn't anything fancy, just a plain white envelope with my name scrawled across the front in loopy handwriting. Blowing out a breath, I ran my finger under the flap and opened it. Stuffed inside were two sheets of paper. The first was a birth certificate.

Name: Carina Ashton Dorsey

I cringed. She'd given the kid my last name. According to the paperwork in my hand, baby Carina was almost six months old.

Mother's Name: Jennifer Ann Johnson

Didn't ring a bell. Not a single one. That shouldn't have been a surprise. It's not like I exchanged contact info with my flings. It was called a fling for a reason. Names never seemed important, except that, at this moment, they were very fucking important.

Father's Name: Hunter Dorsey

No middle name, because why the fuck would she know my middle name when I didn't even know her first? I hadn't signed any paperwork, but my name was there anyway.

Fuck!

Just because this piece of paper pronounced the baby was mine didn't make it true. I wrapped it up religiously. Didn't want a mistake like me to happen.

7

But those blue eyes… they were another piece of evidence that pointed in my direction.

I unfolded the second piece of paper, a note written in the same loopy handwriting as the envelope.

> *Hunter~*
>
> *You may not remember me, but I remember you quite well. You drank yourself stupid at The Sapphire Club where I worked, then offered me ten thousand dollars for a private night in the Jewel Room. It was only supposed to be a bit of fun and the money was too good to turn down. Little did I know that encounter would change my life.*
>
> *I thought I'd be a good mom, but it turned out I wasn't built for motherhood. I'm entrusting you with Carina's well-being, as I'm sure the life you can provide for her will far surpass the life I could provide.*

That alone told me Jennifer Johnson didn't know me at all. I had money. Didn't mean I knew shit about raising a kid. She could have hit me up for child support instead of dropping a baby on my doorstep.

> *Carina likes being snuggled during her feedings.* Yada, yada, yada.
>
> *She's a good girl and shouldn't have to pay for our mistakes. Give her the life she deserves.*

Our mistakes? How could I be part of an *our* when I didn't even know who this woman was? I'd fucked up a lot in my life, but this took the cake. No way was I qualified to be a dad.

I peeked into the diaper bag. There was a can of formula, diapers, and a bunch of other baby stuff I didn't know what to do with. I really should have pushed the carrier in front of Mrs. Hadley's door. She would have known what to do. A sinking feeling took up residence in my chest and stomach, making it hard to breathe. I was in way over my head.

Swallowing down my pride, I called the only person who could help. If anybody knew how to raise a bastard, it was my father.

Chapter 2
Charli

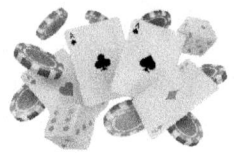

"I need a favor," I said, setting the bag from his favorite deli on my brother's desk.

He peeked in the bag. "You're bribing me with turkey and cheese?"

"Don't be silly. There's extra avocado and salt and vinegar chips." It was a stretch, but I was out of options and Tom was my only hope.

"Spit it out, Charlotte." He opened the bag of chips and offered me one. I shook my head in refusal, never understanding how he could eat those things. He shrugged his shoulders and popped a chip in his mouth, savoring the flavor on his tongue. "You know Trent hates personal distractions, so if we could hurry this up, I'd appreciate it."

"Ugh! I still don't understand why you're someone's personal assistant. You're way too smart for this job." My brother had an IQ of one hundred forty-five and had a perfect score on his SAT in high school. It was a nightmare having him as an older brother. I never lived up to the expectations he set for us with our parents. Imagine their disappointment realizing their daughter was average. Oh, the horror.

He pushed his glasses up his nose. "It's temporary and it pays the bills. I'm this close to making a breakthrough." Tom was a self-proclaimed computer nerd, spending hours holed up in his apartment working on a secret project. He tried to explain it to me once, but he might as well have been speaking a foreign language for all I understood.

"I finished my physical therapy today," I said, starting with the positive. I'd come a long way in the last four months.

Tom looked at the brace on my leg. "How does it feel?"

"It's still sore, sometimes stiff, but they want me to continue strength training on my own." I *was* an aerial performer for one of the biggest shows in Vegas. As a kid, I drove my parents crazy with my constant need to flip and spin, so they signed me up for gymnastics. It didn't take long for me to realize my true passion wasn't just to flip and spin but to do it while suspended thirty feet above a stage. The more challenging, the better.

"When are you getting back in the air?"

I pulled a chair over and plopped in it. "That's where the favor comes in. The doctor said it would probably be another six months before I would be ready. Now that my official therapy is done, the show has put me on leave with no compensation until I can perform again. If I ever can. My apartment lease is almost up, and I'm broke. I need your help."

"Fuuuck... this is worth more than a turkey-and-cheese sandwich."

He wasn't wrong. "Why do you keep dismissing the avocado? You love avocados."

He scowled and shoved another chip into his mouth.

"I'm happy to stay on the couch. Please... only until I find another job. I'm desperate."

He rolled his eyes. "Like I'd say no. I'll clean out my office for you. There's no bed, but there's a couch. Where are you going to look for a job?"

It was a valid question and one I'd been pondering since my skills of climbing a silk rope in under five seconds and twirling without barfing weren't very marketable outside of show business. "I don't know. I can't stay on my feet for very long, so waitressing is out, along with half a dozen other jobs." I tapped a finger against my lips. "Think you could ask Trent about a job at Mystique for me?"

Tom stopped chewing midbite and stared at me. He swallowed the turkey as if it were a rock making its way down his throat. "Absolutely not! You don't want to work for him."

"Maybe not, but I need a job. What did you call this? Temporary? Surely, I can file paperwork, or whatever it is you do."

My brother scoffed. "I don't file paperwork. It's a lot more complicated than that, and the man is… difficult."

A door slammed and the devil himself strode down the hallway toward us. I'd only met him once before. He was handsome, but I'd heard enough stories from my brother to know not to let his good looks fool me. "Tom! Coffee!"

My brother scurried off to the break room like a scolded puppy. I probably didn't want to work for Trent Dorsey, but surely there was something in this hotel I could do. I pushed out of my seat and thrust my hand out. "You probably don't remember me, but I'm Tom's sister, Charlotte. Well, my friends call me Charli." He quirked an eyebrow and I got the message. We weren't friends. "Charlotte Bently."

He ignored my outstretched hand and shoved his fists in his pockets. "I remember. What can I do for you, Miss Bently?"

I let my hand fall as if it hadn't been rejected. "I'm in need of a job. Temporarily. I was wondering if there might be something available here at Mystique."

Trent let out a sigh. "I can send you down to HR and put in a good word for you. It's the best I can do. No promises. No guarantees. I don't like to vouch for people, but Tom has been an excellent employee. I trust it runs in the family and you won't disappoint me."

Without thinking, I lunged at him, knocking him back a step, and wrapped my arms around his tall body. I clung to him a bit too long because… whoa! There was some solid muscle hiding underneath that suit. "Thank you so much! You don't know how much I appreciate this."

"Charlotte!" I unwound myself from Trent at the sound of my brother's voice. "What the hell are you doing?" he growled.

12

I bounced on my toes. "Mr. Dorsey is going to help me get a job. Here. At Mystique. We can carpool together."

Tom handed Trent his coffee. "I'm so sorry about that, sir. My sister is… passionate."

Trent wiped invisible lint from his suit and straightened his jacket. "It's fine. I'm happy to help," he said with a scowl and a sip of his fresh coffee.

If that was his happy face, I certainly didn't want to see his unhappy face. "Thank you again. I can't tell you how much I appreciate this."

"I haven't done anything yet. I'm not even sure we have any job openings."

I nodded in understanding. Honestly, I'd scrub toilets if it meant I'd be able to afford my own place. Okay, maybe not scrub toilets, but anything else. My brother was great, as far as brothers go, but he was a bit uptight and introverted, practically married to his computer.

"Sir, excuse me for asking, but I saw Hunter in the conference room? Is he coming back to Mystique?" My brother asked Trent.

Trent's hand squeezed the foam cup until the dark liquid brimmed. "I don't know. There's a bit of a family issue going on." His jaw ticced. "I need to let Gia know he's here."

As Trent walked away, I whispered to Tom, "Who's Hunter?"

"Trent's brother."

"Who is Gia? And why would she care if Trent's brother is here?"

"Gia is Trent's wife. She works here too. There's bad blood between the three of them," Tom said without further explanation.

"Oh. Care to share?" It was so like my brother to only tell half a story and leave out all the juicy parts.

"Actually, no. I don't care to share," he snapped. "I'm not into spreading gossip and if you plan on working here, you'll need to learn to quell your curiosity. Mystique prides itself on discretion. They pay us well to not see or hear anything."

"Jeez. Lighten up a little. It was just a question."

"Questions like that can get you fired. Keep your head down around here."

I crossed my arms like a stubborn child. "Fine." Living with him was going to be miserable and I already dreaded it.

Trent came back down the hall, followed by a gorgeous redhead. He reached for her hand, and she quickly twined her fingers with his as they disappeared behind a closed door.

Penny hurried over and splayed her hands on Tom's desk, displaying her huge diamond ring. "Did you hear?" she asked, slightly out of breath. I knew who Penny was. She was another PA at Mystique, and I had a suspicion my brother crushed on her a while ago, although he never admitted it to me. She married the most eligible billionaire in Vegas. It was a Cinderella story that had made front page news and was covered extensively by the *Las Vegas Not So Confidential*. The latest stories speculated she was pregnant with a big red arrow pointing at her maybe baby bump. I tried to sneak a peek, but it was hard to tell.

"What's going on?" he whispered and leaned in close. For someone who, minutes before, lectured me about spreading gossip, he was all ears.

"Hunter's bad behavior finally caught up with him. A baby was dropped off on his doorstep. The paternity test results came in and it's his. Can you believe it? This is crazy. Mind blown," she rambled, barely taking a breath.

I didn't know who Hunter was or why this info was so mind-blowing. It wasn't like illegitimate babies were a scandal in Vegas. With all the crazy shit that went on in this city, it was astonishing traditional families existed at all. Even the term *traditional* was challenged on a daily basis. Family was what you chose it to be, not what society decreed. Love was love. Traditional roles were less important than the intensity of the relationship.

"Get the fuck out!" my brother exclaimed. "Ten dollars says he'll try to wiggle his way back into the family business."

Penny visibly shivered. "I hope not. With what he did to Gia and Trent, he can't be trusted."

What did he do to Gia and Trent?

"Yoo-hoo. Just a reminder that I'm standing right here. Care to fill me in?" I asked.

14

"Penny, you remember my sister Charlotte, right?" Tom motioned to me with a flick of his wrist as if I were a pesky child.

Penny smiled at me. "Of course. I'm sorry for being so rude, it's… gah! I love good office gossip, and this is big. Big!" The petite brunette threw her arms in the air and shook her hands like she was in a Broadway musical. "I can't say too much," she whispered. "It's all very hush-hush."

"This is going to throw Trent over the edge," Tom groaned. "He's going to be even more miserable to work for with Hunter creeping around again. Those two are like oil and water."

"We don't even know if he's coming back, but why else would he be here?"

My head ping-ponged between my brother and Penny as they contemplated all the scenarios. For someone who despised gossip, my brother was as invested as a clucking magpie, leaning into Penny and throwing out possibilities.

The gossip was a waste of my time, especially since it was difficult to be invested in the life of someone I'd never met. My top priority was finding a job, preferably one that would pay me enough to make staying with my brother short-lived.

I nudged him with my hip. "I've got to head out. Can you tell me where the HR department is?"

Pulling himself away from Penny, Tom hugged me. "Good luck. I hope they have something available. Go back to reception and hang a left."

The directions were vague, but surely I could find my way. I should have typed up a résumé or something. Going to apply for a job empty-handed was completely unprofessional. I looked down at my black yoga pants and Taylor Swift T-shirt and groaned. Not only did I not have a résumé, but my clothes hardly screamed *give me a job at an upscale hotel*. Tom always looked sharp, even if I thought the bow ties were a bit much.

The door at the end of the hall burst open and a blond-haired man with the eyes of an angry angel clenched his fists and stomped out, turning back to address the people chasing behind him. "I shouldn't have expected more than crumbs from you. You've treated me like a black sheep my entire life!"

15

"Who's that?" I whispered.

"The Dorseys," Tom whispered back. "Mr. and Mrs. Dorsey, Trent and Gia, and the one yelling is Hunter.

"You've alienated yourself from this family, not the other way around. Actions have consequences," the older man said. "You can't start back at the top. You need to earn your trust back in this family. A junior position in the financial office is all I can offer right now."

"We do care about you," the woman said. "Getting a live-in nanny is the only sensible option. I'll send Ms. Peters over. She's a lovely woman and would be wonderful for the baby."

Hunter continued down the hall toward us. "I'm sure she would, but I'm also not under any illusion that she wouldn't report everything I do right back to you. I'll find my own damn nanny."

My ears perked up. *Nanny?* It wasn't exactly the type of job I had in mind, but I liked kids. How much trouble could one baby be?

Reckless.

That's what my mother always called me.

I called it adventurous. Exciting. Exhilarating. I never met a challenge I wouldn't dive into headfirst.

My mind made up, I stepped into the path of the charging bull. "I'll do it."

Hunter jerked to a stop, hands on his hips. "Do what?"

He was even more attractive up close. His features looked sculpted from ice, his eyes cold as the Arctic. "I'll be your nanny. I'm good with babies, and more importantly, I need a job," I said, jutting my chin out.

A collective gasp sounded from Penny and Tom.

Hunter eyed me up and down with a smirk on his handsome face, no doubt taking in my very unprofessional attire. "And who the hell are you?"

I held my hand out. "Charlotte Bently, but you can call me Charli."

Just like Trent, he ignored my outstretched hand. "What are your qualifications?"

Technically, I had none. "I used to babysit. I was good at it."

"When can you start?"

"Today."

16

"It's a live-in position." He glared at me.

I glared right back and crossed my arms. "I assume I'll have my own room."

"Of course." He gritted his teeth. "Twenty-five hundred a week plus room and board. You report to me and only me. My daughter so much as farts and you're there to wipe her ass. Understood?"

Jesus. What was I getting myself into? Twenty-five hundred dollars a week was hard to pass up, especially when I wouldn't have to pay rent for an apartment or crash with my brother.

Everyone—Tom, Penny, and the Dorseys—waited anxiously for my response. Was I crazy for taking a job from this man that so many held animosity for?

Probably.

But to be fair, I didn't know his story. For all I knew, it was a family issue that had nothing to do with me or possibly something that happened at the hotel. Again, it didn't involve me.

He didn't look evil. Yeah, he was angry because of whatever happened in that conference room, but he was also extremely handsome. If the job ended up being a bust, I'd simply quit. It wasn't like I was signing a contract in blood, although it was very possible I was making a deal with the devil.

Tom grabbed my arm and pulled me to the side. "I forbid you to take this job."

I raised an eyebrow at him. "You forbid me? Last time I checked, you weren't in charge of me."

Trent stepped over, shoving his hands in his pockets. "I agree with Tom. I'll find you a job here at Mystique with fair compensation."

"More than minimum wage?"

"I can't make any promises, Ms. Bently."

"No disrespect, but I need more than minimum wage and I'd have a place to stay. This is a win-win."

"Don't do it, Charlotte," Tom begged. "I'll clean out my home office and we'll make it real nice. You can stay as long as you need. Please."

My brother's offer tempted me, but I'd still be stuck in a crap job. There was no way I'd be able to save money for my own place.

Hunter tapped his foot impatiently. "Do you want the position or not? I don't have time to stand around with my thumb up my ass."

Jesus Christ.

His personality left a lot to be desired, but money was money, and I needed it badly.

I looked at my brother and mouthed *I'm sorry,* then turned back to Hunter and straightened my shoulders, trying to look as professional as I could with Tay Tay splashed across my chest. "I want the job."

Chapter 3
Hunter

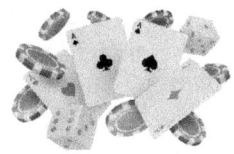

What had I done?

The girl looked barely old enough to be legal. She was a living doll. Something almost too pretty to play with but tempted you to mess up her perfection. Skin smooth as porcelain with pink heart-shaped lips and big blue eyes with long lashes that blinked up at me. Dark hair fell over her shoulders in long waves that nearly reached her waist.

My dick twitched with desire and that pissed me off. Now wasn't the time to fantasize about fucking the nanny.

I scribbled my address on the back of a business card and thrust it at her. "Five o'clock. Don't be late." Then I turned to my father. "Can I speak to you? Alone."

"Of course." I followed my father to his office. I hadn't walked this hall in over a year. In some ways, it felt strange; in others, it felt like home. I was always supposed to be here. I was the son—albeit illegitimate—of the great Edward Dorsey, hotel mogul. It was my birthright.

I had to give it to my mother. When she decided to sleep with a married man, at least she chose well. I'd hit the bastard jackpot. She could have slept with any bum in Vegas. Instead, she landed a multimillionaire turned billionaire.

The only thing that stood between me and my destiny was Trent. I tried to remove him from the equation, but that plan backfired spectacularly, costing me the position of CFO and landing my ass behind a desk at a bank. My skin prickled every time I thought about it. No matter what I did, I'd never be as good as my half brother.

Once inside his office, my father faced off with me. "I don't appreciate your disrespect to your mother."

I rolled my eyes. "Not this again. Rose isn't my mother. My mother didn't give two shits about me."

He puffed out his cheeks in frustration. This was an argument we'd had many times over the last twenty-five years. "She's your mother for all intents and purposes. Rose raised you from the time you were a toddler. You're her son, not by blood, but by choice. I put this family in a bad situation and risked my marriage, but she handled it with grace and loved you as her own."

The *bad situation* was me. "I beg to differ. She never treated Trent and me the same. He was always the favorite."

"Maybe because you walked around with a chip on your shoulder. She tried, she really did, but you fought her at every turn. You intentionally pushed her away with your bad attitude and devious behavior. You made a difficult situation even harder."

Now I was the *difficult situation*. And he wondered why I rebelled so much. There was no way I'd win this battle with him, so I moved on to more pressing issues and finally took a seat. "We'll have to agree to disagree. However, I wanted to thank you for helping me out with Carina. I'm not too much of a man to say I freaked out when she showed up on my doorstep."

My father visibly relaxed at the change of topic and sat behind his desk. "I can imagine. I remember the day I found out about you. It may seem like your world is crashing down, but soon enough, you'll see what a blessing it is."

My father and I always had a decent relationship. He stood up for me, even when I made it impossible, but this was the first time he'd called me a blessing. The pent-up anger that'd been sitting in my chest finally dissipated. "I don't know anything about being a dad."

He chuckled. "None of us do. Trust me, it'll come more naturally than you think. You've always been a quick learner."

Wow! Two compliments in one day. That had to be a record. Who knew it would take a baby to mend our fences? "I don't know about that. Mrs. Hadley, my next-door neighbor, has been doing most of the work." When Carina showed up, I called my dad, and his lawyer got us in front of a family court judge the same day. Because my name was on the birth certificate, he gave us the option of taking Carina home with us or putting her in foster care until the paternity test came back. If she was really mine, I didn't want her staying with strangers. Rose volunteered to take Carina, but I not so graciously declined. Mrs. Hadley was the obvious choice for me, she'd raised three children of her own and had six grandchildren. I generously compensated her, but it wasn't a long-term plan. We paid beaucoup bucks to expedite the paternity test, and now, four days later, she was officially mine, hence the need for a nanny.

The nanny. God, I was an idiot. I should have interviewed a dozen different women to find a qualified caretaker, but I'd been so pissed at Rose's meddling that I hired the first person available. If it didn't work out, I'd find someone to replace her. It was that easy.

My father folded his hands and leaned on his desk. "I'm glad you came to me when you needed help, Hunter. Despite the reasons why, I'm hoping we can use this opportunity to rebuild our relationship. I miss having my son around."

I raised my eyebrow. "Missed me so much that all you can offer me is a junior position in the financial department?"

He sighed. "I know it's not what you wanted, but you broke the trust and sanctity of this family. What you did to your brother not only

21

humiliated him but Gia too. It also put the reputation of this company at risk."

It was bad, yet I'd never admit how low I sank. "Let's not make a mountain out of a molehill."

"It was a mountain, regardless of what you think. It wasn't fair to Trent, and it certainly wasn't fair to Gia. She's your brother's wife and she's damn good at her job. We're lucky she didn't decide to walk away because she's a major asset to Mystique."

Fine. I got it. I fucked up big time. "Point taken, but a junior position?"

My father tapped his fingers on the desk. "Things are changing around here. I haven't announced it yet, but I'm retiring. Trent will be taking my position. If you want to move up in the company, you need to make amends with your brother. And his wife. Show some good faith and then we'll talk."

Fuuuuck! Kissing my brother's ass was at the very bottom of my priority list. "Fine. I'll take the junior position and prove myself. You know that I should be CFO. It's the only acceptable option."

"You do that. Nothing would make me happier than having my two sons running Mystique together. If you're serious, you'll make a genuine effort to make it work."

"I will."

I was serious. When I worked with Trent before, it was a game. I purposely did shit to push his buttons and enjoyed the fuck out of it. Nothing gave me more pleasure than to watch his blood pressure rise to the point that his fists clenched. I loved seeing him try to hold it together when we both knew he wanted to bash my face in.

When Gia started working at Mystique, it only upped the ante. My crude comments about her set Trent on fire. Yeah, I crossed a few lines into sexual harassment territory, but it was only because I suspected Trent had a thing for her. What better way to irritate your brother than to put the moves on the woman he desired but couldn't have?

It wasn't personal with Gia. I had no beef with her. She was gorgeous and competent. Unfortunately for her, she became a pawn in a long-standing feud between two brothers.

Unfortunately for me, that pawn married Trent. I never expected her to stick around after I recorded them having sex and sent it to everyone in the office. The woman had more chutzpa than I gave her credit for.

I'd let Trent punch me in the face again if it meant getting my job back at Mystique. Gia, however, would require a bit more finesse. You know what they say about scorned women. No... she was going to make me crawl and beg for forgiveness.

Luckily, I had a secret weapon and as of today, she was officially mine. No one would be able to resist her. Maybe it made me a piece of shit to consider using my daughter for my own benefit, but I'd never been accused of having high morals. I'd be a fool to not use every weapon at my disposal. Nothing was going to stand between me and my destiny.

Chapter 4
Charli

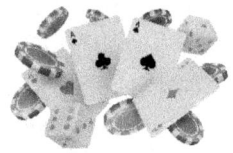

I showed up promptly at five o'clock, dressed in a pink floral sundress and a cute pair of wedge sandals. My first impression might not have been the best, but I intended to prove that I was capable and professional. Smoothing the dress over my legs, I checked the back of his card one more time, making sure the apartment number matched. Raising my fist, I knocked on the door and waited, shifting my weight from one foot to the other.

As I was about to knock again, the door swung open. "You're late, dollface."

Dollface? I stared at the man in front of me. If I thought he was attractive before, it didn't hold a candle to the sight of him cradling a baby to his chest. His green dress shirt was open at the collar, his tie hanging around his neck, and there was a distinct orange smear on the material across his chest. Maybe carrots or squash. It was hard to tell.

"I said you're late," he barked.

My eyes popped up to his and blinked. "I'm not late. You said five o'clock and here I am," I said, holding my arms out.

He held his phone in front of my face. "What does that say?"

My nose scrunched up at the evidence. "Five oh four."

"Exactly," he said as he shifted the baby on his hip. "If you can't be on time your first day, how can I trust you with my daughter?"

Was he serious? I folded my arms across my chest. "I assure you I was here at five o'clock. It's not my fault it took you so long to answer the door."

"Do not blame your shortcomings on me. On time is late and early is on time. A lesson you'd be wise to learn." He leaned out into the hallway, looking in both directions. "Where are your bags, Miss Bently?"

I gulped and adjusted the purse on my shoulder. "I assumed today I'd be meeting your daughter and getting a tour or something."

His eyes narrowed. "Does this look like fucking Disneyland to you? There's no fucking tour. Did you or did you not say you could start today?"

Crap! I did say I could start today. I just thought… It didn't matter what I thought. Clearly, I misunderstood. So far, I'd earned two strikes. If I messed up again, I could kiss this job goodbye. Hunter may have been a miserable human being, but the money was amazing. It was a short-term gig. Something to tide me over until I could get back in the air and on stage, able to support myself again.

"I apologize, Mr. Dorsey. I can start today and will get my things tomorrow." It was no big deal to sleep in my clothes. It's not like I hadn't ever done it before.

He sighed and opened the door wide. "You can start by giving Carina a bath."

She snuggled into her dad's shoulder, sucking on two fingers. Blond wisps of hair stuck up on her little head, and her chubby cheeks were covered in the same orange mess that was smeared across Hunter's shirt. "How old is she?"

"Six months," he grunted. "I've only had her for four days though."

Four days? I couldn't imagine being deprived of my child for six months. "Where's her mom?" I ran my fingers down her face.

"Fuck if I know. Carina showed up at my door with a note. Not even sure who her mom is. I don't know jack shit about her except the name on the birth certificate."

My eyebrows lifted to my hairline. "Oh."

He turned his back to me and hugged the sweet girl tighter to his chest. "Don't you dare fucking judge me. I've gotten quite enough of that from my family. If you have a problem with the circumstances, you can march your ass right back out that door."

I immediately felt bad. Though I hadn't intended to, I did judge him. Maybe because I'd never had sex with someone I wasn't in a relationship with. It wasn't like I didn't know people had one-night stands, but I wasn't one of them. "I'm sorry. I'm not here to judge. I'm here to help. May I?" I reached my arms out to take the sleeping child from him.

"Careful. She's heavier than she looks." Hunter gently set Carina into my outstretched arms. Her eyes blinked open before she settled against my shoulder.

Given his rough demeanor, it surprised me he handled the child like she was made of glass. I rubbed my hand up and down her back. "She's beautiful, Mr. Dorsey. Has your eyes."

He scratched the day-old scruff on his chin. "That she does. Let's hope that's the only thing she got from me." I followed Hunter through the huge sitting room, and he motioned down the hallway. "Bathroom is down there and so is Carina's bedroom. Her furniture isn't coming until tomorrow so put her to sleep in the playpen. Your room is across from hers. Once she's asleep, come back to the kitchen so we can discuss your duties." Then he turned and stalked off in the opposite direction, leaving me alone with his daughter.

I looked down at the sleeping child and wandered down the hallway. "I guess it's just you and me, kiddo." The bathroom was the first door on the right. I flipped on the light and gasped. It was huge. Half my apartment could fit inside.

The apartment where the lease expired in five days, and I hadn't begun to pack. I didn't have that much stuff, but I still didn't have a plan. Yet. I'd figure it out tomorrow.

26

Right then, my priority was getting this sweet girl cleaned up and ready for bed. I laid a towel on the plush rug and set her down in the middle of it. The tub had a bath chair and sitting on the ledge was expensive baby shampoo, a cup, and a clean washcloth. I expected to see a plethora of toys, but the entire apartment, from what I'd seen so far, barely showed any evidence of a child living there.

Four days.

I could barely imagine what that felt like. No time to prepare. No time to adjust. No time to find a proper nanny.

I wasn't qualified for the job, but if my aerial partner, Jasmine, could raise two kids at age twenty-six, surely I could handle one itty-bitty baby. Whatever I didn't know, Google could teach me.

Giving a bath didn't require a degree in parenting. I turned on the faucet and let the water get warm before filling the tub with a few inches. Carina babbled from where she lay on the towel, chewing on her fist. I leaned over and rubbed her tummy. "You're wide awake now, aren't you, sweet girl? Let's get these messy clothes off you. I'm not sure if your daddy got more food in you or on you."

I undid the snaps on her onesie and carefully pulled her legs and arms from the fabric. Her round, soft belly begged to be tickled. I couldn't help but lower my lips to it and blow a raspberry. She laughed and wildly kicked her tiny legs. "You like that, don't you?" I did it again and soaked in the sound of her sweet giggles. A loud toot erupted from her back end, which made her laugh even more. I covered my nose with the back of my hand. "My goodness, girl! That's a stinker for sure."

Looking around the bathroom, I didn't see any wipes or diapers. "Don't you move." I hurried into the next room and found the supplies sitting next to a diaper bag on the floor. The only other things in the room were a playpen and a few clothes hanging over the edge. I grabbed what I needed and rushed back to her, not wanting Hunter to find his baby unattended.

"Let's get you cleaned up." I removed the dirty diaper and wiped her little bottom, then put her into the bath chair. Using the washcloth, I scrubbed her clean from the top of her head to the tips of her toes, rinsing her with cups of warm water. "We're going to have to get you some toys for the tub. Maybe a rubber ducky or a mermaid," I chatted as I worked. Once she was clean, I wrapped her in a fluffy towel and carried her to her bedroom. Picking up the pink kitten pajamas, I worked her arms and legs through the holes and laid her on her back in the playpen. I figured she'd last a few hours before her tummy rumbled, and she'd be ready to eat again. Her little eyes closed, and her fist went right to her mouth. "Good night, sweet girl."

I gave her tummy one last rub and went back down the hall to the kitchen. "She's all clean and down for the count."

Hunter leaned on the counter his head hung down. "She'll be up again around midnight," he growled.

"I figured as much. Show me where everything is, and I'll take care of it."

He showed me where the bottles, formula, and baby food were. "Have a seat, Ms. Bently. We have things to discuss."

I sat at the kitchen table. "You can call me Charli." This didn't need to be difficult, even though it seemed Hunter wanted to make it anything but easy.

Hunter licked his lips and sat across from me. "What did you do before this, Miss Bently?"

Apparently, we weren't going to be friends. I sat up straight, pushing my shoulders back. "Does it matter?"

He chuckled. "Yes and no. I'm wondering why my brother's personal assistant's sister happened to be available when I needed a nanny. What's your angle?"

My angle? Like I had a secret ulterior motive. "I needed a job. I was at Mystique to see if he could help me find one and to ask if I could temporarily reside on his couch."

His lips twisted to the side. "So, I'm to believe that you just happened to be around when I needed a nanny? Seems awfully convenient to me. And this is your dream job?"

I scoffed. "Dream job? Absolutely not. I didn't want a job at Mystique either, but money was money."

28

"So, no one put you up to this? Rose didn't pay you to keep tabs on me?"

I wasn't sure who Rose was, but I answered honestly. "I'm here for money. The fact that your daughter is adorable is a bonus."

He ran a hand through his cropped hair. "I see. And what was your employment before this?"

He was like a dog with a bone, but I couldn't blame him. I wouldn't trust my daughter with a stranger either. "I was an aerial performer at Oasis. Broke my leg and tore my ACL. I have four to six months before I can get back in the air. I needed the money, or I was going to end up on my brother's couch. Not sure if you'd understand why that wasn't appealing to me."

"You don't get along with Tom?" he questioned.

"I get along with him fine, but I don't want to be his roommate. The live-in nanny position solved that problem." Maybe I was being too honest, but a guy like Hunter wasn't going to fall for my bullshit anyway. If this job wasn't going to work out, better to find out sooner than later.

Hunter seemed satisfied with my answer. "I appreciate your candor. Is it going to be a problem to live here?"

"Technically, no. I just need to find a place to store my furniture. My apartment lease ends in five days."

He tapped his fingers on the table. "There's storage space in the basement here. Carina's furniture is arriving at nine, but you can use the rest of the afternoon to move your things. You'll have to take Carina with you." It wasn't a question but a declaration. "I assume you have a car."

"Yes."

He rolled his hand in irritation. "What kind of car? How old?"

Jeez. The man had a way of making me shrink into my own skin with his pointed looks and intrusive questions. "It's an old pickup. Used to belong to my dad."

He harrumphed. "That won't do. No way I'm letting my daughter ride in a beat-up piece of shit." Hunter went to the wall and grabbed a set of keys from the hook, tossing them on the table. "You'll drive my Escalade when you take Carina anywhere. Is that understood?"

My pickup wasn't exactly a piece of shit, but I nodded anyway. "What will you drive?"

"You don't need to worry about that. I have another car. All you need to worry about is getting my daughter from point *A* to point *B* safely." He smacked a credit card on the table. "You can use this for groceries and anything else Carina needs. It's not for your personal use."

I gulped and picked up the American Express card. "Of course."

"You'll be expected to do some light cooking and cleaning, but your main priority is Carina. Help yourself to the kitchen. Any questions?"

Yeah… about a million of them, but I failed to form one coherent thought. "Not at the moment. If it's okay, I'd like to go check out my room, Mr. Dorsey."

He gave a curt nod and stood from the table. Apparently, I was dismissed. I scurried toward the hallway, anxious to catch a breath since my boss seemed to suck the air from my lungs any time I was around him. "Hey, dollface?" I froze and turned on my heel. He refused to call me Charli, but *dollface* was acceptable? "Quit calling me Mr. Dorsey. It reminds me of my father. My name is Hunter."

"Understood." I smirked as I continued down the hallway. For all the sharp lines and hard attitude, something told me Hunter Dorsey was not at all what he seemed. Somewhere under all that gruff was a man who wanted to be accepted for who he was and maybe even… be loved.

Chapter 5
Hunter

Something was seriously wrong with me. My goal was to keep things professional. To, for the first time in my life, not make a complete mess out of something.

Carina deserved better. She deserved someone who would put her needs ahead of their own. Her mother already failed, so the burden fell on me. I wasn't prepared for that type of responsibility.

If I needed confirmation of it, all I had to do was look at my actions over the past couple hours.

Dollface? I rubbed my hand over my face. Jesus Christ. Just because an idea flitted through my mind didn't mean I should vocalize it.

She was my goddamn nanny, not some chick I picked up off the street for a night of fun. We wouldn't be going out for expensive dinners, hanging out at a club or cuddling on the couch eating popcorn and watching Netflix. We weren't friends or fuck buddies. She was the hired help, and it would serve me well to remember that.

I should have taken Rose's advice and hired Ms. Peters. I needed a Nanny McPhee, not a modern-day Mary Poppins. The girl looked so sweet; I wouldn't be surprised if bluebirds sprang from her purse and fluttered around her head. Or maybe that was Snow White. Cinderella? Sleeping Beauty? It didn't matter. The point was I'd hired a goddamn fairy princess to care for my child.

A fact my dick noticed as well.

At least I made one decent decision by putting Carina and Charlotte on the opposite side of the apartment from my own bedroom and office. With any luck, I'd avoid seeing her too much.

Stomping to my office, I pulled out the letter and birth certificate left with my daughter. Charlotte's question about her mother had been plaguing me since the day she showed up. I picked up the card from my father's attorney and angrily punched the numbers into my phone.

It rang half a dozen times before he answered. "What can I do for you, Hunter?"

He knew what I wanted. I'd asked the same damn question since our first meeting at the courthouse. My father warned me about being prickly with Sam Steinberg. Said he wouldn't put up with my bullshit. For what I was paying him, the high-priced attorney should have been willing to dig through a mountain of bullshit. I didn't care if he had to use a spoon.

However, he was the best of the best, so I tempered my annoyance. "Have you found her yet?"

Sam Steinberg sighed. "We don't have a lot to go on. There are literally thousands of women named Jennifer Johnson."

"Jennifer Ann Johnson," I reminded him.

"You do realize Ann is one of the most common middle names for a woman?"

Actually, I didn't, but it shouldn't have been a surprise. Nothing in my life had ever been easy, so why wouldn't I have created a baby with a woman with the most unoriginal name ever. It couldn't have been Adeline Garopoulis or Natalia Kovalenko. No, that would have been way too easy. Jennifer Johnson was about as common as it got.

"Did you check The Sapphire Club?" I told him that's where I met Jennifer, though I didn't know her name at the time. Chances are she wouldn't have given me her real name anyway. I left out the part about paying her ten grand for sex.

"We did."

"And?" His vague answers made my blood boil. Was he purposely trying to irritate me?

"All they confirmed was she worked there about a year ago."

I growled. "Can't you compel them to tell you something? Surely, they have an address, tax information, something."

"Mr. Dorsey, I can't *compel* them to tell me anything. I'm a lawyer, not the damn FBI. Besides, a gentleman's club primarily deals in cash. I wouldn't be surprised if they didn't keep any records on her."

"So now what?" I asked, leaning my head in my hand.

"I'd suggest a private investigator. Rudy Mendosa is the best. He's a goddamn pit bull when it comes to missing persons. Never stops until he gets his man... or woman... in your case. I need to warn you though, he's not cheap."

"Of course, he's not," I grumbled.

"If you want this woman to sign parental termination papers, then he's your guy. Otherwise, the process will take a minimum of six months.

Six months? Six months of waiting for her to show up unexpectedly. Six months for her to change her mind. Six months for her to waltz in and take my daughter away.

Regardless of the fact that Carina was a complete surprise, I'd already decided I wasn't letting her go. I pulled up the camera on my phone that sat over Carina's playpen. She was zonked out on her back in clean pajamas, her tiny lips barely parted. No one thought I was a suitable father, least of all me, but Carina was mine and I'd do what I could to provide her a good life.

"Text me his number. Thanks, Sam." I ended the call before he could reply, but I thanked him, so there was that.

This entire situation had my dick in a twist. I'd been fine living my life alone with an occasional woman to share my time. Since Carina arrived, I decided to reconcile with my family and reclaim my place at Mystique. I also had a twenty-four-seven roommate in the form of a nanny. I enjoyed my solitude, and I'd barely had five minutes to myself over the last four days. Everybody was in my goddamn business, and it made me more surly than usual.

My phone buzzed with an incoming text from Sam, giving me the contact information for the private investigator.

Even though it was after seven, I had no problem calling him. Of course, he didn't answer which made me more annoyed than I already was. I left a curt message with a callback number. I was used to getting what I wanted when I wanted it. All this waiting around pissed me off.

I sat stewing. Patience was not my strongest virtue. Actually, I wasn't sure I had *any* virtues, but patience certainly wasn't one of them.

A quiet knock came at my open door and my head popped up. Charlotte stood there in the dark hallway on her bare feet. "I'm sorry to interrupt."

"What do you need, Miss Bently?"

She tiptoed into my office and stood with her hands clasped in front of her. "Two things actually."

I rolled my hand for her to get on with it. "Did you want me to guess, or are you going to tell me?"

She bit her bottom lip in a way that made me want to nip it between my teeth and then work my way down beneath her dress. I should have insisted she wore pants or maybe bought her a uniform. That would have solved my inconvenient attraction to the brunette. She barely had any tits, but the dress she wore clung to her boobs like a second skin before it fell down her body and skimmed the floor. It wasn't sexy per se, but it had my dick standing at attention nonetheless.

"I was wondering if there was a baby monitor or if that was coming tomorrow as well?"

It was a logical question and showed a sense of responsibility. "It's on an app. Hand me your phone."

She placed her phone in my outstretched hand. "Things have changed a lot since I babysat last. I was looking for a walkie-talkie type thing."

I quirked an eyebrow at her. "And when was the last time you babysat?"

"Ten years ago," she said sheepishly. "I was fifteen."

Jesus. She was older than I thought but still young. "Are you sure you're capable of caring for my daughter?"

She nodded like a bobblehead. "Totally." She cringed at her choice of wording and straightened her shoulders. "I mean, absolutely. Give me a chance."

"I don't give second chances. If you fuck up, I'll send you packing so fast your head will spin. Am I clear?"

"Crystal."

I downloaded the app on her phone and entered the username and password, then wrote them on a sticky note and stuck it to the screen before handing it back to her.

Charlotte pulled the note off and stared at her phone. Her lips tilted up as she watched Carina sleep. "So beautiful," she whispered.

That was my sentiment exactly. Standing in my dimly lit office with her dark hair partly shading her face that glowed from the phone screen, Charlotte was pure perfection. She wasn't just pretty. *Pretty* was an understatement that didn't do her justice. The girl was a stunner.

"Do you have a boyfriend?" The question in my head slipped out without permission.

She tore her eyes from the screen. "Huh?"

"A boyfriend? Do you have one?"

Charlotte pushed her hair behind her ear and shook her head. "No, no boyfriend."

I tapped my fingers on the mahogany desk. The thought of her wrapped around another guy, sharing kisses and whispering secrets, sent needles up my spine. "No fuck buddy or special friend?"

She scrunched up her face. "Not at the moment. Why? Would that be a problem?"

Yeah, it would be a fucking problem. "I don't want my daughter around a bunch of fucking randos, that's all." That wasn't it at all, but it was as good of an excuse as any. "Don't bring guys to the apartment. If you need to scratch an itch, you'll have to do it somewhere else."

Even in the dim light, I could see the indignation in her eyes. "Okaaay."

"I'm serious. This apartment is a no-fuck zone."

Charlotte's mouth twisted to the side and her nostrils flared. "No offense, *Mr. Dorsey*. But if I wanted to be treated like a child, I would have stayed at home in Colorado. Who I fuck is none of your business. I would never bring a man here, but that doesn't mean I won't be fucking someone. Don't you worry... I'll be sure to get a babysitter when I want to *scratch an itch*, as you so eloquently put it." She turned to leave.

I stood and leaned on the desk. "Don't you dare walk away from me when we're talking."

She spun back around. "Oh, is that what we're doing? Talking? Silly me"—she smacked her temple with her palm—"I thought you were giving me a lecture on chastity. You may be my boss, but you don't get to control my life!"

"If it affects my daughter, I do!"

Charlotte stomped back over to my desk and leaned on the opposite side, mimicking my stance. "I would never, and I mean never, do anything to harm Carina or put her at risk." She raised a finger and shoved it in my face. "You know, everyone told me not to take this job and I'm beginning to see why. You're a tyrant and a jerk face."

"Jerk face?" I laughed. "I thought I'd been called every name in the book, but that's a new one."

"If the face fits..." She shrugged her shoulders.

All the tension drained from my body. Somewhere between being called a tyrant and a jerk face, she'd earned some respect. "I'll get you a list of acceptable babysitters to use if needed. Do not take advantage of my generosity."

"I won't. It's smart to have a backup plan. I'd also like a list of emergency contacts in case I can't reach you."

I jotted down a quick note. "Done." It was something I should have thought of myself.

"Thank you."

"What was the other thing?"

"Huh?"

"You said there were two things you needed. What was the second thing?"

"Oh, I was going to ask you if you wanted me to make you something to eat, but I've decided you haven't earned the right to my cooking yet." She shrugged her shoulder. "So, I guess you're on your own."

I stood there and stared after her like an idiot as she sashayed out of my office.

Food was the last thing on my mind, but I was hungry, nonetheless.

Chapter 6
Charli

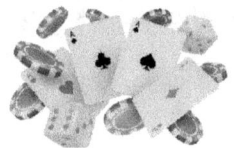

When my alarm went off at six the next morning, I reached over to the nightstand and hit snooze. The sheets were soft, and I was so warm it felt like heaven. After closing my eyes for another minute, they popped back open. "Shit!" I quickly sat up in the bed and grabbed my phone, pulling up the app for the baby monitor.

Thankfully, Carina was still sprawled out on her back, sound asleep. The last thing I needed was Hunter up my ass for being neglectful on my first morning.

Hopping out of bed, I smoothed out the wrinkled dress I slept in last night. Since I didn't have pajamas, I thought it would be strange to sleep in my underwear, especially if Carina needed me in the middle of the night. I certainly didn't want to run into my boss in my bra and panties.

My new room was nice but lacked all traces of personality. The walls were painted dove gray, with sheets and a comforter to match. The black furniture had more than enough space to put my clothes in, and there was a large walk-in closet. The whole room screamed bachelor, but it was clean, and everything looked brand new. If I had to bet, I'd guess I was the first one to ever stay in this bedroom. When I got my things today, it would feel a bit more homey.

I went to the bathroom, quickly took care of business, brushed my teeth with a new toothbrush I found in the vanity last night, combed my hair into a ponytail, and touched up my makeup with the few things I had in my purse. It wasn't fantastic, but given the circumstances, it could have been worse. I wasn't here for a fashion show and doubted Carina would give a crap if I was wearing yesterday's mascara.

After making myself somewhat presentable, I ventured toward the kitchen, peeking into the nursery on my way to double-check that Carina was still asleep. Not only was Carina's room quiet, but the entire apartment was eerily silent.

I needed coffee and I needed it bad. Of course, Hunter had one of those fancy coffee makers with a dozen different settings I didn't understand. After giving it a once-over, I popped a pod in and hit a few buttons, then said a little prayer of thanks when it started to sputter.

My stomach rumbled. All I had to eat last night was a turkey sandwich I made from the meager contents of the fridge. I went to get some eggs for breakfast and stopped to stare at the sheet of paper attached to the front that wasn't there last night. On it were the names of two acceptable babysitters with phone numbers and a list of emergency contacts. At the top of the list was 911.

I rolled my eyes. "Duh." He really did think I was a child.

Pulling the eggs from the fridge, I set them on the island counter. That's when I noticed the second sheet of paper filled with Hunter's perfectly perfect printing.

Today's Schedule:
7:00- Breakfast (see approved list), Diaper Change, Face Washing
8:00- Walk (there is a park across the street)
9:00- Carina's Furniture Arrives (DON'T BE LATE!)
10:00- 6oz. of Formula

12:00- Go to your apartment and pack (Take the Escalade- Spot #32B-Do NOT speed! My daughter is precious cargo and if anything happens to her…)

I stopped reading after that. Hunter had the entire day planned out for me. Under the schedule was a printout of acceptable foods for six-month-old babies that he'd found on a website. Though his attention to detail was admirable, it was also annoying as hell. The man was a control freak. I'd sensed it before, but now I was getting the whole picture.

Staying here actually might not have been better than staying with my brother. It was tough to discern which of them had a stick further up their ass.

I scrambled some eggs, ate breakfast, and washed the pan. There weren't any dishes in the sink, not even a coffee cup on the counter. I had assumed Hunter was still sleeping, but as the time crept closer to seven, I wondered if he was already gone for the day. Tiptoeing down the hall, I peeked into his dark office. Seeing it empty, I went to the next room. The door was barely cracked open, but through the small space, I saw the large bed neatly made.

He wasn't in the apartment, and I breathed a little easier. When he looked at me with those icy eyes, it felt like he was staring into the depths of my soul. Like he saw every insecurity and could shred me to pieces. Seemed strange that he left for work before six, but what did I know? I only met him yesterday. We weren't friends. I was merely the nanny.

I had the urge to snoop but decided to save it for another day. Although getting a peek at what made my new boss tick tempted me, apparently my schedule was already stuffed to the gills.

Instead, I went to wake Carina, only to find her waving her arms wildly and babbling. "Good morning, sweet girl." Picking her up out of the playpen, I changed her diaper and took her to the kitchen. There was no high chair, and I assumed that would be coming today also. There was a stroller by the front door, so I wheeled it over and set her in it.

After a breakfast of peaches and eggs, I took Carina to the park across the street. Although I hadn't noticed it yesterday, the park was beautiful.

There were benches along the walkway and two playscapes, one for younger children and one for the older kids. Obviously, Carina was too tiny to enjoy the playscapes, but I couldn't help imagining her teetering up the ladder for the slide, dropping to her butt, and racing down the smooth surface. I would catch her at the bottom and tell her how brave she was before scooping her up and smothering her in kisses.

A girl could fantasize. I'd thought about the kind of mom I would be, but it wasn't practical at this stage in my life.

Every night I climbed thirty feet into the air and performed choreographed routines most people never dreamed of attempting. Or at least I used to before one false move sent me tumbling down and landed me in the hospital. Honestly, I was lucky I only ended up with a broken leg and some torn ligaments. It could have been worse. So much worse.

As we made our way around the path, the alarm I'd set on my phone went off. "Crap!" I hustled us back to the apartment building and into the elevator. It seemed to take forever to ascend thirty-two floors. The doors slid open to a burly guy pounding on the apartment door. "I'm here! I'm here!" I shouted.

Hunter would have killed me if I missed the delivery. I thought his detailed schedule was overkill, but maybe not. Perhaps I needed more structure in my life.

The delivery guy scowled at me. "I was about to leave. I've got a truckload of stuff to bring up and a team of guys waiting downstairs. There's an upcharge if we need to reschedule."

A team? Jeez. How much did Hunter order? "I'm here now. There's no need to reschedule." I quickly stuck the key in the lock and wheeled Carina inside. She was sound asleep despite jostling her in my rush to get back to the apartment.

The delivery guy followed me inside. "Where are we setting everything up?"

I walked him down the hall to what would be Carina's nursery. "In here. I'll move the playpen."

He barely looked at me. "There's more than furniture," he said, scanning the paperwork in his hand.

"Okay. Well, you bring it in, and I'll find a place for it," I said in my most chipper voice. There couldn't possibly be that much stuff for one tiny baby.

The delivery guy grunted as he left the apartment, presumably to go down to the truck. I guessed being friendly wasn't part of his job.

I checked on Carina and rolled her into the kitchen, then got to work on moving the playpen. It was too big to fit through the door, so I assumed it folded up. But how? I pulled on the sides, but nothing happened. I tried tugging in the corners. Again, zero movement. No matter what I did, the thing didn't want to close. I considered shoving the playpen in the corner and letting Hunter deal with it when he got home.

The thought scared me a bit. It was very domestic. Me waiting for my husband to get home from work to help me. Only Hunter wasn't my husband. He would expect me to figure this out on my own.

I tilted the playpen on its side and looked underneath. Nothing jumped out at me, such as a lever or a button. "Screw it." I began pushing it into the corner.

"Here, let me help." A young guy about my age set down the crib mattress he was carrying and lifted the padding attached to the uprights, pressing buttons on each corner. The thing folded up like an umbrella.

"Thank you," I said, pushing my hair behind my ear.

"First baby?"

My hand flew to my chest. It made sense since I was getting baby furniture delivered, but it still took me by surprise. "Oh, no. I'm not the mom. I'm the nanny."

He stuck out his hand. "Good to know. Now, I won't have to worry about your husband punching me in the face when I ask for your number. I'm Ben."

I giggled and shook his hand. "I'm Charli. Thanks for your help."

"Ben, the truck isn't going to unload itself. Get your ass moving!" His grumpy boss was back with a dolly full of boxes.

"I'm moving," Ben answered with a roll of his eyes.

Over the next hour, a team of men paraded in and out of the apartment with furniture and boxes. Lots and lots of boxes. I'm fairly sure Hunter ordered one of everything. There were boxes on the kitchen counter, stacked in the living room, and all down the hallway. It was a complete disaster.

Ben held up another box. "Where do you want this?"

I inspect the picture and the writing. It was some kind of fancy bottle warmer. "In the kitchen is fine."

Mr. Grumpy appeared. "That's everything. All we have left is assembly and we'll get some of these empty boxes out of the way." He thrust a clipboard at me. "I need you to sign that everything was delivered."

I stared down at the list. It was two pages long. There was absolutely no way for me to know if everything was here without going through the apartment and checking each item off the list. "You sure it's everything?" Hunter wouldn't be happy if I signed for something that hadn't been delivered.

"You're welcome to check," he grumped.

I bit my lip and looked at the mess in the apartment. It would take me an hour to go through everything. "I trust you," I said as I scribbled my name across the line.

"Gee, thanks," he said sarcastically as he walked away.

"Knock, knock," a woman said as she entered the apartment, squeezing by one of the guys on his way out. "I thought I'd stop by to see if you needed some help."

I recognized her as Hunter's mom from Mystique yesterday. We hadn't been formally introduced, but I wasn't going to turn her away. "Mrs. Dorsey, right?" I stuck out my hand. "I'm Charli."

She smiled at me and took my hand in hers. "I remember. And I'm Rose." She looked around at the chaos. "He went a bit overboard, didn't he?"

I pinched my thumb and forefinger together. "Just a tad. I don't even know where to put half this stuff or what to do with it."

"We'll figure it out." She gave me a quick hug. "But first, where is my granddaughter?"

"Believe it or not, Carina's slept through all this madness. She's in the kitchen." I motioned for Rose to follow me.

Rose put her hands to her mouth. "She's so adorable. I expected Trent to give me my first grandchild, but Hunter always has been full of surprises. It might not be traditional, but I'm not complaining. Can I hold her?"

It seemed like Hunter and Rose didn't have a great relationship, however, there was no way I'd tell this woman she couldn't hold her granddaughter. "Of course. I'm surprised she's slept this long. She'll need to eat soon."

Rose rubbed Carina's belly and her little blue eyes fluttered open. She stretched in the stroller and smiled at her grandma. I swear she had to be the happiest baby I'd ever seen. Although I hadn't been here long, Carina hadn't cried once.

"Come to Grandma Rose." Rose carefully lifted her from the stroller and snuggled her. Carina yawned and nuzzled into her grandma's shoulder. "I love her already."

"She's a keeper, that's for sure. Do you mind holding her while I get a bottle ready?" I asked while moving boxes off the counter.

When the bottle was ready, Rose fed Carina, who promptly went back to sleep. Before Rose left, we unwrapped the bazillion other things Hunter ordered and got everything in its proper place. If there was any doubt a baby lived here before, there wasn't now. Every room was now outfitted to accommodate his daughter—from the tub seat to the bouncy chair to the dozens of stuffed animals to the fancy bottle warmer and the high chair. He even bought electrical outlet covers and padding for the coffee table. I doubted very much that those were necessary at this age, but better to be safe than sorry.

The saleslady probably got dollar signs in her eyes when Hunter placed his order. It was one hell of a commission.

If Rose hadn't stopped by, there was no way I would have been able to get everything done before going to my own apartment to pack. She was a godsend. I'm not sure why Hunter didn't seem to care for his mom, but everyone butted heads with their own mother at one point or another. Lord knew my mom and I did. She was still aggravated I'd moved to Vegas to live my dream. My only saving grace was that Tom moved with me. I guessed it gave her a sense of peace, knowing my brother was only a hop, skip, and a jump away.

Overall, it was a good morning. I got to meet Hunter's mom, Carina and I were bonding; everything was unpacked, and the boxes were all taken away by the delivery guys. But best of all, Ben slipped me his number before he left. Who knew? Maybe I'd be using a babysitter sooner than I anticipated.

Chapter 7
Hunter

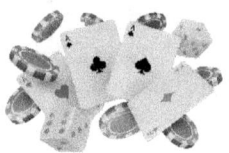

My first day back at Mystique was already a shit show.

I got to work super early to set up my new office, only to find Trent already there, having a new lock installed on *his* office door. I strolled in and took a seat across from his desk, restraining my jealousy of his view of the casino floor. My old office had a view too, but nothing as spectacular as his. Mine overlooked the dumpsters in the back alley, something he never tired of pointing out.

"Don't you trust me?"

Trent twirled a pen between his fingers. "Not even a little bit."

Okay, so I put cameras in his office and recorded him and Gia having sex. Yes, it was wrong, but they shouldn't have been having sex in his office. It was as much their fault as it was mine. No one acknowledged their culpability. All they could talk about was that I had the nerve to record them. And send it in an email to the entire staff in the administrative offices.

Not one of my finer moments, but Trent wasn't supposed to be fucking anyone on staff. My father had warned him. It was my only chance to prove that I was more fit for the CEO position than my brother.

There were worse things a brother could do. I mean... look at Cain and Able. Now *that* would be going too far. What I did was only a bit of humiliation. I'd say he recovered quite nicely, seeing as he'd be taking over for my father when he retired.

"How long are you going to hold a grudge?"

He narrowed his eyes at me. "How long do you plan on living?"

"Longer than you if it means I get to take over your job." I quirked an eyebrow for emphasis. It was no secret I wanted what would be his. It's why I went to the lengths I did to disgrace him.

"Then there's your answer. I don't give a shit about what you did to me. But Gia? You crossed way over the line involving her in your temper tantrum. Just like when we were kids, you never cared who got caught in the cross fire."

He wasn't wrong. With Trent being the perfect child, I often resorted to extreme tactics to get attention. I wouldn't be ignored.

I was born to be at Mystique. Once I had my old job back, I wouldn't have to kiss ass anymore, but until then, I resigned myself to the fact that my lips would be puckered like a duck for the foreseeable future. It didn't mean my tongue wouldn't still be sharp as a blade. This time, I let his insult roll off my back. There were other tactics just as effective but not quite as lethal. "Yes, well, not all of us can be perfect. It's a good thing I have such a wonderful big brother to show me the way."

He threw the pen he'd been twirling onto his desk. "Oh, fuck off with that bullshit. You don't respect me. You never have."

Bull's-eye. I held my hands up in surrender. "I've seen the error of my ways. I'm here to learn and make amends. For the sake of our family. For Carina." He may have hated me, but there was no way he could hate an innocent child. His only niece.

Trent's lips twisted to the side. "How is everything going with her?"

How the fuck did he think it was going? I got on a crazy train the moment Carina showed up and I hadn't gotten off yet. My life turned upside down. I got a kid, and I didn't even remember the fuck that made her. It seemed like the least I deserved. The memory of one good fuck… at least, I hoped it was good. I guess it would be worse if I remembered, and she was a shitty lay. The only thing I was sure of was she had big tits. Those I distinctly remembered.

But I couldn't say any of that.

"Fine. It's only been five days. Between going to court, getting everything legal, trying to find her goddamn mother, and hiring a nanny, I haven't had much time with her. Besides, I don't know what the fuck I'm doing, so Mrs. Hadley, my neighbor, pretty much watched her until yesterday. Other than that, it's going splendidly. She's a good baby."

He leaned back in his chair and tapped his fingers together. "Do yourself a favor and don't fuck the nanny."

"Hardy har. I'm not you. I don't fuck my employees." I would have fucked Gia too, but now that she was my sister-in-law, that ship had sailed.

"Touché. I'm serious, Hunter. She's attractive and your willpower is terrible. Plus, she's Tom's sister. I don't need your drama bleeding over into the office. You should have hired Ms. Peters."

Although I didn't disagree, I really didn't give a shit if she was Tom's sister or the Pope's. Who I slept with was no one's business. "Thank you, oh wise one. I'm sure your wife would be pleased to know how attractive you find my nanny. Thanks for the invite to the wedding, by the way."

"Must have got lost in the mail. What is this world coming to when you can't trust the postal service?" He shrugged his shoulders in a what-can-you-do motion. "And I assure you, I keep my wife incredibly pleased. Speaking of Gia… you still owe her an apology. Not that it will make her hate you any less, but it would be a gesture of goodwill. You know… now that we're being a family and all." His sarcasm was palpable.

"Riiiight… one big happy family. I'll get on that the moment I see her." Apologies weren't my thing. I'd rather pee on an electric fence than apologize. At least then, I'd get a little jolt in my dick.

"And don't be creepy about it. No sexual innuendos or double entendres. A simple *I'm sorry, I'm a fucking asshole* will do. And look in her eyes, not at her boobs."

48

I rolled my eyes. "Geesh! I didn't realize there were so many rules."

Trent pointed at me and growled. "I'm fucking serious. If she tells me you even hinted at something inappropriate, you're done. You can pack up your shit and go back to the bank."

God, I loved ruffling his feathers. Nothing gave me more pleasure than seeing my brother come unwound. I should have brought popcorn. With a dash of salt and extra butter. "Understood. Can you show me my new office now?"

There was a glint in Trent's eyes I didn't trust. "Absolutely."

I followed him past my old office. Peeking in, my replacement sat at my desk wearing wire-framed glasses and a three-piece suit. He looked like a douche. He'd better enjoy it while it lasted because I intended on being CFO again within a few months. He could pack his shit, or he could be my assistant. The choice would be his.

As we turned the corner, a sick feeling slithered down my spine. When we got to the end of the hall, I saw my name placard attached to the wall outside the last door. I could have sworn...

Trent opened the door and motioned inside. "Here you are."

"What the actual fuck." The six-by-six room was filled to the brim with file boxes, office supplies, and all the other things nobody knew what to do with.

"It needs a little cleaning out," Trent said with a smirk.

"It's a fucking closet," I gritted through clenched teeth. Losing my temper wouldn't serve me well, especially on my first day back.

"Well, you see, we're limited on office space. This was the best we could do on short notice. That is"—he tapped his fingers together—"unless you'd be more comfortable in the bullpen with the other assistants."

"There's not even a desk in there," I pointed out.

"Oh, there is. It's buried under a few boxes. We've been meaning to throw this stuff away, but you know how it is when things get busy... all the shit gets thrown into the closet."

His implication was clear. *I* was shit. Suppressing the urge to walk out the door and back to the bank, I loosened my tie. "I'll make it work."

"See? I knew you were a team player. Now you won't have to look at the dumpsters anymore. I've done you a favor." The smug look on his face made me want to punch him. "We have a meeting in the conference room at three. Don't be late."

Trent: 1

Hunter: 0

As he walked away, I flipped him the middle finger. It might have been immature, but it gave me a teeny bit of satisfaction.

This entire situation was temporary. All I had to do was prove my worth to the hotel and make amends with the family. The first was easy. I was the fucking best at my job. I'd have that hack in *my* office packing his briefcase in no time. The second would prove to be more difficult. If my interaction with Trent was any indication, he intended to have me crawling on glass and begging for forgiveness.

This was all a game to him, and I was ready to fucking play.

Within a couple of hours, I'd gone through most of the boxes, which, indeed, were filled with shit. Old time cards, schedules, event invoices, and a bunch of other useless crap at least ten years old. There was no need to keep any of it. I separated the documents to be shredded and set them aside. The hallway was filled with garbage for the janitorial staff to dispose of.

My tie and jacket were long gone, and my sleeves rolled up when my father appeared. "How's it going?"

How the fuck did he think it was going? My hands looked like I'd been sifting through actual shit instead of outdated documents. Everything in this closet had half an inch of dust on it and my Armani suit now looked like something I bought off a sales rack at a discount store. "It's getting there. I can see the desk now," I said with a forced smile.

He looked at my disheveled appearance and stuck his hands into his pockets guiltily. "I know it's not ideal, but it's better than the alternative. This way, you'll have your own space."

"I appreciate that." I scratched the back of my neck, knowing I was probably getting dirt on the collar of my white shirt. "Any chance of getting a new desk?"

He stared at the gray metal abomination and winced. "I'll see what I can do. I'll send maintenance to install a phone line too."

"Thank you." I turned to grab another box off my dented desk.

"Hunter, I'm glad you're here regardless of the reasons why. I always imagined I'd leave this company to both my sons. It broke my heart that you and Trent fought so much, but I think it's because you two are more alike than you realize. Please try to make peace with him. I want my family back."

It was strange seeing the man I'd always admired pleading with me. When I was younger, he seemed so strong and powerful, but as I stared at him now, I noticed more lines creasing his face and smatterings of silver in his once jet-black hair. We looked nothing alike. Never did. The only things I inherited from him were my work ethic and keen sense for business.

I was nothing like Trent. My brother resented me from the day I showed up, and I fueled the fire by following him around like a lost puppy. He hated it. Hated that I stole attention from him. It wasn't my fault at first, but over time, I made a habit of it. Whatever Trent did, I did it twice as well. If he brought home an A on a spelling test, I brought home an A-plus. Trent was responsible for my determination... he just didn't know it.

Nothing much had changed between us, except the stakes were higher. I hoped he enjoyed his time in the limelight while I was gone because my time in the shadows was over.

"Trent and I will be fine. We fight and move on. It's been the same story for almost three decades."

"It's different this time. He's not going to make it easy on you," my father said, rocking back on his heels.

"Obviously." I nodded toward my new *office*. "He never made it easy on me."

"You weren't so innocent yourself," he said with a chuckle. "You used to really push his buttons when you two were kids. You got him good a few times."

I shrugged my shoulder. "Eh. It was all in fun."

"It's going to take more than a tussle in the front yard to fix this."

"I'm aware, but I'm prepared to do whatever I have to do."

My father clapped me on the shoulder. "Glad to hear it. Let me know if I can help," he said before he walked away.

Help? How about kicking that douche out of my *office? That would help.*

I stared at the mess still inside the closet. Day one wasn't exactly what I imagined it would be. Checking my watch, I was disappointed to find it was barely eight thirty. If I was going to make it through this day, caffeine was essential. One thing about Mystique, we stocked the best coffee of all the Vegas hotels. Some things were nonnegotiable. An exquisite cup of coffee being one of them.

After washing the filth from my hands, I headed to the break room. What were the chances my old mug was still in the cupboard? I shuffled the array of mugs around and found mine stuffed in the back corner. I pulled it out and read the white letters etched onto the black. *I'm the accountant, so let's assume I'm right.* This mug always irritated Trent, so it definitely deserved resurrecting.

I washed the mug and poured myself a cup of decadent coffee. No cream or sugar... black like my soul. The aroma kicked my senses into overdrive and the first sip was like a shot of adrenaline straight to the heart. God, I missed this. The bank's coffee tasted like something dredged from the bottom of a lake. Next to the pitiful paycheck, the shit coffee was the thing I hated most about working there.

Carina's furniture was due to be delivered soon. I pulled out my phone to check the cameras installed around the apartment. I wondered what Charlotte was doing. Was she snooping in my shit? I should have locked my office and bedroom, but honestly hadn't given it much thought. After

I checked on Carina this morning, all I wanted to do was avoid an unnecessary interaction with Miss Bently.

It was a mistake hiring her. Hopefully, today, she'd bring a bunch of unflattering sweatpants and T-shirts over. If she wore sundresses every day, I'd be sporting a boner twenty-four seven. An inconvenience I'd rather avoid.

I flipped through the camera feeds and didn't see Charlotte at all. Where the fuck was she? I was about to call her when a tiny brunette practically skipped into the break room humming.

When she saw me, she skidded to a stop and her eyes bulged. "Mr. Dorsey, I didn't know you were here."

"Surprise," I deadpanned. "I started today." She looked familiar, but I couldn't place her.

"Oh... I... well... I'll get out of your way." She backed out of the room.

I snapped my fingers and pointed at her as recognition hit. "Patty, right? You work for Gia."

Her nose scrunched up and she stepped back in, throwing her shoulders back. "Actually, it's Penny. Penny Kingston."

Hey, I was close. It's not like I got friendly with the personal assistants. "That's right. You married Brett. I read all about it in the *Las Vegas Not So Confidential*. Rumor has it you've got a bun in the oven."

"That's not really any of your business," she snapped.

She was pregnant. I was sure of it. "So, tell me, why are you working now that you've married a billionaire? Wouldn't you rather go to the spa and eat bonbons?"

Penny propped her hands on her hips. "I happen to like my job, thank you very much, and I'm good at it. The question is, what are you doing here? Didn't you get fired?"

There was a time when no one dared speak to me that way. I was respected and feared. Now, I was office gossip. "The whys don't matter. I'm back. Get used to it." I pushed past her and headed to my *office*.

Before tackling the rest of the crap in the closet, I pulled up the cameras again. I searched through all the feeds, and Charlotte wasn't in a single frame. Where the fuck was my nanny? It was 9:06 a.m. The delivery guys should have been there already.

I grabbed my keys because there was a more pressing issue. Where was my daughter? This is what I got for hiring some unknown chick without doing a background check. For all I knew, she could be halfway across the state with Carina.

With my phone in my hand and my eyes glued to the screen, I started for the lobby. I jabbed at the button for the elevator but before the doors could open, there she was.

I let out a sigh of relief and ran my hand through my short hair. Charlotte pushed the stroller through the apartment door and let the delivery guy in. I specifically told her nine o'clock, not 9:07 a.m. Nothing pissed me off more than people being late. If she'd missed the delivery, I'd have been furious.

Miss Bently and I were going to have a little talk tonight about promptness and responsibility. If she couldn't handle the job, she needed to go.

Chapter 8
Charli

At noon, I headed down to the parking garage with Carina in tow. I found Hunter's black Escalade in parking spot 32B, as he'd promised. I'd never driven such a fancy car before but figured it couldn't be much different than my old pickup truck.

With Carina fastened safely in the car seat, I headed across town to my own apartment. It paled in comparison to my new accommodations. It was far enough off the Strip that the rent was cheap, but not cheap enough when you hadn't been working. There was no fancy doorman or elaborate lobby, but luckily, there was an elevator. I never appreciated it until I injured my leg. Going upstairs with crutches would have been brutal.

Once we arrived, I pushed Carina's stroller into the elevator. Before the doors could close, I heard, "Hold the elevator." My hand shot out to stop the doors from closing and Mr. Thompson hobbled in with his miniature poodle. "Thanks, Charli."

"Are you and Lucy coming back from a walk?"

He held up his cane with one hand and the dog with his other. "We can't go too far these days, but it's good to get outside. Neither one of us are spring chickens anymore."

I winked at him. "I think you're still dashingly handsome. Any new lady friends?"

"Nope. I'm taking a break. The ladies are crazy. My bump and grind aren't what they used to be."

I chuckled into my hand. I loved Mr. Thompson. He might have been old, but he was young at heart. "I bet your bump and grind are just fine. You're a catch. If I were a few years older…"

He waved me off. "Enough about me." He glanced down at Carina and made a silly face, making her giggle. "How about you? You have a new beau?"

I tickled Carina's toes. "Nope. I have a new job nannying. I'm here to pack up my apartment. I'll be living across town to take care of this little one."

"Hmmm." Mr. Thompson scratched his chin. "Nice family?"

"Single dad, actually," I said, pushing my hair behind my ear.

He perked up. "Rich?"

I had no idea what Hunter's finances were, but he had expensive taste. "Richer than me."

"You know what they say. It's as easy to fall in love with a rich man as it is a poor man. Maybe this'll be the one."

Being my neighbor, Mr. Thompson had witnessed my string of failed relationships over the years. "I'm not looking for a man, but the job pays well."

"Don't close yourself off to possibilities." He bumped me with his shoulder. "*You're* a catch."

The last thing I needed to do was form a romantic connection with Hunter Dorsey. It was a bad idea for so many reasons, the least of which was his sunny disposition. He made the Grinch seem like Man of the Year.

The elevator doors opened, and we both got off on the fifth floor. "I'm moving today, so if I don't see you again, thank you for always being so kind to me." I gave him a hug and patted Lucy on the head. "I'm going to miss you."

"You're easy to be kind to, Charli. Take care of yourself and don't be afraid to fall in love. You deserve it."

We said our goodbyes and parted ways to our respective apartments. Once inside, I let out a sigh. The apartment was small—one bedroom, one bathroom, a tiny kitchen, and a small sitting room—but it was the first place I'd ever lived alone. I'd been so proud when I signed the lease. I felt like a real adult with a real job that paid the bills. Giving it up felt like moving backward instead of forward.

Regardless, it wouldn't take too long to pack. I wished I had the foresight to collect some boxes. It wasn't like I didn't know I had to move; the only question had been where. There were a few shoved in one of the closets, but they wouldn't be nearly enough.

I reached down and pulled Carina from her stroller. "Well, girlie, I guess we better get started." I carried her to the bedroom, laid her down in the middle of the bed, and scattered some toys around her. She seemed perfectly happy, shaking the plush frog and listening to the rattle inside.

Pulling my suitcase from the closet, I began emptying the dresser drawers and stuffing my clothes inside. There was no need to be organized. I'd unpack in a few hours and refold my clothes then. When my suitcase was maxed out, I began stuffing clothes into garbage bags. It wasn't fancy, but it'd have to do.

There was no way I could move everything today. Hunter was insane if he thought I'd be able to move the furniture myself and take care of a baby. Typical man thinking. Even if I found superhuman strength to carry a bed frame and dresser, which was doubtful, there wasn't even enough room in the Escalade. The easiest thing to do was call a moving company and pray they could fit me in before my lease ended at the end of the week. I chastised myself for not having a plan.

Reckless.

Rash.

Careless.

My mother's words echoed in my head.

A knock at the door pulled me from my pity party. It was probably Mr. Thompson. Most of my neighbors kept to themselves. The younger people worked in the casinos or bars. I suspected a few of the women were escorts, but it wasn't my business how people earned their money. We all had to make a living. The older people were much like Mr. Thompson, who hadn't planned out their retirement very well. In their defense, Vegas wasn't called Sin City for nothing. There were a million ways to waste your money here.

Another more urgent knock sounded before I made it to the door with Carina in my arms. "I'm coming!" I swung the door open, and it wasn't Mr. Thompson. Two overly cheery women stood on my doorstep smiling with two very brawny men behind them. If they were selling something, they were out of luck. I needed every penny I had. "Umm. Hello?"

The short blond held up a tape gun. "We're here to help you pack. Mr. Dorsey sent us."

My ears must have been deceiving me. "Hunter sent you?"

"Uh-huh," chirped the taller brunette. "We brought boxes, bubble wrap, and muscle." She hiked her thumb over her shoulder at the guys. "We have a truck too."

I stood there dumbstruck.

The blond leaned around me to look inside. "This shouldn't take too long at all. We'll have you moved in no time." She smiled even bigger at me. "That is if you let us in."

It was a nice surprise. Maybe Hunter wasn't a bad guy after all. "Of course." I stepped back to let them in. "Some things are going into storage, and some are coming to the apartment."

"You're in charge," the brunette answered. "Tell us what's going where, and we'll mark the boxes appropriately. Guys, why don't you start with the couch and TV stand? Us girls will start in the kitchen."

The guys lifted the couch as if it weighed nothing and were out the door without saying a word. The girls, Tina and Carrie, started to empty my kitchen cabinets, carefully wrapping the plates and glasses in bubble wrap like they were fine china. They weren't. I bought them at the dollar store.

"This isn't going to take long at all," I said to Carina as I bounced her on my hip. "Your daddy got us helpers. Wasn't that nice?"

She reached for my hair and gave it a tug, then laughed like I'd said the funniest thing ever.

"Cute baby," Carrie said, or maybe it was Tina. I already forgot who was who.

"Thanks." She assumed Carina was mine, and I didn't correct her. I figured we'd be getting that a lot when we went out, and honestly, it wasn't anyone's business if Carina was mine or not. I was already falling in love with her.

Within a couple hours, my apartment was completely bare. All my prized possessions were packed and loaded into the truck. The only thing left to do was turn in my key.

I sent Hunter a text message with a smiley face emoji. *Thank you for sending the movers. It was a huge help!* Then, I propped Carina on my hip and held up my phone. "Smile for Daddy." Snapping the picture, I sent it too.

All I got back was a thumbs-up emoji.

Chapter 9
Hunter

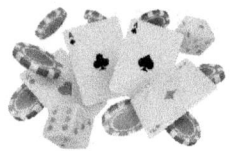

At ten minutes to three, I entered the conference room and took my place next to the head of the table. I'd never arrived late to a meeting. Promptness was not only professional but also showed respect. Seemingly, only one other person shared my opinion.

I ignored the woman at the other end of the table, who looked familiar but I hadn't cared enough to remember her name. I set my portfolio and pen on the table, ready to start on some real work instead of cleaning out a closet that now slightly resembled an office with its crappy furniture and secondhand office supplies. My new boss hadn't even bothered to introduce himself to me. Totally unprofessional. When I was CFO, I made it a point to introduce myself to new employees, even if I forgot their names two seconds later.

My phone buzzed with a text, and I pulled it out of my suit coat. It was from Charlotte. Apparently, the move went well. She also included a selfie of herself and Carina, smiling big for the camera. I gazed at the picture. It was the first one I had of my daughter. I still couldn't believe she was mine, but those cerulean eyes were unmistakable. She was definitely mine.

I saved the picture and sent Charlotte a thumbs-up, then put my phone on silent and set it face down on the table. Distractions were the last thing I needed, and pictures of Charlotte Bently were very distracting.

The table began to fill as employees meandered into the conference room. Trent sat across from me and Gia next to him. "How's the office coming?" Trent smirked at his own perceived cleverness.

"It's perfect." I pasted on a fake smile and set my mug where he could read it. "No complaints." I wasn't going to let him get any more pleasure at my expense than he'd already gotten. There was a quota for that, and he'd reached his limit. I turned my attention to his wife. "Hello, Gia."

"Hunter." If looks could kill, I'd be flat on the floor.

"I'd appreciate a moment of your time after the meeting." Might as well get the apology over with sooner rather than later. I didn't need it lingering between us and I would earn some brownie points with my brother.

She looked me dead in the eye with a bored expression. "I'll check my schedule to see when I'm available. Penny will let you know the time of your appointment."

Appointment?

Trent snickered into his hand. "Burn."

"Of course," I said through clenched teeth. I couldn't really blame her for hating me, but still…

"Ahem." The sound of someone clearing their throat came from behind me. I turned to look at the douche canoe in wireframes and a three-piece suit. "You're in my seat."

To the left of my father had always been *my* seat. I looked at Trent, who raised an eyebrow and motioned with his head for me to move down.

This was fucking bullshit, but I picked up my things and moved to the only empty seat next to Greta, head of housekeeping. She scowled at me as I sat down. In fact, everyone was scowling at me. Not one of them said hello or welcomed me back. I kept my mouth shut and glared at my coworkers. Fuck these people!

My father walked in and took his spot at the head of the table. "Good afternoon, everyone. I want to start this meeting by welcoming back my son, Hunter." He motioned to me, and the staff gave me a lame round of applause. I was about as welcome as a nun at an orgy. Nobody wanted me here.

If I were a lesser man, it would have bothered me, but I really didn't give a shit what these people thought of me. I knew my worth.

During the meeting, I kept my ears open and scribbled notes in my portfolio. Revenue was down and spending was up. Both were bad for Mystique. I couldn't wait to dig into the financial records. When I left here a year ago, we were on our way to being the most lucrative resort in Vegas. According to my father's report, profits were slipping.

When I got back to my office, I planned to examine all the financial records from the last year with a fine-tooth comb. There was absolutely no reason the resort should be losing money. Our shows were fantastic, the cuisine Michelin Star rated, the rooms exquisite, the shopping high end, and the casinos unmatched. We boasted the best customer service on the Strip. Every employee went through strenuous training to ensure it. If we were losing money, it wasn't for lack of quality.

My father prided himself on giving customers an experience they would never forget. With him close to retiring, declining margins would set him back at least another year. Not that I was anxious for Trent to take over, but poor revenue was bad for everyone.

This was an opportunity to seize, a way to get back into the good graces of the family. I made more notes, bullet-pointing areas that required further investigation and possible deficiencies. On a separate sheet of paper, I began conducting a preliminary SWOT analysis, citing strengths, weaknesses, opportunities, and threats for Mystique.

The bank wasted my talent with mundane tasks such as reviewing delinquent mortgages and credit checks for personal loans. Neither took any skills. Any idiot with a degree in finance could do it. I missed the thrill of a challenge—digging deeper, creating spreadsheets, and analyzing facts and figures. Most people found data mining tedious and tiresome. To me, sorting through information to identify patterns and relationships was therapeutic. For the first time since getting fired, my spark and motivation returned.

After the meeting concluded, I took it upon myself to approach my new *boss* and introduce myself since he hadn't had the courtesy to do it himself. I bit the bullet and stuck out my hand. "We haven't been formally introduced, but I'm Hunter and we'll be working together. I'd like to meet with you to discuss my ideas regarding the financial shortfall Mystique is currently undergoing."

He stuck his hands in his pockets and stared at me like a pesky insect he needed to squash. "My understanding is you'll be working *for* me, not *with* me. I'm already conducting an analysis. What I need is for you to oversee payroll while reviewing requests for personal days and vacation time. You think you can handle that?"

Was this guy for real? "All due respect, Leonard..."

"It's Mr. Moroski. All due respect, *Hunter*, but I know who you are, and I won't be extending any special privileges. You'll address me as Mr. Moroski, like all the other employees. I'll have my PA send you the payroll files." He turned on his heel and walked away, leaving me standing there like a complete idiot.

I sat back down and stared at my notes as the room cleared out. This was worse than working at the bank. At least there, people treated me with respect. Maybe coming back here was a mistake. It was unrealistic to think the staff would accept me. The only reason I hadn't been completely exiled was because of my last name.

My salary at the bank wasn't *that* bad. I could go back. All it would take was a bit of groveling. If I worked really hard, maybe in twenty years, I would be promoted to bank manager. Whoop-de-do.

I ripped the pages out of my portfolio, crumbled them in my fist, and threw them across the room. They bounced off the wall in pathetic fashion and dropped to the floor.

Fuck this shit!

No way was I going back to the bank. I pushed my chair back and stormed across the room to pick up the wadded pieces of paper. Smoothing them out, I carefully tucked them back into my portfolio.

There was more than one way to skin a cat. Leonard Morosk-hole was an arrogant dick fucker. I'd spent my whole life hurdling over obstacles bigger than him. He thought he knew who I was, but he didn't have a clue. When it came to playing by the rules, I was nothing like Trent or my father.

He messed with the wrong Dorsey.

Chapter 10
Charli

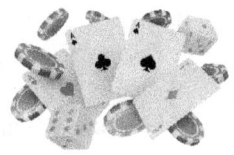

Carina and I had a busy day, productive but exhausting. The last thing I wanted to do was entertain a baby while making dinner. My leg ached and my knee throbbed from being on my feet all day. Sitting on my ass with my leg up while drinking a glass of wine sounded heavenly.

Cooking wasn't really part of my job, but I figured it might get me in Hunter's good graces if he came home to a hot meal. After all, the way to a man's heart was through his stomach. Not that I wanted into his heart, but I owed him for hiring the moving company.

It wasn't quite time to feed Carina, so I sprinkled cereal puffs on the tray of her high chair to keep her busy. She banged on the tray and shoved them in her mouth with her chubby fists, gobbling them down like they were caviar.

I poked around in Hunter's refrigerator, searching for something I could make for dinner. The selection was sparse. He was a typical bachelor. The fridge was stocked with bacon, eggs, yogurt, and protein shakes. I wondered if he had a girlfriend, but I'd say no, according to the inadequate food choices.

The pantry wasn't much better. Did the man not believe in snacks? There wasn't a bag of chips or package of cookies in sight. Not that I needed snacks, but it was nice to have options. I'd put ten pounds on since my accident and my muscles had all but disappeared. Before the fall, I was in the best shape of my life. Performing six nights a week kept me toned and lean. Climbing up the silks like a rope might have looked easy to the audience, but only because I had the strength of a man twice my size. Getting back in the gym topped my priority list right after taking care of Carina. The sooner I got back in shape, the sooner I could get back in the air, assuming my job would still be there when I was ready.

I grabbed a box of pasta and a jar of spaghetti sauce. It was far from gourmet, but it was something. Digging through the bottom cabinets, I pulled out a large pot to boil the noodles in. Filling it with water, I placed it on the stove and turned the heat on.

I wasn't sure what time Hunter got home from work because he didn't include it in the incredibly detailed schedule left on the counter. My best guesstimate was between six o'clock and six thirty. He left the apartment early this morning and I figured he would be anxious to come home to his giggly bundle of joy, although last night, he seemed perfectly fine letting me take care of her.

I looked over at Carina, who had somehow smooshed cereal puffs into her fine hair and across her cheeks. "Well, look at you. You're a mess." She responded by crushing more puffs into the side of her head. "You're going to be a handful, aren't you, baby girl?"

Carina waved her fists in the air and kicked her legs. "Gah, gah!"

I laughed and leaned down in front of her. "Let's try this. Dah, dah, dah."

She blew air through her lips and giggled as puffs sprayed all over my face.

"Nice," I said, wiping the soggy cereal from my cheek. "Now we're both a mess." I grabbed a washcloth and cleaned Carina's hands and face. "No more puffs for you until dinnertime." I suctioned a spinning fish toy to the tray instead and showed her how to use it. "That's right," I took her little hand and helped her hit the fish, "Knock 'em on the head. Knock 'em real good." I started singing. "Bomp, bomp, bomp, ba bomp. Knock 'em real good. Bomp, bomp, bomp, ba…"

"Are you trying to set the house on fire?"

I straightened up, embarrassed Hunter caught me singing. "What?"

He pointed to the stove, where water boiled out of the pot and splashed along the surface, sizzling as it hit the hot burner. I rushed over and turned it off. "It's just a little water."

"Are you aware that most house fires start in the kitchen due to distracted cooking?"

Actually, I wasn't. I'd never given it any thought. "Ummm…"

He sighed. "If you're going to live here, then you need to be more careful. I can't be worried that you're going to burn the house down."

"I won't burn the house down," I promised. Hunter loosened his tie and pulled it away from the collar of his dress shirt. There were gray smudges on the sleeves and on the sides like he'd been standing with his hands on his hips with dirty fingers. Dark circles hung under his eyes and his shoulders slumped. He wasn't the intimidating jerk face from last night. Something must have happened at work today. "Are you alright?"

He ran a hand through his short hair. "I'm fine. What are you attempting to cook?"

"Oh!" I held up the box of dry rotini noodles and shook it. "Spaghetti. Are you hungry?"

"Famished. How did the move go?"

"Excellent. Thank you so much for hiring the movers. It was really a godsend. All I have left to do is unpack the things in my room." I pulled out another pot and dumped the spaghetti sauce into it, then turned the water back on for the noodles. "Carina and I had an excellent day."

"Uh-huh. And were the delivery guys on time this morning?" He raised an eyebrow at me.

There was an edge to his voice that told me to be careful. Had the delivery guy called him and tattled on me for being late. "Yep. Right on time. Nine o'clock sharp." I needed to shut up.

"Is that so?" he asked.

I turned my back to him and stirred the sauce. "Absolutely. They were very efficient too. Set everything up and hauled all the boxes away."

"That's what I paid them for. Everything I ordered came?"

I shrugged and poured the noodles into the boiling water, setting the timer. "I think so."

"You think so? Didn't you check the packing slip before signing the delivery receipt?"

I shrugged again. "Sort of."

He went over to Carina and pulled her from the high chair, snuggling her to his chest. "Sort of? Charlotte, did you check the packing slip or not? If something is missing, I need to know."

Stirring the sauce one more time, I dropped the spoon into the pot and faced Hunter. "Listen, I know you think I'm incompetent, but it was really hectic around here. People coming and going. There were so many boxes, and I didn't know what was what or where to put anything. I eyeballed the list, and it all seemed to be here. If it wasn't for your mother, I'd still be unpacking bottles, hanging up clothes, and assembling the bouncy seat. You said it was going to be furniture, not the entire baby department from Macy's."

His jaw clenched. "Wait. Why was Rose here?"

It was weird that he called his mother by her first name. I might have been younger than him, but I couldn't ever see myself calling my mom Pamela. Maybe that's what rich people did, called their parents by their first names. "I don't know. She came to help and see Carina? I'm thankful she did."

"I don't want her here," Hunter stated.

I let that sink in. "You don't want your mom here? Why?"

He pulled a cereal puff out of Carina's hair and turned his back to me. "She's not my mother. She's my father's wife."

"Oh." That explained why Trent and Hunter looked nothing alike. "She was really excited about seeing Carina. She called herself Grandma Rose." Even if Rose wasn't Hunter's biological mom, would it be so bad for Carina to have a grandma? Someone who loved her.

68

"I bet she did," Hunter grumbled. "That woman doesn't know boundaries."

That woman? Yikes! "What do you want me to do if she shows up again? Kick her out?"

"That's perfect. I'm glad you suggested it."

Wait! What? The timer went off on the stove. I drained the noodles before they got overcooked and soggy, then turned back to Hunter. "I didn't suggest it. Look, I get that you don't have a good relationship with Rose, but I think it would be a mistake to deprive Carina of having a grandma. She already doesn't have a mother."

Hunter considered that for a moment. I could practically see the gears turning in his head. "Not that I asked for your opinion, but I'll think about it." He carefully placed Carina back in her high chair and kissed the top of her head. "Is the spaghetti ready yet?"

"A couple more minutes. Why don't you go change into something more comfortable."

He looked down at his dress shirt and pants. "I am comfortable."

I shrugged. "Suit yourself." Going to the pantry, I pulled out two jars of baby food. "Squash or peas?"

"Squash," he said as he pulled bowls from the cabinet and silverware from the drawer. "The peas make her poop green. It's disgusting."

"Noted." We stood side by side, scooping food into the bowls and took them to the table. My leg throbbed, and I winced as I sat down. Damn this leg. How was I ever going to get back on stage if I couldn't even handle one day as a nanny? I lifted my leg onto the empty chair and pulled the brace down. My knee looked like an angry red balloon.

Hunter looked down at my leg. "Painful?"

"It's fine." I didn't want to give him a reason to take this job away from me. A little pain was worth the paycheck.

"It doesn't look fine. Did you take anything?"

I pulled Carina's high chair between us and fastened a bib around her neck. "I'll take something after dinner. Tomorrow, it'll be good as new." That was a lie. I wasn't sure my knee and leg would ever be *good as new*, but I wasn't going to let it hold me back.

He got up from the table and brought back two little white pills. "Take these. After dinner I want you to finish unpacking and rest your leg. I need you in tip-top condition tomorrow."

I swallowed down the pills greedily. "I still have to give Carina a bath." I put a few plain noodles on her tray and let Carina feed herself while we ate.

"I'm her father. I can give her a bath and get her ready for bed."

"But that's what you're paying me for," I argued.

"I'm paying you to do what I say, and you won't be worth a damn if you're limping around like a gimp tomorrow. Understood?" He dug into his spaghetti like the conversation was over, ignoring me.

God, he was bossy. Why did I find it attractive when he went all caveman on me? I suppressed the urge to argue with him. He was right about resting my leg, even if I didn't want to admit it. "Thank you. It was a busy day, and I'm not used to spending so much time on my feet."

"I'm not worried about it."

We ate in awkward silence as I fed Carina the squash in between my bites of spaghetti. She puckered her lips and spit it out. The orange goo dripped down her chin and onto the bib. "Damn it." I rushed to wipe her mouth before it dripped onto her clothes, but it smeared all over her cheeks, giving her an orange Joker smile. She laughed and blinked at me with her bright-blue eyes. "You're a stinkpot, you know that?" I stuffed another spoonful of squash in her mouth, and she spit it out again.

Hunter grabbed the leg of the high chair and pulled it toward him. "Let me try." I gave him the spoon and he dipped it into the jar. "Open up, princess." He leaned in close as he shoveled it into her mouth.

Carina sputtered her lips, spraying the orange squash all over Hunter's face, and laughed again.

I laughed too, and handed him a napkin over the table. "Nice try."

He wiped his face and frowned. "I don't understand. She ate it fine yesterday."

"She's playing a game with us." I plopped some more noodles on her tray, and she eagerly shoved them in her mouth. "No worries. I'll give her a bottle later."

70

When we finished eating, I limped over to the sink, rinsed our bowls, and loaded them into the dishwasher.

"What are you doing?"

"Cleaning up," I said as I poured the leftover sauce into a plastic container.

"I thought I told you to go rest your leg. I'll clean up and then give Carina her bath."

"I can wash the dishes," I argued. "I'm not an invalid."

"You can do as you're told," he growled as he pulled the pot from my hand. "Go."

I held up my hands and backed away. "Alright, alright. I was trying to help." In his own grouchy way, Hunter was being nice. Truth be told, I *was* exhausted and although the pain pills were helping, my knee was still swollen.

Overall, my first day went well. I almost missed the delivery guy this morning, but Hunter didn't know about that. It would be my little secret.

I was halfway down the hallway when Hunter called out to me. "One more thing, dollface."

"Yes?"

"Nine o'clock does not mean 9:07. Don't be late again."

Seemed it wasn't such a secret after all.

Chapter 11
Hunter

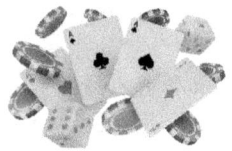

Giving Charlotte the night off wasn't completely selfless.

Although I'd only had her a brief time, I missed my daughter and thought about her all day. I didn't want to be an absentee father. It was bad enough her mother took off without a second thought. One thing I could say about my father, is he was always there for me. He didn't miss Little League games because of meetings or skip out on school functions. I always knew I could depend on him.

Carina deserved someone she could depend on.

Despite Charlotte's pitiful résumé and lack of experience with children, there was no doubt she'd taken good care of my daughter today. I even caught her singing that stupid song when I walked in. Her voice was absolutely awful, but Carina liked it. She needed someone like Charlotte in her life because the last words anyone would ever use to describe me were warm and nurturing.

Also, I liked finding Charlotte in the kitchen making dinner a little too much. I didn't expect her to cook, but she did. Coming home to an empty apartment was my norm. I usually heated something in the microwave or picked up takeout on the way home. It'd been a while since someone cooked for me. Sitting together at the table with Carina felt like we were a family.

We weren't.

I didn't have any delusions about that, but it still felt nice.

I didn't do relationships. Never had anything more than a few repeat dates in my life. I didn't have the time or the inclination. There was no sense getting attached to a woman. When she realized I wasn't a decent human being and I couldn't treat her right, she'd leave anyway.

Sex was easy, love was complicated. I'd never felt that tingly sensation people talked about. Never fell head over heels for a woman. Never needed to have someone to come home to.

I was perfectly happy as a lone wolf. I could do what I wanted when I wanted without having to report to anyone. When I had needs to be satisfied, it wasn't hard to fill them. And when I got the release I craved, I left. No strings. No complications.

It was a good life.

Charlotte was a complication. The less I was around her, the better. I didn't need to see her making my daughter giggle. I didn't need to hear her terrible singing. And I definitely didn't need to see her long legs or perky little tits.

After I cleaned up the kitchen, I took Carina for her nightly bath. Charlotte had lined up all of Carina's new tub toys along the ledge of the tub like little soldiers. I filled the tub with a few inches of warm water, stripped Carina down, and set her in the tub seat. She kicked her little legs in the warm water and giggled.

"You like this, don't you?" I handed her the rubber turtle and let her go to town, squeaking the thing until my ears hurt. She played while I kneeled next to the tub and gently washed her soft skin from her squash-covered face to her tiny toes. She made a grabby motion with her hands, so I tossed a few more toys into the tub. The rubber frog squeaked as she chewed on his eye. She didn't have any teeth yet, but from what I'd read, I expected to see some popping through on the bottom soon.

73

"You got crap luck, kid. Anyone would have been a better father than me. I've got no idea what I'm doing, but I promise I'll try. You'll never want for anything. If you need me, I'll be there. But just so you know, when you get old enough to start dating, I'm going to be a total dick to any boy you bring home. You should know that up front, so there're no surprises later. And don't even think about sneaking out at night. I've done every trick in the book, so you won't get away with it. If necessary, I'll build a moat around our house to keep you safe. What do you think of that?"

Carina reached her arms out to me. "Gah, dah, bah."

I chuckled. "You say that now, but I'm sure when you're a teenager, you'll think I'm an overprotective asshole. And you'll be right. That's exactly what I'm going to be." I picked up her foot and looked at her wrinkly toes. "Time to get out, princess."

I lifted her out of the tub, and she let out a huge fart. It stunk. "Jesus Christ, how can something so little smell so bad?" She kicked her legs and laughed at me. That's when I noticed the brown sludge dripping down the backs of her legs. With one more kick, it splattered across the front of my shirt. "You've got to be kidding me." I held her in the air over the tub. I couldn't put her back in the water and I'd left the towel on the other side of the bathroom.

My stomach turned. I could feel the vomit making its way up my esophagus. I took a deep breath and pushed it down. "Oh, god. Charlotte!" The smell invaded my nose, and my stomach flipped again. The poop dripped off her heels and splashed into the water. I turned and dry heaved over my shoulder. "Charlotte! Goddamn it, where are you? CHARLOTTE!"

Her feet pounded on the hardwood floor and into the bathroom. "What..."

"Help me!"

She stood there slack-jawed. "Oh my god! There's poop everywhere."

"No shit, Sherlock! Do something!" My stomach rumbled and I dry heaved again. If she didn't hurry my spaghetti was going to make a reappearance.

"Are you gonna puke?"

"Charlotte!"

"Right…" She grabbed the pink towel off the counter and held it up, twisting it this way and that. "I don't know where to begin."

"That'll smear it. Grab the showerhead and rinse her off!"

"Smart thinking." She scrambled over me, her crotch practically in my face, and pulled the showerhead down. She turned on the water and the tub began to fill. "I don't know how to work this thing." Charlotte pounded her hand on the sprayer like that was a logical way to turn it on.

"There's a button on the side," I growled.

"Wher—" Water burst from the nozzle, hitting her in the face. She screamed, then frantically aimed it at me. Water drenched my chest and sprayed all over the bathroom.

"Jesus Christ! Get her ass and legs!" My arms were getting tired, and I was afraid of dropping her.

Charlotte finally aimed the sprayer at Carina and began rinsing her off. "I'm so sorry," she apologized as brown water ran down my daughter's legs. "That should be… oh my god, she's doing it again!"

Carina laughed and kicked as more poop ran down her legs.

Fuck! We were never going to get her clean. "Switch places with me! Hurry!" Charlotte dropped the sprayer, and I handed Carina to her. "Hold her over the tub!" I rinsed the poop off, then quickly grabbed a washcloth and some soap, wiped her down, and rinsed her again. I swiped the towel from where Charlotte had dropped it on the floor and wrapped Carina in it. "Quick, go get a diaper!"

Charlotte dashed from the bathroom, nearly falling as her bare feet slipped on the wet floor. She came back with a diaper and a package of wipes. "Just in case," she said as she held them up.

When I finally got the diaper on Carina, I laid her on the dry rug and sat on the floor. Charlotte slid down the wall next to me, looking like a drowned cat. The bathroom still stunk, the tub was full of murky water, and there were flecks of brown on the shower walls. It was as if a bomb went off. A poop bomb.

"That was intense," she whispered as her wet hair dripped down her face.

"Ya think?"

She tilted her head to the side. "Were you really gonna throw up?"

"I have a weak stomach." There was no sense denying it since she'd seen me retching.

"Then maybe I shouldn't tell you… you've got a little… poop on your shirt."

I'd forgotten about that. I looked down and it was even worse now that my shirt was plastered to my chest. Without another thought, I ripped the wet shirt off and threw it to the side. "Hand me the wipes."

"You want one or two?" she asked, pulling them from the container.

"Give me the whole damn box." I could literally feel the poop soaking into my skin as I scrubbed furiously.

"You think it was the squash?"

"I've got no fucking idea, but that was horrible."

"It really was." She laughed. "You should have seen your face." She laughed again, then snorted, which made her laugh even harder. "You were all like… bleh, bleh." Her imitation of my dry heaving made me smile.

"It wasn't that bad."

"It was pretty bad." Charlotte snorted again and wiped the tears from her eyes. "Oh my…" She took a deep breath and immediately covered her nose. "Is cleaning this up part of my job?"

I scratched the back of my neck. "I don't think we discussed hazmat duties."

"I'll flip you for it," she suggested.

I glanced at the murky water and my stomach turned. There was no way I could do it without actually vomiting. "How about I pay you an extra hundred bucks instead?"

She cocked her head from side to side, considering my proposal. "Deal. I hope you have bleach."

"In the laundry room closet." I looked at my daughter, who'd fallen asleep on the rug. "Who knew someone so little could do so much damage?" Picking Carina up, I cradled her in my arms. "I'll put this little terrorist to bed. Thank you, Charlotte."

"I think after what we've been through tonight, you can call me Charli now." She pushed back the wet hair on her face, revealing a black line dripping down her cheek where her mascara had run. She was a complete mess.

I liked it a little too much.

"Good night, Charli."

Chapter 12
Charli

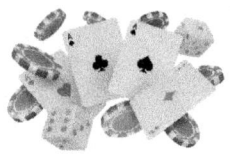

The next morning, I woke up and Hunter was gone again. That bothered me more than it should have. The quiet in the apartment was made worse by the large space. It seemed... lonely. I imagined Hunter living here by himself before Carina and I showed up and wondered if he ever felt lonely.

I brewed myself a cup of coffee and read today's note.

Today's Schedule:
7:00- Breakfast, Diaper Change, Face Washing
8:00- Walk
9:00- Laundry (Collect Carina's clothes from the hamper in her room. Pretreat any stains before washing. I don't want my daughter looking like a hobo.)
10:00- 6oz. of Formula/Nap
12:00- Grocery Shopping (See List)

I rolled my eyes at Hunter's need to schedule every minute of the day for me. It was insulting. I was a grown woman who was perfectly capable of managing her own time. How would he even know if I stuck to the schedule anyway? Did it really matter if we took our walk at eight thirty instead of eight o'clock? As long as I accomplished everything on the list by the time he got home, it was fine.

He was delusional if he thought Carina had any sense of time. Just because he deemed she would take a nap at ten o'clock didn't mean she would. She'd sleep whenever she felt like it. If anything, I was on her schedule.

I hoped nothing like last night happened again. It was a goddamn nightmare. Thankfully, there were two of us to manage it. I'm not sure how I would have fared on my own.

The only thing positive about the experience was Hunter taking off his shirt. Holy crap! He had a pretty face—stunning blue eyes, a chiseled jaw, ample scruff to give a woman whisker burns on the insides of her thighs, and a crop of short blond hair that looked tousled enough to suggest he'd recently had a raucous roll in the hay—but I did not expect what was under his shirt. The man was muscled and cut in all the right places. I'd barely been able to keep my tongue from hanging out of my mouth.

Too bad he was such an uptight asshole.

It was okay though. It would keep me from falling for the jerk.

I scanned the rest of the schedule for the day. Hunter noted at the bottom that he wouldn't be home for dinner and to eat without him. A pang of disappointment smacked me in the chest. It's not that I liked him or anything; he was disagreeable at best. After trying to reconcile my irrational feelings, I moved on to the *second* piece of paper.

Grocery List
Diapers
Wipes (At least 3 boxes)
Stain Stick
Formula
Jarred Baby Food (NO squash)

Cereal Puffs
Eggs
Yogurt
Milk
Bagels
Bacon

The list went on and on. He wrote for me to add what I wanted to the list and to put it on the credit card he'd given me. For someone who'd eaten ramen noodles for the last three months, it felt like I hit the food lottery. I wouldn't go crazy, but it would be nice to buy something that wasn't on the weekly discount.

In the brief amount of time I'd been here, Hunter had dropped an insane amount of money. I wondered what it felt like to spend without thinking about every little penny.

Tom and I didn't grow up rich. We weren't poor, but my parents weren't frivolous either. When the two of us moved to Vegas together, we shared an apartment until I could afford my own. It wasn't anything fancy, but it was freedom. I came here with a dream and not much else. Tom followed me to make sure I didn't end up living on the street. He job hopped a bit until he landed the gig at Mystique. His true passion was computer programming. Fetching coffee for a boss who didn't appreciate him was a total waste of his talent.

Tom had been working on a "secret project" for years and he kept saying he was close to making a breakthrough. He spent hours holed up with his computer, doing God knows what. I hoped whatever it was, it would pay off soon. My brother deserved something of his own... and someone. Life was too short to spend it alone.

I thought about Ben's phone number sitting on my dresser. I'd spent so many nights alone that I'd lost count. It was nice to have someone notice me—not because of my ability to spin endlessly in a hoop thirty feet above the ground—but because of who I was. Not some artistic showgirl, but a normal woman trying to make something of herself. Not that being a nanny was my dream. My dreams had been put on hold as I recuperated from an injury most people would have succumbed to. Not me. More than anything else, I wanted to climb far above a stage and perform acts that would make ordinary women quake in their high heels.

I wasn't ordinary.

I lacked the fear gene. Fear was an excuse for not reaching your full potential. Even after twisting through the silks and crashing, an embarrassing spectacle, the only thing I wanted was the chance to get up and try it again.

My mother had begged me to quit. My father slyly suggested other professional opportunities. My brother felt relief when he didn't have to worry about me night after night.

I was bored out of my fucking skull.

Had been for months. If you had never experienced the shot of pure adrenaline straight to your heart, you wouldn't understand it. I didn't blame my family for wanting something different for me, but that didn't mean I would be deterred. I only had one life to live, and I intended to make the most of it.

At least nannying gave me something to focus my time and energy on. Taking care of Carina was about the best distraction I could ask for. It was a blessing really.

After getting Carina up, dressed, and fed, we went for a walk around the park. It was a beautiful day, and the sun warmed my skin as we followed the path around the small pond. I sat on a bench and pulled Carina out of her stroller to sit on my lap. Pointing at the ducks, I said to her, "See the duckies. What does a duckie say? Can you say quack, quack, quack?"

She waved her hands and made a grabby motion. "Gih, gih, gih."

"That's right, baby girl. "Quack, quack, quack." A brown-headed duck waddled in our direction and Carina squealed with delight. I set her feet on the grass and held her by the waist. She squealed again as the grass tickled her toes. Next time, I'd bring some bread to feed the ducks. Carina would love watching them scramble about trying to get a treat.

"Cute baby."

I looked up at the woman walking her tiny Pomeranian. "Thank you." She was about my age with long blond hair tied up in a ponytail and a body to die for. Her leggings and sports bra showed off every curve she had. Jealousy bloomed. My body was lean and muscular, but my hips and boobs were practically nonexistent. When I was a teenager, I kept waiting for my boobs to grow and they never did. I'd accepted it, but I appreciated a nice pair when I saw them.

"Are you new around here?" the woman asked. "I haven't seen you before."

"Not new to Vegas, but new to the neighborhood." I pulled Carina's hand back from petting the dog.

"It's okay if she wants to touch. Teddy's good with kids."

"Teddy's such a perfect name. He's so fluffy, like a cuddly bear." I let go of Carina's hand and let her touch the soft fur. She closed her fingers and gave it a yank. Teddy licked Carina's face, totally unfazed by her not-so-gentle little hands. "God, I'm so sorry." Hunter would fire me on the spot if he knew I let a dog lick his daughter's face.

"No worries. Teddy's super gentle." The woman bent down and rubbed the dog's fluffy head. "What's her name?" she asked, running her finger along the baby's cheek.

I picked Carina up and balanced her on my hip. "This beauty is Carina. Can you say hi, Carina?" I took her hand and waved it.

"Beautiful name," she mused. "Anyway, I should get going. Teddy gets restless when he doesn't get his walk. Maybe I'll see you around."

"We need to get going too." I put Carina into the stroller and strapped her in. "It was nice meeting you."

"You too," she said as she walked away and waved over her shoulder.

I hoped we would see each other again. It would be nice to have a friend around here. Someone to share coffee with and maybe grab lunch. And Carina clearly adored Teddy, lighting up when he gave her doggy kisses.

Maybe if I was lucky, we'd both make new friends.

With all the bath-time excitement last night I hadn't finished unpacking, so I did that while waiting for the laundry. Carina had been a doll and took a long nap, and while I rarely slept during the day, I snuck in twenty minutes of shut-eye myself.

Now we were off and running again. On our way to the grocery store, I stopped at a coffee shop for a dose of caffeine. I hated getting the stroller in and out of the car, but it was easier than trying to balance Carina on my hip while digging in my purse for money.

Payday couldn't come soon enough. I'd practically run through all my savings from Oasis. If I hadn't found this job, it would have meant months sleeping on my brother's couch. At least at Hunter's, I had my own bedroom, and since he was gone all day, it was practically like living alone.

I stood in line behind half a dozen other people, waiting my turn to order, when I felt a tap on my shoulder. I turned my head and almost melted into the chocolate-brown eyes staring back at me.

"Hey. I thought that was you, Charli."

"Hi, Ben. How are you?" I asked with a smile, glad I wasn't wearing a dress I'd slept in like yesterday. He was cute in a boyish sort of way, round face and shaggy hair that curled around his ears,

He nodded his head. "Good. I'm on a coffee run. Boss man gets grouchy if we don't keep him fully caffeinated."

I laughed. "He must not have had his coffee yesterday."

"Actually, that was him being nice. You wouldn't want to see him when he's in grouch mode."

"Yikes! I can relate. My boss can be temperamental too." The detailed grocery list in my purse proved it.

Ben tilted his head to the side. "I thought maybe you'd call last night. Did I read the situation wrong?"

I tucked my hair behind my ear and shook my head. "Yesterday was my first day and it's been a bit hectic. I'm still trying to get my bearings."

"That's understandable." We moved forward in line. "So, do you live around here?"

"It's a live-in nanny position, so I actually live at that apartment."

"Nice. You've got a short commute to work."

"That I do. Only a walk down the hallway." We took another step forward. "And the clientele couldn't be better." I ruffled Carina's short blond strands that were sticking up on top of her head.

"Yeah, she's cute." He stuck his hands in his pockets. "So, with this job, are you allowed to go out, or do you have to be with her twenty-four seven?"

I remembered the conversation Hunter and I had about my dating. He never said I couldn't, only that he didn't want people coming to the apartment to *scratch an itch*. It pissed me off at the time, but I wouldn't want random people showing up at my house either. "I can go out."

"Cool. How about you give me your number and I'll text you. Maybe we can set something up."

"I'd like that." Ben was a nice guy. There was absolutely no reason I shouldn't go out with him. Nannying was my job, not my life. Getting out by myself with someone who wasn't wearing diapers would be good for me.

I gave him my number and moved to the front of the line. Stepping to the counter, I placed my order and paid an outrageous amount of money for a fancy cup of coffee, then moved to the side so Ben could order. He leaned on the counter and smiled at the barista. "Hi, Kelly. I hope you're having a fantastic day. I'll have four black coffees and cheese Danish."

After paying, he moved next to me. "Do you know her?" I asked.

"Who?"

"The barista. You called her Kelly."

He chuckled. "No. It was on her nametag. I read somewhere that if you use someone's name, it boosts their self-esteem, and you get better service."

"Interesting. Does it work?"

Ben shrugged his shoulders. "It's never not worked. So maybe?"

"Charli!" The barista shouted my name and slid my coffee across the counter, brown liquid sloshing out of the cup.

I grabbed a napkin and wiped up the mess, annoyed by her carelessness and relieved it didn't fall off the counter onto Carina. Not sure how I would have explained that one to Hunter. If she'd been burned, he'd probably come down here, brought the woman to tears, and owned the coffee shop by the time he left.

"Here, let me help." Ben took the napkins from me and finished wiping the counter, then threw them in the garbage. I barely knew him, but he really was a nice guy.

"Thank you. We should probably get going." I took a sip of my coffee and readjusted the purse on my shoulder.

"Wait a minute and I'll walk you out." He winked at me, and I couldn't resist falling for his smile.

The same barista who practically threw my coffee at me—Kelly—leaned across the counter, showing off her cleavage, as she gently handed Ben's order to him. "I gave you lots of napkins and put a little something extra in the bag. Have a great day, Ben. Come back soon." Her voice was syrupy sweet as she shamelessly flirted with him.

He took the cardboard carrier and paper bag. "Thanks, Kelly. You have a great day too."

I pushed the stroller toward the door. Ben rushed ahead and held it open for me. When we were outside, I asked, "What did she give you?" It shouldn't have bothered me. It's not like Ben and I were together, but I was standing right there.

"Not sure." He reached into the bag and pulled out a wad of napkins. He held one up with her name and phone number on it.

I expected him to stick it back in the bag, but he crumbled the napkin in his fist and tossed it in the trash can. "She was nice but not my type."

Relief bloomed in my chest. "What's your type?" The words were out of my mouth before I could stop them.

He tapped me on the nose with his finger. "You. I'll call you."

Ben left me on the sidewalk and disappeared into a white work van. As I watched him drive away, two thoughts flitted through my brain. First, Ben was a gentleman, and I would be lucky to date someone like him. Second, Hunter wouldn't like me going out with Ben.

Then a third thought occurred.

Why did I care what Hunter would think?

Chapter 13
Hunter

Day two back at Mystique sucked slightly less than day one.

First thing in the morning, I left another message for the private investigator, Rudy Mendosa. One of several in the last thirty-six hours. I'd been waiting on pins and needles to hear from him. Patience wasn't my strong suit. Jennifer Johnson was a missing piece of the puzzle I needed solved.

Why hadn't she contacted me when she discovered she was pregnant?

Why did she keep Carina a secret?

How could she drop her child off on my doorstep without so much as a fuck you?

Was she planning on coming back and ripping Carina from my life?

Fuck that! I may not have been there from the beginning, but I was here now, and I wasn't giving up my daughter without a fight.

My old personal assistant, Daniel, poked his head into my corner closet. "Welcome back, Mr. Dorsey."

He was a good kid, young but ambitious. Daniel started working for me right out of college as an intern. He proved to be competent, conscientious, and a stickler for details. I liked him immediately. "Come in, Daniel. What do you think of my new office?" I leaned back in the creaky chair and motioned to the room around me.

He tried not to stare at the dented aluminum desk or the chipped paint on the wall. "It's ummm…"

"A shithole. It's okay for you to say it." I motioned to the plastic chair in front of my desk. "Please, have a seat."

Daniel sat down cautiously on the rickety chair as if it might crumble under his weight. He wasn't a small man, so his chances were fifty-fifty. "You shouldn't be in this room. It's an insult."

"I couldn't agree with you more, yet here I am. I suppose I only have myself to blame, but I'm working on correcting that issue." Leaning forward on the desk, I steepled my fingers. "I assume Leonard sent you here."

He nodded. "I should have come by yesterday to say hello, but yes, Mr. Moroski sent me. He wanted me to train you on doing payroll."

I scoffed. "Train me? I learned how to do payroll when I graduated college. It was my first real job at Mystique." Since almost everything was automated, it was even easier now. "If I'm doing payroll, what will Helen be doing?" Helen had been doing our payroll for the last seven years.

Daniel's lips twisted to the side. "Mr. Moroski fired her."

"What?" How did I not know this?

"As a matter of fact, he fired everyone who used to work for you. I'm the only one left."

My eyes bulged. "Everyone?"

Daniel nodded.

"Fuck. How in the hell did he get away with that?"

"He convinced your dad it was unnecessary overhead."

Interesting. I tapped my fingers together, my mind spinning a hundred miles an hour. "I see."

"He's not happy you're back. I overheard him talking to your dad. I'd watch your back if I were you."

My jaw clenched. "Thanks for the heads-up." Daniel had it wrong though. Leonard was the one who should watch his back. He might have had my father's ear, but I had his blood. It was my family's legacy on the line, and I'd do anything to protect what was ours. Getting rid of Leonard Morosk-hole would be an added bonus. It would make what I did to Trent look like child's play. Getting my hands dirty had never been a problem and mine were going to be filthy.

Already bored to death with payroll, I watched Charli on the cameras feeding Carina and singing her terrible songs. She carted clothes to the laundry room, folded them, and took them back to the bedrooms. I liked watching her, became obsessed with it. It was wrong to spy on her, but she still had her privacy. There were no cameras in her bedroom or the bathroom. I may have been a creep, and my morals were loose at best, but the point of the cameras was monitoring her with Carina, not getting a free peep show.

Charli put Carina in the stroller and rolled her to the front door, then ran back to grab the grocery list from the counter. Although I found her to be a bit free-spirited, I couldn't deny she was a breath of fresh air and exactly what Carina needed.

Both Mrs. Hadley and Ms. Peters would have taken excellent care of my daughter, but they were both in their midsixties with their own families. Neither would be able to dedicate the time, patience, and energy Carina required. Truth be told, I enjoyed having Charli around, which was exactly why I wouldn't be going straight home after work.

I picked up my ringing phone and stared at the screen. *Finally!* "Mr. Mendosa, you're a difficult man to get ahold of."

"And you're a very persistent man, Mr. Dorsey." He chuckled.

I tapped my fingers on top of my metal desk in a rhythmic pattern. "You came very highly recommended. My attorney, Sam Steinburg, said you're the best and the best is what I need."

"I always liked Sam. What can I do for you, Mr. Dorsey?"

"I need to find a woman."

"Don't we all?" he interrupted, clearly amused.

I gritted my teeth. There was no time for bullshit or games. If he found this entertaining, maybe he wasn't the right man for the job. "This woman is the mother of my child. We had a one-time fling, and a week ago, she dropped my six-month-old daughter at my door with a note and disappeared. It's of utmost importance to find this woman. All I have is a name on the birth certificate. Sam already tried to find her, but it seems she's a ghost."

He cleared his throat. "I see. Would you recognize her if you saw her?"

"Doubtful." I rolled my eyes. "She worked at The Sapphire Club, and I was far from sober."

"And you're sure the child is yours?"

"Ninety-nine point nine percent, according to the paternity test."

"All right, then. You should know I charge by the hour. The longer it takes to find her, the more it will cost."

"I don't care what it costs. What I care about is finding this woman before she changes her mind and tries to take my daughter away. I don't want any loose ends. Everything needs to be legal." The more I thought about this faceless woman, the angrier I got. At least Carina was young enough that she wouldn't remember being abandoned. I, on the other hand, didn't have that luxury.

"Email me everything you know, and I'll start looking. I haven't been unsuccessful yet. If she's out there, then I'll find her."

Did he think my daughter birthed herself? Of course, she was out there, unless sometime in the last week, she'd faced an untimely death. Jennifer Johnson might have been selfish, but I had no doubt she was alive.

"I'll send you a contract within the hour," Rudy promised.

I felt only slightly better after the phone call. I wasn't any closer to finding Carina's mother, but at least there was a plan in place. The situation was out of my control, and it bothered me. I strived for control in every aspect of my life. It was why I related better to numbers than people. They didn't lie or drop babies off at your home or leave you. Numbers were safe. They were logical and predictable.

Charlotte Bently was anything but predictable. She was a complete wild card. I thought about her job at Oasis. I'd never seen her perform, but I'd seen enough shows in Vegas to know what she did wasn't safe or logical.

It was reckless.

I shouldn't have cared, but the thought of her climbing high above a stage with no safety net pissed me off. She had zero regard for her own well-being, and it infuriated me.

An alert on my phone reminded me of my "meeting" with Gia in ten minutes. She was going to make me grovel; I was sure of it. The look and tone she gave me yesterday indicated she still held animosity toward me. What I did was wrong, but it'd been over a year. She got the job and my brother. What else did she want?

I wasn't big on apologies, but this was a necessary evil. Getting back on good terms with Gia would help smooth things over with Trent. And although I hated to admit it, I needed Trent on my side to be fully reinstated at Mystique. It was a sticky web I'd trapped myself in.

I locked my computer and headed down the hall toward Gia's office, contemplating my words to her as I went. Passing Trent's office, Charlotte's brother, Tom, sat at his desk like a sentry, making sure he wasn't disturbed by random nonsense. It was the same thing Daniel used to do for me. Now, I was available to anyone at any time. I rarely even shut my door because the lack of windows made me feel claustrophobic.

Before I could stop myself, I stood in front of Tom's desk and stared down at him. "Why did you let Charlotte work at Oasis?"

He slowly lifted his head and looked up at me through his dark-rimmed glasses. "Excuse me?"

"You and Charlotte are nothing alike. You're down to earth, yet you let her climb thirty feet in the air and perform dangerous stunts. Why

90

would you do that?" Tom was a numbers guy. He was rational. Conservative.

"Let her?" He pushed up his glasses with one finger. "You obviously don't know Charli that well yet. My sister isn't someone who can be controlled. She does what she wants when she wants. She wasn't made to be put in a box. She was made to soar above it. If you tell her she can't do something, she'll push back twice as hard to prove you wrong."

"I've already begun to learn that," I said, shoving my hands in my pockets.

"Also," Tom said, standing up, "I may be out of line, but because she's my sister, I feel I have a right. I didn't want her working for you, but she has her own mind and doesn't listen to reason. She doesn't know your reputation, but I do and if you hurt her in any way, there will be consequences. Am I clear? I'm the only one she's got in Vegas, and trust me, I won't hesitate to protect her."

It was hard to take him seriously in his sweater-vest and bow tie, but I appreciated his passion. "Your sister is safe with me."

He let out a sarcastic laugh. "Ha! I highly doubt that. The only one you care about is yourself."

Before I got fired, Tom wouldn't have had the balls to speak to me that way. He used to scurry away like a scolded dog when I entered a room. A lot had changed since I left. "I have no interest in hurting your sister. I'll make you that promise." I stuck my hand out as a peace offering.

Tom stared at my hand, then grasped it with a firmer hold than I expected. "I'm holding you to your word."

"I'd expect nothing less." I let go of his hand and glanced at my watch. "Now, if you'll excuse me, I have a meeting with Miss Romano."

He smirked at me. "You mean Mrs. Dorsey."

I cringed. Like I said, a lot had changed. Although I knew she married Trent, it was difficult to think of Gia as my sister-in-law. "Yes... Mrs. Dorsey."

"Good luck. You're going to need it," Tom said as I walked away.

I didn't need luck. What I needed was to be charming as fuck and get my new sister-in-law to quit looking at me like I was a chewed-up piece of gum stuck to the bottom of her Louboutins—real ones now that she and Trent were married, not the knockoffs she used to wear.

Eating crow had become my specialty since returning to Mystique. It tasted foul in my mouth, yet here I was, willing to eat another huge helping.

"May I help you?" Penny said as she positioned herself between me and Gia's office door.

God, not this again. I was tired of being treated as a second-class citizen instead of a member of one of the most prestigious families in the hotel industry. "I'm here to see Gia."

Penny held up a finger. "Let me see if she's ready for you." She disappeared into Gia's office, closing the door in my face.

I paced back and forth in front of her door. My time was as valuable as Gia's. More valuable, in my opinion. Being kept waiting annoyed me, but that was the whole point. This was a power play to remind me of my disgraced status. To let me know I wouldn't be let off the hook. I glanced at my watch again. It was officially three minutes past our agreed meeting time.

Late.

I hated late.

The door opened and Penny stepped out. "Mrs. Dorsey will see you now."

I pasted on a smile. "Thank you."

Penny held the door open, and I headed toward Gia, who stood in front of her desk. She wore a black pencil skirt, an emerald-green blouse, and sky-high black heels on her feet. Her vibrant red hair was twisted into a professional updo. Diamonds sparkled where they hung from her ears. She was gorgeous. I always thought Gia was attractive, but she'd upped her game. My brother was a lucky son of a bitch.

Speaking of the devil, Trent sat on the leather couch pushed against the far wall with a bag of microwave popcorn on his lap. He gave me a cutesy wave, fluttering his fingers at me.

"I thought this meeting was between you and me," I said to Gia without taking my eyes off my brother.

"Don't worry about me. I'm just here for the show," he said, tossing a few kernels of popcorn into his mouth and chewing obnoxiously loud.

"Trent, I only agreed to let you be here if you kept your mouth closed," Gia chastised him.

My brother mimed locking his lips with a key and tossing it over his shoulder.

"Thank you." She turned to me and motioned to the chairs in front of her desk. "Please have a seat, Hunter."

It was *cute* the way my brother listened to his wife. My father kowtowed the same way to Rose. I vowed to never bow down to a woman. There was a certain order in the world that would turn to chaos if the power hierarchy shifted. If love turned you into a wet noodle of a man, I wanted nothing to do with it. The current situation was humiliating enough.

"Thank you for seeing me, Gia." I forced a smile I didn't feel. Everyone knew I was an asshole. I owned it, lived up to it, and had been rolling around in bed with it for years. Apologizing went against everything I believed in.

She sat behind her desk with an equally fake smile. "Of course. What is it you want to talk to me about?"

As if she didn't know. As if she and Trent hadn't been motherfucking me behind my back for months. "I owe you an apology."

Gia raised an eyebrow and leaned forward on her desk, clasping her hands. "Oh, really? Whatever for?"

"You know what for."

"I'm not sure I do. You did a lot of shitty things to me, so excuse me if I need you to be a bit more specific."

I should have known she wouldn't make this easy. "I'm sorry I invaded your privacy and recorded you and Trent having sex."

She motioned her hand for me to continue.

"And for emailing the video to everyone in the office."

"You humiliated me."

I sighed. "I know. It was the wrong thing to do. I shouldn't have let you become a casualty of my anger with Trent. I was so hell-bent on exposing him that I didn't consider the ramifications."

93

Gia tapped her fingers together. "I see. Anything else you'd like to apologize for?"

Anything else? Did she realize how rare apologies from me were? She'd already gotten more than anyone else in my life. "Like what?"

"Here we go," Trent chimed in from the corner.

Both Gia and I glared at him as he threw more popcorn into his mouth. It irritated the fuck out of me. "Enjoying yourself?" I asked.

"Immensely. Please continue." More obnoxious chewing followed.

Gia turned her attention back to me. "Let's see… what else could you possibly have to apologize for? How about propositioning me like a whore? How about treating me like a floozy instead of a professional? Or maybe for trying to single-handedly destroy my career? For not taking me seriously?" Her neck turned red and her carefully contained rage exploded. "For letting the whole goddamn office see me come! You tried to ruin my reputation and my life!"

Bam! Bam! Bam! The hits kept on coming. When she put it that way, it sounded worse than I remembered. "I'm sorry for all of it. I shit on you, and you didn't deserve it. I have no excuse."

She took several deep breaths through her nose in an effort to bring her blood pressure back to normal. "It's a start. I accept your apology, but I haven't forgiven you and I sure as hell haven't forgotten."

That was obvious. "Tell me, what can I do?" It was a dangerous question. A woman scorned and all that.

Gia tapped a manicured nail against her ruby-red lips. "I'm so glad you asked."

Fuck! Whatever this was, I wasn't going to like it.

"Trent and I haven't gotten to meet our niece yet, and from what I hear, she's quite the cutie. Soooo… I'd like to invite you to our apartment this Saturday for family dinner."

Fuck that! I turned to Trent and glared at him. "That's a firm no."

He shrugged his shoulders. "It was her idea."

Gia rolled her eyes. "Oh, I'm sorry. Did that sound like a request? What I meant to say is we're having a family dinner, and you're expected to be there. I want to meet Carina."

"I have plans," I lied. I had no objection to Gia meeting Carina but spending an entire evening with my family sounded like medieval torture.

"Cancel them. If you want back in this family, then I'm your ticket. I don't know if you know this, but your father adores me. I wouldn't want to have to tell him you're creating a hostile work environment."

I gnashed my teeth. "This is blackmail."

She waved her hand at me dismissively. "Call it what you like. Six o'clock. Casual attire."

"Fine!" I stood abruptly and headed toward the door.

"One more thing," Gia announced.

I halted and looked over my shoulder. "What?"

"Bring Charli."

I ignored her demand and stormed out.

The day kept getting better and better!

Chapter 14
Charli

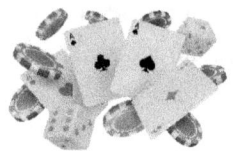

"I'm renewing my objection to you working for Hunter."

Although my brother seemed mild-mannered, he'd always been protective of me. "Acknowledged and noted."

"I'm serious, Charli. I don't trust him."

I held the phone between my ear and shoulder while I fed Carina a bottle. It was almost nine at night and Hunter still wasn't home. "Seriously, Tom, I barely see him. This job pays awesome, and it keeps me off your couch. Plus, you should see Carina. I swear she's the sweetest baby ever."

Tom groaned on the other side of the line. "Promise me you'll keep it professional. Hunter is a smooth talker and a manipulator. Don't fall for him and definitely don't fall into his bed."

An image of Hunter shirtless on the bathroom floor flitted through my mind. He might have been a jerk face, but the man was beautiful. Life wasn't fair. "I'm not going to fall for him, but if I did, it wouldn't be any of your business. I'm a grown-ass woman and I can make my own decisions."

"You know this is going to give me nightmares, right? I can't think of anything worse than having Hunter Dorsey as my brother-in-law."

I laughed. "I think you're jumping the gun. We barely tolerate each other."

"Perfect. Let's keep it that way."

"You're impossible. Stop worrying. You should be happy we don't have to share a bathroom like when we were kids." Carina finished her bottle. I set it on the table next to the rocking chair I was sitting in and placed her over my shoulder to burp her.

"I don't miss that," he admitted. "Your hair was everywhere."

Carina let out a huge burp and I rubbed her back. "Listen, I need to put this munchkin to bed. I'll talk to you later."

"Keep me informed."

"I will. Love you, big brother."

"Love you too. Good night."

"Night." I hung up the phone and set it next to the empty bottle. The apartment was quiet. Had been quiet all day. "Should we read a book?" I carried Carina over to the bookshelf in her room that had more books in it than I'd ever owned in my life. Hunter hadn't spared a dime. Over the last two days, I'd arranged and rearranged everything in Carina's room. It was bursting with books, toys, pillows, and stuffed animals. Painted sunflower yellow with bright pops of color in the decor, the room made me feel... happy. It was every little girl's dream.

I wondered if Hunter picked out any of it himself or if he relegated the job to a sales associate at the store. It didn't bother me that he hadn't come home for dinner, but it did bother me that he was missing time with his daughter.

My fingers walked along the spines of the books. "How about.... this one," I said, pulling one of my childhood favorites from the shelf. We sat back in the rocking chair as I read about a stuffed teddy bear wearing green overalls. Carina's blue eyes fluttered, fighting exhaustion. It didn't take long until her breathing evened out and she was fast asleep.

I carried her to the crib and put her inside. Her little chest rose and fell peacefully. It amazed me how much I already loved her in such a short amount of time.

Having a family of my own had never been much of a priority for me. I was too busy training as an aerial performer to think about kids, but looking down on Carina, I wanted it. Warmth spread through my chest at the thought of being a real mom.

One day.

The guys I dated in the past never really understood me. They were intrigued by what I did for a living and assumed my career in show business equated to being a wild child. Free-spirited? Yes. Irresponsible? No. I didn't participate in crazy after-parties, where drugs and alcohol were consumed like candy. My body was my biggest asset. Like any other athlete, I was careful how I treated it. I couldn't afford to climb silks with a hangover or under the influence. It was dangerous enough completely sober.

One day, I'd find a man worthy of me. One who would put me first. One who would appreciate my goals and support my career. One who would love me for me.

For now, I soaked in the happiness caring for Carina gave me.

I wandered down the quiet hallway, running my hand along the muted gray wall. Hunter's apartment was minimalistic. Not a single picture hung on the walls. There were no photographs or art. With its hardwood floors and black leather furniture the space gave nothing away about its owner. In stark contrast to Carina's room, the rest of the apartment was... functional. It didn't feel warm or cozy. It felt cold and lonely.

In the kitchen, I cut up an apple and smeared peanut butter on the slices. Carrying it to the couch, I turned on the television and watched the latest episode of my favorite show under a blanket from my bed. My eyes began to close, and I forced them back open, readjusting myself on the leather pillows. I wasn't necessarily waiting up for Hunter, but it did concern me that he wasn't home yet. It would be one thing if I knew he was in a meeting or out with friends, but I had no idea where he was. It wasn't my business. I shouldn't have cared, but I did.

Around eleven, I heard the key in the door and Hunter stumbling through it. He dropped his keys on the foyer table with a loud clank and went to the kitchen, not acknowledging me.

I picked up my plate from the coffee table and followed him. "You're home late."

He grabbed a glass from the cupboard, poured some bourbon into it, and tossed back the amber liquor. "Yep."

His tie hung loosely around his neck and his shirt was untucked. I didn't miss the smell of alcohol on his breath. "Are you okay?"

"I'm perfect, dollface," he said, pouring himself another shot.

"Did you drive home?"

"Ubered." Shrugging out of his suit coat, he tossed it on the kitchen island along with his tie and glared at me. "What?"

I flinched. "Nothing. I'm glad you're home."

"Awww. That's so sweet," he said sarcastically. "Your concern is unnecessary and unwanted. If I need a babysitter, I'll let you know. Until then, mind your own damn business. Got it?"

Why the hell was he pissed at me? This job didn't pay enough to get my head bitten off for showing concern. I backed out of the kitchen with my hands held up in surrender and headed for my bedroom. "Understood."

"Where's my daughter?" he demanded.

I turned with my hands on my hips. "I put her to bed two hours ago. I waited as long as I could."

"Fuck," he muttered and pushed past me into Carina's room, shutting the door behind him.

The man infuriated me. Not only did he disappear tonight, but he hadn't bothered checking on us. It would have taken two minutes to pick up the phone. Then, he acted as if I was the one in the wrong. Fuck him.

I went to my room, locking the door behind me. Too wired to go to sleep, I ran myself a hot bath to unwind. I slipped into the tub and rested my head back against the edge. My brother's words echoed in my head. He didn't trust Hunter. Maybe I was wrong in defending the man who snapped at me for no reason. It was great pay, but at what cost? My dignity was worth more than what Hunter paid me for twenty-four-hour service.

Feeling frustrated, I slipped beneath the surface and let the hot water rush over me. He was tipsy at best, drunk at worst. What happened today that made him feel the need to tie one on? Despite the excuses my mind conjured, they had nothing to do with me.

It wasn't my problem.

Yet my heartstrings tugged for him. I had no idea what he was going through. Last week he was a carefree bachelor. This week, he was a single dad trying to pull it together for his daughter. It was enough to rock even the strongest person to the core.

Emerging from beneath the water, I took a deep breath. Everything was okay.

I was okay.

I might have been the target of his anger, but I wasn't the source. Despite his rigid exterior, he was hurting inside. I saw it in his eyes, in the way he tossed back alcohol without a care. His sharp tongue and cold demeanor were symptoms of a bigger problem.

He was right. It wasn't my business, but his daughter deserved better than the man who walked through the front door tonight.

Getting out of the tub, I threw on a pair of shorts and a T-shirt. Whatever was up his ass, we were going to get to the bottom of it.

I stormed down the hallway to Carina's door, which was still closed, prepared to give the man a piece of my mind. Treating me like a punching bag was unacceptable. Pushing the door open, I stuck my head inside, ready to duke it out.

Hunter lay on the shaggy floral rug in front of the crib, curled up in the fetal position with his daughter tucked against his chest. Still in his dress shirt and suit pants, he snored quietly. With all his hard edges softened, he resembled a small child instead of the fierce man he was.

Drip by drip, my anger drained away, leaving pity and compassion in its place.

Gently tugging Carina from her father's grip, I placed her back in the crib. Then I nudged Hunter's shoulder with my foot. "Come on, big guy. Time for bed."

He grumbled and cracked one eye open. "What?"

"You fell asleep on the floor." I reached out my hands for him to grab. He took hold and I heaved him to his feet.

"People suck," he slurred as he wrapped an arm around my shoulders and leaned on me.

I led the big oaf down the hallway. "I know." When we got to his room, I pulled back his comforter and seated him on the bed.

Hunter looked up at me with glazed eyes. "You're pretty."

"And you're drunk," I said with a sigh. "Let's get your shoes off." I knelt in from of him and untied each shoe, slipping them off his feet. For a moment, I let my mind wander. Big feet meant big... hands. Forcing my naughty brain out of the gutter, I set his shoes aside.

"You look good on your knees," Hunter said as he unbuttoned his shirt.

I stood and helped him out of his shirt. "I was going to take off your pants, but you can sleep in them."

"You're no fun."

"I'm plenty of fun, but I'm not a fan of drunken sex." I pushed him back on the bed and covered him with the blanket.

"Like I said, no fun." Hunter rolled on his side and crumpled the pillow under his head. Within seconds, the room filled with his soft snoring.

I plugged in his phone on the nightstand and turned out the light. "Sweet dreams. Tomorrow will be better."

It might not have been true, but I didn't know what I was supposed to say when your drunk boss propositioned you. Chances were, he wouldn't remember any of this tomorrow anyway, but he would have one hell of a hangover.

Chapter 15
Hunter

I woke up in my wrinkled pants and the rest of my clothes strewn about, feeling like demons had taken over my body and dragged me through hell. Last night was a blur. It wasn't the first time I'd come home drunk, and it wouldn't be the last. I'd stopped at The Rabbit Hole for a drink. One drink turned into two, and two turned into three. Before I knew it, the bartender cut me off. The only good decision I'd made was calling an Uber to take me home.

After a shower and a protein shake, I crept into Carina's room. I should have come home right after work yesterday. It was one thing to blow off the nanny; it was another to blow off my daughter. Despite the vow I made to change my ways for her, the selfishness I'd embraced for the last thirty years reared its ugly head. I was determined to show her a leopard could change his spots. Unfortunately, it wasn't going to happen overnight.

"Good morning, princess." I rubbed her tummy. Her eyes fluttered open. It hadn't been my intent to wake her, but I wasn't sorry it happened. She kicked her little legs, cocooned inside her pink pajamas, and her face scrunched up as she started to cry. Carina was such a happy baby that the crying scared me a little bit. Whoever decided I should be responsible for another human being was an idiot.

I picked her up and cradled her to my chest and she quieted instantly. "Shhh, princess. Let's get you changed, then Daddy will get you some breakfast." I hoped to God she was only wet. With the hangover I was sporting, I didn't think my stomach could handle a poopy diaper. Once I got her legs out of her jammies, I peeked inside her diaper. Seeing the all clear, I praised her, "You do love your daddy, don't you?"

I never aspired to be an expert diaper changer, but like every other challenge that'd been thrown my way, I mastered it quickly. You'd never see it on my résumé, but I still counted it as a win. With a clean baby in my arms, I headed to the kitchen and prepared a bottle. My sleepy girl rested her head on my shoulder peacefully.

"Was she crying?" A groggy Charli came down the hallway, rubbing her eyes.

"No. I went in to see her and accidentally woke her up." I screwed on the top of the bottle with one hand and began feeding Carina.

"Do you want me to take her?" Charli offered.

"I got it," I said, sitting on a stool at the granite island. "You can go back to bed."

"I'm up now." She shuffled to the coffee maker and inserted a pod, then pulled a mug from the cabinet. "You got home late."

I didn't owe her an explanation, but since lately I was handing out apologies like candy at a parade, I tossed one her way. "Sorry for making you worry."

"You're a grown man; you can do what you want. A call or a text would have been nice though." The last of her coffee sputtered into the mug. She added creamer to the brew and took a sip. "I found you passed out in Carina's room with her grasped in your arms.

The picture she painted was pathetic. "Jesus."

"No worries. I put you both to bed."

That explained waking up with my pants on. "Thank you for taking care of us."

She shrugged. "It's what you pay me for."

Only half of that was true. "I'm going to do better. That doesn't mean I won't fuck up again, but I'm going to try."

"You're doing your best. I'll give you a pass for becoming an instant parent and starting a new job all in the same week."

"I appreciate that." Carina's little hands reached up in an attempt to hold the bottle. It was the first time I'd seen it happen. Such a little thing, but I'd already missed so much I felt like it was a big thing. "She ever do this when you feed her?"

Charli shook her head. "Nope. That's a first."

Not wanting to seem overexcited, I simply nodded.

"How is the new job going?"

My lips twisted to the side. "Not as well as I hoped. A lot has changed, and I haven't received the warmest welcome."

"It'll get better," she encouraged. "I mean, you're family; they can't hate you forever."

"Actually, they could, but I'm working on it." The family dinner Gia insisted I bring Charli to sat in the back of my mind. I hadn't yet decided if I was going to acquiesce to the demand, so I didn't mention it. "How's your new job?"

Charli took another sip of her coffee and tapped her nails on the counter as she thought about her answer. "The accommodations are amazing, and Carina is about the sweetest baby I've ever seen. I'd say I lucked out, except my boss is a dick sometimes."

I couldn't help but laugh. "What a coincidence, so is mine."

"Yeah. He's a bit ridiculous with the daily agendas and perpetual lists. No offense, but he can also be a grumpy fuck."

That made me really laugh. I appreciated a woman who told it like it was. "I'll speak to management and see what I can do. No promises." Charlotte Bently was a pleasant surprise. The doubts I had about hiring her to care for my daughter were gone. There was no way I'd be having this conversation with Ms. Peters.

"Thanks. Since I don't see an agenda for the day, is there anything you need me to do?"

Carina finished her bottle, so I leaned her over my shoulder and tapped her back with my palm. "I can't think of anything."

"You really should put a towel on your shoulder when you do that in case she spits up."

A few more taps and Carina let out a belch that would challenge a college frat boy. Instantly, I felt the wetness soaking into my back. "Too late."

"Let me take her." Charli took Carina and propped her on her hip while grabbing a dish towel. "Look what you did to your daddy, you silly girl." Carina laughed and buried her head in Charli's neck.

I waved the towel away and stripped out of my dress shirt. Baby spit-up wasn't as gross as the squash from the other night. This I could deal with.

Charli looked away from my naked chest and her cheeks turned pink. *Interesting.* The woman was full of sass. I didn't expect a bit of bare skin to make her blush, not that I could say I minded much.

"There is one thing you can do for me today. I was going to drop my dry cleaning off before work, but I'm getting a later start than I planned. I know it's not part of your job, but would you mind doing it for me? I've been going through shirts faster than chicken wings at an all-you-can-eat buffet."

Charli held out her hand. "Sure. You need me to pick them up too?"

"Thank you. I'll pick them up on my way home," I said, handing her the shirt. "There's a bunch more in my hamper. I'll text you the dry cleaner I use." I glanced at the clock. "Shit. I gotta get going, or I'll be late." I still had to stop at The Rabbit Hole to get my car.

Charli followed me to my bedroom as I went to get a clean shirt. "I've been meaning to ask you… I'm going to look for a gym around here that will allow me to bring Carina. Any suggestions?"

I stepped into my walk-in closet and pulled a pale-blue shirt from the hanger. "There's a fitness center with a pool on the first floor of this building. A perk of living here. Feel free to use it."

Her eyes lit up. "Really? Can I take Carina swimming?"

105

I grabbed a tie and knotted it around my neck. "Only if you protect her with your life," I said, heading back down the hallway to grab my wallet and keys.

Charli scurried behind me, with Carina still on her hip. "I will. I promise. Does she have a bathing suit?"

"No. Order whatever you need and have it delivered. Bathing suit. Floaties. Life Jacket. Don't you need special diapers too? Charge it to the card and don't skimp on quality. I don't want my daughter drowning because you wanted to save a few bucks." My keys were on the hall table but not my wallet. "Damn it! Where is my wallet?" I patted my pants pockets, knowing damn well it wasn't there.

"Maybe in Carina's room." Charli hurried to Carina's room and came back waving my wallet in the air. "It was under the crib."

I sighed. "Thank you." More evidence of my debauchery last night. I quickly pulled up the Uber app and ordered a car. "I gotta go. My ride will be here in four minutes."

"Have a good day." She picked up Carina's hand and waved at me.

I kissed my smiling daughter on the cheek. "Bye, princess. Do Daddy a favor and poop while I'm gone."

Charli swatted me on the shoulder. "Get out of here."

Backing out the door, I headed to the elevator while Charli and Carina waved at me. "I'll be home earlier than yesterday."

"Don't threaten me like that!"

The elevator opened and I stepped inside. Not until I was five floors down did I realize I was smiling.

"Good afternoon, Mr. Moroski."

Leonard glared at me through his wire-rimmed glasses. "What do you need, Hunter?"

The use of my first name didn't escape me. His constant need to remind me of my place grated my nerves, along with his fancy Harvard diploma hanging on *my* office wall. "I wanted to let you know payroll is finished and awaiting your approval."

"Already?"

"Yes. I was wondering what you'd like me to work on next?"

Leonard looked at his watch. "You can get my lunch. Go to the deli downstairs and get me a club sandwich and dark roast coffee with a hint of chocolate."

He had to be joking. I wasn't his personal assistant. "Excuse me?"

"Lunch. Are you capable of getting lunch? Also, I'm almost out of sticky notes. I'll need you to go buy some."

My fists clenched. "I'm sure there are plenty of sticky notes in the supply closet."

"Not the blue ones." He held up a stack to show me. "I only use the blue sticky notes for finances. Being organized is essential to doing this job efficiently. You could learn a thing or two."

Leonard Morosk-hole was walking a razor-thin edge with my patience. I took another step into his… *my* office. The only thing that kept me from pummeling him was my father. I'd never prove myself to my family if I punched my *boss* during my first week. There were other ways to prove myself. Leonard and I might have had the same degree, but he didn't have a clue how my mind worked. With each condescending comment, it went to a darker and darker place. "My time and skills would be better spent dissecting the profit and loss sheets to investigate why Mystique is losing money."

He took off his glasses and rubbed the bridge of his nose. "When I took this job, the books were a mess. It's taken me a year to straighten everything out. I'll let you know if I need them fucked up again."

That was it! Every word out of his mouth was a damn lie. The books were immaculate when I left. Say what you wanted about me, but I took pride in my work. Insinuating my work was shoddy was the last straw. The gloves officially came off.

I smiled at him. "Whatever you think is best. Would you like me to get your lunch first and then get the office supplies?"

"That would be excellent." He pulled out his wallet and handed me twenty dollars. "That should cover lunch and the sticky notes."

Barely. It didn't matter. I'd pay for the sticky notes myself just to get out of the office. When I was the CFO, I regularly bought lunch or coffee for my staff, something I doubted Leonard ever did. "I'll be back in a jiffy with your lunch," I said, taking the money.

I headed down to the deli and ordered a club sandwich and dark roast coffee, minus the *hint of chocolate*. I also got a sandwich for Daniel. Then I stopped into the convenience store where we stocked toiletries, snacks, books, and other last-minute items guests might need and grabbed a box of chocolate-flavored laxatives, which I happily paid for myself. Mr. Morosk-hole was going to get his hint of chocolate. I stirred them into the coffee until they fully dissolved and headed back upstairs.

"Your lunch," I said, setting the bag and coffee on his desk.

He looked at me skeptically. "Did you remember the chocolate in my coffee?"

"Absolutely. I watched it go in the cup."

Leonard picked up his coffee and took a sip, closing his eyes as he savored the flavor. "Perfect. You might have finally found your calling."

"I aim to please. If there's nothing else, I'll head out to get your sticky notes."

He waved his hand at me dismissively.

I took my time and wandered through the casino, pulling the handle of a slot machine a few times before getting to my car. Then I drove down the Strip, windows open and radio blaring, for once not bothered by the congested streets. I'd barely begun my attack on Leonard, and I already enjoyed it more than anything else in the last year. Funny how a stupid college prank could bring so much happiness. Immature? Yes. Satisfying? Also, yes.

After stopping at the office supply store and my favorite electronics store, I made my way back to Mystique. When the elevator opened on the second floor, my body buzzed with excitement. An hour was plenty of time for the secret ingredient I added to Leonard's coffee to kick in.

As I walked toward his office, the smell got stronger and stronger. I held a hand over my nose to keep it from infiltrating my nostrils. Daniel and my father stood outside Leonard's door, holding their own noses. "What's going on?" I asked.

"Mr. Moroski is shouting something about food poisoning," Daniel answered.

"That's impossible. I got his food myself. From *our* deli. It must be something else."

"That's what I said," my father agreed. Loud moans and sounds of flatulence echoed throughout the office. "This is ridiculous." He braved the awful smell of the office and knocked on the bathroom door inside. "Leonard, you're sick. You need to go home."

"I'm not sick. I was poisoned," he yelled.

"Not in my hotel, you weren't. I don't appreciate you saying otherwise. Go home, Leonard. I'm not asking; I'm telling you. Go home!"

There were several flushes and some swearing behind the closed door. Leonard came out red-faced and sweating, buckling his belt. The smell was even worse, and I brought my arm up to cover my nose. I'd take Carina's dirty diaper over this any day, but it was worth it.

Leonard marched over to me and shoved his finger in my face. "You!"

"Me? All I did was run the errands you sent me on." I grabbed the sticky notes out of my pocket and held them up. "You're welcome."

"Oh, fuck off!" Leonard stomped down the hall.

I shook my head in bewilderment. "Okaaay."

My father stared at me. "Hunter, I'm going to ask you this one time and I want you to be honest with me. Did you have anything to do with this?"

"Absolutely not. All I did was what he asked. He sent me to get his lunch from our deli, which I did. Then he sent me to get him sticky notes from the office supply store, which I also did. I wasn't even here."

"It's true," Daniel piped up. "He sent Hunter on errands all afternoon. It wasn't the sandwich because I ate the same thing. My club sandwich was excellent, and I don't have any intestinal distress."

My father looked at me and rubbed his chin. "I'm sorry, but I had to ask. I don't know what's more disturbing, the fact that Leonard thinks he was poisoned or that he's treating you as his errand boy. You have a master's degree, for God's sake."

I held up my hands. "I don't like it either, but I'm trying to be a team player."

"This isn't what I had in mind." He sighed. "Okay, I guess go back to work."

"I don't have anything to do. I finished payroll this morning."

"Payroll?" He looked at Daniel. "Don't you do payroll?"

Daniel shook his head. "I did until Hunter came back. Mr. Moroski wanted him to do it."

My father rolled his eyes. "Daniel, call janitorial and have them do a thorough cleaning of Leonard's bathroom and office. I don't want anyone else to get sick. Hunter, come with me."

I followed behind my father with a shit-eating grin on my face. Stage one of getting my job back was complete.

Chapter 16
Charli

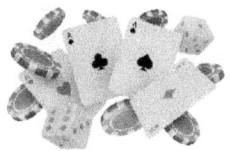

The fitness center was fancy-schmancy. It had all the cardio and weight machines you'd find at a regular gym, two sets of free weights, and a large, matted area with a wall of mirrors that could be used for aerobics, stretching, or whatever you liked. The best part was it didn't cost me a penny.

Carina and I wandered through the locker room, which opened up to the pool. The area was nice, with tables and chairs around it. A hot tub sat at one end and a sauna off to the side.

An older woman swam laps. She had to be almost seventy, but she swam with grace and precision. We watched her effortlessly glide across the pool, dive beneath the water, and head in the opposite direction. Growing up in Colorado, we didn't have a pool and neither did our friends. Pools were a special treat. I could swim, but not nearly as well as the woman doing laps.

The lady popped up at the end of the pool and pulled her goggles off. "Is that Miss Carina in the stroller?"

I lifted Carina and propped her on my hip. "It sure is."

She swam to the edge of the pool and leaned on the ledge. "I'm Sandy Hadley, Hunter's next-door neighbor. I helped him out for the first few days when this sweetheart showed up."

I hadn't met anyone in the building yet and was eager for someone to talk to. Lowering myself to the edge, I tossed my sandals aside and dipped my feet in the pool with Carina on my lap. "I'm sure Hunter appreciated that. I'm Charli, the new nanny."

"How are things going?"

"Okay. Hunter and I are still getting to know one another, but Carina is the sweetest."

"Yes, she is. Hunter showed up at my door a frantic mess. Didn't have the first clue."

I laughed. "I can imagine. He's getting the hang of it though."

She shook her head. "That boy's a smart one. Helped me with my taxes after my Harold died. Likes the ladies too."

That hit a nerve. Although the two of us had a purely professional relationship, I didn't want to think about him with other women. I didn't think he'd bring anyone back to the apartment, but he had gotten home extremely late last night. I thought he was out drinking, but now I wondered. "I'm sure the ladies like him too. He's an attractive man."

"Yes, he is." She grinned.

I chuckled.

"Hey, I might be old, but I'm not dead. I can appreciate a handsome man when I see one. A little eye candy is good for the soul. Must be a nice perk of the job, huh?" She nudged my leg with her elbow.

"It's not like that with us. Taking care of Carina is temporary until I can get back to my real job. Hunter needed a nanny. I needed money and a place to stay. It's beneficial for both of us."

"Uh-huh. And you don't think it's coincidental that he hired a beautiful young woman for the job?"

"I happened to be at the right place at the right time."

"That's called kismet."

"I'm not sure I believe in destiny. We're very different people."

"So were Harold and I. Harold was a hotel investor making his mark on the Las Vegas Strip. I was a showgirl from Boise who came to Vegas with nothing more than a dream. All I wanted to do was be on a stage. Believe it or not, I was a looker back in the day." She patted her swim cap. "Loved the glitz and glam, the sequins and feathers. The costumes were so elaborate and the headdresses, although extremely heavy, were magnificent." Sandy smiled as she reminisced about her glory days.

"How did you and Harold meet?" I held Carina over the water and dipped her toes in the pool. She squealed with delight.

Sandy lifted Carina's feet from the water and kissed her tiny toes. "Harold was in the audience at one of my shows. He waited for me afterward and the rest is history. He was a real charmer, much like Hunter."

The Hunter I knew wasn't much of a charmer. Most of the time, he had the personality of an angry dog, barking at me for no reason. "Did you give up your dream for Harold?"

"Oh, no. I danced for another five years before the younger, prettier girls with bigger boobs took my place. It was time anyway. We wanted to start a family, and no one wants to see a pregnant woman dressed in a skimpy costume. We were married for forty years, had three children and six grandchildren. It was a good life." She sighed.

I bumped her with my foot. "It's still a good life. You look fabulous and have a loving family. I'm certain Harold's always with you."

"I like to think so," she mused. She shook away the memories and focused back on me. "So, how long is temporary?"

"I'm hoping four to six months. I'm an aerial performer at Oasis, but I took a nasty fall a while ago. I was down here checking out the fitness center so I can start training again."

"Hmmm. We're not so different, you and me. It's the adrenaline of performing on stage, isn't it?"

"Yes. There's nothing like the feeling of freedom when I'm up in the air. I can't imagine doing anything else."

She tickled Carina's belly, where she sat on my lap. "Any interest in having one of these? She's awfully cute."

113

"One day. I suppose a time will come when, like you, I'll be replaced with a younger, prettier version."

She patted my knee. "You've got time." Sandy pulled her goggles back in place. "I need to get back to my swimming. Only ten more laps to go. If you need anything, don't hesitate to ask. Even if it's just to chat. I'm right next door." She dove under the water and disappeared.

Mrs. Hadley was a spitfire. I bet she was really something back in her prime.

I never gave much thought to what I'd do when I couldn't perform anymore. I skipped college for my dream, much to my parents' chagrin. I never gave much thought about what I would do when the dream was over.

In the moments when Hunter and I weren't sniping at each other, I could picture myself settling down with a family. In theory, it sounded good… a devoted husband, a house full of children, and perhaps a dog. I wondered if it would ever be enough for me.

"Hello?"

"Hello, Charli, nanny extraordinaire."

I laughed. "Hello, Ben, delivery guy extraordinaire." I lay back on my bed, resting on the fluffy pillows. I'd put Carina down for a nap an hour ago, tidied the kitchen, and threw in a load of my own laundry. My days went faster than I thought they would. The mornings flew by and before I knew it, the afternoon was gone too. I wondered if all moms felt this way or if I was still adjusting to having a shadow with me all day. Although *technically* I had a lot of free time, that time was consumed with the needs of another tiny person, so it really wasn't free time at all.

"I was wondering about that date we talked about. I'd love to take you out on Saturday. Dinner on the Strip, hit a casino or two, and take in the sights. You know, all the touristy stuff."

The thought of getting out and having adult time excited me. "I've lived here for three years. Does that still make me a tourist?"

"It makes you a transplant, like seventy percent of the population. Those of us born and raised here are a minority."

"So I'll see everything from a native's vantage point?"

He chuckled. "I suppose. No matter how long you've lived here, the people-watching on the Strip is top notch. It never gets old."

That was true. It'd been a while since I walked the Strip. No matter how many times I did, it was always magical. The lights, the sounds, the people... that's what attracted me to Vegas in the first place. It was a playground for adults where there were no limits. "I'd love to go out Saturday. However, I need to speak with my boss. I don't know what his plans are, and if he's not going to be home, I need to find a babysitter."

"A babysitter for the babysitter?"

My feathers ruffled. It might not have been the most glamorous job, but it wasn't any worse than delivering packages and furniture. "Yes. It's a twenty-four-hour-a-day job, so when I want to do something without Carina, I need to make arrangements."

"I hope he pays you well," Ben said with a scoff.

I wasn't sure where the attitude was coming from, but it annoyed me. "Very well."

"Is it weird living with your boss?"

"Not really. My room is on the opposite side of the apartment. We rarely see each other." It was true enough. Most of our interactions were quick snippets of time. I barely knew anything about him besides his fondness for lists, sharp tongue, and even sharper cheekbones. Oh, and let's not forget the body he hid under those dress shirts I dropped off at the dry cleaner this morning.

Even though Ben couldn't see me, I buried my head in a pillow. I should not have had those thoughts about my boss. And I definitely shouldn't have had them when I was on the phone with a perfectly nice guy. It was wrong on so many levels.

"Is it weird that I'm a bit jealous of your boss, even though I've never met him?"

"Yes, very weird." I blew off his question, although it had some validity. I may have found Hunter attractive, but it didn't mean the man saw me as anything more than his employee. I'd do well to remember our dynamic. Plus, I was guessing Hunter was at least five years older than me, maybe more. He probably saw me as an immature young woman. Besides age, there were at least half a dozen other differences between us.

He was well educated. I had a high school diploma.

He wore a suit to work. I wore yoga pants and T-shirts.

He had two fancy cars. I drove an old pickup truck.

The guy spent money like it was water while I was thankful not to be sleeping on my brother's couch. Money made the world go 'round and Hunter Dorsey had plenty of it. We were a complete mismatch.

"Charli?"

"Huh?"

"I asked if six o'clock is okay."

"Sorry. I'm just tired. Carina was up most of the night," I lied. "Let me talk to my boss and I'll get back to you."

"Alright. I'll talk to you later, beautiful."

"Sounds good. Bye." I hung up without waiting for him to answer. What was wrong with me? All week, I'd been excited about the possibility of going out with Ben, and then when he called, all I could do was think about Hunter.

It was stupid.

Stupid, stupid, stupid.

I felt like a teenager with my first crush. The crazy butterflies in my stomach refused to settle down. Going to the full-length mirror, I tried to see what Hunter saw when he looked at me. To my dismay, strands of hair were sticking out from the topknot I tied it in this morning, there was a tiny hole in the knee of my leggings, and my Taylor Swift T-shirt had a stain that looked suspiciously like squash but couldn't possibly be since it'd been banned from Carina's diet. "I'm a mess."

I frowned at my reflection. It wasn't like me to let myself go, but ever since the accident, my standards had sunk lower and lower. I blamed it on isolation, a lack of purpose, and a mild case of depression.

It was so easy to fall into the habit of feeling sorry for yourself when your life went sideways, but things were turning around. I had a job, I lived in a beautiful apartment, I could begin training again, and my boss was a superhot asshole. I mean, it would be better if my boss wasn't a superhot asshole—the asshole part, not the superhot part—but beggars couldn't be choosers.

Stripping out of my clothes, I rummaged through my drawers for something more suitable. I settled on a pair of black shorts and tank-style turquoise blouse. The outfit was casual without looking like I was trying too hard. I pulled my hair out of the elastic tie and brushed the long, dark waves down my back. A little foundation and mascara helped a lot.

I'm not sure if it was the clothes, my hair, or the makeup, but I felt better. I checked on Carina then headed to the kitchen to begin making dinner. Hunter never said he would be home for dinner, but he didn't say he wouldn't either. He specifically said I didn't have to cook for him, but what man wouldn't appreciate a home-cooked meal when they came in from work? I pulled the chicken breasts I marinated earlier from the fridge and put them in the oven, setting the timer for forty-five minutes. If I timed it right, the chicken would be done as Hunter walked in the door. Next, I peeled and washed potatoes, then set them on the stove to boil.

Looking at the clock, I realized if I didn't get Carina up soon, she wouldn't want to go to bed tonight. If Hunter stressed anything, it was keeping her on a schedule, and even if the task seemed impossible, I had to try. I went to her room and rubbed Carina's tummy gently until her eyes fluttered open. I rocked her for a few minutes before changing her diaper. As I was finishing the snaps on her pajamas, I smelled something strange, and it wasn't a messy diaper.

Something was burning and it couldn't possibly be the chicken. I scooped Carina up and rushed to the kitchen.

"Shit!"

I plopped her into the high chair, grabbed the dish towel that caught fire on the burner, and threw it in the sink. As I ran cold water over the towel, all I could hear were Hunter's words. *"Are you aware that most house fires start in the kitchen due to distracted cooking?"* I blew him off

117

before for being paranoid, but now I saw the truth of his words. I could have set the entire apartment on fire, putting both Carina and me in danger.

Hunter could never know about this.

Once I calmed down, I wadded up the towel and buried it in the bottom of the trash bin. The burning smell lingered, so I opened the sliding door to the balcony and turned on the ceiling fan. That's when I saw the overhead sprinklers. Thank God there wasn't enough smoke or heat to set those puppies off. It would have been difficult to hide an apartment doused by water.

A fresh wave of panic rolled over me at the thought. In through the nose, out through the mouth. Then again. After a few more calming breaths, I leaned over Carina and rubbed her cheek. "Your daddy is never going to know about this. It's going to be our little secret." I was definitely winning the Nanny of the Year award by asking a baby not to blab. It wasn't that I was afraid of Hunter… much. He wouldn't physically harm me, but I would probably get a severe tongue-lashing and my walking papers. And would deserve it. Although the fire wasn't intentional and it was rather small, my actions were irresponsible. I should have turned off the stove before getting Carina up from her nap.

Lesson learned.

I gave Carina cereal puffs and put some toys on her tray to keep her busy while I finished dinner. The chicken smelled divine and successfully covered up the smell of the burned dish towel. Thank goodness for small miracles. I was whipping the potatoes—adding milk and butter—when Hunter walked in the door.

He dropped his keys and wallet on the hallway table. "Something smells good."

"It's chicken," I said over my shoulder.

Hunter hung his clean shirts on a hook by the front door, then lifted Carina out of her high chair. "There's my princess." He kissed the top of her blond head and held her to his chest. "Why is the sliding door open?"

My spine stiffened. "The apartment was stuffy, and we wanted some fresh air," I said as I scooped the potatoes into a bowl.

"The air conditioning is on and there's an air purifier. It shouldn't be stuffy in here." He walked over to the thermostat and fiddled with the buttons. "It's working perfectly fine."

Hunter was a fixer. If there was a problem, he'd find a solution. I put my hands on my hips and let out a huff. "I didn't say it wasn't working, just that it felt stuffy. It's good to get some fresh air once in a while."

"At the risk of sounding like my father, if you want fresh air, go sit on the balcony. I don't own the goddamn electric company." He walked to the sliding door and slammed it closed with more force than necessary.

"Yes, sir," I snapped.

He raised an eyebrow and pierced me with his eyes. "Careful what comes out of that sassy mouth of yours."

I cowered like a child, but there was a hint of something besides annoyance in his tone. Seduction, maybe? It must have been my imagination, or was it? "Sorry." The last thing I needed to do was lose this job. I pulled two plates from the cupboard and set them on the counter, then took the chicken out of the oven. "Are you ready to eat?" I piled his plate high with chicken, potatoes, and vegetables. If he was in a good mood with a full belly, he'd be more likely to give me the night off so I could go on my date with Ben that I wasn't even sure I wanted to go on.

He put Carina in her high chair and grabbed a container of peaches from the pantry. "She have these yet today?"

"No. Are *you* going to eat?"

"I'm going to feed Carina and then I'll take my plate to my office. I have a lot of work to do."

I tried not to let the disappointment seep into my voice. "Oh, okay." I tossed him a bib for Carina and carried my own plate to the table. There was no sense in letting my food get cold.

He ripped the plastic off the container and held a spoonful of peaches up to Carina's mouth. "You want yummy peaches? Open up, princess."

She opened her mouth, and Hunter shoved the fruit in. "Mmm mmm mmm," she hummed.

"So, Charli... anything interesting happen today?" he asked as he continued to shovel peaches into his daughter's mouth.

119

For a brief second, I thought he knew about the fire, but there was no way he could. Hello, paranoia. I chewed the piece of chicken in my mouth and swallowed. "I met Mrs. Hadley today. She was swimming laps in the pool."

"Is that right?" He continued to feed Carina without looking at me.

"Yes. She's really nice. Did you know she was a Vegas showgirl back in the day?"

"I didn't know that." Hunter stole mashed potatoes from my plate to go with the peaches.

I might as well have been having this conversation with the walls for all the attention he was giving me. Feeling frustrated, I got up and filled a small bowl with mashed potatoes and put it in front of him. "She seems to think you're the cat's pajamas and adores Carina."

Hunter wiped his daughter's mouth with the bottom of the bib. "Is there a point to this idle conversation?"

Crossing my hands, I leaned forward on the table. "I'm glad you asked. I'd like to ask Mrs. Hadley to watch Carina Saturday night unless you plan to be home."

Looking bored, he fed Carina another spoonful of mashed potatoes. "And where exactly would you be going?"

He may have been my boss, but he didn't get to approve my social calendar. "Does it matter?"

"Actually, it does." He dropped the spoon into the bowl and finally focused his attention on me. His intensity made me wish I was still talking to the walls. "Are you helping a sick aunt, shaking your ass in a bar, or getting your clit tickled by some random loser?"

I could feel the heat rising up my neck. Never in my life had I met someone so forward and crass. Worst of all, now I was thinking about his tongue and the things it could do to me. My pussy tingled and pulsed. Dammit!

I squirmed on the chair. "I don't have an aunt in Vegas. Not that it's your business, but I have a date."

He narrowed his eyes. "So, it is to get your clit tickled."

Slamming my hand on the table, I shouted. "Stop saying that! It's totally inappropriate. It's a first date. There won't be any tickling of any sort."

"No."

I let out a measured breath. "No, what?"

"No, you can't have the night off."

"Why not? I've been working twenty-four hours a day all week."

"And you're being compensated for that. Quite well, I might add."

He wasn't wrong. "Come on. I'm going stir-crazy. I need adult interaction."

"What am I? Last time I checked, I was an adult and also the one who signs your paycheck."

My shoulders sagged. "You're barely ever home."

"Hence why you have a job. Besides, you just got finished telling me you spent time with Mrs. Hadley."

"That doesn't count. It's like spending time with my grandma. All I'm asking for is one date. I don't even know if it's going to go anywhere."

"And if it does, you'll want more time off. Where did you meet someone anyway? Don't tell me it's a Tinder date."

Why did this inquisition feel like I was talking to my father? He had me defending myself when I owed him nothing. "It's not a Tinder date." I sank down in my seat and resigned myself to telling him the truth. "His name is Ben and he's one of the guys that delivered Carina's furniture."

"A delivery guy? Really, Charli? You're better than that."

Definitely daddy vibes. I threw my hands in the air like a petulant child. "Oh, sorry we can't all be gazillionaires like you."

He chuckled. "I'm not a gazillionaire, only a millionaire. And the answer is still no."

"Why? I've earned some time off."

"Because I'll be needing your services Saturday night. You'll be attending a dinner with me and Carina at my brother's home."

I pulled back in surprise. Here I thought he was just being a dick when his reason was somewhat legit, even if it stank like yesterday's fish. "Why do you need me?"

He went back to feeding his daughter. "Your presence was specifically requested by Gia, my brother's wife. They want to get to know you."

Still sounded fishy. "Again, why?"

"I don't fucking know why. It's a family dinner I'm being blackmailed into going to. If Gia wants you there, then you're going. End of story. Tell your fuckboy you've got other plans." He stood, grabbed his plate from the counter, and stormed down the hallway.

I winced when his office door slammed. The discussion was over. My request was heard and denied. I was having dinner with Hunter's family. If I found Hunter intense, I couldn't imagine what the rest of his family would be like. Certainly, they couldn't all be arrogant assholes.

After cleaning the kitchen, I played with Carina for a while, gave her a bath, then put her down for the night. Then I texted Ben and gave him the bad news.

My head was all over the place. On the one hand, I was annoyed that Hunter cockblocked me, but on the other hand, I was semiexcited about spending more time with him. Truth be told, I wasn't all that upset about my canceled date. If Ben was really interested, he'd ask again.

When I went to bed, I couldn't get Hunter's words out of my head. He might have been a jerk face, but I had a feeling he was an expert at clit tickling. Not that anything like that would happen at a family dinner. I fell asleep thinking about the big jerk and everything he could do to my body.

In the morning, I woke to another note.

The fire extinguisher is under the sink.

P.S. Don't lie to me!

The burned towel I'd buried at the bottom of the trash lay next to it. Fuck!

Chapter 17
Hunter

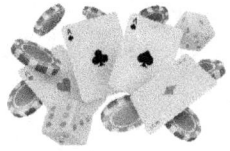

The memory of Charlotte squirming on the chair and the blush that crept up her cheeks had me sporting a semi. I'd been out of line with her, but there was no way I was approving of her going out on a date with some fuckboy who delivered furniture. It only took one phone call to solve that problem.

Buh-bye, Ben.

I was a selfish prick and even if she did almost burn my apartment down, I wasn't letting her go that easily. Charli Bently was a wild thing that needed taming. I could think of a dozen ways to shut that sassy mouth of hers, starting with my cock shoved between her pouty lips. She could *yes, sir* me all she wanted on her knees while staring up at me with those big blue eyes.

I made sure to leave the apartment early this morning to beat Leonard to Mystique if he even showed up at all. For all I knew, he was still shitting rivers from his specialty coffee with a hint of chocolate.

While in his office, I strategically inserted the camera I bought yesterday into the frame of the picture of his too-hot-for-him wife and their pimply teenage son. I checked the feed on my phone and angled the frame toward Leonard's keyboard. You'd think I'd have learned my lesson with Trent, but unlike taping my brother having sex, this wasn't for my entertainment. It was strictly research.

Leonard was as shady as a crack dealer selling bibles. If he was hiding something, I was going to find it.

Before leaving, I placed the package of blue sticky notes on his desk along with the receipt and his change. Three pennies. It was more of a *fuck you* than anything else.

I slipped out of his office and locked the door with the key no one had bothered to take back from me when I was fired. With my work done, I headed to the break room to get coffee.

Gia sauntered in a few minutes later for her own dose of caffeine. "Don't forget about tomorrow," she said.

"I'll be there will bells on," I drawled sarcastically.

"Good to hear. And Charli?" She filled her pink mug with coffee. The mug said *A woman's success is not measured by the size of her feet.* I internally rolled my eyes. Feminism was overrated.

"I'll drag her along too, although I'm not sure of the purpose."

Her bright-red lips turned up in a smile. "Because I invited her. Does there need to be another reason?" She casually added cream and sugar to her brew, enjoying our little interaction way more than I was.

Because you're dead set on making my life hell and making me pay for that damn video. "I suppose not."

"Perfect. We'll see you tomorrow then. I can't wait to meet my niece. Ta-ta, Hunter."

The thought of going to Trent and Gia's was about as appealing as a rectal exam performed by Edward Scissorhands. I'd rather bleed than make small talk with a family who pretended I didn't exist for the last year. Not even a goddamn Christmas card or a fucking cookie bouquet for my birthday. It was poor manners.

124

When I crawled to my father and begged for my job back, I didn't realize it was going to include family dinners. What was next? Cake, streamers, and fucking piñatas?

Hard pass.

I took my coffee and left the break room, practically bumping into a haggard-looking Leonard, pallid skin and dark circles under his eyes. "Good morning, Mr. Moroski. I hope you're feeling better today."

He glared at me. "What do you want, Hunter?"

"The question is, what do *you* want, Mr. Moroski? I'm here to help. Would you like a cup of coffee?" I held up my mug of freshly brewed java.

"No," he grumbled as he stomped away.

"You sure? It's a fresh pot," I yelled at his retreating form, the devil on my shoulder throwing a fist pump in the air. That dick fucker deserved the stomach cramps and burning asshole I gave him yesterday. He fucked with the wrong person.

"I see you're making friends." Trent clapped his hand on my shoulder.

I took a sip of my hot coffee. "What do you know about Leonard?"

"Guy keeps to himself mostly. Seems competent enough."

That was the least glowing recommendation I'd ever heard. "But is he trustworthy?"

Trent raised an eyebrow. "I trust him more than you."

"I'm not talking about most likely to fuck your wife, I'm talking about money."

My brother gritted his teeth. "I'm going to pretend you didn't say that unless you want me to knock you on your ass again."

I gave him a big grin. "Don't worry about it. Unlike you, I don't screw our employees. And anytime you want to go a round, let me know. Last time you hit me, it was a cheap shot. I'd be happy to even the score."

"God, I did not miss this shit."

"Awww... you're a liar. You totally missed me."

"Not even a little bit."

I looked at my watch. "Wish I had time to call you out on your bullshit, but I have a meeting with Dad."

"Wait! So do I."

125

We looked at each other and scrambled off in opposite directions, ties flying, to our own offices. Within seconds, we both arrived at my father's door, jockeying for position to get through it first. Trent beat me by seconds, but I was right on his heels with my laptop and notes.

At our anything-but-smooth entrance, my father looked up from his computer and smiled. "You two are early. Come in, boys." *Boys.* Like we were children and not grown men. It took me back to the days when Trent and I would wrestle on the back lawn beating the crap out of each other, only to face the consequences with our father. Trips to his office never boded well for either of us.

I wasn't in the mood for a disciplinary lecture. Trent and I, for the most part, had been amicable this week. It was the best-case scenario. If he was hoping we were going to sing "Kumbaya" and roast marshmallows, he was out of luck.

"Why are we both here?" Trent asked.

I wanted to know that answer too.

"Have a seat." Our father motioned to the leather chairs in front of his desk. Trent and I shared a wary look and sat. "I wanted to do some brainstorming with the two of you."

Trent scowled. "He's a junior financial assistant."

Anger boiled inside me. I used to be the CFO. I didn't need my fall from grace shoved in my face any more than it already was. The closet office. The junior position. The snide remarks. The jeering glances. The kowtowing to Leonard and anyone else who felt the constant need to remind me of my status. The whole thing humiliated me, although I was sure that was exactly the point.

Humiliation.

Before I could say anything, my father held up his hand to stop me. "He's my son, same as you. The two of you have been around this hotel your entire lives. Besides your animosity for each other, the two of you are the most qualified to bring Mystique into the future. We're losing profits and we need to figure this out. Something is out of whack."

"You're right," Trent conceded.

126

It was more than I expected from him. Despite my bad behavior, I had a great work ethic. This hotel and casino resort was like my second home. Rose would bring us here when we were kids to see our dad. When we were old enough, we had our first jobs here. From the mail room to administration, we knew everything there was to know about Mystique.

"As I told you both, I want to go back to basics." He went over to the huge whiteboard hanging on the wall and drew two lines in the form of a plus sign that divided it into quadrants. He wrote the word "strengths" in the first box. "Go."

Trent and I had both done our homework. We filled the box with all the amenities Mystique offered from restaurants to shows to gambling to the luxurious rooms and spa. Dad wrote down each one, having to squeeze some into the box sideways.

"We know what we do well. Now, let's move on to weaknesses. He wrote the word in the next box. "Give me all your thoughts."

I stood and took the marker from my father and wrote one word in capital letters. LEONARD.

"For Christ's sake!" Trent rolled his eyes. "Just because you don't like the guy doesn't make him a liability."

"Trent's right. You sound like sour grapes." He picked up the eraser and I swiped it from his hand.

"Hear me out. Why did he fire my entire team except for Daniel?"

"It was unnecessary overhead," my father answered.

"Bullshit. Trent has a team of people who work underneath him. Everyone has a specific job. My team was the same way. It's too much for any one person."

"Leonard's more efficient than you were. Deal with it," Trent scoffed.

"Again, bullshit. When you're dealing with the type of money we bring in, there needs to be a system of checks and balances. Accountability. All it takes is one misplaced number to lose thousands, possibly millions of dollars."

"What are you suggesting?" my father asked.

"I'm not sure yet, but something doesn't sit well with me. How could we go from being one of the most successful casinos on the Strip to hemorrhaging money in less than a year? It doesn't make sense."

"I agree, it's concerning, but what you're proposing is a serious accusation." My father let out a ragged breath.

"If you accuse him of wrongdoing and you're wrong, he'll sue the crap out of us for defamation and a handful of other offenses," Trent pointed out.

"I'm aware of the risk, which is why I have another suggestion."

"Which is?"

"I want to do a complete audit of all the financials over the last year. We keep it between the three of us." It was a ton of work, but the only way to determine if Leonard was as shady as I suspected.

"And if you're wrong?" Trent asked.

"I'm not wrong."

"That's all well and good to say, but you have to prove it." My father never doubted me before, and I took this as a challenge.

"I will." When I proved Leonard was a piece of shit, I'd be reinstated as CFO. It was a risky move on my part.

I hoped I was right.

I stayed late at work to download and print the necessary documents. It was a shitload of paperwork, but I was giddy when I got home. I dropped my keys and wallet on the hallway table. "Hello?"

"In here!" Charli and Carina were on the living room floor playing. The coffee table had been pushed to the side and they lay in the middle of the fluffy, black rug. Carina was on her back while Charli held a stuffed frog to the side and made her reach for it. "Do it again, sweetie." Carina rolled onto her tummy and laughed.

"Did she roll over?"

Charli smiled. "Yep. I've been working on it with her all week, and today, she's been rolling around like it's second nature. I was starting to worry because she should have been doing it by now."

I didn't know that. I didn't know shit about baby milestones. I added it to my list of things to research. She also needed to see a pediatrician. It should have already happened, but I'd been so busy it took a back seat to everything else.

Getting down on the rug with them, I buried my face in Carina's tummy and nuzzled her. "That's my big girl." She laughed and hit me on the head with her tiny hands. "You gonna get your daddy? Huh? I scooped her up and rolled on my back, zooming her around like a miniature airplane, arms and legs flailing. The sound of her laughter caused warmth to spread through my chest. I'd never loved anyone like I did my daughter. "Who's got you now? Huh, princess?"

"Hunter, stop!"

"She's tough. Aren't you, girl?" I zoomed her again and brought her down to kiss her forehead.

"Hunter..."

Carina opened her mouth to laugh and... puked all over my face. Putrid liquid covered my eyes, nose, and mouth. It dripped down the sides of my face into my ears. I froze because what the hell else was I supposed to do? "Hel—" I slammed my lips closed, but it was too late. The contents of Carina's stomach already seeped through and infiltrated my tongue.

"Oh, god! I was trying to tell you I just fed her a bottle." Charli snatched Carina from my arms and laid her on the rug. Then she rushed away and returned with a wet washcloth. "Hold still." I wasn't going anywhere. Charli gently rubbed the cloth along my eyelids, down my nose, and over my lips. "Don't move." She left and returned with a fresh cloth, wiping away any of the mess she missed the first time.

All I could do was stare into her big blue eyes. They weren't the same blue as mine. Hers were darker, like the ocean at midnight, with long lashes that fanned her cheeks when she blinked. I was mesmerized.

"How's your stomach? You're not going to throw up, are you?" She gently patted my face with a dish towel as she hovered over me, her long hair falling around her face like a curtain.

My weak stomach was the last thing I was thinking about. "Thank you."

She smiled. "You're welcome."

I reached up and pushed her hair behind her ear. "Not only for this but for everything. I know I'm not the easiest person to be around, but I don't know how I would have survived this week without you."

"You're not that bad. You have a loud bark, but deep down"—she put her hand on my chest—"I think you're a good person who got thrown into a difficult situation."

She had no idea what she was talking about. Didn't know my past. Didn't know the lengths I'd go to to get what I wanted. "You're wrong. I'm not a good person."

"I've seen the way you are with Carina. You're going to be a great dad."

Not *you are a great dad*. Couldn't blame her. I'd missed the mark more than a few times. "Regardless, you've made this much easier. I've ridden you hard and you barely complain." I internally winced at my choice of words.

She still leaned over me. Maybe even closer than before. Her breathing shallowed. "Not that hard yet."

The conversation was veering into dangerous territory. Unprofessional. Not able to help myself, I brushed her cheek with my thumb. "There's still time."

"Yeah?"

Her soft voice made my cock swell. "Yeah. You're not quitting on me, are you?"

Charli smiled. "Not planning on it."

Carina screeched, the high-pitch squeal cutting the sexual tension between us. I wouldn't be winning any Dad of the Year awards for flirting with the nanny while my daughter, who just threw up, lay on the rug ignored. I rolled away from Charli and picked up Carina.

130

She should have been my first priority, not getting my dick hard with the nanny. "I'll give her a bath tonight. You're officially off duty."

Charli pulled back at my sudden change in demeanor. "Off duty?"

I stared down at her. "Yes. If you want to go out with the fuckboy tonight, you're free to do so." It came out angrier than intended. Did I want her to go out with some other guy? No, but I was afraid if she didn't leave, I'd have her on her back by the end of the night. A bad idea for more than one reason.

"Oh, wow! That's so generous of you," she said sarcastically. "I guess I'll pick up some rando off the Strip. Sounds fun." She stalked to her room and returned with her purse. "Hope she doesn't shit on you tonight." Before I could respond, she was out the door.

My keys on the hallway table rattled when the door slammed. I should have felt relieved that Charli was no longer sucking the air from my lungs, but all I felt was a sinking in my chest. I'd never felt guilty in my life, but I was sure that's what this was. I took an intimate moment and turned it into something dirty.

Made her feel dirty.

How many times had I picked up a woman for a night of fun? More times than I could count. She had every right to find a man to make her forget about me, but I really hoped she wouldn't.

Chapter 18
Charli

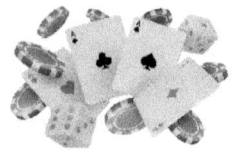

Hunter pissed me the fuck off.

How could I have ever thought there could be something between us? He'd shown me who he was over and over again. Everyone warned me he was an asshole.

Surprise… he was!

The way he stared into my eyes and caressed my cheek, I thought he was going to kiss me. Thought he might be seeing me as more than the nanny.

And then he ruined it.

I made my way to the parking garage and hopped in my old pickup truck without a destination in mind. I didn't care where I went as long as it was away from my boss.

Boss.

Yes, I needed to get that through my thick head.

The little moments we shared were nothing. They were natural consequences of two people being in the same space for an extended amount of time. There would be no more cooking him dinner or dropping off his dry cleaning. That's what a girlfriend was for, and I certainly wasn't that. I was the fucking nanny. My only job was caring for Carina. From now on, if it didn't directly affect her, I wouldn't be doing it.

I'd keep it strictly professional.

Should have from the very beginning.

Driving through the downtown traffic, I found myself in the employee lot behind Oasis. It was my second home. Where I spent most of my time before I fell, and everything went to shit. The people here were like family to me.

I couldn't complain to my brother about Hunter. I'd been warned. Multiple times. Telling him would only lead to *I told you so* and being chastised like a child. And there was no way I could admit I was falling for the jerk face. Subjecting myself to Tom's criticism was as bad, if not worse, than putting up with Hunter's disrespectful words.

Jasmine was my best friend in Vegas. She'd listen without judgment.

The show didn't start for another two hours. Hopefully, Jasmine was working tonight. A group of us rotated shows because it would be physically impossible to perform two shows a day, three on Saturday. If my replacement was here instead of Jasmine, I think I'd puke. She was a reminder of my failure. Her position was temporary and conditional upon my return.

I was coming back. There weren't any other options for me.

After staring at the building for ten minutes, I got out of the truck, walked to the back entrance, and hit the buzzer. Big Mike opened the door and gave me a bear hug. "Hey, Charli. Are you back?"

I shook my head. "Not yet. Is Jasmine here?"

He motioned down the long hallway. "She's in the dressing room."

"Thanks." The back entrance was a stark contrast to the glitz and glamour of the front theater. It was dark and dusty, with props strewn about. Light and sound people rushed by with headphones, making last-minute checks. Performers milled around half dressed, engaged in preshow rituals, some practicing and others sneaking in a few minutes of meditation. The air buzzed with anticipation.

If the audience ever got a look behind the scenes, they'd get a shock. We were an eclectic group of people, weird and bizarre, who all had a passion for performing, but when the curtain went up, everything gelled into something nothing less than magical. It was an illusion, produced with lights, music, and extravagant costumes.

I loved it.

Every little thing about this place was what I lived for, and I missed it terribly.

I poked my head into the third dressing room on the right. "Hey, bitch."

Jasmine's hand stopped midswipe of her metallic-green eyeshadow as she screeched, "Charli!" She abandoned her makeup brush and ran to me. We collided and smashed together, arms wrapped around each other and swayed back and forth. "I've missed you so much!"

My eyes misted. "I've missed you too." I hadn't been back since my accident. The pain of not being able to perform was too much.

She held on to my shoulders and inspected me from head to toe. "How are you?"

"I got the all clear from the doctor, but I'm so out of shape. Now that I have the green light, I'm hoping to be back in a few months."

She squeezed my bicep. "They are puny."

I slapped her hand away with a laugh. "They aren't puny, but my legs and core aren't what they used to be." I kept up my workouts while in rehab, but there's only so much you can do with a messed-up knee. "I'll be back before you know it."

Jasmine held a hand to her chest. "I'm so glad. If I have to share a dressing room with Zaria much longer, I'm going to rip every feather from her headpiece and shove them down her throat. Her area is a complete mess and all she does is talk, talk, talk. Sometimes, a girl needs some peace and quiet, you know?"

I did know. Six of us shared this dressing room, but never all at the same time. It depended on what shows we were doing and how much time there was between performances. With two aerialists per show, my preferred partner was Jasmine.

134

We clicked right from the beginning. She'd been working here for two years when I started and became a mentor to me. She taught me the art of seduction and that a truly spectacular routine was about more than the cool tricks I could do but the way I made the audience feel. Jasmine was a pole dancer before coming to Oasis, and let me tell you, she had seduction down to a science without removing a single piece of clothing.

The show was called *Deep Desires*. It was a fantasy, a tease, a sensual experience without the sex and nudity. It wasn't exactly what I thought I'd be doing when I moved to Vegas, but after my audition, they hired me on the spot. The offer was too good to pass up. Not many people got to make a living by pursuing their dream but I was one of the lucky ones. If it were up to my parents, I'd be teaching third grade in Colorado. I couldn't think of anything worse.

Jasmine sat back at her vanity and continued applying her winged eyeshadow. "You should come by the training facility and get some practice in. I can show you this new move I've been working on."

I straddled a chair and leaned on the back of it. "I'd love that, but I'm not sure I'd be able to get off work."

"Work?" She lifted a penciled brow.

"Yes, work. Oasis cut my disability check. I had to get a job."

"Well, that sucks," she said as she carefully glued rhinestones from the outside corner of her eye to the tip of her eyebrow. "What kind of job did you get?"

"I'm a live-in nanny for a six-month-old baby girl."

She blinked at me through the mirror. "And how's that, Miss I'm Not Ready For Kids Yet?"

I sighed. "It's actually really good. The pay is amazing, and my boss is hot as hell."

She clapped her hands together excitedly. "Ooooh! I'm loving this plot twist. Single, hot daddy falls for the nanny who is all kinds of flexible and sexy. I'd read that book. Can you imagine the things they would do in bed?"

I'd be lying if I said I didn't imagine exactly what we could do in bed. Right up until he rejected me and made me feel stupid. "Only this isn't a book; it's my life. He's a jerk, but once in a while, I get a glimmer of the man he could be."

"That's even better. You could be the woman who reforms his bad-boy ways."

I laughed. I'd never thought of Hunter as a *bad boy*, but if you looked up *asshole* in the dictionary there was no doubt his picture would be right there. "I don't want to reform him." Okay, maybe I did a little bit. "And even if I did, I think it's a dead issue. I thought for a minute he was going to kiss me, but then he told me I had the night off and, basically, to go find some random dude to fuck."

"Ouch! That's harsh. Do you like him?"

"More than I should. He's my boss."

She wiggled her fingers at me. "Technicalities. If you like this guy, then you have to act completely unaffected by him."

"That seems counterproductive. How will he like me if I act like I'm not interested?"

Jasmine turned and took my hands in hers. "Oh, my sweet Charli, men like a chase. They want what they can't have. It's an evolutionary instinct to conquer. Take Nick, for example. He came to the show night after night to see me. Left flowers in my dressing room with cute little notes. Every time I ignored him, he stepped it up another notch. It made him crazy, and he tried harder. Men like something they have to work for, they don't want it handed to them on a silver platter."

"And now you're married with two sons," I concluded.

"I made him work for it, but yes. Let me tell you, it wasn't easy to keep pushing him away. I wanted to run right into his arms every time I read one of his cheesy notes. Now he appreciates what he has because I wasn't easy to get. He knows I'm independent and wouldn't hesitate to leave him if he treated me poorly."

"You think this strategy will work with Hunter?"

She fanned herself. "God, even his name is hot. If you like him, then it's worth a try."

I hugged her over the top of the chair. "Thank you. I totally needed this pep talk. I've missed you like crazy."

"Miss you too, bitch. Call me and we'll set up a time to meet at the training facility. I can watch the baby while you practice."

"That would be awesome."

I wasn't sure if I wanted Hunter to fall for me or not, but either way I was done letting him think he had any effect on me. From now on, my focus was only Carina.

I had my mind made up. I only hoped my heart would listen.

It was quiet when I got back to the apartment. I quickly checked on Carina, who was fast asleep, then went to my room. I lay back on the bed with pillows propped behind me and flicked on the television. Flipping through the channels, I settled on a murder-mystery show about a guy who disappeared outside a pizza shop in Seattle, never to be heard from again. It was mindless, and after the events of the evening, mindless was exactly what I needed.

A half hour into the show, a light knock came at my open door. Since I'd moved in, Hunter had never come to my room, so I figured it had something to do with Carina. I turned down the volume on the television. "What's up?"

Wearing a pair of plaid pajama bottoms and a plain black T-shirt, he leaned against the door. In the last week, I'd never seen him look so casual and comfortable. It instantly softened some of his hard lines, making him seem younger and more approachable. "Just checking in. You're home early."

His words seemed innocent enough, but I saw them for what they were. Probing. "Yep."

"Where'd you go?"

He'd lost his right to know where I went with his crass accusations and insinuations. "Does it matter?"

"Shit," he muttered and blew out a measured breath. "I shouldn't have said what I said earlier. It was wrong."

"And rude," I added. "If this is your attempt at an apology, it's lame."

"Lame?" He chuckled. "I suppose it is. I'm sorry for being rude and lame."

"Apology appreciated. Is there anything else?"

"It's been a stressful week," he said, as if it excused his behavior. "You've been the only thing that's kept me from pulling my hair out, knowing that if nothing else, Carina was being well-cared for." Hunter pushed off the door and sat on the edge of my bed, although I hadn't invited him to do so.

I scooted back an inch. I could still feel his almost kiss feathering against my lips, and I didn't trust myself. "Even though I almost started your kitchen on fire."

He growled as he ran a big hand through his hair. "No harm, no foul. I'm hoping you scared yourself enough that it won't happen again."

"I did." I still didn't know how he figured it out, but now didn't seem like the time to ask. "It won't happen again."

"So, where did you go?"

I folded my arms across my chest. "I don't owe you an explanation. You're not my father."

"Oh, trust me, I'm very well aware." His eyes moved from my face to my small breasts that were pushed up from my arms.

It wasn't my imagination. The attraction was an electric current that zipped between us. Thinking I would be able to resist him was useless. My arms relaxed and I leaned back on the pillows. "What do you really want to know?"

"Did you go see Ben?"

I shook my head, letting my long hair brush against my bare shoulders.

"Another guy?" he questioned, his jaw tense.

The man looked as if he were about to erupt. I could have told him a lascivious story that made his blood boil, but what would be the point? "I went to Oasis."

His brows furrowed. "Getting ready to leave me already?"

"Not yet. Why? Are you going to miss me?" It was a bold question I had no business asking.

Hunter ran the back of his fingers down the side of my face. "I may. I'm getting used to having you around."

A tingle raced down my spine, and my resolve weakened. "Then give me a reason to stay."

"Careful what you ask for, dollface." His eyes pierced mine so deep, I swear he could see into my soul.

I should have backed away. I should have run. I should have done something to preserve myself, but I didn't. Instead, I leaned into his touch. "I'm not afraid."

"You should be. I'm not a good man."

"I don't believe you."

He growled. "Don't say I didn't warn you." Then those fingers that'd been dancing along my cheek wrapped around the back of my neck and pulled me in.

The moment our lips touched the air crackled with energy. His mouth moved over mine possessively, his tongue pushing between my lips. My breath caught in my throat, taken aback by the force that was Hunter Dorsey.

He knew what he wanted… and it was me.

Chapter 19
Hunter

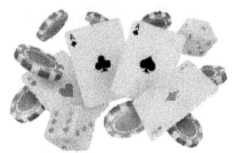

Fuck me.

What was I doing?

I should have stopped myself, but I couldn't.

She wasn't mine to take, but damn if I didn't want her anyway.

I was a selfish bastard.

It was one more reason she should have pushed me away, yet she surrendered submissively. The silly girl had no idea she was playing with fire. We'd be lucky if we both didn't go up in flames.

My arm wound around her waist and pulled her to straddle my lap. Ending the kiss, I took her face in both my hands. "So damn pretty. I've wanted to kiss you since the first moment I saw you. I promised myself I wouldn't touch you, but you're too damn tempting. Tell me no."

"I'm not telling you no." She blinked those big blue eyes at me.

The woman was infuriating. She had no self-preservation whatsoever. "Damn it, Charli. Tell me no. Tell me not to kiss you. Not to touch you."

"I want you to kiss me."

I squeezed her cheeks harder. "You're trouble with a capital *T*."

She wound her arms around my neck. "And you're bossy, so I guess we both have our flaws. What are you gonna do about it?"

If she knew all the dirty, depraved things I wanted to do to her, she'd be running for the door. It was one thing to lust after the nanny, but quite another to act on it. Every warning Trent gave me, telling me not to get involved with her, was overshadowed by need.

I flipped her back onto the mattress and caged her in with my arms. "I don't do relationships."

"I'm not asking for one. I've got dreams bigger than you," she said, jutting out her chin.

This girl. "Must be some pretty big dreams." I pressed my hard cock into her soft body that was trapped beneath me.

She gasped. "They are. I'm not going to be here forever."

"Who said anything about forever?" I knew better than most that no one ever stayed. Eventually they left, taking pieces of you with them. Staying unattached was my specialty. "While you're here, you're mine. Understood?"

"See? Bossy."

"I'll show you bossy." I grabbed her by the chin and lifted her mouth to mine, sealing our lips together in a scorching kiss. My tongue pushed into her mouth and twisted with hers.

It wasn't gentle.

It wasn't seductive.

It was pure lust.

Want.

Need.

Desire.

This woman had me tangled up in knots. Wanting things I shouldn't. Pushing boundaries and crossing the lines I'd drawn between us.

I lifted both her arms above her head on the pillow and clasped her wrists in one hand, holding her captive as I pressed my body into hers. She wrapped her long legs around my waist and pulled me in tighter until there was no space between us. Separated by only the thin layers of fabric from

141

my pajama pants and her shorts, there was no doubt she could feel how much I wanted her. The heat radiating from her pussy made my cock even harder.

My fingers danced along the strip of bare skin between her shorts and shirt. It was as soft as I imagined but toned in a way I rarely saw on a woman. Her ab muscles were clearly defined under her silky skin, and I was surprised that it turned me on. Charli was full of pleasant surprises.

Although I shouldn't have, I slid my hand under her shirt and grabbed a handful of one of her breasts. Despite my affinity for big-boobed women, Charli's tiny tits turned me on. They fit her long, lean body perfectly. My thumb flicked the stiff peak of her nipple through the lace of her bra.

"God, Hunter, that feels so good!" She began rubbing her pussy along my dick, seeking her release.

"Fuck! You're a very bad girl, Charli, trying to come on my cock without permission. You like when I play with your tits?"

"Yes, yes," she moaned. Her hips moved faster over my cock as she raced for an orgasm.

I pulled back the lace of her bra and pinched her nipple, then did the same to the other one. Her body arched into mine, responding to my every touch. If she didn't come soon, I was going to explode in my pants, and I refused to let that happen, but the woman was wrapped around me like a damn spider monkey.

When I thought I couldn't take anymore, her body pulled impossibly tight and stopped writhing. Her back arched and mouth fell open as she let out a cry of pleasure. A sound so sweet I wanted to hear it again and again.

I swear, Charli coming was one of the sexiest things I'd ever witnessed, and I was afraid I might become addicted. With her eyes closed and little pants coming from her pouty lips, she was the picture of perfection.

My cock was painfully hard, but the urge to come subsided. It was manageable until I had the privacy to handle it myself. We'd crossed enough lines for the night.

I ran my fingers along the side of her face. "You good?"

142

She opened her eyes and nodded, looking blissed out and relaxed. "Very."

"Then will you kindly unlock your death grip on my hips," I said with a smirk.

Her eyes widened. "Oh, shit. Sorry." She unhooked her ankles and let her legs fall off my waist.

I released her wrists and rolled onto my side, propping myself on my elbow. "Well, that was the most fun I've had with my clothes on in a while."

Charli covered her face with her hands. "I'm so embarrassed. I shouldn't have done that."

I pried her hands from her face. "Nothing to be embarrassed about. Perfectly normal for the nanny to get herself off on her boss's cock."

She groaned. "Why do you have to say shit like that?"

"Because I like watching your cheeks turn pink." Her already flushed cheeks turned a shade darker. "Yep. Just like that."

Her hands covered her face again and she peeked through her fingers at me. "Do you need me to… you know… take care of you?" Charli's eyes zeroed in the outline of my hard cock clearly visible behind my pants. She lifted her foot and poked it with her toe.

"Hey!" I grabbed her ankle and pushed her long leg away. "Where's the respect?"

She laughed. "I'm trying to cop a feel."

I quirked a brow at her honesty. "I think you got enough feels for one night. And no, I don't need you to take care of me."

"You sure?"

"Dollface, you should know, in Vegas, you don't play all your chips on the first night. You save some for later." I tapped her on the nose and left to deal with the situation in my pants. My apology might have been lame, but her orgasm wasn't.

Chapter 20
Charli

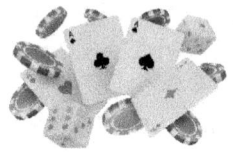

In the morning light, I was even more mortified about using Hunter's cock as my own personal vibrator. My resolve vanished into thin air when his lips touched mine. It was even more humiliating when he denied my offer of returning the favor.

Of course, with it being Saturday, the chance of avoiding him was minimal. And then there was the dinner at his brother's we were attending in the evening. More together time. If neither one of us made a big deal about it, then maybe it wouldn't be as awkward as I feared.

Determined to seem as unaffected as Hunter was last night, I bustled around the apartment in my normal morning routine, thankfully without getting a glimpse of my boss. I even tiptoed down to his room and peeked inside. The bed was neatly made and the room completely silent. He wasn't in his office either.

Although it was a relief to not have to see his stupid-hot face, it annoyed me that he was gone without even leaving me one of the notes he was so fond of. He didn't owe me an explanation of his whereabouts, but as another person sharing the same living space, I felt I deserved one.

How would he feel if he woke up and I was gone? No note. No text. Nothing. He was going to find out, that was for sure.

I packed up Carina and headed down to the fitness center. It wasn't ideal, but after seeing Jasmine last night, I was more determined than ever to get back in the air and that meant weight training and practice. Since Carina wasn't crawling yet, I laid a big blanket on the mat and set her up with some toys. I put on some music and hit the weights first. They were my least favorite, but a necessary evil. Part of the magic of performing on silks was to make it look effortless to climb to the top, when in fact it was hard as fuck.

When my muscles burned, I plopped down on the floor with Carina, tickling her tummy and making silly faces. She giggled and was so cute that my chest ached. I wasn't under any illusions that most babies were as happy as Carina, but I wanted one of my own someday. Although I took this job knowing it was temporary, I wasn't looking forward to the day when I walked away. I would miss her so much. Maybe Hunter and I could come to an agreement where I could still visit. It was months away, but my mind was already thinking five steps ahead.

Training should have been my first priority, not the little person in front of me, so I cued up my music and started a carefully choreographed routine in front of the mirrors to stretch my muscles. Flexibility and control were as important as strength. I pressed up into a handstand and balanced my weight while lifting one hand off the mat and extending my arm out to the side, then repeated the process with my other arm. With both hands firmly back on the mat, I opened my legs into an upside-down split and moved my hands to turn my body in a circle. My arms shook with the weight and movements, proving to me that I was definitely out of practice.

For the next thirty minutes, I twisted and bent my body into the unnatural positions that were required to return to Oasis. My muscles ached, but it was worth every minute of the pain. I would not let a stupid injury derail my career. I was tougher than that. My parents always encouraged me to chase my dreams, they just never realized where it would take me, and despite their objections, they supported me. Failing now wouldn't only be letting myself down, but them as well.

As I stood on my hands again, I bent my back and brought my legs down to touch the top of my head, then straightened them parallel to the floor.

"Who knew you were a human pretzel?"

Hunter's gruff voice startled me, and my body wobbled. Using all my strength, I straightened my legs back to the ceiling and walked out of the handstand. "You scared me," I said as I shook out my arms, trying to get the blood flowing again.

"Sorry. I didn't mean to distract you."

It wasn't his words that distracted me though. He stood with his hands on his hips wearing only a pair of shorts and his running shoes, his shirt carelessly thrown over his shoulder and his chest dripping with sweat. Every muscle glistened and I had the urge to lick every ridge of his defined abs. He was a perfect male specimen, and I wondered how he kept his body looking like that while working behind a desk all day. "It's fine. I was finishing up anyway."

He tilted his head to the side and stared at me for longer than was comfortable. "Is that what you do at Oasis?"

I chuckled. Up until now, he hadn't shown much interest in what I did. "Yes and no. Same thing but from way up there." I pointed to the extra-tall ceiling.

"Explain," he said as he used his shirt to wipe the sweat from his chest.

Keeping eye contact was difficult as he rubbed the shirt over his pecs. I could have easily gotten lost in the back-and-forth motion. "Usually, I perform on silks or in a hoop that hangs from the ceiling. Since I don't have the equipment, I'm making do with practicing from the floor."

He stared up at the ceiling. "That's dangerous and reckless. Why would you want to do something that risks your life?"

It was a bit dramatic, but I understood his thinking. Pretty much everyone in my life asked me the same question at one time or another. "I like the challenge. There's an adrenaline rush doing something that very few people can do. An immense feeling of satisfaction mastering a trick

146

that seems impossible, and even more satisfaction when I do something everybody tells me I can't do."

Hunter rubbed at the scruff on his chin while he shook his head. "I don't get it. You already fell once, why risk it again?"

I let out a huff of irritation at having to explain my life choices. "Did you ever fall off your bike as a kid?"

"Of course."

"But you got back on that bike and tried again. It didn't stop you, did it?"

"That's totally different. If I fell, I wouldn't crack my skull open."

"That's not true. Hundreds of people die in bicycle accidents every year," I said, crossing my arms. "Why do you even care?"

He rolled his eyes. "Excuse me for not wanting to see my nanny splattered on the floor like a pile of wet dog shit."

"Nice analogy." I picked up Carina and grabbed her blanket. "What time do we have to leave for dinner?"

"We'll leave by five thirty." I gave him a thumbs-up and headed toward the door when he called my name, "Charli!" I stopped and glanced at him over my shoulder. "You should have told me *no* last night."

For a moment I wondered if he regretted what happened between us, but his wolfish smile told me otherwise. "Maybe I will next time."

But I knew damn well I wouldn't.

Hunter and I successfully avoided each other for the rest of the day. I never wanted to kiss and simultaneously punch someone in the face before. It seemed an impossible juxtaposition, but somehow Hunter managed to achieve it with his beautiful, smug face, godlike body, and smart-ass mouth. It was infuriating, only made worse by my lack of self-control last night.

I acted like a porn slut and that definitely wasn't me.

And now I was getting ready to officially meet Hunter's family. Since my brother knew the Dorseys, I asked him for advice.

Listen attentively.

Don't offer your opinion unless asked.

Keep your sass in check.

Basically, don't be me.

"Remember, these people are our livelihood," he said as if I wasn't nervous enough. Needless to say, my talk with Tom wasn't helpful at all. If anything, it made my stomach churn.

I dressed Carina in the cute pink dress with matching bloomers that Rose brought over. I figured she'd be tickled to see Carina wearing it. With a pink bow in her wispy hair and sandals on her feet, she was damn adorable.

Dressing her was way easier than dressing myself. Hunter said it was casual, but casual for rich people was different than for us ordinary folk. I was fairly certain a T-shirt and leggings would be frowned upon. Searching through my closet, I pulled out two sundresses and held each one in front of me while I looked in the mirror. "What do you think, baby girl? Yellow or blue?"

"Buh, buh, buh," Carina babbled.

"Blue it is." I slipped the dress off the hanger and shimmied into it. Turning in front of the mirror, I admired the way it enhanced my barely there curves. Paired with my black wedges with ribbons that wrapped around my calves, it was perfect. Casual with a hint of elegance and sexy with a side of innocence. Ideal for a nanny trying to impress her boss's family.

Not even sure why I was trying to impress the Dorseys, except that I wanted them to feel confident that I was taking good care of the newest member of the family. And yes, I was very aware that my behavior was also a reflection on my brother. When I returned to Oasis, Tom would still be working at Mystique. For how much longer, I wasn't sure, but he had a good thing going there and I didn't want to mess it up.

I brushed out my long, dark waves and secured them back from my face with a black headband, pushed small silver hoops through my ears, and fastened a simple chain with a heart pendant around my neck. Slicking my lips with a coat of red, I carried Carina to the kitchen, where Hunter was already waiting. He tapped the face of his watch.

"I'm not late," I insisted. "It's only a quarter after five."

"You're almost late," he said with a scowl.

"Almost late is not late. All I need to do is pack her diaper bag." I handed Carina to her father, noticing his freshly pressed dress shirt and tie. "Wait! I thought you said tonight was casual. You're dressed like you're going to work."

"I'm not wearing the jacket. This is casual." He lifted Carina high in the air and made funny faces at her while she giggled.

I looked down at my dress, second-guessing my wardrobe choice. "Should I change into something nicer?" I wasn't even sure if I owned anything nicer.

Barely giving me a glance, he said, "What you're wearing is fine."

I cringed. *Fine?* It was such a blasé word. No woman wanted to be told she looked *fine* unless it was in the context of *fine-ass bitch.* "Are you sure?"

Hunter finally quit playing with Carina and held her to his chest, trying to keep her from stuffing his tie in her mouth. His eyes swept up and down my body with a gaze that felt like I didn't have any clothes on at all. "You look good, Charli. Actually, you look beautiful."

"Thank you. I don't want to embarrass you."

"You couldn't embarrass me if you tried. My own actions are more questionable than yours."

I teasingly waggled a finger at him. "Don't be so sure about that, mister. I've been known to do a few questionable things myself."

"Like last night?" He raised a brow at me.

"Exactly like last night." I hurried to the cupboard and began gathering food for Carina to hide my embarrassment.

"You're doing it again."

I turned and faced him with my hands on my hips. "Doing what?"

"Blushing. I fucking love that," he said smugly.

"Shut up. I'm not blushing."

149

"You are." He chuckled.

I rolled my eyes. "Whatever. Can you check to see if there are enough diapers in the diaper bag?" Deflect and avoid, that was my strategy.

He rooted around in the bag and pulled out a handful of diapers. "You think five is enough?"

"God, I hope so. Unless she has a blowout, I think we're good." I handed him the containers of baby food.

He held them up, reading the labels. "No squash, right?"

I let out a huff of exasperation. "You told me not to buy squash. I'm a good listener and can follow directions. Chicken and carrots should be safe."

He tapped on the container of carrots. "They're orange. I don't trust them."

I swiped the containers from his hand and stuffed them into the bag. "So are sweet potatoes, but she hasn't had an issue. You can't cross off everything that's orange."

"Fine, but if she shits all over, you're cleaning her up," he grumped like a petulant child.

"You're ridiculous." I zipped up the bag and threw it over my shoulder. "Are you ready to go?"

"Me? I've been waiting on you."

I tapped on my bare wrist. "You're the one grumping and making us late."

Hunter shook his head and laughed. "You're something else, Charlotte Bently."

Chapter 21
Hunter

We pulled up in front of Trent's building with ten minutes to spare. Plenty of time to park and get upstairs. I grabbed Carina's car seat from the back of my Escalade and started toward the elevator.

Charlotte's heels clicked on the cement floor of the parking garage. "Jeez, slow down, will ya?" Her legs weren't short, but she was practically running to keep up with my long strides.

I dreaded this dinner. "The faster we get in, the faster we can leave." I hit the elevator button repeatedly, urging the doors to open.

Charli put her hand on mine and gently pushed my finger away from the call button. "What's the problem? Why don't you get along with your brother?"

"Because he's a pompous asshole who thinks he's better than me."

The elevator doors finally opened, and we stepped inside. "And you don't think you're better than Trent?"

"Of course, I'm better than him. I'm smarter, better looking, and I have a winning personality." I gave her a big, toothy grin that was about as cheesy as you could get.

She rolled her eyes. "So, it's sibling rivalry."

The elevator started rising and my heart rate ticked up. "This goes way beyond sibling rivalry. I never stood a chance. Trent has always been my parents' favorite. I've been trying to catch up my entire life."

"I'm sure that's not completely true." Charli grabbed Carina's sandaled foot and gave it a little shake, making her giggle. "You have the first grandchild. That should be worth something."

I let out a huff. "Yeah, because I didn't wrap up my dick properly, not because I planned it."

Charli's eyes narrowed. "Are you saying you regret her?"

Looking down at my daughter, the only thing I regretted was the words that came out of my mouth. I never wanted her to feel unloved or unwanted. "I don't regret her. I feel sorry for her that she ended up with a father like me and a mother who didn't care enough to stick around. I wouldn't give up my daughter for anything, but she deserves better."

Charli put her hand on my arm. "It's a tough situation, but you're doing the best you can. No one expects you to be a perfect parent in a matter of weeks."

"Obviously, you don't know my family. The minute we walk through the door, everyone will be judging me. Watching my every move and waiting for me to fuck up again." I felt like an idiot for telling the nanny my insecurities. Verbal diarrhea wasn't normally a problem for me. I guessed I was more anxious about this dinner than I'd admitted.

She crossed her arms. "Then don't fuck up. Be the doting father I know you can be and forget about everyone else. The only one that really matters is Carina."

The doors opened on the top floor and Charli stepped out of the elevator, leaving me standing there with my mouth open. She managed to scold me and give me a pep talk in a matter of a few sentences... and honestly, I felt better.

I don't know how she did it, but Charli never stopped surprising me. She turned over her shoulder. "Are you coming or what?"

"I'm coming," I grumbled as I stepped out behind her. I still didn't want to go to this dinner, but having Charli with me made it more tolerable. Leading her to Trent's penthouse, I knocked on the door, hoping no one would answer and we could go home. I looked at my watch. Six o'clock on the nose. No one could say I wasn't punctual.

Luck was not on my side because Gia answered the door within seconds. "You actually showed," she said with disbelief.

Knowing my brother, those two had probably bet on it. I wondered which one of them won. "I didn't think it was optional. Are you going to invite us in or make me stand in the hallway holding this carrier?"

Gia's eyes dropped to the bundle I was carrying, and her hands flew to her mouth. "Oh my god! She's beautiful." My sister-in-law backed away from the door to make room. "Come in, come in!"

We moved into the sitting room, and I set the carrier on the floor. For a little thing, Carina was heavy to lug around.

"You must be Charli," Gia said, reaching her arms out and wrapping them around my nanny.

"That's me," she answered, returning the hug and giving me a confused look.

"What? No hug for me?" I asked.

Gia propped her hands on her hips. "You haven't earned a hug yet, but I would like to get my hands on that baby of yours."

"Let me get her out of the carrier," Charli offered.

I let the girls fuss over Carina while I stood awkwardly staring out the window. Of course, Trent had a penthouse with a magnificent view, the city lights shining in the distance. He'd never been shy of flashing his money around. My apartment was nothing to sneeze at, but it wasn't... this.

"Where is my dear brother?" I asked. If nothing else, I knew he'd have top-shelf booze, and I was in desperate need of a drink.

"He's in the kitchen."

153

I wandered through the dining room—taking note that the table was set for eight—and into the kitchen to find Trent shoving aluminum containers into the trash. When he saw me, he closed the trash can lid and stood in front of it, trying to hide what I'd seen.

"Don't judge," he said. "Gia's not a good cook, so we decided to order food from Valentino's. Trust me, you'll thank me later."

I chuckled. Gia was always so put together at work; it was nice to know she had some flaws too. "Did you order lasagna?"

"That and about a half dozen other entrées, along with salad and bread. Don't tell her I told you. She wanted to make a good impression on Mom and Dad."

That explained two of the extra place settings. "Who else is coming besides Dad and Rose?"

"Brett and Penny are coming too. Everyone was excited to meet Carina."

"Jesus Christ!" I ran a hand down my face in an effort to calm my irritation. "Carina is my daughter, not a goddamn circus sideshow. You might as well have invited Tom too, then the gang would all be here."

"I hadn't thought about that. Do you think I should have? I don't want him to feel left out, especially with his sister being your nanny."

This dinner party was getting worse by the second. "Absolutely not. It's already too much." I started opening cupboard doors, searching for the liquor. "Please tell me you have booze. And don't hold out on me; I want the good stuff."

He frowned at me but took out two rock glasses and poured us each a splash of Glenfiddich.

I motioned with my fingers for him to fill it up. "Don't be stingy. You dragged me here. The least you can do is ply me with liquor."

"Technically, it was Gia's idea."

God, he was whipped. I didn't sign up for this. It was bad enough Rose was coming, but Brett and Penny too? Brett and Trent had been best friends forever. I used to try hanging out with them when we were kids, but they always ditched me, making me feel like a dingleberry on a dog's butt that had been shaken off. Eventually, I quit trying.

Although I resented that Gia insisted I bring Charli, I was thankful she was here. Charli was the only one that didn't make my skin feel too tight. I genuinely enjoyed her company, something that couldn't be said about the rest of the guests.

Downing my drink in one gulp, I motioned for Trent to fill it back up. "You sure that's a good idea? You need to drive home." Sometimes his big brother tendencies were annoying as fuck. I wasn't a child.

"It's a perfect idea. Charli can drive if necessary." We carried our drinks back out to the girls, where Charli was telling Gia about her job at Oasis while Gia held my daughter, making funny faces at her and eliciting a ton of giggles. The sound had become one of my favorites.

Over the next few minutes, my father and Rose arrived, along with Brett and Penny. I prepared for one of the most miserable nights of my life.

Everyone sat around the table while Gia and Trent brought out the food. Gia had transferred all the take-out food into fancy bowls and platters. It looked homemade, even if I knew better. I could have called her out on it but figured I should count my blessings instead. Valentino's was one of the best Italian restaurants in town.

I had Carina on my lap, and she squirmed, not wanting to be held. "That's not going to work," Charli whispered. "There's no way you'll be able to eat while holding her. Why don't you let me take Carina to the other room so you can enjoy your dinner? It's my job as the nanny."

"You're not going in the other room while we all eat. That's ridiculous. She'll be fine."

"What about another chair? We could put her carrier on the chair between us."

It could work. "Trent, do you have another chair?"

"Oh my gosh! I totally forgot," Gia interjected. She motioned to Trent, who hurried off and returned with a high chair.

"You bought Carina a high chair?" I asked, flabbergasted. "Thank you. I think that's the nicest thing you've ever done for me."

Trent rolled his eyes. "It was Gia's idea, and we did it for Carina, not you." He wedged the chair between Charli and me. "We were going to need one anyway," he said.

Rose snapped her attention to Gia. "Are you pregnant?"

Gia shook her head. "Not yet, but we're trying." She crossed her fingers and smiled sheepishly.

Funny how that worked out. I hadn't been trying, nor had it ever been an inkling in my mind, yet here I was with the first grandchild. I lifted Carina into the high chair while Charli fastened a bib around her neck.

"It'll happen," Penny said as she began to pass the food around the table. "Things have a way of working out when you least expect it."

Rose clapped her hands excitedly. "I can't wait to have two grandbabies to spoil. Though Hunter's done a good job of keeping that little angel all to himself."

I scooped a piece of lasagna onto my plate along with a slice of fresh bread, skipping the salad. "It's barely been two weeks. We're still getting adjusted."

"Well, just so you know, I'd be happy to watch Carina for you."

"That's what Charli is for," I grumped. It was a dickhead thing to say, but the last thing I wanted was Rose being all up in my business and criticizing how I raised my daughter.

"I understand, but surely Charli needs some time to herself."

I doubled down. "I pay her to be available twenty-four seven."

Charli kicked me under the table. Hard. "Actually, Rose, that would be wonderful," she said. "I need to get into the training center a couple days a week. You taking Carina for me would be super helpful."

Rose beamed while I scowled. Rose hadn't been a bad stepmother per se, and she would probably be an excellent grandmother if I gave her a chance. She said all the right things, did all the right things, provided for me as a mother should, but I never felt like her heart was in it. I guessed that's what happened when a kid showed up on your doorstep from an affair you didn't know your husband had. I was a little prick, and she was resentful. We were both thrown into a situation neither of us wanted.

"That sounds like a great plan," my father said. He still wanted to pretend we were one big, happy family.

Happy wasn't a word I'd ever used to describe our family. Dysfunctional would be more accurate. "We'll see."

"Call me, Charli," Rose said with a wink. "I'm more than happy to help."

"Absolutely." Charli smiled.

It was like I wasn't even in the room, which pissed me off even more.

"Did you hear back from the investigator about Carina's mom?" my father asked.

I gnashed my teeth together so hard I was liable to crack a molar. "You mean birth giver. Just because she pushed a kid out of her vagina doesn't make her a mom. A real mother wouldn't abandon her kid with a note. There's a right way to do things and a wrong way."

"Fair point," my father said with a nod. "Don't worry. Rudy will find her."

My body vibrated with anger. "The only thing I want from her is a signature. Then she can fuck right off back to where she came from."

Charli put her hand on my knee under the table and gently rubbed it. The heat from her skin seeped through the fabric, calming me a fraction.

Needing an outlet for my aggravation, I turned to Brett and Penny. Brett was born with a silver spoon and probably shit gold bricks every morning. He'd been a thorn in my side for almost as long as Trent. Penny, although relatively harmless, was guilty by association. The girl really moved up in the world since marrying the golden boy. It was a classic Cinderella story, and the two of them were fodder for the *Las Vegas Not So Confidential*.

I pointed my fork at them. "Rumor has it you two have a bun in the oven. Any truth to that?"

"You can't believe anything in that gossip rag," Gia said.

"Actually… this time you can," Penny answered with a barely contained smile.

"What?" Trent practically choked on his chicken piccata. "I thought you guys were waiting."

Brett wrapped his arm around Penny's shoulders. "Things have changed. It's early, so we didn't want to say anything yet."

Congratulations erupted around the table, and everyone started talking at once. It pissed me off that they were so happy.

I'd been deprived of this moment. I missed the joy of anticipating my own damn daughter's arrival. Instead, she showed up like a dirty secret that'd been shoved under a rug.

Carina deserved better.

When I finally found Jennifer Johnson, I was going to destroy her.

Chapter 22
Charli

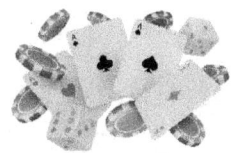

Hunter barely spoke to me on the ride home, the tension so thick it nearly suffocated me. It continued in the elevator and into the apartment. Carina had conked out in the car, so I put her to bed, knowing she'd be up again in a few hours.

When I came out, Hunter's hands were shoved in his pockets as he stood on the balcony and stared out at the starry night.

I should have left well enough alone, but my feet moved in his direction on their own accord. With no sense of self-preservation, I slid the door open and stepped outside. My hands wrapped around the warm metal of the railing. "It's beautiful tonight."

He grunted. "You come out here to talk about the weather?"

So much for small talk. "No."

"Then what do you want, Charli?"

My fingers gripped the railing tighter. "Did I do something wrong tonight?"

His eyes swung to me for a brief moment then returned to the dark abyss. "No. You were perfect. Everyone loved you."

"Then why do you seem so annoyed?"

"I'm not annoyed. Tonight went better than I expected. Everyone was… nice."

I peered up at him. "That's a good thing. What's wrong with nice?"

He shrugged. "Nothing. I'm just not used to it."

"Sounds like you haven't always made it easy."

"I haven't."

"And why is that?"

"I never felt like I belonged. My dad cheated on Rose. That's how I came into the picture. I was a little kid, but I remember the day my mom dropped me off at their house. I thought she was coming back, but she never did. Rose didn't want me there any more than I wanted to be there. I wanted to go home. Rose wanted a reality where her husband didn't fuck a stripper. Neither one of us got what we wanted."

Everything he said at dinner was put in a different context and I finally understood his bitterness. Not knowing what to say, I said the lamest thing possible. "I'm sorry you went through that."

"Everybody goes through shit. It could have been worse. I could have ended up with a dad who lived in a cardboard box. I hit the jackpot in that department." He waved a hand in the air dismissively. "Rose tried. I have to at least give her that much. I fought her tooth and nail every step of the way. The situation wasn't her fault, but I took it out on her anyway. Guess I still do."

"For what it's worth, I think you did a great job with Carina tonight."

Hunter cupped my cheek in his hand and stared down at me. "Only because you were there. Thank you for going with me."

His ice-blue eyes hypnotized me. This was intimate. More intimate than the messing around we did last night. Last night was fun and lustful. This was something completely different, and I didn't know how to deal with this version of him. "It's my job to be available twenty-four seven."

He backed me up against the wall. "Are you still mad I messed up your date with Fuckboy Ben?"

My breath caught in my throat, so I shook my head.

Pressing his muscular body up against mine, he caged me in with his hands against the wall. "Tell me no, Charlotte."

My insides turned to lava. Hunter was the kind of man that would wreck me for all others. He was all jagged lines and fortified walls. He wielded his sharp tongue like a weapon to keep everyone out.

Including me.

During the last week, he'd cracked the door open to his fortress and I'd gotten a glimpse of who he really was.

What he wanted more than anything else was to be accepted.

Approved of.

He was still that little boy searching for his mother's love.

He had a heart, but it was caged behind razor wire.

I'd be a fool to think he'd trust me with it.

I wasn't sure I was ready for that kind of responsibility, but I was willing to try. "I can't tell you no."

Hunter pounded his fist against the wall over my head. "Damn it, Charlotte! Tell me no. I'm not good for you or anyone else. I'll ruin you."

My own reckless heart thrashed in my chest and my chin jutted up. "I'm not afraid." Though inside, I was shaking, knowing I might regret it later.

"Stupid, stupid girl."

Hunter's lips crashed against mine in a feral kiss that had my body pushing off the wall and my arms clinging to his neck. It was all teeth and tongue and desperation.

In a move so quick it nearly knocked the breath out of me, he scooped me up and threw me over his shoulder like a caveman. A sharp smack came down on my ass and I yelped. "You're mine," he growled.

Hunter carried me into the apartment and down the long hallway that led to his bedroom. He tossed me on the king-size bed and stood over the top of me, hands on his hips and a glare that would make most men's testicles shrivel up and fall off. "I knew from day one that it was a mistake to hire you, dollface. You're too pretty, too innocent, too perfect."

I sat up on my elbows and shook my hair over my shoulders. "I'm not that innocent." I'd been with men before, but as I looked at Hunter, I realized they were merely boys compared to him. This was a dangerous game I was playing. He was older, more mature, and most definitely more experienced.

"We'll see." He undid his tie and threw it on the bed. "I have a feeling our definitions of innocent aren't the same."

A shiver ran down my spine. With the way he was looking at me, I was a hundred-percent sure he was right about that. Hunter Dorsey was a force to be reckoned with.

He grabbed me by the ankles and dragged me to the end of the bed. Kneeling between my legs, he lifted my heeled feet over his shoulders. "I've been dying to see what's under this dress." His hands ran up my thighs, taking the material with them.

"I still have my shoes on," I blurted.

Hunter chuckled. "I'm aware. They're staying on your fucking feet. If I don't feel them digging into my back, then I'm not doing my job right."

Alrighty then. "And what job would that be?"

He flipped my skirt up and groaned when he saw my electric-blue lace panties. "Eating your pretty pussy. Do you want that, Charlotte? Do you want me to tickle your clit with my tongue?"

I covered my face as heat crept up my neck and into my cheeks. "Stop saying that!"

"And miss out on watching your cheeks turn pink? Never." His fingers ran along the edge of my panties and over the silky material, tracing my seam. "Answer me, Charlotte. Do you want me to eat this pretty pussy?"

I'd never been with anyone who had such a dirty mouth, and it made my panties flood. No doubt he could feel it through the thin material. I peeked at him through my fingers and whispered, "Yes."

He held his hand up and cupped his ear. "I can't hear you, dollface."

If he wasn't stroking my clit, I would have given him shit about being bossy, but all I could do was drop my head back and gasp. "Yes!"

"That's what I thought." He grabbed my thighs and yanked me closer to the edge of the bed, then pulled my panties aside and feasted.

162

My god! The man had a magic tongue. He licked up my slit and circled the sensitive nub he'd been taunting me about for days. Lazy strokes lightly lapped at me, then disappeared. A tease of what was to come, but never finishing the job. He brought me to the brink then let it fade, my orgasm just out of reach.

It drove me crazy.

My back arched off the mattress.

My hands fisted the comforter.

My hips shifted, trying to get his tongue exactly where I needed it.

Hunter lifted his head and peered at me from between my thighs, chin glistening from my arousal and a shit-eating grin on his face. "You need something, dollface?"

I growled in a most unladylike fashion, my frustration and impatience bleeding out like a child having a temper tantrum. "You know what I want. You're teasing me." I refused to say the words he wanted to hear. Giving in felt like losing a high-stakes game. A game we'd been playing since I walked through the door on my first day. A power struggle I thought I could win but was clearly outmatched.

"I'm not sure I do. Tell me."

His tongue lapped at me again and my pussy clenched. "Do it!"

"Is this what you want?" He circled my clit with a finger and speared his tongue inside me, so fucking close but missing the mark. The man was sadistic.

I could only take so much before my willpower snapped, my head thrashed and the forbidden words poured from my lips. "Tickle my clit!"

"Fucking finally." Hunter ripped my panties at my hips and tore them away from my body.

"Hey! Those were expensive!"

"I'll buy you new ones." Then he buried his face in my pussy, his tongue zeroing in on my clit, attacking it with laser-like precision. It was pure ecstasy, an overload of stimulation.

His fingers dug into my ass, refusing to let me squirm away from him. I wanted to pull away and get closer, both at the same time. I'd never experienced this level of intensity. When the man committed to something, he was all in.

"Yes! Don't stop!" My breath came in short gasps and every muscle in my body tightened one at a time. It was the click, click, click of a roller coaster climbing the highest mountain. There was no way I could take much more.

Hunter growled from between my legs and thrust two long fingers deep inside me. They massaged that magic spot, that until this moment, I thought was a myth. It wasn't a myth... it was totally real and made my mouth sputter stupid words even I couldn't understand. A mix of every filthy word I had ever heard, with Hunter's name thrown in the middle.

And when he sucked on my clit, I free-fell from that mountain I'd been teetering on. Every nerve ending was set on fire as sparks ignited from the top of my head to the tips of my toes. I lost control as my body pulsed and clenched without my permission. My head swam in a dark abyss of pleasure I'd never experienced. Every thought disappeared and all I could do was... feel.

Complete euphoria.

My body buzzed and hummed, the white noise blocking out everything else, my brain light and foggy like that sensation you get right before you pass out.

When the feeling subsided, I opened my eyes to find Hunter propped up on the bed, staring down at me, his lips tipped up in a rare smile. "Welcome back."

"Hi," I croaked out. My throat felt like I'd walked a mile in the Sahara.

His fingers played in my hair, twisting the ends around and around. "You're beautiful when you come."

I licked my dry lips, stalling at the unexpected... compliment? I stared up at him with wide eyes, not knowing how to respond.

Hunter ran the back of his hand along the side of my face. "The correct response is *thank you*."

"Thank you." The man gave me whiplash; so domineering and bossy one minute and unbelievably sweet the next. I wondered how many people knew this side of him even existed.

He leaned down and gently pressed his lips against mine. "You're welcome." His fingers danced up and down my arm like it was a piano. "You've proven to be a pleasant surprise, Charlotte Bently."

"So are you," I said dumbly. "You're a good man, Hunter."

"I think I short-circuited your brain," he said with a laugh. "Giving orgasms doesn't make me a good man. If I was a good man, I wouldn't have touched you."

It wasn't just an orgasm. It was an earth-shattering orgasm. "I didn't tell you no."

"You should have. You're my nanny and you're too young. It was a mistake. I'm sorry if you felt pressured."

I was so confused. And embarrassed. Maybe I *was* too young. I'd obviously misread the situation. Made it into something it wasn't. It was an impulsive decision that he now regretted.

God, I was so stupid.

I let my heart take over instead of using my brain. Tonight felt nice, like we were a family of three. It was a stupid illusion I created. I wasn't Hunter's wife or Carina's mom. I was the fucking nanny. I was paid to be there, nothing else.

Suddenly feeling very exposed, I pulled down the dress that was still bunched up around my waist. "I didn't feel pressured. No worries."

In the distance, I heard a soft cry and hopped off the bed, thankful for the distraction. As I left to get Carina, Hunter called my name. "Charli?"

I looked at him over my shoulder. "It's not a big deal. Forget about it."

Walking away, I tried to tell myself the same lie, but I knew there was no way I would forget about it.

Chapter 23
Hunter

I slammed my fist against the shower wall, pissed at myself for fucking up.

Again.

Why couldn't I have left good enough alone? Seeing her with my family, blending in better than I ever could, made the hollow thing in the middle of my chest pump full of blood. I didn't deserve her compliments or support. I hadn't exactly made her time here easy, yet she still gave them. Like a pixie cheerleader standing on the sidelines, shouting, "Go, Hunter! You can do it!" The woman had more faith in me than I had in myself.

I didn't deserve her, but damn, I wanted her.

I squirted shampoo in one hand and leaned the other on the wall. My fist wrapped around my cock as the hot water scalded down my back. I could still see her pretty pink pussy glistening for me, wet and plump and swollen. It would have been so easy to slide my cock into her, taking what I wanted without a care of how it would affect her.

My hand moved in lazy strokes as I imagined it sliding in and out of her hot, little body. Long, toned legs that wrapped around my neck and dug into my back as I ate her pussy, making her come on my tongue. I still hadn't seen her tits, but imagined they were as amazing as the rest of her. I licked my lips, tasting the remnants of her arousal.

It was addictive.

She was addictive.

I squeezed my dick as my hand shuttled up and down its length. Jerking harder and faster, I imagined her pushed up against the shower wall, her long hair cascading down her back and her ass pushed up and out as she stood on her toes, waiting for me to take her. To shove my cock in her tight hole and ruin her.

A tingle started at the base of my spine. My head dropped back, and a prayer fell from my lips. "Charlotte!" Thick ropes of cum landed on the wall and slid down the wet tiles.

When I felt empty and depleted, I leaned my head against the wall and chastised myself.

I was always in control, but when it came to her, I had none. She twisted me up inside, a beautiful temptress with midnight-blue eyes I got lost in. I should have been turned off by her careless and reckless ways, but somehow, they made her more appealing. She gave the whole world a big middle finger, chasing her dreams no matter what anyone else thought.

I admired Charlotte Bently.

And maybe that was the problem. She wasn't some bubbleheaded blond with big tits and zero ambition who hung out in bars trying to reel in a man who would bankroll her future. A woman like that was easy to fuck and forget. Zero fucks given.

No, Charli wanted more out of life. She had a career, albeit an unconventional one. There was a sense of pride when she talked about performing. A passion. I understood passion and wanting to be the best. I'd done it my entire life.

It was exactly why getting involved with her was a bad idea.

After changing into lounge pants and a T-shirt, I crept down the hallway to Carina's room. It was quiet inside, but my girl was still wide awake.

I rubbed my hand over her belly and picked her up. "There's my princess." I took her over to the rocker and cradled her in my arms. She was so tiny. It was hard to believe I was her father. The kid had shit luck right from the beginning.

I rocked her back and forth, getting lost in the hypnotic rhythm. She cuddled into my chest and sighed. It was crazy that I was responsible for her well-being. I'd never kept a plant alive, let alone a living, breathing human. Her birth giver really was an idiot to trust me.

"So, I wanted to talk to you about Charli." Speaking to someone who couldn't judge me was cathartic. There would be no eye-rolling or smart-ass remarks. All she could do was listen.

"I think I fucked it up. I like her. More than I should. I know you like her too. She's good for us. I've never had a long-term relationship, but I think I could do it with Charli."

Carina squirmed and stuck her thumb into her mouth, little eyes fluttering shut. "I wish she was your mom, but she isn't. Your mom fucked off and left us both to figure shit out on our own. It isn't fair to ask Charli to fill that gap. She's young and determined. This is a temporary job for her. In a couple of months, she'll be gone as abruptly as she came into our lives. It wouldn't be fair to get attached. Not fair to you or me, and definitely not fair to her. You haven't learned this lesson yet, but I'm going to give you some harsh realities."

I readjusted her head and leaned back in the rocking chair. "No one ever stays. The only one you can depend on is yourself. I've learned that the hard way. But I'll tell you something, baby girl, you'll always be able to depend on me. No matter what shitty decisions you make or trouble you get into, I'll always be here for you. I may be a colossal dick, but I'll be there for you. That doesn't mean I won't make mistakes. You were not part of my plan, but you're the best thing I've ever done in my life. You and me, kiddo. We might both be bastards, but I'll never ever let you feel like you're less. You'll be my princess forever."

With my daughter asleep in my arms, I placed her in the crib. "Good talk, Carina. Sleep tight, don't let the bedbugs bite." I kissed her forehead and backed out of her room, still feeling like shit.

Tomorrow was a new day, a new opportunity to set boundaries between the nanny and me. No matter how mad she was, I knew I did what was best for her and that made me feel one notch better than the raging asshole I was.

Chapter 24
Charli

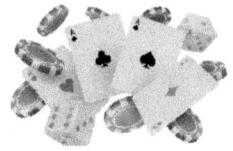

I lay in bed last night and listened to Hunter over the baby monitor. Part of me felt slimy for intruding on his private thoughts. The other part felt sad.

It wasn't only me he rejected.

The man rejected anything that resembled warmth and love.

He had to be one of the most broken men I'd ever met.

He wasn't wrong that I planned on leaving, but it didn't have to be forever. When I went back to Oasis, there was no reason we couldn't still be together. He'd need a new nanny, but not a live-in one. Preferably one over sixty with gray hair and sagging boobs.

Maybe I was being ridiculous. I'd only known Hunter for a short time, but he'd grown on me. I saw the man behind the mask he wore around everyone else and I understood why he wore it. Hunter was about control and letting anyone see him as anything other than the confident man he portrayed wasn't acceptable.

It was clear from what I'd heard that Hunter did see me as more than just the nanny. He and I had crossed a line that couldn't be uncrossed, but it would only be awkward if I let it be. Yes, my feelings were hurt last night. However, if I wanted to prove to him that I wasn't too young, I'd have to buck up and move forward.

Hunter was a no-show in the kitchen for breakfast the next morning. He showed up after working out, kissed Carina on the head, and went right to his room, barely sparing me a glance. Not much of a shocker since I'd anticipated his avoidance of me. For someone who thought I was too young, he was the one acting childish.

Exhausted by his Jekyll and Hyde routine, I packed up Carina in the stroller and took her to the park. We both needed some fresh air.

As we walked around the pond, I thought about the way Hunter touched me last night. No one had ever made me feel so beautiful. Gentle fingers cupping my cheek. Blue eyes peering into my soul. Husky voice demanding I tell him no. The filthy words that came out of his mouth when I didn't, and the way he feasted on me like I was his last meal.

I should have been upset about how the evening ended. But for a few glorious minutes, sprawled out on his bed, I felt wanted.

Desired.

Beautiful.

My core clenched as I thought about it.

Carina babbled as the ducks came into view. I pulled out the bread I brought and threw pieces on the grass, close but not too close. The ducks waddled toward us, and Carina let out a loud screech. Her little hands clapped together as she laughed and laughed.

"You like the duckie, don't you, baby girl?"

"U…u…uk"

I immediately realized my mistake. If her first word ended up being *fuck,* Hunter would not be amused, although he'd have to shoulder some of the blame. "Can you say quack? Duckies go quack, quack, quack, quack."

"Uk!"

I winced and tried again. "How about da da?"

171

"Uk."

I gave up. "Yep, that's a fucking duck." I threw some more bread, and the ducks waddled closer, pecking at the ground with their yellow bills. Carina waved her arms around and squealed with delight.

"Someone's a happy baby today."

I looked up at the woman with the Pomeranian we'd seen last week. "Yeah. She really likes the ducks."

"I can see that. Mind if we sit with you?" Without waiting, she sat on the bench while her dog, Teddy, put his front paws on Carina's stroller.

Carina laughed and smacked the dog on the head with her tiny hands. "Gentle, baby girl." I took her hand, showing her how to pet the pup. "I was hoping we'd see you two again," I said.

"Oh, me too. That baby is too cute. You must be a proud mama." She stared as Teddy licked Carina's hands. Carina immediately shoved them in her mouth.

I cringed. That dog had probably licked his butt less than ten minutes ago. "I'm not her mom. I'm the nanny," I said, pulling out a pack of wipes from the stroller. I took each hand and gave it a thorough wipe down. A dog's mouth was supposedly cleaner than a human's, but I wasn't sure if that was fact or fiction. After tossing the wipes in the trash, I held out my hand. "I'm Charli."

She grabbed my hand with her perfectly manicured fingers. "Ginny. Sorry, I just assumed."

"No worries. It happens all the time." I lifted Carina from the stroller so the dog couldn't give her another tongue bath.

"How long have you been her nanny?" She tilted her head to the side and gave me a head-to-toe glance.

"Only a week, but it seems like a lot longer."

She gave me a big, toothy smile. "Hmm. That's understandable. Babies are a lot of work." Ginny stood and began petting Carina's soft hair like she was a dog instead of a human being. "How are the people you work for? It must be hard taking care of someone else's baby?"

I bounced Carina on my hip. "It's a single dad and he works a lot, so sometimes we're like ships passing in the night." It was a half-truth. Last night, we were like two ships running off course and colliding. "Plus, Carina's an easy baby."

Ginny ran her finger down Carina's cheek. "I bet her daddy is hot, huh?"

I didn't have much experience with this, but the question seemed bold. It wasn't like we were friends; we barely knew each other. "We don't have that kind of relationship."

She rolled her eyes. "But you're not blind. Come on. You can tell me. Who am I gonna tell?"

Good question. It felt like a trap. I assumed our meeting was random, but I didn't put it past Hunter to test me. "He's a decent-looking man." Downplaying our relationship—considering I didn't even know what that was—seemed like a good idea.

"Rich too, I bet."

"What makes you say that?"

She motioned toward Hunter's apartment building. "Honey, nobody poor lives there."

I shrugged my shoulders in a noncommittal way. Hunter's money was none of her business. Or mine, for that matter. "All I care about is that my paycheck clears."

"Okay, I see how it is. We're not talking about your hot, single sugar daddy."

I pulled Carina closer to my chest. "Whoa! He's not my sugar daddy, just my boss."

"Hey, no judgment here. Can't blame a girl for trying to move up in the world."

"I don't need a man to take care of me." It was only half-true. If I was so great at taking care of myself, I never would have ended up working for Hunter Dorsey in the first place.

She held a hand against her chest. "I didn't mean to offend you. I'm sure you can take care of yourself. I'm all for women being independent, but a man with money never hurts. It's how I got these." Ginny cupped her boobs and pushed them up in her sports bra. "If you play your cards right, you could get some too," she said with a wink.

My jaw dropped as I looked down at my tiny boobs. Hunter didn't seem like the type of man who would pay for breast implants, but what did I know? Maybe he was into big boobs. I mean, what man wasn't?

Suddenly self-conscience, I readjusted Carina to hide my tiny titties. "I wouldn't count on it."

Teddy let out a yap and pulled on his leash. "Someone's anxious to get moving," Ginny said with a smile as if she hadn't insulted me. "We better get going. It was great seeing you two." She leaned in and kissed Carina on the head. "See you soon, sweet girl." Then she turned on her heels and wiggled her fingers at me over her shoulder. "Toodles, Charli."

I stood there stunned. It was one of the strangest interactions I'd ever had. I'd thought maybe the two of us could have been friends, but now I wasn't sure I wanted to. Reading people was my specialty and something about her set all my alarm bells off.

It wasn't like she was the only female in Vegas obsessed with men and money. However, she was the most blatant one I'd ever met. She was a walking red flag, and I pitied any man who was fool enough to fall for her.

Chapter 25
Hunter

"I approve."

My head snapped up from where I'd been poring over spreadsheets for the last three hours to find Gia leaning against my open "office" door with her arms crossed. It was fucking annoying. It was bad enough that I got shoved in the closet, but having people stop by like it was a normal situation was even more humiliating.

I tossed my pen on the gray metal desk. "Am I supposed to be a fucking mind reader?"

"I'm talking about Charli. She's great and so good with Carina."

"Thank god!" I pressed a hand to my chest. "I've been waiting for your approval since the day I hired her. I can't tell you what a relief it is to finally have it."

She waltzed in uninvited and took a seat across from me. "Don't be an asshole."

"Did you expect something different? Did you think because I had a kid, all of a sudden, I was going to *poof* turn into a nice guy. Sorry to disappoint you, sweetheart," I raked a hand down my body, "same leopard, same spots."

Gia tossed her red hair over her shoulder and huffed out a laugh. "I'm not so sure about that."

I narrowed my eyes at her. "Would kicking you out of my office convince you?"

"After I graciously invited you and your family over for a homemade dinner, it would be rude."

Two things were wrong with that statement. "Yes, *your* cooking skills were phenomenal," I said with a smirk.

She squinted her eyes. "Did Trent tattle on me?"

I nodded.

"I'm going to kill him." Gia's fists clenched and I almost felt bad for my brother. He should have known not to trust me with that kind of information.

I let Gia stew and attacked the second point. "Also, Charli's not family. She's the nanny. That's it."

"So you say."

"What's that supposed to mean?"

"It means I watched you. It was cute the way you two worked in tandem with Carina, like a well-oiled machine. The way you gave her little looks during dinner and the way she didn't seem at all affected by your sour attitude. There's definitely a connection. You two look good together; she's completely adorable and you're not totally unfortunate looking." She smiled proudly as if she'd solved the mystery of Atlantis.

I steepled my fingers and tapped them together. "Well, aren't you clever. A real Nancy Drew, snooping into stuff that's none of your business. Unfortunately, your evidence proves nothing. Charli is an employee and I'm her boss. There's nothing going on between us."

Gia rolled her eyes. "I don't believe you, but whatever. Just don't jerk her around. She's not some nameless, faceless bimbo. I liked her and so did Penny. And Rose... she's practically got the two of you married already."

176

"Fuck." This, I didn't miss. People being all up in my shit. For the past year, no one cared who I slept with or what I did. "Rose is going to be sorely disappointed. I'm hardly the marrying kind."

She lifted a manicured eyebrow. "Neither were Trent nor Brett. A good woman can make all the difference. Plus, you've got Carina to think about now."

I scrubbed my hands down my face. "I fucking know. Charli's young and she's got her own career to think about. She doesn't need someone like me to screw her up."

"Aha!" Gia pointed at me. "You do like her."

"That wasn't an admission. I'm simply stating facts. Don't go getting all gossipy."

Gia tossed her hair over her shoulder. "I don't gossip."

"Sure you don't." This little meet-and-greet session exhausted me. "Is there another reason you're in my office?"

"Actually, yes." Gia set a manilla folder on my desk. "I was wondering if you would go over the financials from last year's fundraiser. It didn't pull in as much money as we anticipated. Something seems off."

Picking up the folder, I thumbed through it. "It's not my job. Leonard should be going over this."

"He already did, but I trust you more."

I nearly choked. "I'm sorry?"

"The guy is shifty. For all your faults, I know your bookkeeping is impeccable. I've looked it over a dozen times, and I can't find anything amiss, but that doesn't mean something's not fishy."

A shit-eating grin stretched across my lips. "Did you compliment me?"

She lifted her chin in defiance. "Yes. I don't think you're a horrible person, but you did do horrible things to me."

"I've apologized." There was no sense denying the wrong I'd done to her. Even I could admit, in hindsight, it was shitty.

"And we're moving forward," Gia said with a stiff nod. "So, will you do it?"

Not gonna lie; the boost to my ego felt good. "I'll do it."

177

"Thank you."

"Can you get me the financials from the previous year so I can do a comparison?"

"Of course. And let's keep that folder between us. It's only a hunch on my part."

"What folder?" I shoved it in my desk drawer.

Gia unfolded herself from the uncomfortable chair. "Thanks again, Hunter. I appreciate it."

"No problem." Truth be told, I couldn't wait to dig into the financial reports. I scoured documents all weekend and came up empty on Leonard's misdoings. The guy was shady as a tree, even Gia saw it. I wouldn't stop until I took Leonard Moroski down. I couldn't wait to kick his pompous ass out of my soft, cushy chair and send him packing with his tail between his legs.

"Look at us getting along. Who would've thought?"

"Hey, Gia?" She turned over her shoulder. "Thanks for the high chair on Saturday. It helped a lot."

"You're welcome."

"And good luck with the… baby-making." I could barely get the words out. The last thing I wanted to think about was her and Trent doing the dirty.

She laughed. "That about killed you, didn't it?"

"Every part of my black soul."

"Maybe it's not as black as you think." She winked at me on her way out.

Doubtful.

Back at home, I hunkered down over spreadsheets until my eyes crossed.

Charli poked her head in. "You want anything to eat before we go down to the pool?"

"Kinda late, don't you think?" I asked without looking up.

"What are you, my father? It's only seven o'clock and she's restless. Don't be such a fuddy-duddy."

My head popped up. "First, I'm a jerk face, now a fuddy-duddy?"

She crossed her arms and leaned on the doorframe. "Like I said before, if it fits. There's no reason we can't have fun in the evening."

Fun. Yes, I'd like to have a bit of fun with her—on my bed. Spread out like a buffet. My head between her toned thighs. That's the only kind of fun I'd thought about over the last few days.

"Why don't you come with us? It'd be good for you to get out of these four walls." Charli ventured farther inside and leaned on my desk. "Or are you allergic to fun?"

My eyes zeroed in on her clothing or lack thereof, and I scowled. "You can't go down there dressed like that."

Her eyes bulged. "Now you really are acting like my father. It's a bathing suit and I'm wearing a cover-up. Get over it."

I'd hardly call it a bathing suit. It was more like a few scraps of fabric held together with string and said cover-up was so sheer, it did nothing to hide what was underneath. My cock stiffened and my muscles tensed. There was no way I was letting her walk around the apartment building practically naked. "It's inappropriate. There could be perverts creeping around."

"Then I guess you should chaperone us," she said with a sly smile. "Or are you afraid of people thinking you're the pervert? I am awfully *young*, you know. I mean, what would people think of a young girl hanging out with such an old fuddy-duddy?"

"Quit calling me a fuddy-duddy. I know how to have fun." Although my idea of fun over the last few years consisted of drinking myself stupid and picking up a willing woman to fulfill my needs.

"Then stop acting like one and go put your bathing suit on."

179

The girl tested my nerves. "You're a brat. I should take you over my knee and—" I stopped myself before I completely lost it. My hand twitched with the need to spank her ass. Every day I spent with Charli, the closer I came to losing complete control and fucking her right on top of this desk.

She turned, clasping her hands together behind her back, and sauntered away, wiggling her ass as she went. "Promises, promises. Are you coming with us or not?" The back of her bathing suit was worse than the front. The ruffle on her butt barely covered anything.

Goddammit! "I'm coming. Don't forget Carina's life vest."

"Already packed," she called over her shoulder.

This girl! I don't know what kind of spell she had on me, but I couldn't tell her no. She had me changing into my swim trunks and pulling a T-shirt over my head. I occasionally swam laps, but I'd never used the complex's pool for fun. It seemed so juvenile for a man in his thirties.

When I got to the front door, Carina looked adorable in a teal swim suit, babbling away. Charli had a bag over her shoulder and her arms were full of towels and a unicorn floaty. I grabbed everything from her and slung the bag over my shoulder. "You look like a pack mule."

She shrugged. "Babies require a lot of stuff."

"Don't I know it," I said with a huff.

"Hey, no one is making you come with us. We're perfectly fine on our own."

Like hell she was. "Not dressed like that."

Charli rolled her eyes and opened the door. "Let's go, fuddy-duddy."

In the elevator, a couple of teenage boys got in on the fifth floor. Their eyes roamed over Charli's body before landing on me. I gave them my best death glare and stepped in front of her, shielding her from their view. Busy fussing with Carina, my nanny was completely oblivious to their wandering eyes, proving she was too naive to be left to her own devices.

When the elevator reached the athletic complex, I shook my head at the teenagers and ushered out Charli, then pressed the button for the lobby and sent them on their way. If they thought they were going to get a show, they were sadly mistaken.

Thankfully, no one was in the pool area. I dropped everything on a table and slipped off my shoes. Charli strapped Carina into her life vest. "Did you get those arm thingies?"

She riffled through the bag and pulled out two uninflated armbands. "She already has a life vest on. Do you really think she needs water wings?"

Water wings… right. Honestly, I didn't know if she did, but I wasn't taking any chances. "Better safe than sorry."

"Here." She held Carina out for me to take and then blew up the inflatables. I watched her mouth work with rapt attention. The way her lips pursed, and her cheeks hollowed out…ugh! All I could imagine was Charlotte on her knees, head bobbing, as I kept her sassy mouth full of my cock.

My dick very inconveniently twitched, and I berated myself for my filthy thoughts while holding my daughter. It wasn't right. Not even close. "Are you almost done?" I grouched.

"Hold your horses. I can only blow so fast."

Seriously? I looked away and pretended to find the wall incredibly interesting while willing my semi to shrink by thinking unpleasant thoughts. *Leonard Morosk-hole. Family dinners. My shoebox office.* With each thought, the problem in my shorts subsided.

"You want me to take her?"

My attention snapped back to Charli, who'd already put the water wings on my daughter and stripped off her sheer cover-up. This was cruel and unusual punishment. How was I supposed to resist my nanny when she looked like that? All lean, toned muscle, perky little tits, and an ass that made me want to bite it. Fucking brutal.

"Why don't you two start and I'll join you in a few? I've got to check a couple messages."

Charli reached out with grabby hands to take Carina. "Fine, but all work and no play makes Hunter a very dull boy."

I handed Carina over and sat at the table with my phone and pretended to check my email, while sneaking glances at Charli as she carried Carina into the shallow end of the pool. I was a creeper, no better than the teenage boys in the elevator. With her dark hair tied up on top of her head, it elongated her neck that would look so pretty with my hand wrapped around it.

Fuck! This wasn't helping.

I opened my email for real and read the message from Gia with last year's fundraiser financials attached. I shot her a quick reply and opened the next email from Leonard, reminding me that payroll was due tomorrow. If he wanted to treat me like a child, then that's exactly how I'd act. My mind already reeled with the possibilities for my next show of opposition.

"Are you coming in or what?"

For a brief moment, I'd forgotten about Charli. In the water up to her chest, she was now sufficiently hidden from view and my dick stopped acting like it was attached to a prepubescent boy.

I stripped off my shirt and dove into the water, surfacing on the other end of the pool.

"Perfect ten, Mr. Dorsey. I'm impressed." She set Carina in the water and held her hands, pulling her around in small circles. My daughter resembled a marshmallow with her life vest and water wings on, safe as could be in Charli's care as she giggled and giggled.

I waded over and picked up my daughter, bobbing her in the water. Carina squealed and laughed. I was more than fortunate to have such a healthy, happy child. Although I hadn't planned on her, every day I grew more and more attached. I never believed in love at first sight, but it happened with Carina.

And maybe with Charli too.

Chapter 26
Charli

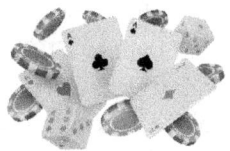

By the end of the week, we'd settled into a routine that was somewhere in the flirty friend zone. He stopped sneaking out of the apartment at an obscenely absurd hour and we began having our coffee together before Carina woke up.

In the evenings, the three of us ate dinner together, and Hunter had completely taken over feeding Carina. Sometimes I stared at him as he zoomed the spoon around and made airplane noises before popping it into her waiting mouth. It was ridiculously adorable. Watching him with Carina sent my ovaries into overdrive.

Neither of us ever mentioned the box full of expensive panties that arrived after Hunter ripped mine to shreds. He bought me a dozen pairs in every color of the rainbow. They came from a high-end retailer I could only dream of shopping at. I hoped it meant we would have more sexy rendezvous, and he planned on ripping apart more of my panties.

My cheeks blushed as I sat across from him at the kitchen island. Taking a sip of my coffee, I broached the topic I knew he was going to fuss about. "Don't forget Rose is watching Carina today while I'm at the training center."

In typical fashion, Hunter's brows knitted together. "Remind me again why you need to go there instead of the fitness center downstairs."

I sighed. "The fitness center is great for weights and cardio, but it doesn't have the specific equipment I need for practice."

"Like what?" He gulped down the rest of his coffee and set his mug down harder than necessary.

"Like the silks hanging from the ceiling or a hoop. It's hard to practice without the actual pieces of equipment I'll be performing on." The issue wasn't me going to the training center. It was about Rose coming to watch Carina. "I don't know why you're making such a big deal out of this. Rose is very capable of watching Carina. She wants to bond with her granddaughter. Is that such an awful thing?"

"It's not an awful thing. You're making me sound like a grouchy asshole who wants to keep Carina all to myself."

I lifted a brow at him.

"Fine. I'm a grouchy asshole, but in my defense, I'm still getting adjusted myself. I don't know if I'm doing any of this right. What if I'm a terrible father? I don't need Rose coming here and pointing it out."

I reached for his hand and gently rubbed my thumb over his knuckles, trying to ease his fears. The man was confident in everything, except where Carina was concerned. "You're not a terrible father and no one would say you were. You're doing the best you can. You're going to make mistakes, but I'm pretty sure every parent has, even Rose. Maybe helping with Carina is her way of righting those wrongs."

"She's going to snoop," he huffed.

"Lock the rooms you don't want her in. Are you afraid she's going to find your box of whips and chains?" It was a joke but also a little snooping on my part. Hunter completely dominated me the other night and I was curious how far he would take it.

Hunter chuckled. "I'm not into whips and chains. There's no red room here."

"Good to know." I could handle a little kink but had no intention of being submissive. And there went my head again, imagining things that would never happen. "Anyway, Rose is coming at ten. I'll be home before you, so you won't even have to see her."

"Fine." He grabbed his keys and tucked his wallet into his pocket.

I poured the last of the coffee into a travel mug and handed it to him. "Have a good day, Mr. Dorsey."

"You too, dollface."

Although I initially hated the name and found it demeaning, it grew on me. No man had ever given me a special nickname. It wasn't generic like *sweetheart* or *honey* or *darling* that could be used for anyone, including a first date or a one-night stand.

Dollface was just for me and that made my insides flutter.

Chapter 27
Hunter

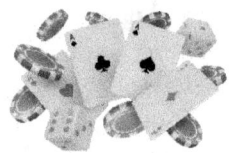

Ten minutes before Rose was supposed to arrive, I logged into my home security system and set up my phone where I could watch the cameras. I bought the system long before Carina arrived, but it never showed me anything interesting until I hired Charli. At first, I used it to spy on the stranger I'd invited into my home.

It quickly became an obsession.

Watching Charli was my favorite pastime.

Her hair was in a high ponytail as she rolled on the floor with my daughter, giving her the extra little nudge she needed to flip herself over. Carina smiled and laughed as Charli praised her hard work.

Although I doubted Charli's qualifications when I hired her, I didn't have a single regret. Besides the small kitchen fire, she'd done an amazing job, proven to be responsible and attentive to my daughter's needs.

Mine too.

I didn't hire Charli to take care of me, yet she seemed hell-bent on doing it. Morning to-go cups of coffee, evening meals, laundry washed and folded—I appreciated all of it. But the thing I valued most was the way she quietly listened and offered encouragement.

I'd fought my way to the top, never showing weakness. I might have shown up on my father's porch as a toddler in stained and tattered clothes, but I spent the rest of my life proving I deserved to be a Dorsey. I worked harder, aimed higher, and achieved more than Trent, yet he still came out on top. The golden boy who couldn't be touched. The heir to our father's legacy.

When Gia got hired at Mystique, I saw my opportunity and I took it. Wanted to prove Trent wasn't so perfect after all. That his weakness for women would be his demise.

Releasing that video backfired spectacularly. All it did was prove I was exactly who they thought I was—the black sheep who put ambition above integrity and family.

Being ousted from the company and the family was a relief from working day in and day out to be accepted, appreciated, and respected. Being alone wasn't a hardship, it was my destiny… or so I thought.

Then a tiny pink bundle with chubby cheeks showed up and the neat, orderly life I'd built no longer existed. Calling my father and admitting I needed help was one of the hardest things I'd ever done. I expected judgment and condemnation, but what I got was understanding and empathy.

It was the first stone in rebuilding the bridges I'd blown to smithereens with my family. Yes, I hated my new job, but I'd be lying if I didn't say it felt like home to be back at Mystique. Since returning, everyone was dead set on inserting themselves into my life.

It unnerved me.

I didn't trust it.

No one ever stayed.

But what if someone did?

I watched the camera as Charli answered the door and let Rose in. They greeted each other with a warm hug, something I rarely got as a kid. I was almost jealous that Charli was able to bond so quickly with Rose when I'd struggled my whole life to feel wanted.

187

It was best for Carina.
It was best for Carina.
It was best for Carina.

I continued the mantra over and over as I watched Rose pick up my daughter and kiss her round face. She bounced the baby on her hip as Charli showed her around the apartment, opening cupboards and giving instructions.

It made me twitchy, but knowing I could watch what was going on in my apartment gave me a bit of reassurance that everything would be fine. Rose wasn't my biggest fan, but there was no way she would do anything to put her granddaughter in danger. It was a seed of trust planted by my nanny.

The woman who continued digging herself further into my life, making me rethink my stance on relationships and... *love?*

I depended on Charli. Respected her. Trusted her. Bathed in her positive energy. She filled my tank when I had nothing left.

It didn't hurt that she was gorgeous and sexy as fuck without even trying, such a contrast from the women made of plastic and paint trolling Vegas, searching for their next payday in the form of a wealthy man who would tend to their every need. Obviously, Charli took the job because of the money but she was intent on returning to Oasis and earning her own way.

She was a go-getter, and I admired that.

I watched Rose on the screen, still not a hundred percent comfortable with the situation. The longer I watched, the more I realized there was nothing to worry about. Her attention was on Carina, not going through my drawers or snooping in rooms where she didn't belong.

"Excuse me, sir." My head snapped up, breaking me from the haze of staring at my daughter and her grandmother.

When I worked here before it was a power trip to be called *sir* but now it irritated me. Maybe it was that everyone knew I'd been previously fired. Maybe it was my new shitty office. Or maybe it was guilt because the only person I wanted to call me *sir* was this guy's sister. Preferably on her knees, blinking up at me with her big blue eyes. "What can I do for you, Tom?"

"Mr. Dorsey would like to see you in his office." He hitched a thumb over his shoulder.

"I'm Mr. Dorsey," I said with a straight face.

Tom pushed his glasses up with one finger. "The other Mr. Dorsey."

I knew who he was talking about but decided to fuck with him anyway. "My father?"

"No, sir." I had to give it to him, Tom barely cracked. If it weren't for the slight twitch of his jaw, I'd think he was completely unaffected.

As much fun as this game was, I didn't enjoy it like I used to. "Listen, Tom, I'm yanking your chain."

He folded his arms and leaned on the doorframe. "Honestly, I thought you were just being a dick."

My eyebrows shot up. "Wow! Didn't realize the snappy one-liners ran in the family. Although Charli has never called me a dick, she's partial to jerk face."

His lips tipped up. "If the face fits."

I chuckled. "You two are definitely related. On a more serious note, don't call me sir. It makes me feel old and there are too many Mr. Dorseys around here, so Hunter is fine."

"I was trying to be respectful."

Tom was actually one of the few people here, besides family, who hadn't treated me like a pariah when I returned and, considering my current circumstances, it spoke to his integrity. "I appreciate that."

He edged his way into my office. "So, how is my daredevil sister? I haven't heard from her recently."

I leaned back in my rickety chair and folded my hands behind my head. "She's at the training center, climbing and spinning or whatever it is she does."

"Damn. I was hoping she'd give it up after her accident, but she's too damn stubborn. Every time I see her up in the air, it gives me a heart attack, but then she does her thing, and I forget it's my sister. She truly is amazing."

189

I let out a sigh. Thinking about the risks Charlotte took with her life gave me heart palpitations. "I understand passion. What I don't understand is her addiction to danger and taking the chance of killing herself."

Tom tilted his head to the side. "You actually sound like you care."

"She's a damn good nanny."

"That's it?"

"What else would it be?" The last thing I needed was Tom snooping around in my business too.

"Right," he said with a nod as he backed out of my office. "Anyway, Trent wants to see you."

"Tell him I'll be down in ten minutes."

I wasted the next few minutes responding to inconsequential emails and checking on my daughter. Trent was trying to pull a power play by sending his lapdog to fetch me. I'd accepted the uneven footing we had, but that didn't mean I had to run every time he snapped his fingers. I'd get there when I was good and ready.

When I showed up in his office exactly twelve minutes later, I found him staring out the window that overlooked the casino floor. Even in the middle of the day, it was packed with people flirting with Lady Luck. The odds weren't in their favor, but that didn't stop them from throwing around an exorbitant amount of cash like it was Monopoly money.

"It doesn't make sense to me," he finally said. "How can we possibly be losing money?"

I shoved my hands in my pants pockets. "Because dad hired a scam artist to replace me."

Trent narrowed his eyes at me. "You got proof of that yet?"

I'd been scouring spreadsheets for two weeks and came up with zip. There wasn't one thing out of order, but that didn't mean I was wrong. "Not yet, but I will."

"I hope you do. I've never been a fan of Leonard's. He's arrogant and walks around here like he owns the place. It pisses me off."

"Finally, something we can agree on." Lord knew the list was short.

Trent huffed. "Might be the first time ever."

"That why you sent Tom to fetch me or is there something else?" I hated having my time wasted and Trent knew it.

"There's something else."

"Is this a guessing game, or are you going to tell me?"

"Hold your fucking horses." He looked up at the ceiling in exasperation. "Why do I even listen to my wife?"

"Because she carries your balls in her purse," I deadpanned.

"Fuck off." Trent opened his desk drawer, pulled out two tickets, and shoved them in my hand. "You're welcome."

I stared down at the tickets with confusion. "Rissa Black is playing here?" Tickets were notoriously hard to get and highly coveted.

"Yeah, Gia reached out to her agent and offered her a residency here. She declined the offer but agreed to add a show at Mystique to her tour schedule. One night only. The tickets sold out in minutes. Gia snagged six of them for the front row with backstage passes. It's going to be Gia and me, Brett and Penny, and you and Charli. If you don't want them, no big deal." He reached for the tickets and tried to take them from my hand.

I yanked my hand back and pushed the tickets into my pocket. "What makes you think I'd take Charli?"

"Why wouldn't you take Charli? You have a girlfriend I don't know about?"

Trent and I weren't close growing up. I tried to forge a bond with him when we were teenagers, but the constant rejection was a hard pill to swallow.

I moved on. Went to a different college. Made new friends. Got my own apartment.

Through all of it, I never had a girlfriend. I had friends who were girls. Plenty of dates. Women who I hooked up with.

Never a relationship. No one I trusted enough to keep around for more than a few nights.

"No. No girlfriend."

Trent threw his hands in the air. "Exactly." Then he narrowed his eyes and tapped a finger against his lips like I'd seen Gia do. "Wait. Is there a guy friend? I mean, it's cool if there is…"

I held out a hand to stop his train of thought from running off the track. "No guy friend. No girlfriend. Just Charli."

He gave me a smug smirk. "That's what I thought. We're going to dinner before the concert if you want to join us."

"I'll think about it." The amount of thought required to decide if I wanted to take Charli to the concert was zero. The amount of thought required to decide if I *should* take her... was infinite.

She was my employee.

I was her boss.

There were plenty of reasons we shouldn't be together.

And one really big reason why we should.

At ten minutes to two, I strolled into the conference room and sat next to Gia. She'd become an unexpected ally in my quest to take Leonard down. I wasn't quite sure why she forgave me so quickly for the atrocities I committed against her, but I didn't question it. An ally was an ally, and there was no one better than someone who shared my suspicions.

Despite our rocky start when I returned to Mystique, my sister-in-law transformed into somewhat of a cheerleader for me, both professionally and personally.

Weird, but nice.

Leonard strolled in with his cocky attitude seconds before the meeting started, taking the seat on the left side of my father that belonged to me. The sooner he was gone, the better.

I bided my time, not making eye contact with him. I took my standard notes and participated in the meeting as if I were any other head of department. I wasn't—and technically I shouldn't have been included in these meetings—but I was grateful my father insisted I attend. It was nepotism at its finest and there wasn't a damn thing Leonard could do about it.

Twenty minutes into the meeting, a tentative knock came at the door. Teresa, our administrative receptionist, stuck her head into the conference room with an apologetic look on her face. "I'm sorry to interrupt, Mr. Dorsey, but there seems to be a problem."

My father, who hated interruptions, furrowed his brows. "What kind of problem?"

Two female officers pushed their way into the conference room. "We're looking for Leonard Moroski," the blond officer said.

My boss spun around in his chair. "I'm Leonard."

"Mr. Moroski, we're going to need you to come with us," the brunette said.

All eyes were on Leonard and his lips flattened into a thin line. "I'm not going anywhere until you tell me what this is about."

"That's fine," the blond responded. "We can do this right here." She yanked him by the arm and pushed him up against the wall, roughly pulling his arms behind his back and handcuffing him. "You're under arrest."

"Holy shit," Trent blurted, his gaze focusing on me.

I subtly shook my head with wide eyes. The scene playing out during our meeting had everyone in shock.

Leonard's face turned bright red. "Under arrest? For what?" he shouted. "This must be a mistake."

"Sadly, it's not," the brunette said as she pushed him back down into the chair. "You're under arrest for not having enough fun on your birthday."

Music began to play and both women ripped open their uniform shirts to reveal tiny sequined bikini tops covering their big breasts. One woman began to ride Leonard's leg in a sexy lap dance, as the other woman tore away her pants revealing a matching thong with her ass cheeks hanging out. She loosened Leonard's tie and unbuttoned his shirt. The whole thing was completely absurd.

"What the fuck!" my father yelled.

Unfazed, the woman giving the lap dance pushed her pants down her legs and wiggled her ass in Leonard's face. The other woman lifted his chin with two fingers. "Apparently, Lenny's been a very bad boy. He refused to take the day off of work on his birthday and go golfing with his buddy. Greg said to tell you if you wouldn't come out to have fun, he'd bring the fun to you."

"Oh my god!" Gia gasped. The other employees were trying to have the decency not to watch the spectacle, but how could they not?

"This is ridiculous! Uncuff me right now!"

"And move this show out of my conference room!" my father screamed. "This is a place of business not a strip club."

"Edward, you have to believe I didn't know about this," my frazzled boss pleaded.

"We'll discuss this later. Take the rest of the day off, Leonard. Enjoy your birthday somewhere else."

"But, but…"

"Go!" My father pointed at the door.

"Boo! You're no fun," the blond complained with a pout as she uncuffed *Lenny*. The brunette picked up their clothes from the floor, giving the entire room a spectacular view of her ass.

The trio exited the conference room, Leonard looking like a scolded puppy.

The room was bathed in silence, everyone still shocked. "Well, that was unexpected," someone finally said.

"It's Vegas," said Greta, head of housekeeping. She was older than dirt and had worked at Mystique forever. "I'm just disappointed it wasn't two young bucks instead of those floozies."

I tried to keep in my laugh, but it bubbled up my chest and escaped, starting a chain reaction. Soon everyone was talking at once and laughing it up, even my father, who ended the meeting when he realized he'd lost control.

Trent turned to Gia and me. "What the hell was that?"

"Apparently, ol' Lenny boy is a freak." Gia laughed.

"Completely unprofessional," I added.

The camera and audio equipment I planted in Leonard's office hadn't revealed anything about Mystique's finances, but they gave me a little nugget of information that was almost as valuable.

Best five hundred bucks I'd ever spent. The look on his face was worth every penny.

Chapter 28
Charli

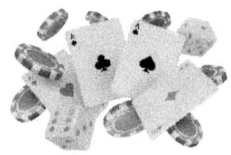

Sweat trickled down my back as I let myself slide down the silks to the floor. It was my job to make the performance look effortless, but truth be told aerial acrobatics completely worked your body from head to toe. My muscles burned from the lack of training over the last few months. I needed this more than I realized.

Jasmine sat down on the mat beside me. "You looked great up there. You'll be ready to return to Oasis in no time."

I groaned and flopped onto my back. "I know."

"Not exactly the response I was expecting," she said, cocking her head to the side. "I thought you wanted to come back."

"I do. That's the problem."

"I'm not following."

I propped myself up on my elbows. "I love this. It's my dream come true. When I took the nanny position, I figured I'd be there for a few months, make some quick cash, and go. It was a win-win for me. I never thought I'd actually like the job."

Jasmine smirked at me. "You like the hot daddy. Any progress on that front?"

A rough laugh escaped my lips. "Nope! First of all, I suck at playing hard to get. All he has to do is say my name and I melt into a gooey puddle. We've messed around a couple times, but he refuses to sleep with me."

"Because you work for him?"

"Yeah, that's one of his excuses. He thinks I'm too young or some stupid shit and he calls it"—I finger quoted— "*doing the right thing.*"

"Let me guess, you don't think those are the real reasons."

I looked up at the exposed metal beams that ran along the ceiling. "I overhead him talking to Carina on the baby monitor."

"You were snooping," she accused.

"Not on purpose, but yes. He doesn't want to get attached because he's afraid I'm going to leave. And you know what? He's right. I never planned on staying. When I go back to Oasis, I'll have to quit the nanny job. He'll go his way, and I'll go mine."

"Doesn't have to be that way. You won't be able to nanny full time, but that doesn't mean the two of you can't be together."

"I'm falling in love with him," I admitted.

She gave me a lopsided smile. "I already knew that. It's written all over your face whenever you talk about him. You get this goofy grin."

My poker face wasn't the best. I ran a hand down my face, trying to erase all traces of my feelings for Hunter. "Better?"

"Not really. You need more practice." Jasmine grabbed my hand and pulled me to my feet. "Do the routine one more time, then go home and give that man an epic blow job. That should help."

I rolled my eyes. "Great advice." I wished life was that easy. That one blow job could make the man see me as more than a temporary solution to his problems.

There wasn't any reason the two of us couldn't be together. The air crackled with electricity every time we were within three feet of each other. The only things keeping us apart were his weird sense of morality and the twenty-foot wall he'd erected between us.

197

Jasmine turned on "Earned It" by The Weeknd and I ascended the silks, letting the fabric guide me until I was high above the mat below. The new routine was alluring and seductive, even in the harshness of the training center without the magic of special effects and dramatic spotlights.

Suspended only by the delicate material, it became an extension of my own body as I twirled and spun, making the silk ripple in waves. With every carefully choreographed pose, I was more at ease in the air, a reassurance that one fall hadn't ruined my years of training. The silks became my dance partner, supporting me through daring, yet sensual, maneuvers. Stretched between the two pieces of fabric, my body felt as weightless as a feather fluttering through the air. In this magical place between the earth and the sky, I controlled my own destiny.

I was the master of my dreams.

And lately my dreams featured a man with chiseled cheekbones, ice-blue eyes, and a wicked tongue.

I took the lasagna Rose prepared from the oven and set it on the stovetop. The scent of savory tomato sauce, oregano, basil, and garlic mingled together and wafted throughout the kitchen, making my mouth water. She said it had been Hunter's favorite since he was a boy.

Although Hunter harbored resentment toward his stepmother, he couldn't deny she was trying to make things right. Maybe it was the sudden appearance of Carina in their lives, but whatever the reason, I hoped Hunter would give Rose a chance. The dinner party at Trent and Gia's gave me a glimpse of what it could be like for Hunter to have a supportive family around him. He needed to give them a chance.

Hunter's keys jingled in the door, announcing his arrival. "Something smells amazing," he said as he entered the kitchen.

I popped the garlic bread in the oven and set the timer for ten minutes. "You're right on time. Dinner is almost ready."

He came over and inspected the lasagna. "That looks heavenly." His tongue came out to wet his bottom lip and his eyes closed as he took in the aroma. "It's the perfect ending to a perfect day."

"I can't take the credit for this. Rose put it together before I got home." I cocked a hip and leaned against the counter, gazing up at him. "There's something different about you... you look... happy."

Hunter barked out a laugh. "I'm not always a miserable asshole."

I laughed along with him. "Yes, you're decidedly less of an asshole than when I first met you. Definitely progress."

"I'm glad I have your approval." He opened the oven door and peeked inside. "Garlic bread too?"

"You must have been a very good boy today," I teased.

"Actually, I was a very bad boy, but it felt good."

My face fell. No wonder he was so happy. Good sex will do that to you. It made complete sense, even if I had hoped he might be interested in me. A man like Hunter wasn't likely to be celibate. "She's a lucky woman."

His eyebrows scrunched up. "Who's a lucky woman?"

"Whoever it is that put you in this happy mood," I said nonchalantly. I shouldn't have cared what or who Hunter did. We weren't a couple, and we weren't in a relationship, but my stomach sank anyway.

"It was actually two women."

I playfully punched him in the shoulder. "Good job, Romeo. Should have known you were an overachiever."

"I am, but it's not what you think," he said, shrugging out of his jacket and hanging it over the back of the chair.

"It's not my business." I pulled plates from the cupboard and silverware from the drawer to keep myself busy. "Are you eating in the kitchen or in your office tonight?"

Two big hands gently grasped my shoulders and spun me around. "Charlotte, look at me. I didn't have sex today, if that's what you're thinking. In fact, I haven't been with anyone since before Carina arrived."

I looked everywhere but at him. "It's not my business. I'm just the nanny."

Hunter leaned down so we were nose to nose, and I had no choice but to look in his eyes. "That's bullshit and you know it."

"Do I?"

He huffed out a breath and ran one hand through his hair. "I don't know what we are, but we're something."

"Something?"

"You're in my head twenty-four seven, even if I don't want you to be. I've become quite accustomed to you being here and the thought of you with someone else drives me crazy. So yes... something. I'm not making any promises."

My heart skipped a beat because this was a step in the right direction. "I'm not asking for promises. I'll be going back to Oasis, but that doesn't mean—"

Hunter held a finger over my lips. "Let's not get ahead of ourselves. One day at a time, yeah?"

"One day at a time." I nodded in agreement. "So you gonna kiss me?"

"Fuck, yes." He held my face in his hands and pressed his lips against mine. His tongue ran along the seam of my lips, and I opened for him, wrapping my arms around his shoulders. Our tongues tangled together in a slow dance I wasn't expecting. It was gentle yet passionate, and somehow that made the kiss better.

The timer on the oven dinged, shattering the moment as I pulled back from the kiss. "That's the bread."

His lips turned up on one side. "Don't want to burn the bread. Where's Carina?"

I grabbed a mitt from the counter and pulled the bread from the oven. "Rose tired her out. She'll probably sleep through dinner." Although I wouldn't say it aloud, I was thankful it would only be the two of us.

"I'm going to go check on her and then we can eat."

"Aye, aye, captain," I said with a salute.

He shook his head in exasperation as he walked down the hall to Carina's bedroom.

This day had taken a positive turn. Something was better than nothing, and that was everything. I grabbed two wineglasses and set them on the table along with the lasagna and bread. Lastly, I grabbed the bottle of Cabernet Sauvignon from the counter and a corkscrew.

Hunter sauntered back into the kitchen. "She's totally out. Does that mean she'll be up all night?"

I shrugged my shoulders. "Maybe, but I doubt it. I'll wake her after we eat so she doesn't stay up too late."

"Alright. Maybe we can take her for a walk or something after dinner."

"Sounds good," I said with a smile. Hunter wasn't big on the three of us doing things together, maybe because it made us seem like a family. We weren't, but from the outside looking in I wouldn't blame someone for coming to that conclusion. Now that he'd decided we were *something*, perhaps we'd be spending more time together than early mornings and meals.

Hunter sat and picked up the bottle of Cabernet Sauvignon. "Wine?"

"Courtesy of Rose. She said no Italian meal is complete without wine."

"She's right about that." He uncorked the bottle and poured us each a glass. He held his up. "Salute."

I clinked my glass with his. "Salute."

"Now let's dig in. This looks fabulous." Hunter wasted no time cutting us each a piece of lasagna and plating them. When he took his first bite his eyes closed. "So good."

"Tell me about the two women who made you happy today." I should have left it alone after his confession of not being able to get me out of his head, but my curiosity was killing me.

His fork froze halfway to his mouth. "I shouldn't tell you. You'll think I'm a bad person."

"You realize now you have to tell me, right?"

"Two conditions. First, you can't tell a single soul. I mean it. Not your brother, not anyone. It would be bad for me." I ran a finger over my heart in the shape of an *X*. "Second, know that I had a good reason for doing what I did."

It was unlikely, but I gave him the benefit of the doubt. "Of course, you did. Now dish the dirt." I stuffed a forkful of lasagna into my mouth.

He took a sip of his wine and eyed me over the glass as if deciding whether I could be trusted. "You remember me talking about Leonard?"

"Your boss at Mystique? The guy you hate?"

Hunter winced. "Yes, to both. He's got my job, and I intend on getting it back. He's crooked as shit, and I can guarantee he's the reason Mystique has been losing money. I've been going over the books and I haven't found anything yet, but in the meantime, I've been making his life miserable."

I dropped my fork and let it clatter on the plate. "What did you do?"

Hunter leaned back in his chair and crossed his arms. "Hired two strippers dressed as police officers to *arrest* him today. Our entire staff was in the conference room for our weekly meeting when they showed up. You should have seen his indignation when they pulled out the handcuffs, but when they started taking off their clothes he was horrified." A low chuckle rumbled up from his chest turning into a full-blown belly laugh. He wiped the corner of his eye, catching the tear that formed. "It was priceless. My father was so mad and all I could do was sit there looking as shocked as everyone else."

My hand flew up in front of my mouth. "You didn't."

"I absolutely did, and I don't regret it one bit. It's his birthday after all." He kept laughing like he'd been holding it in all day long.

My own giggles broke free. "That's horrible. Funny as hell, but still horrid."

"Not as funny as the day I put laxative in his coffee. Guy practically shit his pants. Stunk up the entire floor."

I laughed so hard my belly hurt. For as serious as Hunter was, I didn't think he was capable of such shenanigans. "Oooh, oooh... you should get him cupcakes tomorrow to wish him a happy birthday."

Hunter snapped his fingers and pointed at me. "Excellent idea. Let's go to the bakery after dinner and you can help me pick them out. Maybe I'll get some candles too."

"Absolutely." A soft cry interrupted our laugh fest. "We must have woken her up." I pushed away from the table to get Carina.

"Charli, wait." Hunter pulled two tickets out of his pocket and handed them to me. "You wanna go?"

They were for the Rissa Black show at Mystique. "Oh my god, I love her. That song 'Broken Wings' gets me every time. Tickets for her shows are almost impossible to get. How did you get these?"

He shrugged like it was no big deal. "Gia. Helps when your sister-in-law is the director of entertainment and events."

I was stunned. "Is this like… a date?"

He stood and came around the table placing his hands on my hips. "Yeah, dollface, it's a date. Will you go with me?"

Looking up into his blue eyes, I nodded. "Yes, I'd like that very much."

Hunter leaned down and kissed my forehead. "Then it's settled. I'll go get Carina while you decide what kind of cupcakes we should buy."

Then he casually walked down the hallway like he hadn't flipped a one-eighty and asked me out on a date. Like us going out was the most normal thing in the world.

If this was the start of *something*, I couldn't wait to see where it went.

Chapter 29
Hunter

"Happy birthday, Leonard." I set the box of cupcakes on his desk.

Lenny Boy scowled at me and opened the box. "I'm not eating a damn thing from you."

I scowled back. "That's not very nice. I picked these up special since I missed your birthday yesterday. Even brought a candle." I pulled the candle out of my pocket and poked it into one of the cupcakes.

He pushed the box away. "If you don't think I know you were behind yesterday's events, you've got another think coming."

Stuffing my hands in my pockets, I rolled back on my heels. "I think you're being paranoid. Didn't the ladies say they were sent by a golf buddy? If my friend sent me a stripper for my birthday, I wouldn't be mad about it. I would have sat back and enjoyed it."

"My friend didn't send them." He stood and leaned on his desk, his face turning red. "It was you! You're trying to make me look bad."

"No disrespect, but all I've done is be at your beck and call, even if you've treated me like a servant. I tried to do something nice by bringing you cupcakes and all I get are accusations."

Leonard pointed a finger and shoved it down on top of his desk. "I don't trust you!"

I shrugged my shoulders. "Is that a no on the cupcakes then?"

"It's a hell no."

"Suit yourself." I extracted a cupcake from the box and took a huge bite out of it. Chewing slowly, I hummed my appreciation. "These are delicious. I'll put them in the break room for the rest of the staff." I grabbed the box and turned on my heel.

"I want payroll done by the end of the day," he barked at me.

"Finished it this morning. Check your messages." With that, I strolled out of his office. Leonard might have thought he had me all figured out, but there wasn't a shred of evidence against me. Paranoia was a dangerous place to be, and Leonard was well on his way.

My father showed up in my office doorway with a shit-eating grin on his face. "I have a surprise for you."

I hated surprises. In my experience, they weren't a good thing... moving to a new home without my mom, getting fired when my brother broke company policy, a baby showing up at my apartment. Well, the last one *did* end up being a good surprise, even if I wasn't ready for it. Now I'd rip out the heart of anyone who dared try to take Carina away from me.

Which reminded me to follow up with Rudy. For a private investigator who came highly recommended, I wasn't impressed. You'd think I'd asked him to find out what happened to Amelia Earhart instead of a stripper in Vegas. In this day and age, it was nearly impossible to be completely off the grid, yet Jennifer Johnson had evaded every attempt to locate her. It pissed me off. I didn't like loose ends and that's exactly what

Miss Johnson was... a loose end who could show up at any time and threaten the custody of my daughter.

Where the fuck was she?

"Hunter?"

I snapped out of my thoughts and focused on my father. "What's the surprise?" Perhaps he'd already decided to sack Leonard. That would be the best surprise ever.

He motioned for me to step into the hallway. "Ta-da! It's a new desk."

It was indeed a new desk, but nothing like the expensive mahogany one that was now being used by Leonard Morosk-hole. That desk probably wouldn't even fit in the closet where I worked.

Instead of seeming ungrateful, I plastered on a smile. "Thanks, Dad. This is great."

His face lit up. "I hope you like it. I'll have maintenance swap it out with your old one immediately." He peered into my office and scrunched up his face when he looked at the metal hunk of junk my computer sat on. "God, that's really awful. I'm sorry it took so long to replace."

I clapped him on the back. "No worries. It hasn't interfered with my ability to do payroll."

My father's brows furrowed. "What else does he have you doing?"

"Honestly?"

He nodded. "Of course."

"Not a damn thing. I am helping Gia with something, but other than that... nada. It's a waste of my degree."

My father was known for his patience, but Leonard was testing it. "I'll have a talk with him. There are a million things you could be doing, and I'm not talking about getting his coffee."

I motioned with my head for him to follow me into my office and shut the door behind him. "About the other project we talked about... I need access to more records. There's nothing obvious popping up. I need a list of vendors, all accounts payable, invoices, daily transactions... the full gamut. I know he's stealing from us."

I could tell by the look on his face that my father didn't want to think it was true because if it was, it called into question his decision to hire

Leonard. He was a prideful man and a mistake like that would devastate him. "I'm not sure—"

"I am, Dad. Don't let that asshole steal your family's legacy." My father had the power to do whatever he wanted. The fact that he was stalling concerned me. He'd been shrewd in his younger years but was losing his edge. Getting soft in his older years.

Luckily for him, I had no such affliction.

He sighed. "Come to my office. I'll give you everything I've got."

Finally. "Thank you." I didn't expect to find anything in the company records. I was sure the evidence I needed was on Leonard's computer.

Guess I was working late tonight. That camera I installed in his office was about to pay off.

"Are you telling me she fucking vanished into thin air?"

"What I'm saying is that every Jennifer Johnson we've found isn't her. I'm starting to wonder if it's even her real name."

I was irritated I had to call Rudy Mendosa for an update. I was irritated he hadn't found her yet. And I was irritated she ended up being more conniving than I first thought. *When I got my hands on that woman...*

What?

What was I going to do?

I wanted to say that I was going to ship her off to Timbuktu in a wooden box, never to be seen again, but... she was Carina's mother, so some type of legal agreement that didn't include sending her to the middle of the Sahara Desert would probably be more appropriate.

I'd barely given the woman a second thought since Charli came into my life. Although Charli took the nanny position as a temporary job, she fell in love with Carina. I couldn't ask for someone better to take care of my daughter. And me for that matter.

"Keep looking," I instructed Rudy. "I don't want any loose ends where she's concerned. I need her to relinquish her parental rights."

"Hunter…"

"What?"

"I'm on your side here, but I have to be honest with you. When we do find her, you can't force her to sign the paperwork. You'll have to prove that Carina is better off with you than her mother."

"She abandoned her daughter!"

"I understand. However, I want you to be prepared. What seems like common sense doesn't always hold true in the courts."

Fuck that!

Getting upset with Rudy wasn't going to help the situation. For once in my life, I needed to think with my brain instead of my emotions. "You just find her; I'll deal with the legalities."

No one was taking my daughter away from me.

Chapter 30
Charli

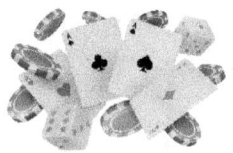

"Thank you so much for taking care of her." I handed Carina over to Rose, who was taking her back to their house for the night.

"Are you kidding me? I'm thrilled. Edward and I have been waiting on Trent and Gia. We never thought Hunter would have the first grandchild."

"Are you sure you don't want to stay here? It might be easier."

"Pfft!" She waved away my concern. "I already have a room ready for my granddaughter. Gave me an excuse to do some redecorating. Besides, you two kids could use a night off. Go enjoy yourselves." Rose spoke like we were a couple, yet it was still very unclear exactly what we were.

Hunter rushed in the door, throwing his keys on the hallway table. "Thank god you didn't leave yet." He stole Carina from Rose's arms and covered her with sloppy kisses. "I missed you, baby girl." Over the past month he'd changed from a reluctant father to a man whose whole world revolved around his daughter.

Rose put a hand to her lips. "I never thought I'd see this day. This makes my heart so happy."

Hunter gave her a rare smile. "You're not the only one. I didn't even know I had a heart until this little munchkin arrived." He lifted Carina high into the air and nuzzled her belly, while she laughed and tried to kick him in the face. "Be good for Grandma and Grandpa tonight."

Carina squealed and waved her arms wildly.

"She will be." Rose ran her fingers through Carina's short hair.

Hunter put Carina into the stroller, then grabbed the car seat base and two diaper bags I prepared. Yes, two. Who knew little people required so much stuff? I wanted to make sure she had everything she needed. "I'll help you get her in the car," he said.

Rose chuckled. "I've done this a time or two."

"But it's been a while. Things have changed a bit in the last thirty years." Hunter leaned over and kissed me on the forehead. "I'll be right back."

As Hunter made his way to the elevator, Rose gave me a conspiratorial smile and hugged me. "I'm so happy you're in his life. You make him a better person."

I hugged her back. "We're undefined at the moment."

"Young people. You all have to do things the hard way when the answer is right in front of your face. Trent and Gia did the same thing. Mark my words, it won't be undefined for long." Then she followed Hunter and left me standing there speechless.

Rose was a sneaky little matchmaker, and it seemed she had her sights set on Hunter and me. I wasn't complaining, but I couldn't see how we would work out in the long term. Once I returned to Oasis, my schedule would be crazy. I'd worked too hard to give up my dreams for a man.

With a sigh, I returned to my room. If I worried about the future, then I wouldn't enjoy today. Life was a journey, not a destination. Every day a new adventure awaited. The only regret in a risk was not taking it.

I finished curling my hair and touched up my eye makeup, going a little darker than my normal everyday look. *Now what to wear?* I pulled distressed jeans from my closet and paired them with a silver, sequined tank top. Casually fancy and perfect for a concert in Vegas.

Hunter knocked on my door as I fastened black, strappy heels onto my feet. "Are you almost ready? We're supposed to meet them for dinner in a half hour." He stared at his watch impatiently. It was only a ten minute drive, but with traffic on the Strip, I didn't blame him for wanting to leave early.

Standing, I walked over to him and put my hand on his chest. "I'm ready."

His eyes scanned me from head to toe. "Wow! You look great."

"You don't look so bad yourself." I laughed. "I didn't even know you owned jeans." The black button-down shirt he had on was rolled at the sleeves, showing off his muscular forearms. "Just one little thing." I undid the top two buttons of his shirt and fixed the collar. "Much better."

"Thanks."

"Do you have the tickets?"

He pulled them from his back pocket. "Right here."

Of course he did. Hunter was nothing if not meticulously prepared. I grabbed my purse from the dresser as Hunter led me from the room with his hand on the small of my back.

"Do you think Carina will be okay with my parents?" he asked as we waited for the elevator.

I was surprised he hadn't brought this up earlier. "She'll be fine. They're excited to have her."

The doors opened and we stepped inside. "What if she gets fussy?"

"Then they'll feed her, change her, rock her... this isn't their first rodeo." It was cute how worried he was, although he really had no cause.

"What if she has a poop blowout? That's a totally valid concern."

I pressed my lips together, trying to contain my amusement. "Then they'll clean her up. I packed plenty of diapers, wipes, and extra clothes."

"Do you think they'll know how to handle it?"

I couldn't suppress my laughter anymore. "Do you really think you or Trent never had a blowout as a baby?"

"Not me. I was fully potty-trained by the time I moved in with them."

I winced at my mistake. Although I knew his history, I still managed to put my foot in my mouth. "Sorry. That was insensitive of me."

Hunter took my hand and squeezed it. "It's okay. I get your point. It just feels weird knowing Carina won't be there when we get home."

"You can call to check on her if it makes you feel better, but I can assure you your daughter is in good hands."

He gave a curt nod, and I knew he'd be making more than one phone call tonight.

I understood his concern, but part of me was excited we would have the apartment to ourselves. We'd never been *completely* alone, and I was hoping not having a baby in the house would be the inspiration Hunter needed to *completely* take advantage of me. And that thought made tonight even better.

Turned out Hunter was justified in his concern about being late. Traffic was a nightmare. We were only running behind by five minutes, but the way he dragged me through the parking lot you'd think we were meeting the president, not friends, at the bar and grill.

Well, not my friends. I was more of a friend by acquaintance. Come to think of it, I wasn't sure if they could be classified as Hunter's friends either. I mean obviously, Trent was his brother... so maybe family and friends? But I got the notion that Hunter and Brett weren't close.

Whatever.

It didn't really matter. The point was these people weren't worth twisting my ankle over. "Slow down. I can barely keep up with you in these shoes."

Hunter ran a hand through his hair. "I'm sorry. You know how I feel about being late." He slowed down a little, but his long legs still ate up the distance faster than mine. The man was wound so tight, one day that little vein in his forehead was going to burst.

212

I was practically panting by the time we made it to the hostess stand and seriously rethinking my choice of footwear. "We're with the Kingston party of six," Hunter said in a rush.

The hostess smiled at him. "Brett Kingston?"

"Yes," he said roughly, almost to the point of being rude.

"You're the first to arrive." She gathered up some menus and led us to a semiprivate corner table. "Your waitress will be with you shortly."

"Guess we didn't have to worry about being late." I didn't mean for it to come out sarcastic, but my feet hurt and armpits were damp. It wasn't exactly what I had in mind to start off our evening.

"I already said I was sorry. I know it's only dinner, but punctuality is important to me, especially with my brother and Brett."

Our waitress came with water and took our drink orders, mine a rum runner and Hunter's a bourbon. When she walked away, I turned back to my date. "Explain."

He rolled his neck, letting it crack on both sides. "When we were kids, they were like two peas in a pod, the best of friends. I used to follow them around like a damn puppy. I was only a year younger, so I didn't think it was that big of a deal. They ditched me at every opportunity, making me feel like a defective third wheel. In high school, they weren't *in* the cool crowd. They *were* the cool crowd. Girls got in actual fistfights over them."

The waitress returned with our drinks and Hunter picked his up, taking a big sip. "Anyway, not much has changed. They still make me feel inferior, like I'm not good enough. I guess I still feel the need to prove myself worthy, especially after getting fired."

I understood more than he knew. I spent my whole life trying to live up to the standards my brother set... his accelerated classes, his valedictorian-worthy GPA, his amazing test scores, and the scholarships that fell into his lap. Unfortunately for my parents, their second child was painstakingly average. I felt guilty Tom worked for Trent as his personal assistant. If it weren't for him following me to Vegas, he'd probably be making big bucks somewhere in Silicon Valley.

Putting my hand on top of his, I gave it a squeeze. "Thank you for sharing that with me, but can I tell you something?"

213

He nodded.

"Your value doesn't depend on what others think of you. Nobody, and I mean nobody, agreed with my choice to move to Vegas to become an aerialist. The only one who really supported me coming here was my brother, although begrudgingly. You know he's got mad computer skills, right? His job at Mystique is so far below him that it makes me feel selfish and guilty. He only took it to be close to me. When I fell and couldn't perform anymore, all I could think was what a terrible person I was for putting my dreams above his."

"You're not a terrible person. I know Tom really cares about you and he's very protective of you. He threatened that if I didn't treat you right that I'd be sorry. I have to be honest; I didn't see him as that big of a threat, but I respected him for standing up for you."

I threw my head back and laughed. It was so typical of my brother. "Oh, you should be afraid. He'll never throw a punch, but he'll make your life a living hell regardless. He'll hack every device you own, installing malware and viruses that will affect every electronic platform you use…bank accounts, social media, email… everything."

Hunter's eyes went wide. "I did not know that."

"Yeah, he might seem innocuous, but I can promise you he's as dangerous as they come. Anyway, my point was that you're too old to worry about being in the cool kids' club. You'll never get everyone's approval. If people don't like you… fuck 'em."

"That hasn't exactly worked out well for me."

I tilted my head to the side. "Were you being yourself or were you trying to be part of the cool kids' crowd? Just be yourself, minus the assholeness."

He chuckled. "Point taken, but being an asshole is pretty much part of my personality. Call it my trademark."

"Well, how about you work on taking it down a couple notches? You've made mistakes but you're making amends and that's important. I think you're harder on yourself than anyone else could ever be."

"Thank you." He picked up my hand and kissed my palm. "You don't know how much I needed to hear that."

214

"Are we interrupting?" Gia raised her eyebrows. The rest of our group arrived, and all eyes were on us.

Hunter dropped my hand and tapped on his watch. "You're late."

"Traffic was awful," Trent said.

"A total gridlock," Brett added.

Penny looked at Gia and gave her a wink. "Looks like you two were doing fine without us."

Yes, we were.

Gia and Penny accepted me easily into their fold, showing genuine interest. It probably helped that they knew my brother, so we had that in common.

I tried to apply the cool kids pep talk I gave Hunter to my current situation. Both of these women wore designer clothes and looked like they'd stepped out of the salon. I never worried too much about my no-name-brand jeans or discount shoes before, but it was difficult when sitting across the table from Gucci and Chanel.

"I love that top. Where did you get it?" Penny asked.

I looked down at my shirt. "Oh this? I picked it up from a little boutique called Second Chances." Boutique was a euphemism for thrift store, but I hoped they wouldn't know the difference.

"Oh my god, I love that store!" she shrieked. "I used to shop there all the time. They have some terrific finds." Then she turned to Gia. "You know that red polka dot blouse I have that ties at the waist. I got it at Second Chances."

"Wait. You shop at Second Chances?" I asked in astonishment. I couldn't help but stare at the rocks both of them were sporting on their ring fingers. Gia's was enviable, but Penny's was almost obscene. Her diamond alone could probably feed a small third-world country.

"Well, not so much anymore, but before I married Brett, every little penny counted. It's not like I make a killing being her personal assistant." She motioned to Gia.

That was true. I knew my brother made decent money, but it was nothing to write home about. He and I were surviving, not thriving.

Gia put a hand to her chest. "Don't blame me. I'm not in charge of the salaries. Without Trent, I might still be living at the hotel."

"Oh, I doubt that. You make more money than me, and I was able to afford a condo. It wasn't fancy, but it was mine."

My head ping-ponged between the two of them. I admired their easy friendship and candor.

I snuck a peek over at Hunter and was pleasantly surprised to see him engaging with Brett and Trent, laughing even. It made me sad that Hunter wasn't close with his brother, and I hoped they could repair their relationship.

Being estranged from my brother would devastate me. We were super close when we were kids. Although Tom liked to bitch about the things I did, I knew he'd always have my back. Moving to Vegas with me proved that.

Hunter squeezed my knee under the table. A shiver ran up my spine and my lady parts clenched. As much as I didn't want to be attracted to him, my body didn't agree. There was an electric chemistry between us since day one, despite his assholeness. Beneath his hard exterior was a decent guy not many people got to know.

After finishing off a burger and my second rum runner, I was a tad tipsy, so I switched to water. I wasn't a big drinker, and my tolerance was low. Also, I didn't trust myself to be a drunky skunk around Hunter. Although we were officially *something*, I didn't quite know what that meant or if we were going public. It was better to keep my wits about me and follow his lead even if the group had caught him kissing my hand.

Penny leaned in close and whispered, "What is going on with you two?"

"I don't know what you're talking about." Playing dumb wasn't my strong suit, but I tried it anyway.

"Don't play coy with me, missy. He can't stop looking at you."

"Okay. It's just a little… something."

Gia clapped her hands together. "I knew it!"

"Wait! Are you actually encouraging this?" Penny asked.

"Yes," Gia said with the widest of grins.

Penny lowered her voice even more. "Why? He's a total jerk."

Pushing a strand of dark hair behind my ear, I whispered back, "He's not that bad." It wasn't a glowing recommendation, but I didn't know what else to say. It would betray his trust to tell them about the conversations we shared.

"Something has changed in him. He's not the same guy since Carina showed up. I would have never believed it before, but he has a soft side. I saw it the night of the family dinner."

The family dinner. Hunter had eaten me for dessert, and I couldn't stop thinking about it. Of course, I wouldn't share that information.

"It's risky," Penny insisted.

"It's Vegas. What isn't risky?" I asked.

"Be careful, or you'll end up gambling your heart away," she said.

I heard her warning loud and clear, but I'd never backed away from a challenge. Because I might get hurt wasn't a reason not to try. I'd been taking chances my whole life and this one felt right.

Chapter 31
Hunter

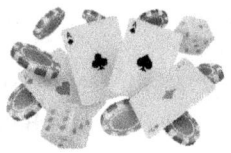

I glanced down at my phone again and stared at the picture Rose sent me. Carina was nestled into my dad's arms, looking happy and safe.

"How many times have you texted them?" Charli nudged me with her shoulder.

"Only three." It took a lot of self-control not to text my parents every five minutes. It was weird that when I went to work, and Charli was alone with Carina, I never worried, but now I was a Nervous Nellie.

"Three is not so bad." She laughed. "They've got this. Be assured neither your dad nor Rose would ever let something happen to Carina."

She was right. I knew she was right, but it didn't help settle my nerves. Sliding the phone into my pocket, I put a hand on the small of her back and led her into the packed theater. "I'm trying."

Charli smiled at me over her shoulder. "I know you are."

We followed Brett and Penny to the front row and settled into our seats, waiting for the show to start. I didn't know much about Rissa Black but could feel the energy pulsing through the crowd. "What kind of music is this again?"

"Seriously? Rissa Black is only the hottest ticket this summer. She's got country roots, but mixes it with pop, rock, and grit. Her voice is freakin' amazing. I can't believe we're getting to meet her after the show." Charli held up her VIP backstage pass that hung around her neck and bounced on her toes.

Her enthusiasm was adorable, and I began thinking of ways to keep that look on her face. I never particularly cared about the happiness of my dates, but I cared with Charli. Maybe because she understood me more than any other person in my life ever had. And maybe because she was helping me understand myself better too.

I decided right then and there that I couldn't stand the thought of anyone else putting that smile on her face.

Charli wasn't just a date; she was quickly becoming my person. I'd become attached to her more than I should.

Nobody ever stayed.

People came.

People went.

Charli might leave too, but she was worth the risk. I couldn't imagine a life where she wasn't part of it.

She threw her arms around my neck. "Thank you so much for this, jerk face," she said with a laugh. It was nothing more than a tease.

My arms circled her tiny waist, lifting her off the ground. "You're welcome, dollface." Without thought, my lips pressed against hers and she melted against me, giving me a taste of that sassy mouth. I claimed her as mine and I didn't care who saw. This girl was everything I never knew I wanted.

"Get a room!" Brett shouted over the din of the crowded theater.

Dropping Charli to her feet, I flipped him off and placed another kiss on her forehead.

Penny giggled as she bumped Charli with her shoulder. "Just a little something? Ha! Looks like a whole lot more to me." Clearly, they'd been gossiping, but I didn't take Charli for someone who'd spill all the dirty details.

Gia came barreling down the aisle with a squeal, Trent following behind. They'd been backstage to *make sure everything was running smoothly.* I took it for what it was, using their positions at Mystique to their advantage.

"Oh my god! I met her and she's even more beautiful in person. She's supersweet and has the most adorable Southern accent. She invited all of us to her private suite after the show!"

The women huddled together, sharing their excitement in hoots and hollers. I couldn't have cared less about the concert, but it made me happy to see Charli happy.

The lights dimmed and Charli grabbed my hand, giving it a gentle squeeze. She threaded our fingers together and refused to let go as the theater went black.

A drumbeat echoed in the air, followed by the riff of a guitar. A single spotlight shone on the stage, lighting up Rissa Black as she started her first song. Although I wasn't a fan per se, I could see why Charli was so enthralled. The woman's voice demanded your attention as her fingers flew over the strings of her guitar.

When the song ended, she set the guitar aside and grabbed the microphone. "Hello, Las Vegas! Y'all sure know how to make a girl feel welcome."

Charli jumped up and down, waving her arms in the air as she screamed at the top of her lungs. There might have been thousands of people in the audience, but all I could see was one—the sassy brunette I'd decided was mine.

By the third song, I moved Charli in front of me. My arms hung loosely on her hips and my chin rested on the top of her head as we swayed to the music. Her body rubbed against my cock, and it sprang to life. "Bad girl," I whispered in her ear.

She gave me a devious smile and blinked up at me with her big, blue eyes. "I don't know what you're talking about."

I pressed my cock into her back. "Sure you don't, little troublemaker."

Charli shrugged her shoulder innocently. "Doesn't seem like a problem to me."

She was right. The only problem was having to wait to get her into my bed tonight.

We stumbled through the door, drunk on lust. The entire concert was nothing but foreplay, filled with sexual innuendos, stolen kisses, and forbidden touches.

Charli stretched up on her toes and kissed my cheek. "Thank you for tonight. I had the best time."

"Nuh-uh. That's not how this night ends." I scooped her up and threw her over my shoulder, giving her ass a hard smack.

"Eek! Give a girl some warning." She laughed, playfully swatting at my back.

"Behave, or I'll have to spank you," I said with another smack to her ass as I walked us to my bedroom. She wiggled her butt, daring me to smack it again, to which I gladly obliged before tossing her onto the middle of the bed. "You are nothing but trouble."

She bounced once before sinking into the mattress. "Guess you better decide if I'm worth it, Mr. Dorsey."

"Oh, I've already decided, Ms. Bently," I said while unbuttoning my shirt.

"And what is it you've decided?"

I grabbed her by the ankles and dragged her to the edge of the bed, removing one shoe and then the other. "That you're mine. Your sassy mouth. Your pert little tits. Your long legs and the pussy between them."

She placed her bare foot on my cock and wiggled her toes. "Those are some big assertions. Are you sure you're ready to deliver?"

I grabbed her foot and pressed it harder to the front of my pants. "I always deliver, and my assertions aren't the only thing that's big."

"Mighty confident there, boss."

I cringed at the reminder of why we shouldn't be doing this, but as Charli shimmied her tank top over her head and tossed it aside, all apprehension washed away. "I'm confident in everything I do. Tell me I'm wrong. Tell me you don't want this."

"You're not wrong."

I leaned over the bed, unbuttoned her jeans, dragged the zipper down, and pulled them off her long legs. In a pink bra and panties, she was a vision of perfection—toned muscles and lean lines. "You're beautiful, Charli."

She shook her head, dark hair swishing over her shoulders. "Don't be cheesy."

"I'm nothing if not honest to a fault. I wouldn't lie about something like that."

Charli crooked her finger at me. "Come here."

Wasting no time, I crawled over her luscious body and caged her in, then captured her mouth. Her arms wrapped around my shoulders and her hips lifted to meet mine.

Fuck, she was hard to resist. Luckily, I didn't have to anymore.

"You're wearing too many clothes," she cooed as she forced my open shirt off my shoulders.

Pushing to my knees, I shrugged it off and threw it on the floor.

"Pants too."

"Somebody's impatient," I said as I stood and slipped out of my shoes.

"I've been waiting a very long time."

"Too fucking long." I undid my belt and pants, letting them fall to the floor. With my pants and socks gone, I stood before her in only my boxer briefs, with my cock straining to get free. "Better?"

Charli bit her bottom lip and nodded. "It's a shame you hide all that behind a suit every day. It's a disservice to women everywhere."

I rolled my eyes. "Now who's being cheesy?"

She reached out with grabby hands. "Get over here."

I'd fought with myself over this exact scenario since the day she showed up at my door in that sundress. Trying to stay professional was torture. Sipping coffee across the island while she wore tiny sleep shorts and a tank top sent me off to work every morning with a hard-on. While I used to work ridiculously long hours, I found myself eager to get home to whatever meal she cooked.

And seeing her with my daughter did weird things to my chest, making my heart flutter in a way it never had before. When I closed my eyes, I could almost imagine that Charli was mine and wanted to fill the role of mother to my child.

Almost.

We only agreed to *something*, not *everything*.

There was a big difference between fucking and committing to a lifetime together.

Wasn't even sure if I wanted a lifetime with her, or with anyone for that matter.

Charli poked me in the leg with her foot. "You changing your mind?"

I shook my head. "Not at all. Just looking at you."

She pulled the straps of her bra down her shoulders and undid the front clasp, letting the material slide down her arms. "Stop looking and start touching." Although her breasts weren't big, they were round and perky, with dusky-rose areolas and tightly pebbled nipples.

I crawled back onto the bed and my mouth crashed into hers, our lips moving in perfect rhythm. I was giddy with a feeling I'd been missing for years—a sense of want, need, possession. Pressing my chest to hers, I relished the feel of her soft skin. Our tongues twisted and tangled while her fingers scraped through the short hair at the nape of my neck. It felt so right having her in my arms.

Rolling us to the side, I took her tit in my hand, squeezing it and pinching her nipple. She moaned and bucked her hips forward, one leg wrapping around my hip. "You like that, dollface?"

"So much. Feels amazing." She moaned again as she grabbed my ass and threw her head back, exposing the slender column of her throat.

I peppered kisses down the trail of her neck and over her collarbone to her breast. My tongue circled her nipple, giving it a flick before sucking the taut peak into my mouth.

223

"Yes, yes, yes," she chanted as she ground her hips against mine. My cock thickened, nestled between the heat of her legs. The thin material of our underwear barely provided any barrier at all as we dry-humped on the bed.

Every muscle in my body tightened and my balls started to tingle. *No, no, no!* I hadn't come prematurely since I was a teenager. That was embarrassing enough.

This would be mortifying.

The weeks of sexual frustration between us had built up so much tension I was ready to explode. Jacking off hadn't quelled my need for her one bit. Now that I actually had her in my bed, I'd be damned if this ended before it barely started. I had to slow this train down.

I pulled back and stared at her gorgeous face—dark-blue eyes you could drown in, pouty lips that would look phenomenal wrapped around my dick, high cheekbones with a slight blush to them, and a smattering of freckles across the bridge of her nose that I'd never noticed before.

"Why are you looking at me like that?"

"I'm thinking about eating your pussy."

Her giggle was like music to my ears as she buried her head in my chest. "Oh my god, don't say that. It's embarrassing."

Wrapping my hand in her hair, I pulled her head back. "I don't want you ever to be embarrassed with me, especially when you come all over my face. Now take those panties off."

She bit her lip. "So bossy."

"I won't ask twice," I growled. "Next time, I'll rip them off."

"Not my new panties!" Charli quickly pushed them down and flung them off her feet to join the rest of our clothes.

I rolled to my back and pulled her on top of me. "Sit on my face. I'd suggest you hold on to the headboard."

Charli sat astride me, her tits nice and perky, and frowned. "I'm not sitting on your face. I'll suffocate you."

I reached up and pinched her nipple. "You let me worry about breathing, you just hang on tight." With one fell swoop, I lifted her above my face.

"My god! Give me some warning," she shrieked.

"I did. You didn't listen," I said with a smack to her ass. My mouth watered from the smell of her, and I didn't waste another minute before burying my tongue in her pussy. Fucking sweet heaven. I lapped and licked and devoured her as she squirmed and muttered unintelligible words.

All of it music to my ears.

"Hold still," I demanded with another smack. With her juices running down my chin, I held her hips and nibbled on her clit.

"Oh, fuck! That feels so good!"

Using the tip of my tongue, I ran it back and forth over the sensitive, swollen pleasure point, giving it a good lashing.

"Oh god… oh… shit…don't stop! I'm gonna…"

And that was my cue. I stuffed two fingers in her pussy, crooking them in a come-hither motion while sucking her clit between my lips and giving it a good tug. Her walls clenched tight around my fingers as her body tensed and she let out a scream. My mouth worked double time to extend her orgasm and wring every bit of pleasure from her body.

When Charli came down from the high, her body sagged, and she collapsed onto my chest with a satisfied smile on her face that made her look as content and dazed as a cat that'd rolled in a field of catnip. "That was fucking incredible, Hunter," she whispered. "I don't think I've ever come that hard."

My name on her lips was a prayer and an answer all in one. "Oh, we're not done yet." I flipped Charli on her back and leaned over her to grab a condom from the nightstand drawer.

She hooked her fingers in my briefs and pulled them down my ass, releasing my rock-hard cock. Her fingers wrapped around my shaft and gave it a long, slow rub from root to tip. A bead of precum glistened on the tip and she greedily lapped it up. Her tongue working its own magic tricks.

My length swelled and pulsed. "Bad girl. Did I give you permission to lick my cock?"

Charli smirked at me and did it again, this time taking the whole head into her mouth and sucking it down her throat.

Pure fucking heaven.

Tingles ran down my spine and my muscles tightened. "Very bad girl." I pulled away to roll the condom on. No way was I coming in her mouth when I'd waited this long to get her in my bed.

"Only in the very best way," she said, reaching for my dick again.

I grabbed her wrists and held them over her head on the pillow. "You're trouble, dollface. Knew it from the first moment I saw you."

"And you're not trouble?" she asked, spreading her legs farther apart.

"Oh, I think we both know that I am." Talking was done. It was time to get to the fucking. I lined myself up with her entrance and slowly pushed in a couple of inches to let her body adjust to mine. Her pussy was so warm and tight it felt like she was made for me. Pure perfection.

Charli's back arched as she bit her lip and moaned. "Don't tease me, Hunter."

"Think you can take all of me?"

"Yes. Please," she gasped. "I need to feel you."

It took every thread of control I had to ease into the warm well of her body instead of impaling her with one strong thrust. She wasn't some random woman I met at the club. I wanted her to enjoy this as much as I did. I felt the need to care for her, to be gentle, to connect on a deeper level. Once fully seated, I stared down into her eyes. "You still good?"

"So good."

Leaning down, I pressed my lips to hers and ran my tongue along the seam. She opened and kissed me deeply as her legs wrapped around my waist. Our fingers twined together, and our hips began to move in the perfect rhythm. With every stroke in and out of her body, I rubbed against her clit, making her moan. "I'm not going to last long if you keep making those sounds."

"We have all night. I'm not going anywhere," she cooed.

Fuck it. I let go of her hands and grabbed the back of her thighs, practically tossing her legs over my shoulders. She let out a gasp when her ass lifted off the mattress, but not a single complaint. I grabbed her hips and pistoned into her body like a man on a mission, sweat dripping down my temple. "Play with your clit. I need you to come again."

Her fingers worked furiously, rubbing in tight, little circles. "I'm... I'm gonna... come!"

Thank god! I couldn't hold back much longer.

Her walls clenched around me, pulsing and squeezing my dick like a vise as she screamed my name. Sparks shot down my spine and my balls pulled tight. With one final thrust, I buried myself deep inside her and came so hard that spots dotted my vision. Wave after wave of ecstasy rolled through me as I pumped my hips to wring out every last drop of cum.

"Holy fuck!" Charli shouted.

Holy fuck, indeed! Completely spent, I slipped out of her and fell to the side, huffing and puffing. Hands down, the best sex I'd ever had, and I'd had a lot of it.

Charli wiped the sweat from my head with the tip of her finger. "You alright there, old man?" she asked with a goofy grin taking up her whole face.

"I'm not old. There's plenty more where that came from."

She wiggled her eyebrows at me. "I'm counting on it."

Chapter 32
Charli

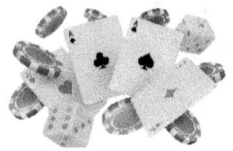

Hunter stood from the bed and walked to the en suite bathroom, giving me a fantastic view of his perfect ass. I lay on the bed staring, completely spent despite the electrical impulses zipping through my limbs. Having sex with him was well worth the wait. I could only compare it to liquid sunshine infiltrating every part of my body—a brilliant, dazzling radiance that made me content and dopey.

"Spread your legs, dollface."

I lifted my head and reached for the washcloth in his hand. "I can do that."

He tugged it away. "I got you dirty, so I'll clean you up. This is me taking care of you."

Reluctantly moving my legs apart, I let him gently wipe up the mess. Though I wouldn't admit it, the warm washcloth felt divine as it soothed my delicate skin. "Thank you."

Hunter tossed the cloth into the bathroom and lay next to me on the bed. "Are you sore? I didn't hurt you, did I?"

His concern was another shot of that sunshine, making me feel cherished and cared for. "A little, but not enough to keep me from doing it again."

He chuckled and kissed me on the head. "You're a greedy little nymph, aren't you?"

I stroked his dick, hoping to bring it back to life. "I'm only greedy because you kept me waiting."

"You can't fault me for trying to do the right thing." He wrapped his hand around mine, helping me pump him up and down. "Staying away from you has been one of the most difficult things I've ever done. I've never been big on making the right decisions. In fact, most of the decisions I've made in my life have been the wrong ones, but I can't say I regret this."

"There's nothing to regret. I had a choice too and I wanted this as much as you."

"Because you're a very bad girl," he said, looking down at our hands that were gripped around his now erect cock. "Look what you did to me."

"Let me show you how bad I can be." I shimmied down the length of his legs to kneel between them. Pushing his hand away, I fisted his manhood with both of mine and licked the pearl of precum from the tip.

"Now who's teasing?"

"Not teasing, just warming up." I ran my tongue up his length, tracing the vein on the underside, then swallowed him one inch at a time until he hit the back of my throat.

Hunter lifted his hips. "Fuck! You look so good on your knees for me with my cock down your throat." He brushed the hair out of my face and held it on top of my head. "Let's see what that sassy mouth can do."

I wasted no time sucking him down with my lips suctioned tight. There was no way I could take all of him, so my head bobbed up and down while my hand stroked the base of his velvety smooth yet iron-hard shaft. My other hand played with his balls, giving them a gentle tug and massaging the soft skin behind them.

He growled so deep I felt the rumble against my throat. "You. Are. Magnificent. Let's see if you can take more of me, shall we?" When I took him as far as I could, Hunter held my head and applied the slightest pressure. "Breathe through your nose and swallow like a good girl."

I gagged and drool dripped down my chin, but I was determined to comply. Swallowing through the uncomfortableness, my throat opened and took him a little deeper.

"Fuck, doll, you're doing great. A little bit more." He increased the pressure on the top of my head, so I had no choice. "Easy…"

I swallowed repeatedly, taking more inches than I thought were possible. His fingers massaged my neck, easing the discomfort.

"Fucking perfect," he growled again with a thrust of his hips, going even deeper. Every possible curse word spewed from his mouth, including some very creative combinations.

Of course, I'd given blow jobs, but I'd never deep-throated a man before. It felt dirty, but also empowering to make a man, who demanded control in everything he did, lose his mind. It satisfied me immensely.

My eyes watered and I gagged repeatedly before he pulled out and held my face in his hands. "You did so good." Using his thumb, he wiped the drool from my chin and kissed my forehead.

"But you didn't come."

"Only because I'm saving myself for your pussy." He reached for another condom and rolled it on, then patted his thighs. "Now, get up here."

I crawled from between his legs to hover above his erect cock, slowly lowering myself onto him while bracing my hands on his defined abs. My body stretched and molded itself to his large size until I was fully seated. I gave myself a moment to adjust before lifting up and sliding back down. "You feel so good inside me."

"Being inside you is my new favorite thing." Hunter rested his hands on my hips. "Play with your nipples for me."

Sliding my hands up my body, I cupped my small breasts. I'd never been embarrassed by their size, but I'd be lying if I said it didn't make me feel insecure. Most men liked big boobs, and I doubted Hunter was any different. Padded bras worked wonders, but here in dark with the lights of the city casting shadows across my skin, there was no hiding their inadequacy. I tried to cover them with my hands, hoping he wouldn't notice how small they actually were.

Hunter grabbed my wrists and pulled them away. "Don't hide from me. I've already seen your tits. It's too late to be shy."

I'd changed clothes in rooms full of other performers. Shyness wasn't the problem. "I'm not shy. It's just that…"

"It's just what?"

"They're not big," I blurted, stating the obvious.

Hunter frowned. "Do you hear me complaining? Your body is beautiful. Anyone who tells you otherwise is full of shit." He sat up and wrapped his arms around me, capturing a nipple between his teeth and giving it a little tug.

Sparks shot through me as I rode the thin line between pleasure and pain. I'd never experienced it before but found I quite liked it. The hum. The zing. The zip that coursed through my body. My head dropped back, and my nails scraped down his spine, scoring his skin and returning a bit of that pain. "Hunter!" He licked and bit and pulled and pinched. I'd never come from someone playing with my breasts but at the rate he was going, it was entirely possible. Every inch of my skin tingled and my pussy throbbed, stuffed full of his cock.

His tongue ran a line across my chest, over my shoulder, up my neck, and to my lips where he devoured my mouth with such a voraciousness that my head spun. I couldn't think. All I could do was feel. The need inside me overwhelmed my senses.

"Ride me, Charli."

I braced my hands on his shoulders and rode him up and down, each stroke rubbing against my clit and bringing me closer to the release I craved. His hands gripped my hips so hard as they lifted me, I was sure I'd have bruises in the morning, but I didn't care. I needed to come.

We weren't gentle with each other. We were wild and untamed, like feral animals mating in the moonlight.

My pussy clenched and my muscles tightened, the tension almost unbearable and building by the second. When I thought I couldn't take any more, Hunter reached between us and rubbed my clit.

That was all it took for me to detonate. Like a rocket lifting off, a firework exploding, a bomb igniting. My body spasmed as liquid fire consumed every part of me and I screamed a litany of profanities. My head swam with pleasure and white lights spotted my vision. All I could hear was the pounding pulse of rushing blood as my head grew lighter.

I was barely aware of Hunter pulling out and flipping me like a rag doll. My knees and chest hit the mattress. He held my hip and fucked me from behind at a furious pace, as one arm wrapped around my waist and his thumb thrummed my clit. "Give me one more, Charli. Come for me!"

"I can't," I moaned, but even as the words left my mouth, I could feel another climax building.

"Yes, you can, dammit!" Not one to be denied, he doubled down his efforts as he savagely took me from behind.

The orgasm hit me hard and fast, an eruption so intense and fierce I lost all sense of space and time. Wave after wave of euphoria consumed me, the high so spectacular I never wanted it to end.

"Fuck, yes! Fuck...fuck... you're squeezing my cock so tight. Fuck! Fuck!" Hunter collapsed over my back and panted in my ear. "So fucking good. My god, you're going to wreck me."

"I think you've already destroyed me. I can barely breathe," I huffed.

Hunter rolled to his back, taking me with him. "Are you okay?"

"Mm-hmm." I snuggled into his side, completely exhausted from the powerful orgasms that racked my body. Darkness settled in and I let it take me as I drifted away into nothingness.

A sliver of light fell across my closed eyes, rousing me from the best night of sleep I'd had in forever. I rolled to my back and stretched my achy muscles, arms reaching above my head and toes pointed down. My body groaned in protest, everything tight and coiled. The sheets were soft against my bare skin, slipping down to my waist as I arched my back.

"Good morning, dollface."

My eyes popped open to find Hunter already dressed and fastening his watch onto his wrist. Acutely aware of my nakedness, I gripped the sheet and pulled it up to my chin. I might have been brave last night, but in the light of day things felt different. Hunter was still my boss, and I was still the nanny. "Good morning."

He sat on the bed next to me. "Sleep well?"

"Immensely. What time is it?" I asked with a yawn.

He chuckled. "It's only seven. You should go back to sleep."

I sat up, holding the sheet to my chest. "No wonder I'm still tired. Why are you up so early?" It wasn't unusual for him to be an early bird, but it was after three before we went to sleep. Or I passed out. I couldn't remember which one it was.

"Things to do. I'm going to get Carina, stop at the office for some paperwork, and pick up breakfast. Any requests?"

As if on cue, my stomach rumbled. Loudly. Heat crept up my neck at the unladylike sound. "Banana pancakes?" I squeaked out. "They have them at that little diner down the street."

He smiled. "Banana pancakes it is."

The conversation was so domestic, and I wondered what it meant. "Are we okay?"

He cocked his head to the side. "I'm okay. Are you?"

"I mean… is this going to be weird? I'm still working for you. I think we crossed some lines."

"Sweetheart, we bulldozed over those lines. There's no going back. Nothing has to change except the fact that were fucking. It's not a problem for me. It's preferred, actually, because I won't have to hide my hard-on every time you're around." He yanked the sheet away from my body, exposing my breasts. "And I told you not to hide from me. I plan on seeing you naked as much as possible."

Still feeling self-conscious, I pulled at the sheet to cover myself, but it was no use. He wasn't letting go.

Hunter leaned over and licked one nipple, then ran his tongue across my chest and licked the other one. "I like your tits. Get over it." Then he kissed me on the forehead. "I'll be back in a couple hours with pancakes."

"Banana pancakes," I corrected.

"Banana pancakes. Now, go back to sleep," he said as he stood from the bed and walked to the door.

"Thank you," I shouted as he left.

"You're welcome. Go back to sleep, Charlotte."

I snuggled back into the pillow with a dopey grin on my face. For as gruff as Hunter could be, he was also incredibly sweet. As I closed my eyes and remembered everything that happened last night, I knew there was no way I was falling back asleep.

For the first time in my life, my reality was better than my dreams.

Chapter 33
Hunter

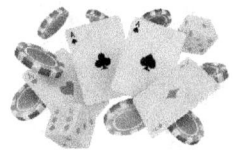

I'd been locked in my home office most of the day, searching for the inconsistencies in Mystique's financial documents. Nothing jumped out at me. Wherever Leonard was hiding money eluded me.

I rubbed my eyes and cracked my neck. The last thing I wanted to be doing was going over spreadsheets, especially when Charlotte was walking around my apartment in tiny shorts and a tank top. I should have been bending her over the couch and giving her a good fucking since she decided to tease me by going braless. My cock strained at my zipper every time I thought about her nipples poking through the thin material of her clothes. The girl was nothing but trouble.

"Think, Hunter. Think. Where is the money going?" I mumbled to myself.

"Knock, knock." Charli appeared in my office doorway with Carina on her hip. "I made meatloaf if you're hungry."

I'd been smelling the goodness coming from the kitchen for the last hour, but I didn't have time to stop. "Can you bring a plate in here?"

She twisted her lips to the side in disapproval. "You've been at it all day. It's time to take a break. Come have dinner with your daughter and I'll help you once I put her down."

I ran a hand over my scruffy chin in frustration. "I wish you could help, but you can't."

"Hunter Dorsey, I may not have gone to college but I'm not stupid. I'll have you know I finished top of my class in high school. I can help."

High school? Jesus Christ. It was a reminder I didn't need about our age difference. Not only was I her boss, but I had eight years on her. "Bring me a plate, Charlotte."

"No. You will take a break. If not to spend time with me, then to spend time with Carina. We'll be waiting in the kitchen." She turned on her heel and walked away with a slight sway of her ass.

Dammit! Just once I wished that woman could do as she was told. She wasn't wrong, but still. It was a dick move to fuck her last night and ignore her today. Plus, Carina deserved better than a dad that put work before his daughter. No matter how busy my father was, he always made time for me. I needed to do the same.

Closing my laptop, I made my way to the kitchen. Carina was in her high chair stuffing puffs into her mouth while Charli plated our dinner. I kissed Carina on the head. "Daddy's sorry he's been busy all day, princess." Then I turned to Charli. "What can I do to help?"

She turned and waved a spoon at me. "Absolutely nothing. Sit with your daughter and I'll bring the food over."

I sat down and grumbled, "And you said I was bossy."

She slid a plate in front of me piled high with meatloaf, mashed potatoes, and green beans. "You are."

It looked delicious and smelled even better. I'd skipped lunch and hadn't realized how hungry I was, but that wasn't the point. "I didn't hear you complaining last night."

Her cheeks turned pink. "That's different."

I lifted an eyebrow at her comment, but kept my mouth shut. Yeah, she liked my bossiness in bed. The way she screamed my name proved it and I couldn't wait to make her prove it again tonight, but right now was about spending time with my daughter. I cut a small piece of meatloaf off with my fork and held it out to Carina.

She opened her mouth and gobbled it up, squealing for more while banging her fists on the tray. My little girl had a ravenous appetite for such a tiny thing. Once Charli moved her to more solid foods, she quit spitting everything out, which I greatly appreciated. Couldn't blame her, most of the jarred food looked and smelled disgusting.

I finally took my own bite of dinner, and it practically melted in my mouth. One thing I could admit was that Charli was a damn good cook. She might have almost set my kitchen on fire, but the food was top notch. "Where'd you learn how to cook?"

She took her own bite and swallowed. "From my mom. My parents are very traditional. She made sure I knew how to cook and clean the house. How to be a good wife."

"I'm guessing she's not too happy you ended up in Vegas."

She let out a self-deprecating laugh. "Not at all. She thought my obsession with acrobatics was a phase. If she had her way, I'd be teaching elementary school with a husband and two kids."

I didn't like the picture she painted of herself with another man. "Yeah, that doesn't sound like you."

"Don't get me wrong, I do want kids of my own, but I'm not ready to quit on my dreams yet. It'd be pretty hard to climb the silks being eight months pregnant." She laughed.

I pictured what she would look like, big and round, carrying my child. It was stupid. I was barely qualified to take care of the child I had, let alone add another one to the mix. "Maybe one day you'll meet a man who will change your mind," I said gruffly.

She set her fork on the edge of her plate. "Hunter Dorsey, are you jealous of my hypothetical husband?"

"Don't be ridiculous. We spent one night fucking. That doesn't mean I want to marry you, or any woman for that matter."

Her face fell. "Of course not. I wasn't implying that."

If I was planning on hurting her, which I wasn't, I'd say I hit the bull's-eye. "I'm sorry." She didn't deserve me reverting back to being an asshole.

"For what? Being honest? I'm a big girl, I can take it. Let's not make a big deal out of nothing. I was teasing. No biggie." Her words said one thing, but her actions told a completely different story. Charli pushed the potatoes around on her plate before she scooped some up and fed them to Carina.

My instincts told me it was better not to press the issue. I'd only dig myself a bigger hole. "Do you still want to help me later?"

"Actually, I'm more tired than I thought. After I clean up the kitchen and give the princess a bath, I'm gonna call it a night. I've got a busy day tomorrow."

I wasn't sure how to deal with this version of her. Usually if I bit her head off, she bit back. Right now, she looked like a puppy who'd been slapped on the nose with a newspaper. "Alright. You want me to help clean up?"

"Nope. I got it. You should get back to your work. I'll do my job and you do yours."

The entire mood of the room changed, and we continued eating in silence. The lump of regret in my stomach had me pushing away my plate. "I'm going back to my office."

Charli carelessly waved her fingers at me in dismissal as she continued to feed my daughter.

Way to fuck things up, Dorsey.

I went back to my office but couldn't concentrate worth shit. Pots and pans banged in the kitchen, a clear sign I'd royally pissed Charli off.

It was better this way, wasn't it? The last thing I needed was her getting attached to me, especially when she planned on leaving anyway.

Last night was mutual. We both got what we wanted. It didn't have to be more than that. Sex was sex. It wasn't personal. It was a means to an end.

If all that was true, why did I feel like a piece of dog shit?

I pushed the feeling aside and focused on my singular goal since returning to Mystique—proving Leonard Moroski was a thief.

After three hours of scouring documents and finding nothing, I gave up. My head wasn't in it.

Nope.

My head was still on the brunette I insulted with my crass words. *Fucking idiot.*

I pushed away from my desk, walked past the kitchen, and headed toward her room. The door was mostly closed, the laugh track of whatever sitcom she watched floating out into the hallway. Like a Peeping Tom, I put my eye to the crack, hoping to get a glance at Charlotte.

She lay on her bed doing some contortionist's move with her leg next to her head. Her shorts stretched tight against her pussy leaving little to the imagination, although I didn't need to imagine shit. I knew what was hiding under her clothes and it made my dick hard. I backed away before she could see me being a creeper and went to check on Carina.

My girl was sound asleep, sucking on her thumb with a stuffed rabbit clenched under her arm. She looked like an angel, but one day, she'd grow into a woman, and some sick pervert would defile her the way I did Charli last night. I scuffed a hand through my hair. If I was protective now, I was going to be a lunatic by the time she turned sixteen. There was no way I would let her date until she turned twenty-one.

Maybe twenty-five.

Hell, thirty sounded reasonable.

I'd move us to the middle of North Dakota if it meant keeping her away from an asshole like me.

There wasn't a single thing I wouldn't do for my daughter. Mama bears had nothing on me.

I ran my fingers through her soft hair and kissed the top of her head. "Don't ever grow up, princess. The world is full of fucking assholes. If one ever tries to break your heart, they'll regret the day they messed with you. I can promise you that."

Going back to the kitchen, I warmed a plate of leftovers and ate them while scrolling through my phone. If I hadn't been such a jerk, Charli would have been here keeping me company. I should have been used to the silence after spending so many years alone, but the only thing worse than the silence was knowing I wasn't alone. That the silence was a choice made by the other person in my home.

I don't even know why I said what I did. I made her sound like a casual fuck when she was more than that. I screwed up. Big time.

Rinsing my plate, I stuck it in the dishwasher and went to my room. After the events of the last few hours, all I wanted was sleep. I brushed my teeth and crawled between the sheets, tossing and turning because all I could think of was her.

The faint aroma of her perfume and the scent of our mixed arousal wrapped around me like a cocoon. It invaded my senses and sent my head spinning. I could practically hear her screaming my name as her pussy squeezed around my cock. I remembered how her body molded to mine and her contented sigh as she snuggled in next to me at the end of the night.

Sleep didn't come.

Instead, I spent the night staring at the ceiling, thinking of how to repair the damage I'd done. How I could put the smile back on her face. Because if I didn't... someone else would.

And that? I'd be damned if I let that happen.

Chapter 34
Charli

When I woke, Hunter was already gone for work. No good morning, no coffee together. No silly quips to start our day.

It was as if Saturday night never happened.

I got Carina up and ready for our walk. She was such a happy baby, babbling and blowing spit bubbles. I cooed at her while I put the flowered dress over her head and pulled the matching bloomers up her chubby legs. "Your daddy is a complete jerk face, you know that? Yep. I would have thought things were changing between us moving forward. Instead, I feel like we've taken ten steps backward."

She couldn't understand a thing I said, but it felt cathartic to tell someone. I couldn't very well talk to my brother about it for fear he'd immediately start hacking Hunter's life. Not that I would tell my mother the dirty details, but she didn't need an excuse to beg me to come home. Gia and Penny? We weren't really friends, more like acquaintances. I barely knew them. And Jasmine? She'd definitely have an opinion, although I wasn't sure I wanted to know what it was.

It was sad to think that in the two years I lived in Vegas I'd hardly made any friends at all. Perhaps that's what happened when you put all your time into your job. You ended up lonely and alone.

I picked up Carina and bounced her on my hip. "Good thing I have you, baby girl. You're a good listener and you keep your opinions to yourself."

I decided to start our day by walking down to the corner diner where Hunter bought our breakfast. Yesterday we were sharing banana pancakes and today we were pretending like each other didn't exist. If I'd known a joking comment about being jealous was going to elicit his reaction, I would have kept my mouth shut.

The more I thought about it, the more I stewed. How dare he speak to me that way? I never asked him for marriage. I never even asked him for a relationship. All I asked for was some respect, which I definitely didn't get. I wasn't some floozy he picked up off the street.

It was my mistake to think he actually cared about me. I lived there. I was convenient.

He didn't care.

I thought it would be hard to leave this job when it was over, but it was getting easier by the minute. Of course, I'd miss Carina, but Hunter could go fuck himself for all I cared. It would be strictly business from now on. I was hired to be the nanny and that's it. There would be no more home-cooked meals or travel mugs with fresh coffee or neatly folded clothes on his bed or any of the other dozen things I did to be nice.

Nice was done.

If he had no intention of ever getting married, then it was high time I quit playing wife to him.

My mind was made up by the time the bell above the door jangled when we entered the diner. The place was busy for a Monday morning, but I found us a table in the corner where the stroller wouldn't be in the way. I ordered scrambled eggs for Carina and a full country breakfast for myself, with bacon, pancakes, an omelet, and toast. Being mad made me hungry and I was starving, especially since I did little more than push my

242

food around the plate last night. It pissed me off that my meal was ruined by Hunter's assholeness.

As we waited for our food, a familiar face walked in. I felt bad about canceling my date with Ben, but maybe he'd be up for still going out sometime. It was obvious that Hunter and I wouldn't be dating. In hindsight, it was stupid of me to cancel my plans with a nice guy for someone who saw me as little more than the hired help.

I waved my arm at Ben and shouted his name. He raised his hand in acknowledgment and came over to our table. "Hey, Ben. I'm sorry I never got back with you. Things have been really hectic with this little one. How have you been?"

His eyebrows knitted together. "I've been better, Charli. I see you're still doing the nanny thing." His voice held none of the friendliness it did a few weeks ago.

I guessed he was mad about me canceling. "Yes, she's a doll. Do you want to join us for breakfast?"

He shook his head. "I don't think that's a very good idea."

Definitely still mad. "Oh, come on. What could it hurt? I thought maybe we could reschedule that date."

Ben blew out a frustrated breath. "Are you for real right now?"

Okay, maybe more than mad. That was not the reaction I expected. "I'm sorry I had to cancel on you."

"That's not it, Charli. I was fine with rescheduling. You really don't have a clue, do you?"

It was my turn to shake my head. "I don't understand."

"Your boss"—his nose flared—"got me fired."

"Fired? For what?"

"Inappropriate behavior with a customer."

My eyes went wide. "What?"

"That's right. Apparently, me asking you out crossed the lines of appropriate workplace behavior. No offense, but I recently started a new job, and I don't need your boss fucking it up for me. So, forgive me if I don't take you up on that rain check."

"I'm so sorry, Ben. I had no idea." My apology was completely inadequate. "He had no right to do that to you."

"Yeah, well, he did it. I'm trying to move forward. Have a nice life, Charli." He turned and left the diner without even eating. The man couldn't get away from me fast enough.

I fumed. Talk about crossing lines… Hunter crossed a huge one. Not only did he make me feel like shit last night, but he ruined my chance to go out with an actual good guy. He might as well have pissed on me like a territorial dog.

If things had worked out with Hunter, I never would have called Ben anyway, but that wasn't the point. He got Ben fired *before* we slept together. Hunter's whole plan from the beginning was to keep me for himself. For what? To control me?

Screw that!

Pulling out my phone, I began typing furiously.

Me: You got Ben fired?

I stared at the screen and waited for his reply, tapping my fingers on the table impatiently. He could have been in a meeting or knee-deep in his beloved spreadsheets, but it annoyed me that a response didn't come.

Our breakfast arrived and I tried to enjoy my time with Carina, but my mind wouldn't stop turning over the conversation with Ben. Mad didn't even describe my feelings. Furious? Horrified? Embarrassed?

Yep, yep, and yep.

When Carina and I finished our breakfast, I whipped out Hunter's credit card to pay the bill. It was a small act of defiance, and he probably wouldn't even care, but it gave me some satisfaction. Twenty bucks was nothing to him, but if I wanted to move back out on my own every dollar counted.

We went from the diner to the park and Carina waved her arms in delight when she saw our feathered friends waddling about. Seemed the ducks recognized us too because they headed in our direction in search of food. I grabbed the bag of stale bread from under the stroller and threw it to the birds, who gobbled it up.

Across the pond, I saw Ginny walking with Teddy. I quickly threw the rest of the bread on the ground and headed toward the apartment. My last interaction with her was weird and intrusive. I thought she had the potential to be a friend, but something was seriously off with that woman. I couldn't put my finger on it, but something was definitely odd.

My day kept getting worse. I planned on working out to rid myself of the pent-up frustration but there was a sign in the lobby noting the gym was closed for maintenance.

And I still hadn't heard from Hunter. He'd read my message but didn't bother replying to it.

I started wondering if the money was worth the aggravation of this job.

Nannies were a dime a dozen. I could easily be replaced.

While Carina napped, I looked for an apartment. With the money I saved, there had to be something I could afford.

The way I saw it, the sooner Hunter and I went our separate ways, the better.

Chapter 35
Hunter

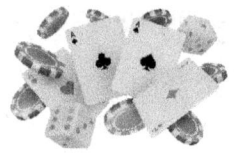

When I walked in the door from work, Charli was already feeding Carina her dinner. From the lack of aroma in the air, it was obvious she hadn't cooked. I couldn't really blame her after what happened last night.

I set my briefcase on the kitchen island and kissed Carina on the head. "Hello, princess. Did you have a good day with Charli?"

Carina reached for my face and patted my cheeks. I never thought such a little gesture would mean so much, but warmth spread through my chest at the feeling of her chubby hands on my skin.

"And how was your day?" I asked Charli.

The look on her face told me her pisstivity level hadn't subsided any. She crossed her arms and scowled at me. "Did you get Ben fired?"

I'd seen her text but conveniently ignored it all day. I leaned against the counter and crossed my ankles. "He wasn't good enough for you."

She stomped her foot like a child. "That wasn't your decision to make. Getting him fired was selfish. I know you have beaucoup bucks, but for us normal people a job is everything. You can't mess with someone's

246

livelihood like that. Not to mention he's a good guy. Acting like a jealous prick makes you an even bigger asshole."

As fierce as she tried to be, I found her rant amusing. "You about done?"

"Not even close." She poked me in the chest. "I may work for you, but you don't get to control my life. You crossed a line. A big one!"

"I'm not going to apologize for looking out for your best interest."

"MY best interest? You've got to be kidding me!"

"Yes, your best interest. What did you even know about him? Did you know he had a sexual assault charge against him last year?" Her jaw dropped. "So, yes, although you might not approve, it was in your best interest. You're welcome." When I found out that little nugget of information, I had zero guilt about my actions.

"But... but... he... shit." Her shoulders sagged. She couldn't come up with a single retort. "He seemed so nice. How could my radar have been so off?"

"Because that's what sexual predators do. They come off as nice guys and lure you into feeling safe. Ever heard of Ted Bundy? Perfect example."

"That's a bit extreme. Ben isn't a murderer," Charli said, rolling her eyes.

"I wasn't willing to take that chance with you."

She crossed her arms tighter and doubled down on her anger, not willing to concede. "I'm still mad at you. I know we're *just fucking*, as you so eloquently put it, but you acted like a total ass face last night. It was completely rude and uncalled for."

I chuckled. "So I've graduated from jerk face to ass face?"

"Like I said before, if the face fits."

Even mad, she was adorable. I held out my arms to her and she reluctantly walked into them. I held her tight and rested my chin on her head. "I'm sorry about last night. You're right, it was rude and uncalled for. I'm not good at relationships of any kind, so I freaked out. I'm sorry. It's more than *just fucking*."

She looked up at me with her big blue eyes. "I don't want to fight with you."

"I don't want to fight with you either. I really am sorry. Can you forgive me?" Charli was the one good thing in my life besides Carina. I didn't know where it would go, but I wanted to find out.

"You're forgiven. For now. Pull that shit again and it'll be a different story."

"Understood."

"Are you hungry? I can heat up some of last night's meatloaf for you." She moved to the fridge and began pulling containers out. "Also, I need to go to the training facility tonight. I can take Carina with me if you can't watch her.

I took the containers from her hands and set them on the counter. "You don't need to go to the training center tonight."

She began to puff up again. "Yes, Hunter, I do. It's bad enough that the gym was closed today, and I didn't get to work out, but I've got to get more practice in. This isn't negotiable."

I picked up Carina from her high chair and walked to the door. "Come on. I want to show you something."

Charli squinted her eyes at me. "What are you up to?"

"Come on." I motioned with my head for her to follow. "For once, be a good girl and do as you're told."

"You're not the boss of me." She scowled but followed anyway.

Putting my hand on the small of her back, I led her to the elevator. "Technically, I am."

When the doors opened, she stepped inside. "Professionally, not personally."

I smirked at her and hit the button for the athletic center. "We'll see."

The whole way down, Charli eyed me suspiciously. I could practically see the gears turning in her head as she tried to figure out what was going on.

Once the doors opened, I led us to the gym and handed Carina to Charli. "Close your eyes."

"Why?"

"For fuck's sake, woman, close your eyes, or I'll have to blindfold you with my tie."

"Kinky, but not in front of the baby," she said with a huge grin.

I lifted her chin. "That sassy mouth of yours is going to be the death of me. Now close them." When her eyes were firmly shut, I opened the door and guided her inside. "Keep them closed."

"I am." She laughed.

I turned on the lights and took Carina from her arms. "Okay, you can open your eyes."

The look on her face was worth every penny I spent and every string I pulled to make this happen. "Oh, my god! What is this?" Her hands came up to cover her face and a single tear ran down her cheek.

"What does it look like?"

She tentatively walked toward the equipment hanging from the ceiling and ran her fingers through the long silks. "It looks like a dream." Charli pulled herself into the hanging hoop and sat on the edge, causing it to spin without any effort at all.

"It's your own personal training center." I kicked the thick industrial mat beneath the equipment. "Complete with safety precautions, god forbid you need them. And when you're done for the day, everything ties up off to the side." I pointed to the rope that would pull the equipment out of the way for the other tenants.

"You did all this for me? Why? It's too much." She wiped at the tears that kept falling down her cheek.

"See that's the thing. It's not too much. You have no idea how much I appreciate everything you've done for us." I held up Carina's hand. "You've made our lives so much better. You deserve the world, but for now, you'll have to settle for this. I care about you, Charli, and I want you to chase your dreams."

She flew off the ring and launched herself at Carina and me, wrapping us in her arms. "I love it so much. I don't know how to thank you."

"You can thank me by showing me what you do. I want to see you in action."

She nodded her head furiously. "I'm so excited."

"Do your thing, dollface."

Charli kicked off her shoes and grabbed hold of the silks to pull herself up, hooking her feet into the fabric and effortlessly ascending. With every twist and twirl, she defied gravity in her show of strength and elegance. She wrapped herself in the silks, the fabric clinging to her like a second skin, accentuating every curve and muscle. I was hypnotized as she spun and stretched her body, with only the support of some flimsy material to hold her weight when she let go.

Nothing had ever been so beautiful as watching Charli in her element—the sheer joy and determination painted across her face.

Every maneuver spellbound me.

Amazed me.

Tantalized me.

Made me fucking hard.

Then a rush of adrenaline raced through my veins as she recklessly unraveled, falling toward the floor at an astonishing rate. My heart stuck in my throat, and I only caught my breath when she dangled from the fabric by her ankles. Damn near put me into cardiac arrest.

The woman was as crazy as they came.

Bold.

Fierce.

Fearless.

This was her passion, and I knew when it was time for her to leave, I had to let her go.

I wouldn't be the one to hold her back.

For the first time in my life, I would be selfless instead of selfish.

I just wasn't ready for her to go yet.

Chapter 36
Charli

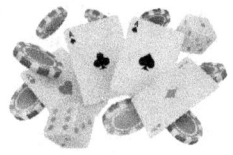

It'd been two weeks since Hunter apologized. Two weeks since I'd slept in my own bed. Two weeks of passionate nights and blissful mornings.

Life was good.

I rode the elevator up to the Mystique offices, then pushed the stroller into the reception area and asked for directions to Hunter's office. Making my way through the maze of hallways, I stopped to see my brother first.

"Hey, you."

He looked up from his computer and smiled. "Hey, Charli. What are you two doing here?" He made a googly face at Carina and patted her on the head like a dog.

"Bringing our favorite men some lunch." I held up a paper bag and jiggled it in front of his face.

Tom groaned and snatched the bag from my hand. "Men? Please tell me that doesn't include Hunter."

"Don't be like that. We may have had a rough start, but things are going really well."

"Professionally or personally?"

"Both actually," I said with a smile. "And I've been training like crazy, so I'll be able to return to Oasis soon." A little deflection never hurt.

"Nothing would make me happier. How's your leg?"

I gave it a tap. "Good as new. No soreness or lingering pain. Don't even need a brace. I guess the doctor was right, I am a quick healer."

"So you'll be quitting the nanny job and getting your own apartment soon?"

Subtlety was not my brother's forte. "I'm not sure what I'll be doing. We'll cross that bridge when we get there." I didn't want to make any assumptions that Hunter would want me to stay. It was a conversation we needed to have, but I wasn't in any hurry. The last thing I wanted to do was freak him out again.

"Charli?" my brother growled.

"Nothing is set in stone, so cool your jets. Relax and enjoy your chicken salad."

His face perked up. "Homemade?"

"Mom's recipe," I confirmed.

He opened the bag and pulled out the sandwich, taking a larger-than-socially-acceptable bite. His eyes closed as he chewed. "Holy cow! This is why you're my favorite sister."

"I'm your only sister."

"Yes, but it's still a true statement." He polished off the sandwich in record time, then wadded up the bag and tossed it in the trash. "I'll take you to see Hunter." Carina and I followed him down a long hallway, around a corner and down another hallway. I peeked into the open offices, impressed with their size and elegance. Mystique didn't cut corners, that was for sure. "Here we are," Tom said, waving his arm toward the door at the end.

I gave him a hug and proceeded to Hunter's office, knocking on the closed door.

"Come in," he said gruffly.

Hoping he wouldn't be mad I was disturbing him at work, I twisted the knob and poked my head in. "Surprise."

His office wasn't anything like I imagined. It was small. *Really* small. A large desk was crammed inside, with two plastic chairs in front of it. His bathroom at home was bigger than this room.

"Hey." He climbed out from behind the desk and squeezed by it to greet me with a hug. "This *is* a surprise. What brings my girls by?"

My heart fluttered in my chest. When he said *my girls*, it made me feel as if Carina and I were a package deal. Like he wanted to keep me. Like I belonged to him.

I looked around his office, taking it all in—the peeling paint, the noticeable crack in the wall, and the stain on the carpet that looked as if a box of pens exploded. Honestly, it was disappointing. I thought for sure Hunter's office would be huge. This one lacked all of the opulence of the others I passed in the hallway. "Did you draw the short straw or something?"

He looked back over his shoulder at the space. "This is all Trent. My punishment for humiliating him. He's teaching me a lesson. I'm making it work, trying to be a team player, but I will get my old office back once I prove Moroski is a thief."

"How's that going?" I whispered.

"Not great." He stepped out into the hallway and closed the door behind him. "Let's go into the conference room, where there's more space." He picked up Carina and placed a kiss on both our foreheads. My heart fluttered again from the sweetness of it.

"I hope you didn't eat yet; I brought you lunch," I said, pulling out the bag with his sandwich in it.

"Thank you. I'm starving."

"Hunter!" A middle-aged, balding man huffed down the hallway in our direction. "I'm waiting on the payroll. You don't have time to fraternize. This is a place of business, not a day care."

WTF? Seriously, what the fuck? "Who is that guy?"

Hunter straightened to his full height and his eyes turned to ice. "Well, Leonard, if you looked at your inbox, you'd see payroll was completed

253

two hours ago. And this"—his arm tightened around Carina—"is my daughter. The granddaughter of your boss."

Leonard waved his arm in the air. "This is completely inappropriate!"

Hunter's jaw ticced. I shrunk into myself as much as I could, trying to disappear completely. It was dangerous to get between him and his daughter. He handed Carina to me and met Leonard head-on. "What's inappropriate is you! I know you're new here, but Mystique is and always has been a family business. It's family above anything and *everyone* else. So if you have a problem with my daughter being here, then I suggest you speak to my father!" His voice echoed off the walls and I swear I felt the vibrations in my bones.

Leonard didn't have to go to Hunter's dad because every person on the floor was standing in the hallway, observing the shit show. *The* Mr. Dorsey pushed through the crowd. "What's going on here?" He looked between Hunter and Leonard, who shot daggers at each other, neither of them backing down.

"Children don't belong in the workplace and neither does she," Leonard spewed as he pointed at me.

Hunter took another step forward, getting in Leonard's face. "*She* is my girlfriend and my daughter's caretaker. Charli is family, unlike you, you piece of—"

I hugged Carina against my chest. "I'm sorry. I shouldn't have come here. I didn't mean to cause a problem."

Mr. Dorsey took Carina from me and bounced her on his hip. "Having my granddaughter here is never a problem, Charli. You're always welcome." He kissed Carina all over her chubby face and handed her back to me. "Leonard, in my office now!"

"But…"

"My office!" He stomped away and Leonard reluctantly followed behind. I jumped when the door slammed.

"I'm so sorry…"

Hunter put a finger to my lips. "You have nothing to apologize for. That guy has had a hard-on for me since the moment I came back."

Trent came down the hall, slow clapping theatrically. "Finally put that surliness to good use. That guy is a total douchebag." He stopped in front of us and stuck his hands in his pockets. "How are you, Charli?"

"How the fuck do you think she is?" Hunter snapped.

"Right." He waggled a finger at Hunter and me. "Now, this is interesting. I like it."

With all the commotion, it hadn't even registered that Hunter called me his girlfriend. If I wasn't still shaking, I would have been preening at his public declaration. Seemed our *something* had progressed.

Employees lingered in the hall, staring at me and whispering. Hunter gave them a death glare. "Show is over, people. Nothing to see here." Everyone scurried back into their offices.

Trent followed us into the conference room. "The girls are excited Carina is here. I'll tell them to give you fifteen minutes before they bombard you."

I set Carina back into her stroller and opened the paper bag, taking out the sandwich and placing it in front of Hunter. "I made chicken salad."

Trent clicked his tongue. "You made him lunch? How cute." Then he pouted, turning his lips down dramatically. "Where's mine?"

"I... umm..."

Hunter pushed him out of the room. "Have your wife make your lunch." He closed the door and leaned against it. "Finally, a moment of peace."

I laughed. "Is it always so crazy around here?"

He shrugged his shoulder and sat at the table. "Usually it's boring as fuck." Unwrapping the sandwich, he picked it up and took a bite. His eyes rolled back as he chewed. "Oh my god, this is so good."

I reached into the bag and pulled out an apple, brownie, and bag of barbeque chips and set them neatly on the napkin I remembered to pack. Then, I sprinkled some puffs on the tray of the stroller to keep Carina busy. She promptly picked up a handful and shoved them in her mouth. "So that's Leonard, huh?"

"That's Leonard," he said between bites, pushing the bit of chicken salad on his lip into his mouth with his thumb. "Total dickbag."

255

"Why does he hate you so much?"

"He's threatened by me. Knows I'm here to take his job, therefore he treats me like an enormous pile of donkey shit."

"What does your dad say about it?"

Hunter scratched his chin. "I think, in the beginning, he thought it was all me and got a bit of satisfaction out of seeing me struggle, but that"— he swept his arm toward the door—"should be proof enough."

"You mean besides the tainted coffee and the strippers?"

"Hush now." He cupped a hand over my mouth. "We don't talk about such things."

I giggled behind his hand. "Alright, alright, alright,"

A knock sounded at the door and Tom's face flashed in the window. I motioned for him to come in. He opened the door and poked his head inside. "I wanted to make sure you were okay. That was brutal."

Hunter plastered on the biggest fake smile I'd ever seen. "I'm fine. Thanks for asking."

Tom sighed and opened the door farther, squinting his eyes at Hunter. "Not you. My sister."

"I'm okay." Even though I was still a bit shaken, Hunter's antics made me laugh.

My brother stared at me, probably trying to figure out if I was telling the truth or not. "You're sure?"

"I'm sure."

He nodded and scanned the table where Hunter's lunch was laid out. "Wait! He got a brownie and chips? I only got a sandwich."

"Boyfriend privileges," Hunter said with a smirk as he unwrapped the brownie and took a bite.

Tom scowled at him, then leaned across me and grabbed the chips. "I'm taking these. Later, Charlotte."

I waved goodbye to his back as he left. "Later, big brother!"

"I think he's really starting to like me," Hunter said sarcastically.

"Maybe you should hold off on the matching shirts just to be safe."

Chapter 37
Hunter

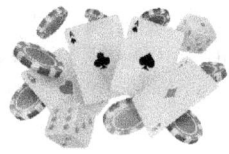

Charli made chicken piccata for dinner. I'd never eaten so well in my life, and to be truthful, my pants were getting a little tight in the waist. She spoiled me, and I didn't know how I'd go back to living alone when she left. Not completely alone, of course. Carina and I would have each other, but the void in our lives would be hard to fill.

While she did the dishes, I gave my daughter a bath. Since removing the squash from her diet, thank fuck, she didn't have any more bath-time blowouts.

It was amazing how much Carina had grown. She was still all squish and dimpled legs, but she splashed more in the water and had taken to shoving every bath toy into her mouth, her favorite being the frog.

Even though I washed and disinfected the toys after every bath, I worried about the germs she was putting into her body. But from every article I read, it seemed stuffing everything into her mouth was actually good for her immune system. So, although it grossed me out, I let her do it. Charli said I was overprotective. I preferred to think of myself as cautious.

Her preoccupation with the frog did make bath time easier though. Or maybe I was getting better at it. Probably a little of both.

When she was all clean, I lifted her from the tub and wrapped her in a clean towel and gently patted her dry. She laughed and twisted, making it difficult to get her diaper and pajamas on. "You are a squirmy little worm, princess," I said, tickling her tummy.

She grabbed my finger and shoved it in her mouth, like she'd done a million times. She sucked and slobbered all over my hand, drool running down the side of it. I didn't even want to think about the *great* germs she was getting.

Something sharp poked my finger and I pulled it away. I inspected my finger and sure enough, there was a tiny indent on it. Feeling around inside her mouth, there was a sharp spot on the bottom. I squeezed her cheeks, forcing her mouth open, and peered inside. There was the tiniest tip of white sticking out of her gums.

"Charli! Come here! Quick!"

Footsteps pounded down the hall and she came racing into the nursery. "What's wrong?"

"Carina's got her first tooth."

"Are you sure?" she asked, crouching down to get a better look.

I squeezed Carina's cheeks and tapped my finger on her bottom gums. "Right there."

"She sure does. Hold on, let me get my phone. We need to document this." Charli returned with her phone and took several pictures of my daughter's first tooth, her smile wide as she showed them to me. "I'll text these to you."

"Is it weird that I feel incredibly proud right now?" I asked, puffing out my chest.

"You didn't actually grow the tooth, so it's a little weird, but considering you're a first-time dad, it's cute."

Carina yawned and rubbed her eyes. "Somebody's getting sleepy."

"I can put her to bed." Charli reached out her arms.

"I'll do it." Charli did so much for us, and it was time I stepped up my game. Soon enough, she'd be gone and I tried not to think about all the other firsts she would miss.

"You're working too much." Charli walked in wearing the tiniest shorts and a tight tank top. It was distracting enough that her perky nipples poked through the shirt, but if she bent over, her ass cheeks would be on full display too. She set the cup of coffee on my desk among the piles of spreadsheets.

"It's here. Somewhere. I know it. I've been going over everything for weeks and it's all starting to look the same. My eyes are fried." I scrubbed a hand over my face.

She leaned her butt on my desk and crossed her arms. "I told you I would help. I'm not sure what I'm looking for, but maybe you need a fresh set of eyes."

"That's the problem… I don't know what I'm looking for either. I was sure something would jump out at me, but it hasn't."

"Then let me help."

Resigned to the fact that I needed help, I handed over the stack of papers Gia gave me from the fundraiser and the documents I copied from Leonard's computer. I'd been so consumed with other financial data; I hadn't gotten a chance to look at the fundraiser yet. "Compare these two sets of documents. Gia's convinced something is off."

Charli gave me a salute. "Aye, aye, captain."

"Ummm… here, let me clear off part of my desk," I said, starting to rearrange the papers that covered the surface.

"No need. I can work right here." She plopped down on the oriental rug and spread her legs, putting the papers between them.

"Your back is going to kill you."

"Don't worry about me. I prefer to be on the floor where I can spread out." She leafed through the papers, making organized stacks on the rug. "I need some sticky notes and a pen."

I tossed her the requested supplies, and she got right to work. I watched as she started entering numbers into her calculator and writing notes, sticking them to the stacks of papers. "What are you doing?"

She scrunched up her shoulder. "Some preliminary calculations to make sure the formulas are right. I was really good at math. Never really liked it, but I got straight A's."

Jesus Christ! I must have been desperate to let her help, but there wasn't anything she could do to make it worse.

The pages and pages of numbers blurred in front of my eyes. If Leonard was on the up-and-up, I'd never live it down. Play stupid games, win stupid prizes. Outright calling Leonard a thief might have been the stupidest game I'd played yet.

I needed my job back.

My position as CFO at Mystique.

My cushy office.

My self-respect.

I'd lost all of it over a stupid grudge against Trent.

The need to one-up him.

The need to be right.

The need to feel superior for once in my life.

All of it turned to shit because of my big fucking ego.

They wanted to humble me? Mission accomplished.

But I was nothing if not determined.

Charli and I worked in silence. Her nails continually clicking on the calculator was somewhat distracting, but not nearly as distracting as the tiny outfit she wore or the light scent of floral perfume that filled my office.

I couldn't help but watch her. The way her long legs flexed, showing off defined muscles, and her ass cheeks peeking out as she leaned over, stretching in a way my body never could. She pulled back her long hair and twisted it up on top of her head, showing off the column of her neck.

When she reached up, stretching her arms above her head and pushing her chest out, my sanity snapped.

My dick was so hard it hurt.

"Come here," I growled.

She looked up at me and blinked. "What?"

"Come here." She went to push to her feet, but I stopped her. "On your knees. Crawl."

Charli's lips formed an *O* as she registered what I was saying. Without a word, she crawled toward me like a cat stalking its prey, her ass swaying back and forth.

I pushed my chair back and spread my legs. She stopped between them and kneeled. "Arms up." Without arguing, she lifted her arms toward the ceiling. I grabbed the hem of her tank, lifting it up and over her head, and tossing it to the side. My thumbs ran over her taut nipples and a visible shiver ran down her back. "I love your fucking tits, and I love seeing you on your knees for me." I put her hand on the bulge in my pants. "Look what you do to me."

Charli's tongue darted out and licked her bottom lip. "I can help with that."

"Can you now?"

"Uh-huh." She deftly undid my pants and reached inside my boxers, pulling my cock out. She stroked me from root to tip until a bead of precum formed. "How does that feel?"

"It'd feel better with your mouth wrapped around it. Suck my cock, dollface."

She wasted no time stuffing as much of me into her mouth as she could, her hands making up for the rest. I leaned back and watched her work me over like a porn star. Applying the slightest pressure to her head, she took me deeper and gagged, the pulsing of her throat nearly making me come.

I pulled her head back with one hand and swiped everything on my desk to the side with the other. Making her stand, I pulled her shorts and panties off in one fluid motion, then I perched her ass on the desk. I lifted one leg and set her foot onto the edge and then did the same to the other, so she was completely exposed. "God, you're fucking beautiful. Look at that pretty pussy all pink and wet for me."

She leaned back on her hands and lifted her hips. "It's all yours."

Not able to resist a second longer, I dove between her thighs and ate her pussy with one solitary goal: to make her come all over my face.

Chapter 38
Charli

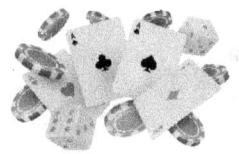

Oh my god!

The way Hunter worked my body was divine. His mouth did delicious things to me, licking and laving and nipping. Every time an orgasm crested, he backed off and let it subside, then dove in again.

By the fourth time, I was ready to take care of the issue myself. My hand crept toward my clit, and he swatted it away. "Please, Hunter! I can't take it anymore!"

He looked up at me from between my legs, his chin shiny from my arousal. "You can and you will."

I fell to my back and threw an arm over my eyes. It was sweet torture.

He stuck two fingers inside me, working them in and out, then added a third. My body stretched to accommodate the sweet intrusion. His fingertips tapped on that secret spot inside me only he'd been able to find and gave my clit a long, hard suck. My pussy clenched around his fingers, and everything tingled. I rode a razor-thin edge between pleasure and pain, heaven and hell, frustration and bliss.

Higher and higher I climbed, every muscle in my body coiled tight. With one last flick of his tongue, I exploded. A beautiful array of colors burst behind my eyelids, like confetti being shot from a cannon. My back arched and my hips lifted from the desk, my pussy pulsing. Wave after wave of euphoria flowed through my veins, little prickles of electricity zapping every neuron. My head thrashed back and forth, and a scream ripped from my throat.

Then Hunter was on top of me, filling me with his cock. "Please tell me you're on birth control."

"Yes, yes! Fuck me, please fuck me!" I couldn't wait. I needed him now. Needed him to fill me up.

Hunter pounded into me furiously. I wrapped my legs around his waist and held on for dear life. It didn't take long to feel him swell inside me and fill me with his warmth. Buried to the hilt inside me, he pushed my hair back and stared into my eyes. "Charli…"

"I know." Maybe it was love, maybe it was lust. We didn't need words to define it. We felt it. Saying it aloud would only complicate it.

I loved this feeling and wanted it to last for as long as he was willing to have me.

And maybe I was falling in love with him too.

The next night, snuggled into Hunter's side with his arm wrapped around me, a distant wail filtered into the bedroom. Someone was either wet or hungry.

I scooted out from beneath Hunter's arm and walked bleary-eyed to the nursery. Hunter and I worked again tonight and then he fucked me until my bones turned to Jell-O. I was exhausted but happy. Deliriously happy.

As I entered Carina's room, her wails got louder. "It's okay, baby girl." I picked her up and cradled her to my chest, rocking her back and forth. She continued to cry, huge sobs and tears running down her cheeks.

I set her on the changing table and checked her diaper. Dry as a bone.

She had to be hungry. I warmed a bottle and tried to give it to her, but she kept pushing it away with her little hands.

I sat in the rocker and talked to her, hoping the motion and my voice would soothe her. "I don't know what's wrong with you, honey. Do you not feel good?" Maybe she had an upset tummy, and a good burp or fart would do the trick. I put her on my shoulder and patted her back. When that didn't help, I got worried something else was wrong. I put my hand on her forehead. "Oh no!" She was way too hot. God, I was so stupid. I should have done that first.

Hurrying down the hallway with Carina in my arms, I shook Hunter awake. "Hunter, get up!"

He rolled over and looked at us through slitted eyelids. "What's wrong?"

"Carina's burning up. I think we need to take her to the hospital."

He shot out of bed like someone lit him on fire. "Shit!" He quickly pulled on some sweatpants and a T-shirt. "Where are my keys and wallet?" he asked, patting his empty pockets.

Carina wailed again and rubbed her ears with her fists. "Hold her while I get dressed."

Back in my room, I threw on the first thing I saw and slipped into my flip-flops. I didn't really care what I looked like. Grabbing the diaper bag and my purse, I met Hunter back in the kitchen.

He already had Carina strapped in the carrier and was talking to her. "It's alright, princess. Shhh. I know you don't feel good but Daddy's gonna get you all better."

I sat in the back with Carina, trying to calm her, while Hunter drove. It was probably better for me that I wasn't in the front. His careful driving ceased to exist as he barreled down the road at excessive speeds and made questionable stops. "Slow down, Hunter! It's not going to be helpful if you get us in an accident."

"I know, I know. It's just that—"

"You're worried. I get it, but please slow down."

If I thought Hunter was overprotective before, it paled in comparison to a daddy in distress. We pulled into the parking lot, and Hunter took Carina in while I parked the car. Of course, even in the middle of the night, the closest spot wasn't close at all. My flip-flops flapped loudly as I speed-walked across the lot.

The emergency room was complete chaos. A group of about fifteen people took up half the waiting room, crying and hugging each other. A man in the corner threw up into a garbage can while his girlfriend rubbed his back. A bleary-eyed mom tried to wrangle her three children who decided they weren't tired at all and played chase around the chairs. An elderly man with a cut on his head sat in the other corner, his wife continually dabbing it with a towel.

And in the center of it all was Hunter arguing with the receptionist. "I'm not sure you're understanding me! My daughter has a fever. I need to see a doctor immediately."

The woman waved her arm at the chaos. "So does every other patient here. We'll call you when it's your turn."

"How long will that be?"

"As long as it takes." She passed him a clipboard with forms to fill out.

"That's completely unacceptable! She's a baby!"

The receptionist sighed. "Mr. Dorsey, I understand your frustration, but yelling at me isn't going to get you in any faster. We're doing the best we can. We're two doctors and a nurse short tonight. Please have a seat."

"Come on, Papa Bear," I said as I took Hunter by the arm and led him to some empty chairs, mouthing *I'm sorry* to the woman.

"This is bullshit! Can't they see my daughter is sick? I'll pay extra to get her in before these other people."

"Careful, your entitlement is showing," I said as I took Carina out of the carrier and rocked her in my arms. She was still fussing, but the sobs had stopped.

Hunter leveled me with a glare. "Do I look like I care?"

266

"No, but you should. No one wants to be here in the middle of the night, yet everyone is here for a reason. Try to relax and fill out the paperwork."

"Relax, my ass," he grumped, scribbling furiously on the forms.

Three hours later, we walked out of the hospital with antibiotics and a much calmer baby. The culprit of Carina's fussing: an ear infection.

Although Hunter's protectiveness was over the top, there were no lengths he wouldn't go to for his daughter and that was admirable. The way he defended me to Leonard proved I was under his protection too.

I hadn't asked for it or expected it, but I liked it.

Chapter 39
Hunter

Carina slept on the bed between Charli and me when we got home from the hospital. Her fever broke and this morning she was much more content. I wanted to stay home from work, but Charli convinced me she had it under control and there was nothing I could do that she wouldn't already be doing.

Because of our late night, I didn't get in to work until eleven. Leonard gave me a dirty look even though I'd sent him a courtesy email I certainly didn't owe him. I went right to my dad's office and plopped into the chair opposite his desk. "Sorry I'm late."

"No apologies necessary. I remember those days, staying up all night with a sick child. I could run a billion dollar empire, but I couldn't help my own kid. Rose was always so calm, and I felt helpless."

"Exactly," I said with a huff.

"I don't know how I would have done it without Rose."

"Same. Charli was a lifesaver. She knew exactly what questions to ask while I scowled at the doctor."

He chuckled. "Why doesn't that surprise me?" Then he leaned forward, arms resting on the desk. "I don't know if I've told you lately… I'm really proud of you. You're a good dad and Carina is lucky to have you. I know coming back to Mystique was hard for you, but I'm glad you're here."

"Weirdly, I'm glad to be back too. I never thought I'd step foot in Mystique again, but it's kind of been like coming home despite the shitty office and horrible boss. Can't we fire Leonard?"

My father tapped his fingers together. "Trust me, with the stunt he pulled the other day, I was close. Then I started thinking about your theory of why Mystique is losing money. It makes sense and the timing aligns. If you're right, he's not walking out of here unscathed. We need solid proof though. Find anything yet?"

I shook my head in frustration. There was nothing I wanted more than to see Leonard go down in flames. "His recordkeeping is solid. Whatever he's doing, he's hiding it well, but it's there. I can feel it. There's something I'm missing."

"I have faith in you. If you find he's stealing money from us, the CFO job is yours."

It was what I'd been working for, but to hear my father say it out loud gave me the extra incentive I needed.

Leonard didn't know it yet, but his ass was getting kicked to the curb, preferably in handcuffs.

That night, Charli and I were back at it. Despite my skepticism, she was really good with numbers, and we were able to get through the documents twice as fast.

"I think I found something."

If only… My heart beat double time at the prospect of finally finding evidence of wrongdoing. "What did you find?"

"It's not a lot, relatively speaking, but there's an almost ten thousand dollar discrepancy in the silent auction earnings from the fundraiser. At first, I thought it was a simple adding error, but it's not. It looks like"— she compared the two sets of papers—"that some numbers were transposed."

"Show me." I pushed away from my desk and leaned over her shoulder.

She pointed to the lines she'd highlighted. "Here, here, and here. There's five of them, and in every case, the numbers were reversed to show a lower amount." She looked up at me and chewed on her bottom lip. "I mean, it could be an honest mistake."

I took the papers from her hands and inspected each line. "Son of a bitch! Once would be a careless mistake. Five times is purposeful."

"What does this mean?"

"It means I was right. Leonard is stealing money. There has to be more. I'm sure of it." I grabbed Charli by the cheeks and kissed her. "Excellent work, dollface."

She beamed. "What's my reward?"

"Anything you want."

Over the rest of the week, Charli and I found hundreds of *errors* that involved transposed numbers, dating back to the month after Leonard started at Mystique. At first, the errors only equated to a few dollars here and there, but over time, the differences became greater. I figured in the beginning, he was testing the waters to see what he could get away with, and when no one questioned it, he got greedy. In total, we'd found over a million dollars in *mistakes*. Since he'd fired almost my entire staff, no one kept him in check.

There was only one question left to answer. Where was the money?

Chapter 40
Charli

I had just put Carina down for a nap when the doorbell rang.

Who in the hell could that be? My best guess was Mrs. Hadley next door. She and I chatted quite a bit and she absolutely adored Carina.

Looking through the peephole, I was surprised to see Gia and Penny. I threw the door open. "Aren't you two supposed to be at work?"

"We're playing hooky," Gia said, pushing her way inside.

Penny followed, carrying greasy take-out bags. "We brought lunch. Have you ever had Tico's Tacos?"

"The food truck? I've seen it, but I've never stopped."

Penny opened the bag and held it out for me to sniff. "Brett took me there on one of our first dates. It's to die for."

Somehow, I had a tough time reconciling a billionaire with a food truck. "I thought he'd spring for something a bit more fancy."

Penny shrugged. "Good food is good food. Doesn't matter where it comes from."

Gia looked around the apartment, taking in the high chair, toys, and playpen. "So this is where Hunter lives. It's very bachelor-ish, well, except for all the baby stuff. Gah! I still can't believe he's a dad. Where is the little munchkin anyway?"

"She's taking a nap. You've never been here before?"

"Nope. Never had a reason... until you."

"Me?"

Penny put the bags on the kitchen table and emptied them, doling out the tacos. "Yes, you. Inquiring minds want to know."

"About?"

Gia shook her finger at me. "Don't play dumb with us, missy. We all saw Hunter come to your defense and call you his girlfriend. I mean... you two looked cozy at the concert, but obviously, things have progressed."

"Spill the tea, *girlfriend*." Penny sat at the table and motioned for us to do the same. "Is it terrible that I know these tacos are going to give me heartburn, but I'm going to eat them anyway? I never had that problem before I got pregnant."

I reached into the cabinet next to the sink and pulled out a bottle of antacids. "Eat the tacos."

She took a bite and hummed. "This is how I know we're going to be great friends."

I didn't know these women well, but they seemed hell-bent on showering me with friendship. "I'll tell you on one condition. When and if this thing with Hunter ends, I get to keep the two of you."

Gia made a face. "Like we'd ever dump you for Hunter. Granted, he does seem like a different man since Carina showed up, but we knew him before. Wasn't a fan. Not only did he say the most inappropriate things, but he videoed Trent and me during a private moment. Everyone in the office saw me orgasm. It was completely humiliating."

"True story." Penny nodded her head as she chewed. "At least you weren't naked or had your boobs hanging out."

Gia practically face-planted into her tacos. "I guess, but it still sucked," she groaned.

The picture they painted wasn't a pretty one. I didn't know what to say, so I took a bite of my taco. "Oh, wow! These really are good." The flavors burst on my tongue, creating a fiesta in my mouth. I pushed away from the table. "Diet Coke for anyone?"

"Me," Gia reached out with grabby hands. "You know the way to my soul, Charli."

I laughed at her theatrics.

"Water for me. I'm trying to lay off the caffeine for the sake of this little one." Penny rubbed her belly, which had popped out significantly since her announcement. "The things you do for your kids."

"Enough stalling," Gia said, popping the top of her can. "Are you and Hunter a thing or what?"

I wobbled my head back and forth. "Yes and no. Yes, for now, but he hasn't committed to anything beyond my time as Carina's nanny. When I go back to Oasis, things will be different."

"He'll have to get another nanny," Penny said, putting the pieces together.

"I assume so. I mean... I could still be with Carina some of the time, but with scheduled practices and shows..." I shrugged my shoulders.

"Rose would watch Carina," Gia said. "I know she was hurt Hunter didn't ask her from the beginning."

"Seems there's some history there. I'm not sure it's an option."

"It's totally unfair that men don't have to give up their jobs to have kids, but women are expected to stay home. And the price of childcare is ridiculous. I want to keep working once the baby is born. We can afford childcare, but then I'd miss everything. There has to be a better solution."

Gia tapped a finger against her lips. "You're totally right. I don't really want to give up the job I worked so hard for when we get pregnant. What if there was in-house day care at Mystique? You'd be assured your child was well taken care of, but you could see them on breaks and at lunch."

Penny sighed. "That would be a dream. I know other employees would appreciate it too." She snapped her fingers at Gia. "You should get on that. You're married to the boss's son. If anyone can make it happen, it's you."

"Hunter did say Mystique is all about family," I agreed.

"It's definitely something to bring up to Trent. If we came up with a solid plan, I don't think Edward would object."

It was a decent idea, but it wouldn't help me. I would be back at Oasis in less than a month. There was no way they'd get a day care up and running in that short amount of time. Besides, day care wasn't really the issue between Hunter and me.

"I don't know if he wants to keep me," I blurted.

"What? Why?" Gia asked.

"I don't know. I jokingly brought up marriage once and he freaked out."

"He's scared," Penny concluded. "Brett had the same issue. What is it about men and commitment? They don't even know how good they have it until we're gone."

"Hunter seemed to do fine before I came into the picture."

"He was a miserable human being," Gia said. "Since you've come into his life, he's much more tolerable. Sometimes, dare I say, nice. Even I can see the changes and I have every reason to hate him."

"Behind every successful man is a kick-ass woman. History is full of them: Jackie O, Coretta Scott King, Eleanor Roosevelt, Yoko Ono, and let's not forget the most important one... Penelope Quinn Kingston. I swear Brett would be lost without me." She waved her hand in the air like it was an undisputed fact.

Gia laughed. "Girl, you've come so far in the time I've known you. You used to be so insecure, and now you're one half of a power couple. A badass in your own right."

"Thank you, thank you very much." Penny's face glowed from the compliment. "Charli's a badass too. Any woman who can tame Hunter deserves an award."

"I don't think I've tamed him. He can still be grumpy and boorish with everyone else. I just know how to put him in his place when he acts like a jerk."

"As a good woman should. Unfortunately for you, it's a full-time job," Gia said with a smile.

"That man would be a fool to let you go," Penny added.

Or maybe I was the fool for thinking he wouldn't let me go.

Chapter 41
Hunter

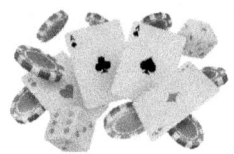

I couldn't fucking believe it!

All these months of looking at spreadsheets and it'd been here all along.

Well, not exactly.

I'd copied every folder from Leonard's computer, searching for something useful. It was buried in a secret folder on his desktop named "family photos." The dumbass was so confident he didn't even password protect it. And he would have gotten away with it too, if I hadn't come along.

Among photos of his idiot kid and unfortunate-looking wife was a single document. A document that showed dozens of money transfers to a company called Intentional Hospitalities Corporation.

The name of Mystiques holding company was International Hospitalities Corporation. Two little letters separated the companies. A strategy to mislead and camouflage transfers if anyone had gone snooping.

I picked up my phone and called Trent. "Come to my office and bring Tom."

"Hello to you too."

"I'm serious. I need to see you both. Immediately." I hung up the phone without waiting for a response. He'd be pissed, but he'd come. This wasn't the type of conversation to be had over the phone.

Ten minutes later—because, of course, he was going to make me wait—Trent showed up with Tom in tow. "What crawled up your ass?"

"Come in and shut the door."

"Is this about Charli?" Tom asked, puffing out his chest.

"It's not about your sister," I assured him.

Trent closed the door and sighed. "What *is* this all about?"

I gestured toward Tom. "Do you trust him? Like would you trust him to keep a secret if your life depended on it?"

"Oh, for fuck's sake! Yes, I trust him."

"If your life depended on it?"

"Yes, if my life depended on it."

Tom pushed up his glasses. "Good to know, but I'm not sure you pay me enough for that responsibility."

"Don't worry, I'm pretty sure my life isn't in the balance," Trent said, patting Tom on the shoulder. "Hunter tends to like hyperboles."

"Nothing I say leaves this room." I leaned on the desk, clasped my hands, and rested my chin on them. "I found something."

Trent threw up his hands. "Oh my god! Is this whole thing going to be a guessing game? You found what? A mouse in your pocket? A quarter under your couch cushion? What?"

I ignored his ridiculousness and gave him a devious smile. "I found something on Leonard."

"Why didn't you start with that?" Trent asked in frustration.

"I guess because I like seeing you get all flustered, but I'm over it now." I picked up two stacks of papers from my desk and handed them to him. "He's definitely stealing from us."

Trent scanned the papers. "What am I looking at?"

"The numbers are transposed," Tom said, looking over Trent's shoulder.

I snapped my fingers at Tom. "Exactly. In each of the highlighted lines, the numbers were reversed to show a smaller amount. Gia was right to be concerned about the fundraiser. The silent auction alone is missing almost ten thousand dollars."

Trent's fingers clenched around the papers. "Son of a bitch."

I held up a finger. "And that's not all. Charli and I found hundreds of incorrect documentations from original paperwork to Leonard's official reports."

"You let Charli help?"

"Yes. She's the one who found the first discrepancy. Turns out she's not just beautiful, but smart too. So far, we've found over a million dollars."

Tom let out a low whistle. "That's a lot of money."

"Bet your ass it is! And with most of the financial staff gone, none of it was cross-checked."

"Where is the money going?" Trent asked through clenched teeth.

"That's where I was stumped. I couldn't find a damn thing until I examined the files on Leonard's personal computer."

"Do I even want to know how you got into Leonard's personal computer?"

I waved away his concern. "Probably not, but that's beside the point. My tactics were totally justified."

Trent rolled his eyes as I handed over the records from our bank. "What am I looking at?"

"Look closer. All the money that comes into Mystique is distributed to vendors, employees, operating funds, etcetera. A portion is also transferred to our holding company."

"I'm aware."

I handed over the single document from Leonard's computer that itemized the illegal transfers. "See it now?"

His eyes went wide. "Fucking hell! How come nobody caught this?"

"Because our father put blind trust into an outsider. There were no checks and balances."

Tom took the papers from Trent and looked at them. "What's Intentional Hospitalities Corporation?"

"That's where you come in," I told Tom. "Charli said you have mad computer skills. What's the chance of you following the money trail and finding out who owns the company? What we have is good, but we need to prove the money is going to Leonard."

Tom swallowed. "It'll take some time, but I can do it. I have to warn you though, I'll have to do some hacking. It won't all be completely legal."

I looked at Trent. "Are you on board?"

"Fuck yeah, I am."

"Good. We don't have to disclose how we found the information, only that it exists."

"Have you told Dad about this yet?"

"Not yet. I wanted to wait until we had solid proof. And when we do, it'll be bye-bye, Leonard Moroski."

And hello, Hunter Dorsey, CFO.

Chapter 42
Charli

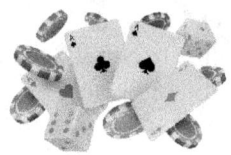

Hunter poured us each a glass of wine. "Tonight, we're celebrating!"

"What exactly are we celebrating?"

He handed a glass to me. "I found out where the money is going. We're waiting on Tom to confirm it."

"You got my brother involved?" I don't know why this surprised me, but it did.

"You said he was the best and I need the best. Plus, Trent trusts him a thousand percent."

I smiled. "Look at you, making amends with your brother."

Hunter lifted his shoulder. "He's still an arrogant asshole, but he's alright."

It made me happy to see him so happy. After everything he'd gone through in the past few months, he deserved this.

Hunter set his glass on the kitchen island. "I'm taking us out to dinner. Go put on something fancy, and I'll get Carina ready."

I didn't have many fancy clothes, but I did have one little black dress I wore to my cousin's wedding that would be perfect. Once I touched up my makeup, put some curls in my hair, and zipped myself into the dress, I looked in the mirror. The woman staring back at me looked happy. Her cheeks were rosy, and her smile was vibrant.

I was in love with my boss, and I couldn't deny it a moment longer. Gia and Penny were right; Hunter and I could totally make this work when I went back to Oasis. I was willing to try, and I hoped he was too.

Timing was everything though.

I wanted him to make the decision.

I wanted him to ask me to stay.

I wanted him to say the words.

Hunter and Carina were waiting for me in the kitchen. "Wow! Doesn't Charli look beautiful, baby girl? How did we get so lucky, huh?" he asked as he bounced her on his hip.

I tickled Carina's belly. "I'm starting to wonder that myself."

"I called ahead and reserved us a table at Imperial Steakhouse. I hope you're hungry."

"I'm starving."

Twenty minutes later, we were seated in the fanciest restaurant I'd ever been to. Waiters wearing black tie carried sizzling plates steaming hot from the kitchen that smelled so good my stomach growled.

Hunter handed me a menu. "Their steaks are delicious, but so is the seafood. You really can't go wrong, no matter what you choose."

I opened the menu and scanned my choices. Everything looked good, but there was one minor problem. "Ummm… there aren't any prices," I whispered.

He lifted his eyebrow. "You're not paying the bill, so you don't need to worry about that."

"But…"

"But nothing. Get whatever you like. If I want to spoil you tonight, I will. Get used to it."

I gave him a tight smile and tried to choose something I thought would be reasonably priced, although no prices usually meant everything was expensive as hell. I'd never been spoiled before, and it wasn't something I thought I'd ever get used to. In my world, if you wanted something, you worked for it. Nothing was ever given for free.

It didn't take long for our food to arrive—steak and lobster for Hunter, a filet for me, and a bowl of mashed potatoes for Carina. I loaded buttery potatoes on a spoon and popped them into Carina's waiting mouth. She smacked her lips and clapped her hands. I thought it might disturb the other guests, but I was wrong.

The woman at the next table smiled at us. "What a cute baby. She's totally adorable."

"Thank you," Hunter said, puffing out his chest.

"We're due in three months. With twins," her husband announced, taking his wife's hand over the table.

"Congratulations!" Her husband was so proud, taking credit for his big accomplishment as if he'd won a gold medal for a triathlon.

"I'm sorry about that," his wife said, rolling her eyes. "He's been telling everyone we meet. It's getting embarrassing." Then she looked at Hunter. "You have a lovely family."

"That I do." Hunter smiled at me across the table. "I'm a very lucky man."

Heat crept up my neck and into my cheeks. It was only natural that people would think I was Carina's mother, but Hunter's words made my heart swell with hope.

I cut a piece of steak and chewed it slowly as I thought about how to approach the topic that'd been running through my mind nonstop. "I wanted to thank you again for getting the equipment for me to train in the gym. It's been really helpful."

Hunter took a sip of his wine. "I'm glad. That was the whole point."

I said the next part quickly, afraid of what it was going to mean for our relationship. "My routines are getting better every day. I think I'll be ready to go back to Oasis soon."

He froze. "Are you putting in your two weeks?"

Two weeks? I hadn't really considered how this would work. Of course, Hunter would want a two-week notice. This was a job. "Not exactly. I haven't even talked to the producer."

Hunter let out a breath of relief. "Good. I'm not ready yet."

I grabbed his hand. "I am going back to work though and I'm wondering what that means for us."

His lips twisted to the side. "Do you want to leave?"

I shook my head. "No. Do you want me to leave when I go back?"

He looked at his daughter. "I want what's best for her and you're what's best. For both of us."

It wasn't exactly the answer I was looking for. I wanted him to tell me he loved me. I wanted him to tell me to stay. I wanted him to say he wanted a future with me. Not because he needed someone to take care of Carina but because of me. "Are we in a relationship? I know you don't like labels, but I need one. I need to know…"

Hunter reached across the table and put his finger over my lips. "You're my girlfriend, Charli. I've never felt for anyone what I feel for you. I want you to stay, but I also want you to live your dreams. I don't want to hold you back. I'm not sure of all the logistics, but I want to try to make this work."

Finally, he'd said the words I'd waited so long to hear. My eyes welled with tears. "I want to try too. I'll still be able to help take care of Carina, but I wouldn't want you to pay me. You'd have to find someone else to fill in, like maybe Rose, when I have to go to work. I don't want to be your employee anymore. I want to truly be your girlfriend."

"You already are."

Carina was fast asleep in Hunter's arms as the elevator made its way up to the apartment. Seeing him cuddle her made my ovaries kick into overdrive. I didn't want a baby anytime soon, but I did want one or two or possibly three.

"I'll put her to bed while you change," he said, as we stepped in the door. Hunter had been doing the night routine more often and it was good for both of them. When he first hired me, he was more of a provider than a caregiver, relying on me to carry most of the load. With me going back to work soon, I was glad to see him stepping up his game.

"Alright. Don't forget her stuffed rabbit. It's her favorite."

He kissed me on the head. "I won't forget."

I went off to my room to put on some comfy clothes. Although Hunter and I had been sleeping together for some time now, I still kept a separate bedroom with all my things. Hopefully, that would change soon, and I'd move my clothes into his room like a real couple.

Once I'd changed into a T-shirt and shorts, I went back to the kitchen and poured us each a glass of wine to finish off the bottle we started before dinner.

It didn't take long for Hunter to join me. "She didn't even wake up."

"Did you remember to change her diaper?" Although Hunter was taking on more responsibility, I still felt the need to check.

"Yes, ma'am," he said with a smirk. "Changed her diaper, put on her jammies, and made sure she had her rabbit."

I handed him the glass of wine. "You've come so far," I teased.

"Thanks to you. I don't know how I would have ever done this without you."

"It's my job."

"True, but you've gone above and beyond for both of us. I want you to know how much I appreciate it."

"How about you show me how much?" I waggled my eyebrows at him.

He backed me up against the kitchen counter and pressed his lips against mine. His tongue ran along the seam, and I gladly opened to him, tasting the sweet wine on his tongue. The man knew how to kiss, and it sent tingles right down to the tips of my toes. His large hands skated up the side of my body and squeezed my breast. If we didn't make it to the bedroom soon, I was going to explode.

And then a sharp knock came at the door. "You've got to be kidding me," he growled into my neck.

"Maybe they'll go away."

He continued kissing me while groping my breast in one hand and my ass in the other.

The knock came again, this time more insistent. He groaned and rested his head on top of mine. "I better get that."

I followed Hunter to the door and got the shock of my life when he opened it. "What are you doing here?"

Hunter stared at the woman on the other side of the door and then turned to me. "Do you know her?"

Not only did I know her, but she was the last person I would have expected to show up on our doorstep. Gone were the expensive leggings and sports bra. Instead, she was dressed in tight jeans, sky-high heels, and an off-the-shoulder top. Her hair and makeup were impeccable.

"I met her at the park," I said, wondering how the hell she found out where we lived, and more importantly, what she wanted.

"Long time, no see. I'm Carina's mother."

Chapter 43
Hunter

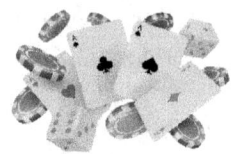

What the actual fuck?

I stared at the woman and tried to place her but came up totally blank. I'd been searching for this woman for months, to no avail, and here she was at my fucking door. "You got proof of that?" I barked.

She tilted her head to the side. "Sapphire Club. You were drunk off your ass and took me to a private room, mumbling something about how unfair life was and getting shafted again. You were pissed at the world. For ten thousand dollars, I took away your troubles for the night."

All that sounded familiar. Too familiar. "You got a name?"

"You didn't really care about names that night." She laughed.

There wasn't a damn thing funny about this situation. "You got a fucking name or not?"

She reached out and ran her finger down my chest. "What do you want it to be?"

I grabbed her hand and pushed it away. "Stop fucking around!"

"Officially, I'm Jennifer Johnson, although I haven't used that name in years."

"You told me your name was Ginny. You lied to me." I'd almost forgotten Charli was still standing there. The shock on her face mirrored mine. One minute we were about to have sex, the next we were confronted by a woman claiming to be Carina's mother. *What a clusterfuck!*

The woman waved away Charli's accusation. "Honey, in my business, you change your name all the time. One day, I'm Ginny; the next, I'm Darla. It's all part of the job."

"Give me your driver's license," I demanded. She dug through her purse, pulled out a tattered card from her wallet, and thrust it at me. I inspected it, turning it over and checking the back. The Michigan license indeed said *Jennifer Ann Johnson.* "It's expired."

"What are you, the police? You gonna arrest me for an expired driver's license?" she asked as she ripped it from my hand.

"You tricked me," Charli blurted. "You knew who I was the whole time, and you never said a word."

"I don't owe you anything. I wanted to see my daughter. Where is the little munchkin anyway?"

Jennifer, Ginny, Darla—whoever she was today—tried pushing her way into my apartment. With a hand to her chest, I pushed her back into the hallway. "You're not seeing Carina."

The woman stomped her foot. "She's my daughter!"

"You should have thought about that when you abandoned her."

"You can't keep her from me!"

"The fuck I can't!" I slammed the door in Jennifer Johnson's face.

This was exactly the scenario I'd been worried about. It's why I hired Rudy Mendosa to find her before she showed up claiming parental rights. Mr. Mendosa was getting a call in the morning. If he thought I was an asshole before, he hadn't seen anything yet.

"I swear I didn't know," Charli said, wringing her hands together. "She had this little Pomeranian that Carina loved. She kept showing up when I was at the park. I knew something was off, but I never thought… I'm so sorry."

287

I grabbed Charli's face between my hands. "It's okay. There's no way you could have known."

"She said her name was Ginny. What if she had tried to kidnap Carina?"

"You would have never let that happen." I wasn't sure who was freaked out more, Charli or me.

"She's going to come back. What do we do?"

There was no doubt Charli was right. This wasn't the last time we'd see Jennifer Johnson.

The next morning, the conference room at Mystique was full, not with employees, but with everyone who'd fallen in love with my daughter. Even Sam Steinburg, our attorney, was here and I'd tested his patience plenty.

Charli bounced Carina on her lap while I addressed the room. "I'm sure you're wondering why I called this meeting. Some of you I've known my whole life, others much shorter, and I can guarantee I've done something to piss each and every one of you off."

There were grumblings of agreement around the room. Finally, Brett spoke up. "Why am I missing a meeting with investors right now?"

"I need your help. I need everyone's help. I'm asking for Carina." I finally had everyone's attention. "Her birth giver showed up at my apartment last night."

"What?" Gia exclaimed. "She's been gone for months."

"It was a shock for us too," I assured her. "Apparently, she's been keeping tabs on Carina. She befriended Charli at the park."

"I didn't know who she was," Charli defended when all eyes landed on her.

"I know I can be an overprotective big brother, but I don't want Charli alone at the apartment to deal with this woman. We don't know what she's capable of," Tom said.

"I couldn't agree more."

"She can come stay at the house with me during the day," Rose volunteered. "We have a top-notch security system."

"Or our place," Penny offered. "The building is totally secure, and nobody can get up to the penthouse without a key card."

It was amazing seeing my family and friends rally around us, if not for me, then for my daughter. "I appreciate that, but it's only a temporary solution."

My father looked at Sam. "What are our options?"

Sam tapped his fingers together. "I was afraid this might happen. Right now, you have physical custody per the court, but she still has joint legal custody. Since it hasn't been six months since the abandonment, she still has rights."

Fuck! "So, what do we do?"

"She could claim postpartum depression, financial troubles, or a change of heart. The chances of the court granting her physical custody are minimal, but that doesn't mean they wouldn't grant her visitation. They're going to do whatever is best for Carina and most of the time, they side with the biological mother."

This was a fucking nightmare. "How is visitation best for Carina? The woman dropped her off without a second thought."

"Obviously, she did have second thoughts," Trent piped in.

Even though he had a point, I scowled at him. "What can I do?"

"There are two routes," Sam said. "Route one is you go through the court system. It's risky. The court could grant the mother visitation. In that case, she'd be allowed to take Carina on a predetermined schedule. You wouldn't have any say in how that visitation time was spent. If she's desperate enough, she could take Carina and run."

I folded my arms across my chest. The thought of Jennifer Johnson disappearing with my daughter was enough to make my blood boil. "That's not an option. What's route two?"

289

"The fact that she didn't go through the court system works to your advantage. Route two is that you handle it on your own. Get to know this woman. Allow her supervised visitation with Carina in your home, where you can monitor the situation. Get as much information about her as you can, starting with a maternity test. You need to be sure she is who she says she is."

The last thing I wanted was this woman in my home, but my options were limited. "And then what?"

"You either find evidence that she's an unfit parent and get the court to terminate her rights or maybe you find out she's a decent woman who deserves a second chance."

"If she were decent, she would have come to me to begin with. I wouldn't have had to wait until Carina was six months old to find out I had a child."

"Be that as it may, you have to think about Carina."

I threw my hands up in the air. "What do you think I've been doing? She's the only one I'm thinking about."

"Are you? If Carina has the chance to know both her parents, shouldn't you give that to her?" Sam asked.

My father put his hand on my shoulder. "He's right, son."

I didn't like it.

At all.

I thought about how my life might have been different if my mother had come back for me.

Maybe I wouldn't have felt like the black sheep.

Maybe I would have felt good enough.

Maybe I would have felt loved.

If I wanted to save Carina from the fate I endured, I didn't have a choice.

Jennifer Johnson was going to get a chance to prove herself.

Chapter 44
Charli

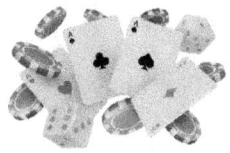

The last twenty-four hours made my head spin. I had no legal rights to Carina, but over the last few months, I started to think of her as mine.

That was a mistake; I wasn't her mother.

Hunter insisted on dropping me off at his parents' house this morning and picking me up after he got off work. I was thankful to have a place to go, because I didn't want to deal with Ginny—or Jennifer—on my own, but it felt restricting.

Carina and I spent the afternoon in Rose and Edward's pool, and I lay in the sun while she napped, but I couldn't help but think the novelty would wear off over time. How long would I have to hide out at someone else's house? Technically, Hunter's apartment wasn't my home, but it sure felt like it.

We'd just started to make a life together and then *she* showed up. I wasn't jealous, per se, but it definitely complicated things.

I didn't trust her. I remembered all the little comments she made to me about having a sugar daddy and moving up in the world. She should have been honest with me from the beginning. My intuition told me her motives were purely selfish and had nothing to do with Carina.

It was a terrible thought. One I should have been ashamed of but couldn't bring myself to care. The woman was a problem.

We'd barely made it into the apartment when the knock at the door came. "For fuck's sake, she could give us a minute to get settled. I bet she was at the park waiting for us to get home."

Hunter kissed me on the head. "I don't want her here any more than you do, but you heard the attorney. We have to play nice for the sake of Carina."

"*You* have to play nice. I don't have to."

"Are you jealous?"

"I don't trust her," I said, crossing my arms.

"That makes two of us. She'll never be alone with Carina, so there's no need to worry."

"Fine." I sounded like a petulant child, which made Hunter laugh.

He opened the door, and sure enough, Miss Multiple Names stood on the other side. "Hello, Jennifer," Hunter said coldly.

"I want to see my daughter."

"Of course you do. Come in." Not expecting that answer, she cautiously stepped into the apartment. "We have a bit of housekeeping to do before I allow you to see Carina."

"What does that mean?"

Hunter led her to the kitchen and motioned for her to sit at the table. I was supposed to stay out of this, but I couldn't help waving my fingers at her. "Hello, *Ginny*."

She rolled her eyes and turned back to Hunter. "Where is my daughter?"

"She's taking a nap right now, but as I said, there are a few things we need to discuss."

"Such as?" she huffed.

"Verifying your identity. You say you're Carina's mother, but how do I know that for sure?"

"Oh my god! You know me from The Sapphire Club. Are you in the habit of impregnating women?"

"To the contrary," he said calmly. "I never fuck without a condom. And as far as knowing you, I don't remember shit. I don't know you."

"You wore a condom, but you're a sloppy drunk," she said, jutting her chin out.

"If we didn't exchange names, how did you find me?"

Jennifer laughed. "You don't think I look at the name on a credit card when someone lays down ten grand?"

Well, that explained part of the mystery. I couldn't imagine there were many Hunter Dorseys running around.

Hunter leaned on the back of the chair. "Fair enough, but why didn't you contact me sooner? I've been trying to figure out how any mother could drop her child at a stranger's door."

"You think I wanted some rich guy to run my life? Had I told you, that's exactly what would have happened. Being a single mom was a lot tougher than I anticipated. I couldn't do it anymore and I knew you had the means to give her a good life. Better than I could. Is it wrong to want more for my daughter?"

He sighed. "I appreciated the sentiment, but your execution was flawed. Why now? Why come back?"

Her eyes welled up. "I thought I would be okay knowing she was well taken care of, but I miss my daughter. So damn much." A tear fell down her cheek and she wiped it away with the back of her hand, smearing her otherwise flawless eyeliner.

The tears were real, but I was still skeptical. This was not the same woman I met in the park who didn't seem to have a care in the world. The woman that freely admitted a man paid for her boobs. I didn't doubt she missed Carina; I mean… how could she not? But something wasn't adding up.

"You want to see her, then you play by my rules now." He handed her a stack of forms. "I'll need these completed in full."

She looked at the papers. "What's this?"

"Basic background information. Like I said… I don't know you. I'm not taking any chances when it comes to *my* daughter. I'll need your driver's license too."

"This is bullshit!"

Hunter motioned to the door. "You're free to leave and you can take me to court. I'm sure the judge will love that you left your kid on a stranger's doorstep."

Hunter was playing with fire. Going to court was a gamble and he knew it. There was no telling what a judge would say. Sam Steinburg made that clear.

Her eyes widened. "Fine. I'll fill out your fucking papers."

"Perfect." He held out his hand. "I'll take that driver's license now."

She rummaged through her purse, pulled it out, and handed it to him. He gave it to me. "I want copies of both sides."

I nodded and rushed off to make the copies. Once inside his office, I felt like I could breathe again. That woman sucked all the air out of the room. It was difficult to stand there and say nothing. I couldn't tell if Hunter bought her bullshit story, but I didn't. Fool me once…

When I got back to the kitchen, Jennifer had finished filling out the paperwork. "Now, can I see Carina?" she pleaded.

"One more thing." Hunter handed her a plastic tube with a swab inside. "I'll need your DNA to prove you're Carina's mother."

"This can't be legal," she huffed.

Hunter shrugged his shoulders. "It's your choice. Swab your cheek or walk out the door."

Jennifer reluctantly opened her mouth and ran the cotton along the inside of her cheek, then tucked it back into the plastic tube. She thrust it at him. "Where is my daughter?"

Hunter tapped the tube against his palm. "When I get the results of this, I'll call you. Don't come back until then."

"Are you serious?"

"As a heart attack. There's nothing I won't do to protect my daughter, even from the woman who claims to be her mother."

She picked up her oversized purse and slung it over her shoulder. "I'll see you soon. You better call or I'll show back up."

"I have no doubt about that." He ushered her to the door and leaned against it once she was gone.

"Now what?" I asked.

"Now we wait."

Chapter 45
Hunter

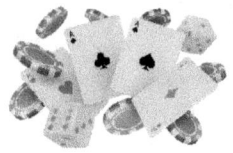

I passed Jennifer Johnson's information to Rudy. Since he'd failed to find Carina's mother, he owed me. I had him run a complete background check on the woman while we waited for the results of the DNA test.

"What did you find?"

The private investigator cleared his throat. "She has no employment records for the last three years, hasn't filed taxes for longer than that. She's probably worked for cash; there's no shortage of those jobs in Vegas. Her last record of employment was at a diner in Michigan."

"What about the address?"

"The apartment is leased to a Brenna Houston. I went over there and showed her picture to the leasing office and the neighbors. Both confirmed she lives there. The only thing attached to her social security number is a phone. No utility bills, no car, nothing. This woman seriously wanted to disappear, and she picked the right city to do it in."

"Disappeared so much that you couldn't find her, could you, Mr. Mendosa?" It still pissed me off that the woman caught me off guard by showing up at my home.

"To be fair, you didn't give me much to go on."

"You're supposed to be the best!"

"I am, but I'm not a fucking miracle worker. No one could have found her."

I tapped my fingers on my desk and let out a sigh. "I guess we'll never know, will we?"

"You want the rest of the report or not?"

"Proceed."

"She's been arrested twice for petty theft and once for prostitution. Never served time and was let out on bail. Pretty typical for Vegas. Other than that, her record is clean."

"Anything else that throws up a red flag?"

"Besides the fact that she barely exists… nothing."

The arrest record wasn't great, but Rudy was right, in Vegas those were minor infractions. Part of me was relieved she seemed legit. The selfish part of me was annoyed he didn't find anything that would give me just cause to keep her away from Carina.

I couldn't imagine letting that woman take my child for visitation. What would she be exposed to? Would she be in danger? Would she be taken care of? Would Jennifer try to disappear with her?

The last question felt like a knife to the gut. I already knew Jennifer was good at disappearing and not being found. Having my daughter stolen away would destroy me.

After hanging up with Rudy, I stomped down to Trent's office. In a weak attempt to stop me, Tom held out his arm. "He's on a phone call."

"Do I look like I give a fuck?" I pushed open the door without knocking and signaled for Tom to follow. He did but remained by the door while I parked myself in front of my brother's desk with one leg crossed over the other.

"I have to go," Trent said into the phone. "An unexpected pest scurried into my office, and I need to call an exterminator. I'll talk to you soon." He hung up and scowled at me.

Like I cared. "You shouldn't be telling people you need to call an exterminator. They'll think Mystique has a cockroach problem."

"It kind of does," he deadpanned.

This back and forth with my brother felt good. Normal. Almost comforting. With the chaos my life had become, I needed it. "God, you've always been such a drama queen. I thought since you've been getting laid on the regular that would have stopped."

Trent stood and leaned forward on his desk. "I always got laid on the regular. You were the one who had an intimate relationship with your right hand."

"Left, actually, but that was before I stole your girlfriend in tenth grade."

Trent jabbed his finger into the top of the desk. "You didn't fucking steal her. She and I were done long before you came snooping around. She had the IQ of a fish."

My lips tipped up and I chuckled. "She kinda smelled like one too."

"There may be some truth to that." He tried to hold back his laughter, but it slipped free as he sat down. "What do you want?"

"I need Tom."

"Okay, but that doesn't explain why you're in *my* office."

"Because yours has the better view and since my life is a gigantic shit show right now, I thought I'd come annoy you." I turned to Tom, who was still standing by the door and beckoned him to join us. "This"—I pointed between the three of us as Tom sank into a chair—"is the triangle of trust. I need to know where we are on the Leonard situation. With Carina's mother showing up, I can't take any more bad news."

"Did you confirm she's actually her mother?" Trent asked.

"I'm still waiting for the DNA test results and since I'm really shitty at waiting, I figured I'd obsess over Leonard. I need something positive. Please tell me you have good news."

Tom cleared his throat. "Intentional Hospitalities Corporation is owned by a shell corporation. Two actually."

I threw my hands in the air. "So you've got nothing!"

"Calm down," Trent said. "Let him finish."

"It's not nothing. I dug into those shell corporations and guess what? They're also owned by shell corporations. Whoever set this up knew what they were doing."

"And?" I asked impatiently.

"And it's going to take some time. You're asking me to hack into financial institutions with top-notch security and massive firewalls."

"This sounds too risky. If he gets caught, we're all going to jail. This whole scheme is crazy. Maybe it would be better to turn it over to the FBI or something," Trent said.

"Don't be a pussy. The only one going to jail is Leonard." I turned to Tom. "You're not going to get caught, right?" Charli told me he was the best, but I needed to hear it from him.

Tom sat up straighter. "I know what I'm doing. I've rerouted my IP address through ten different countries. No one can trace it back to me or Mystique."

I gave him a smirk. "I'm almost jealous of what goes on in that brain of yours."

"You don't even want to know."

After making the phone call I dreaded, Jennifer Johnson was now sitting on my couch. Much to my chagrin, she was indeed Carina's mother.

"I told you I was legit," she said, crossing her arms.

"Well, excuse me for not believing the first woman who showed up at my door. You're the one who made this difficult, not me."

"Can I please see my daughter now?"

She looked up at me with her green eyes, but all I could focus on was the cleavage spilling out of her low-cut shirt. *Good god!* No wonder I slept with her. I remembered the big boobs and blond hair, but that was about it. In my state of mind that night, I didn't need anything else. "One more question. How did you know I was the father?"

Jennifer sighed. "I'm a stripper, not a prostitute. I don't normally sleep with my clients. I give them a lap dance and maybe a blow job then send them on their way. You fit the time window."

"You have an arrest record for prostitution," I pointed out.

Her lips puckered. "Mighty judgy of you, considering you paid me too."

"Touché."

"Besides, I never said I was perfect. I did what I had to do to survive when I moved here. I don't do that anymore."

Except that she did, or we wouldn't be sitting here right now. It didn't matter what I thought. It's not like I could take the moral high ground when most of my life I did whatever served me best. I was the king of deception and amorality.

I had to face facts; this woman was going to be part of my life. It wouldn't do me or my daughter any good to tear her down.

"Let me get Carina." I went down the hallway to the nursery. Charli sat in the rocking chair rubbing Carina's back as she sang to her. "It's time."

Charli turned to me, eyes wide. "I don't like this, Hunter."

I stuck my hands in my pockets. "Neither do I, but we don't have a choice."

"There's always a choice."

"Yeah, and none of them are good. This is the best option." At least that's what the lawyer told me. I had to believe this was in Carina's best interest. She deserved to know her mother.

"Alright. Let me carry her out?"

I nodded and Charli hugged Carina tighter as she carried her. This process was difficult, and I was glad to have Charli on my side. We were partners, not only between the sheets but in loving my daughter. Although

I initially questioned my decision in hiring her as Carina's nanny, I knew now that it was the right choice.

The only choice.

Jennifer squealed when we entered the room. "Oh my god, my baby! I missed you so much! Come to Mama." She reached out for Charli to hand her over.

Carina buried her head in Charli's neck, and Charli protectively squeezed her tighter. I understood her hesitation, but this had to be done.

I pried Carina from Charli's arms and gently handed her to Jennifer. "Careful, she's getting heavy."

Jennifer rolled her eyes. "You act like I didn't carry her in my womb for nine months. I'm perfectly capable of handling my daughter."

Carina's face scrunched up and her lips began to quiver. She reached out for Charli. "Ma….ma…ma."

Jennifer held Carina up and scolded her. "I'm your mama."

Charli held a hand over her mouth and her eyes welled. "That's her first word."

Jennifer glared at me. "Well, isn't that sweet? You've allowed our daughter to call the nanny *Mama*. Jesus!"

Fucking hell! The whole first-word moment was ruined by this woman. "It's understandable that Carina would be confused. She hasn't seen you in months."

"I plan to be around a lot," she said. "Isn't that right, my little boo-boo bear?" She nuzzled into Carina's belly.

Charli backed away into the kitchen. She leaned over the sink as she got a glass of water and guzzled it down, then filled the glass again.

I went over and put my hand on her shoulder. "You okay?"

She waved away my concern. "Yeah, yeah… it's just… her first word."

"I know."

Charli pointed to her chest. "She called me *Mama*."

"I know."

It was a monumental moment that neither one of us fully got to appreciate. I looked over at Jennifer, who had Carina on her back, tickling her belly. My daughter smiled and laughed. As much as I didn't want this woman a part of our lives, she made my daughter happy.

And that's all that really mattered.

Chapter 46
Charli

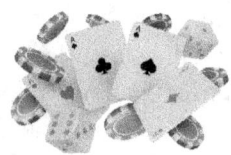

I was sick of Jennifer Johnson.

Ever since she came into our lives, she'd been sucking the life out of me.

Every day it was the same. She'd show up shortly after Hunter got home from work and then stay well into the evening. I barely got any alone time with him anymore.

I was sick of her shrill laugh.

I was sick of her too-sweet perfume.

And I was sick of her cleavage popping out like a jack-in-the-box.

Worst of all, she treated me like a servant who was there to meet her every need.

Carina needs her diaper changed, Charli.

Oops! She spit up on the carpet, Charli.

Can you get her snacks, Charli?

Guess what, lady? Handling those things was part of being a mother. Besides playing with Carina, she was completely useless. I wondered how she raised Carina for six months on her own because she didn't have a freakin' clue.

Hunter and Jennifer sat on the couch drinking wine while Carina played on the carpet with her toys. The two of them laughed and chatted like they were old friends while I was in the kitchen making dinner. Yes... she'd been having meals with us, too.

It made me ill.

"Oh, my god! Look! I think she's getting ready to crawl," Jennifer shrieked. "I need to record this."

I turned the vegetables on the stove down to simmer and hurried into the other room where Jennifer had her phone aimed at Carina. Sure enough, Carina was on all fours, rocking back and forth. She moved one tiny hand forward, then her opposite leg followed. She repeated the process with her other hand and took another step forward. Three more movements forward and she fell on her butt, looking incredibly pleased with herself.

I'd been practicing with her for weeks, getting her comfortable on her hands and knees and encouraging her to move, but usually, she fell to her belly and laughed. This was a huge milestone.

I rushed around the couch and wrapped my arms around Carina. "Good job, baby girl! I'm so proud of you," I said with a kiss to the top of her soft, blond head.

"You're ruining my video."

"What?"

"I was recording my daughter, and you got in the picture. Ugh! I'll have to cut that part out." Jennifer huffed. "Can you move, please?"

Reluctantly, I backed away. "Sorry. I got excited."

"No worries," Hunter said. "I think we're all excited." Then he turned to Jennifer. "Can you send that to me?"

"Yep. No problem." She pushed some buttons on her phone. "All sent."

Hunter's phone pinged with the incoming message.

They were texting each other now? Huh? I wondered when that started. For a guy that wanted nothing to do with the woman a couple weeks ago, they seemed super chummy.

"Dinner smells good," Jennifer said with a fake smile. "Is it almost time to eat?"

"Umm… almost. It'll be ready in a few more minutes."

"Charli's a phenomenal cook. She only tried to burn down my kitchen once." He chuckled. "The stove's not on right now, is it?"

"Of course not," I lied. It pissed me off that he even brought it up, especially in front of Jennifer. Was he trying to be cute? Because it wasn't cute at all.

I retreated back to the kitchen and drained the vegetables, then pulled the chicken and potato wedges from the oven. Usually, I would cut my own potatoes and drizzled them with olive oil and seasoning, but Jennifer didn't deserve my fresh potato wedges. I bought these in the freezer section and dumped them on a cookie sheet. Same with the green beans. Frozen. I'd be damned if I slaved away in the kitchen while those two cavorted on the couch. "Dinner's ready!"

Hunter carried Carina and put her in the high chair. "Everything looks great," he kissed me on the cheek. "Thank you."

Jennifer plopped her ass in my chair—the one right next to Hunter—and scooted closer to him than was necessary. She helped herself to heaping portions before I even had a chance to sit down. "Are these fresh green beans? They're healthier than canned or frozen, you know? My daughter needs proper nutrition."

That was it! I was fucking done.

"She's not eating regular green beans yet." I slammed down a jar of green bean puree. "If you have a problem with the nutrition, take it up with Gerber."

I made my plate and took it to my bedroom, closing the door behind me. Eating on my bed was better than sitting across the table from *her*. I couldn't stand to be around that woman for one more second.

I'd been the one caring for Carina for the last few months, while she spied on us and gallivanted around town.

I'd been the one feeding Carina. Bathing her. Changing her diaper. Tucking her in at night. Making sure she felt loved. If she wanted to do it, she should have never abandoned her daughter.

I was still stewing when Hunter knocked on my door and came inside. "What's wrong with you?"

"What's wrong with *me*? What's wrong with *you*?"

"What do you mean?"

"She's absolutely awful to me and you're all chummy-chummy with her." He stared at me with a blank look on his face. "When are we going to get our life back? Why does she have to be here every day?"

His eyebrows knitted together. "Do you hear yourself right now? You sound like a teenager having a tantrum. There's nothing wrong with Jennifer. Yes, she's made some mistakes, but so have I. You can't blame her for wanting to get to know her daughter again."

"I'm not saying she shouldn't. What I'm saying is you need to put her on a schedule or something. This is getting ridiculous."

"If anyone is being ridiculous, it's you. Are you jealous? Is that it?"

"I'm not jealous!" Okay, I was a little bit jealous. The differences between the two of us were glaring. Where I had mosquito bites for boobs, she had the fucking Rocky Mountains on her chest. I was practically a beanpole next to her voluptuous curves. A woman like me couldn't compete with a woman like her. Not physically anyway.

"Then stop acting like a child and do what's best for Carina. Give Jennifer a chance. If anything, you should feel sorry for her."

"And why is that?"

He leaned against the doorjamb. "Come on, Charli. She's obviously had a rough life, especially if she felt giving up her daughter was her only choice. Have some empathy."

I couldn't believe what I was hearing. After all the bitching he did when she showed up, now he was on her side? It was pure craziness, but the last thing I wanted to do was fight with Hunter. "I'll try harder."

"That's all I ask. Do it for Carina." He hiked a thumb over his shoulder as he backed out of my room. "I should get back out there."

Do it for Carina?

Who the fuck did he think I'd been doing it for? Everything I did was for that little girl.

And how dare he call me jealous? Even if it was a teeny bit true, he had no right to call me out on it. I mean, who wouldn't be jealous of her curvy body, perfect hair and flawless makeup? It wasn't like she was going to steal Hunter away from me.

I slapped a hand over my mouth.

That was totally it! Subconsciously I was afraid Hunter would fall for her and kick me to the curb. Our relationship was tenuous at best; it was possible.

I *was* being a jealous bitch.

I was not a jealous person. Ever.

Jennifer was turning me into a person I didn't know. I was letting her have too much power. Hunter was with me. I was the one he shared his feelings and his bed with, not her. I was the one he depended on. I was the one he called his girlfriend.

Not her.

Jesus Christ! What was wrong with me?

When I finally got up the courage to leave my bedroom, I found Hunter giving Carina a bath. I went in and sat on the edge of the tub. "I'm sorry."

"It's okay. I know this has been a stressful situation for both of us."

"You want me to finish her bath?"

"Nah, I got it. Why don't you go tidy up the kitchen. Then have a glass of wine and limber up. I plan on having your ankles next to your ears tonight." He waggled his eyebrows at me.

Alrighty then.

I guessed I didn't have to worry about Jennifer, but a part of me wouldn't let it go. I trusted her about as far as I could throw one of her silicone-filled implants, which wasn't very far.

Chapter 47
Hunter

I looked everywhere… in my suit pants from last night, under a stack of mail on the counter, by the bathroom sink. Hell, I even looked in the refrigerator because that was a totally logical place.

"What are you looking for?" Charli asked as she made my to-go cup of coffee.

"Have you seen my watch? I must have taken it off when I gave Carina a bath last night and I can't find it anywhere. I don't even remember taking it off." At this rate, I was going to be late for work. I really didn't care what Leonard thought, but I didn't feel like hearing him berate me again.

"It'll show up." She handed me the cup. "I'll do a thorough search when Carina goes down for her nap."

"Thank you, dollface. I owe you one." I owed her way more than one. The woman practically saved my life when Carina showed up. I didn't know how I would have done this without her.

Charli lifted Carina's hand and waved it at me. "Bye, Daddy. Have a good day at work."

Every time she did something like that, it made my heart swell. I'd never given a lot of thought to being a father, but I now realized it was the best thing in the world. I kissed them both. "I hope my girls have a great day too." The whole situation was so domestic, and I didn't hate it. I loved it.

What I didn't love was not being able to find my watch. My father bought one for both Trent and me on our twenty-first birthdays. Trent lost his to a woman who robbed him blind. It was so stupid, and I loved rubbing it in his face.

My wrist felt naked without the watch, but Charli was right. It would turn up. She'd probably find it at the bottom of my clothes hamper or under the bed.

When I got to work, my father called me to his office. Usually, I dreaded it, but I couldn't think of anything I could be reprimanded for except maybe my covert mission to get rid of Leonard. He wouldn't be happy if he knew I had Tom digging into shit he shouldn't be digging into. I had to believe the triangle of trust was solid. Trent might not be my biggest fan, but he wouldn't rat me out. When we had issues, we handled it like civilized human beings... with our fists.

I poked my head in my dad's office, and he motioned for me to sit. I took the seat opposite his desk and crossed one ankle over my knee, trying to look relaxed when I felt jittery as fuck.

"How's the Leonard investigation going?"

"I actually found some stuff, but I'm still playing detective. I have a feeling it's just the tip of the iceberg."

"Fuck. I was afraid you were going to say that." He ran his fingers through his hair in a very uncharacteristic manner. "I can't believe I let this happen."

"It's not your fault. The man is shady as shit. He went to great lengths to hide what he was doing." It was kind of his fault for not keeping better tabs on Leonard but pointing that out would only make him feel worse. "I'll let you know when I have my full report finished. Then we can say goodbye to him for good and hopefully stop him from doing this to anyone else."

"Right." He nodded. "How are things going with Carina's mother?"

"Not as awful as I expected. She's not a bad person, but she definitely got on the wrong track. Carina seems to love her, so that's a positive. Charli hates her, but honestly, I think she's jealous of another woman coming into the picture."

"That's totally understandable. Not that it's the same, but Rose practically threw me out when your mother showed up. I regret not being faithful in my marriage, but I got you, so something good came out of it. I wish I hadn't hurt Rose. It took years to convince her she was the only one for me."

"Why did you cheat on her?" It was something I always wondered but never had the nerve to ask.

He rubbed his clean-shaven chin. "We got in a fight one night shortly after Trent was born. It was over the curtains, of all things. Stupid really. We were both under a lot of stress. Trent was a colicky baby and neither one of us were getting any sleep. One night, we both snapped and said things we didn't mean. Next thing I knew, I was sitting in a dive bar, drinking away my sorrows. Men make bad decisions when they're drinking."

"Don't I know it. I was pissed at everyone the night Carina was conceived, so drunk I barely remember the night."

"Anyway, I knew it was wrong taking your mother to a hotel. I promised myself that Rose would never know and that it would never happen again."

"Then I showed up."

He nodded. "Then you showed up. I was as shocked as Rose, but looking back, it was one of the best days of my life."

I rubbed my wrist where my watch was supposed to be. "What was she like?"

"Your mother?"

"Yeah. I've always wondered about her."

"I don't remember much except that she was beautiful and a really good listener. I wish I could tell you more. I have the paperwork she signed locked in my safe. If you ever want to find her, I can give it to you."

Did I want to know my mother? Of course, I did. All these years, I wondered how my life would have been different had she not given me up. But what if meeting her was an epic disappointment? With everything going on in my life, I wasn't sure if I was ready for that emotional roller coaster. "What was her name?"

"Her name was Angela."

"Oh." I don't know why I never asked before. Guess it never seemed like the right time.

"Why all this interest in your mother? I mean... why now?"

"I'm wondering if I'm doing the right thing for Carina. I don't want to fuck this up."

"You're not going to fuck it up. With things like this, there is no right or wrong answer. We do what we think is best with the information we're given. Whatever happens, you'll know your heart was in the right place when you did it and no one can fault you for that."

I hoped he was right, because everything I was doing was for my daughter and I didn't want to let her down.

When I got home, Jennifer was already there, which surprised me because I thought we had an agreement.

I threw my keys and wallet on the kitchen island. "You're here early."

She smiled up at me from where she was feeding Carina something that looked like applesauce. "I got off work early, so I figured I'd get a little one-on-one time with my little boo-boo bear. It's not a problem, is it?"

Fuck! It might have been a problem. Hell if I knew. "Where's Charli?"

"Umm. I think she's in the laundry room." She waved her arm in the general direction.

I found Charli rinsing one of Carina's onesies under the water and scrubbing at a brown stain on the material. "God, that smells foul." I held my hand up over my nose.

"You're telling me. She had a blowout right after Jennifer arrived. I had to give Princess Poops-a-Lot a quick bath."

I chuckled. "Did you just make that up?"

"The name fits. How can so much disgusting stuff come out of such a tiny baby?"

"It's a mystery." I motioned to the kitchen with my head. "How long has she been here?"

"I don't know. What time is it now?"

I looked at my naked wrist and shrugged.

"I guess about an hour."

"You're okay with her here?" After last night, I didn't want a repeat.

"Being a team player." She pasted on a huge smile that she couldn't even pretend was real. "Oh, and no luck with the watch, but I'll keep looking."

"That's so weird. I felt like I was walking around with my hand cut off today."

Charli rolled her eyes. "Don't be so dramatic. It's just a watch. I'm sure you can buy another one."

"It's not just a watch. My father gave it to me, and it was superexpensive."

She sprayed some spot cleaner on the stain and rubbed more, before tossing the onesie in the washing machine with the rest of the clothes. "Well, I'm sure it'll turn up." She scrubbed her hands and dried them with a towel. "What do you want for dinner tonight? I've been too busy to even think about it."

"How about I order takeout?" Despite her tantrum last night, Charli had been a trooper cooking dinner for all of us every night. It was way beyond her nanny duties and maybe I'd gotten a little too comfortable having her around, taking advantage of her good nature.

She slumped back against the washer. "That would be fabulous. Would you mind if I took a quick shower before dinner? I feel like I've been running all day."

"I'm thinking Chinese."

"Perfect. I haven't had Chinese food in forever. Can you order me chicken chop suey with white rice and an egg roll?"

"Yes, ma'am. Go shower and I'll order the food." I swatted her ass as she left and then went back to the kitchen. Jennifer scrolled through her phone while Carina banged on the tray of her high chair with applesauce on her cheeks and in her hair.

I sighed. "I presume she's finished eating."

Jennifer looked up from her phone. "Oh yeah. She was starving. Are you sure Charli's feeding her enough?"

"Charli has her on a schedule. The doctor said she's right on target for weight gain." I pulled a washcloth from the drawer and wet it, then wiped Carina's hair, face, and hands, making sure to get every bit of the sticky mess. I removed her bib and threw it on the counter, then picked up my princess. "Did you miss Daddy today?"

She patted my cheeks with her chubby hands. "Da... da... da." There was nothing better than holding my girl and hearing her call me *Dada*. In the few short months since Carina arrived, she'd stolen my heart, and I never wanted it back.

"You want Chinese food?" I asked Jennifer.

She finally put her phone down. "I can't afford it, but thanks for asking."

"That wasn't the question. I asked if you wanted it."

"Oh well, in that case... yes, I'd love some fried shrimp. I've barely eaten today." Jennifer took Carina from me and gave her a stuffed dog, which my daughter immediately squeezed to her chest. When her phone pinged again, Jennifer frowned at the screen.

"Is there a problem?"

She bit her lip. "It's my landlord. I'm late on my rent and he's threatening to evict me."

My eyebrows shot up. "How late are you?"

313

"Two months," she said, as her face scrunched up. "I've been trying to get on the straight and narrow for Carina, so I quit my job dancing and started waitressing. It doesn't pay close to what I used to make. God, I can't afford to lose my apartment."

"How much do you need?"

She folded her hands in her lap and bowed her head. "I'm behind four grand."

I rhythmically tapped my fingers against my lips. Everything inside me said not to give her any money, but I didn't want to see her out on the street either. I could easily afford it. What kind of person would I be if I let the mother of my child become homeless? "I can give you the money."

"Oh no… I couldn't possibly accept that. It's not your responsibility," she insisted.

"Let me do this to help you. I'll give you five thousand to help with next month's rent too." It was the right thing to do, no matter what my gut told me.

Her face broke out into a huge smile. "That's incredibly generous. It would help so much!"

"I'll write you a check."

"Actually, cash would be better."

Chapter 48
Charli

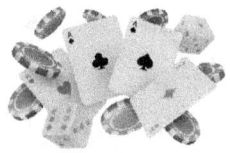

Jennifer showing up early today almost pushed me over the edge. When Carina had her blowout, the woman had no problem handing over the baby like she was a hot potato. Cleaning her up wasn't the most pleasant job in the world, but as they say… shit happens. A mother should've been able to deal with it.

My shower was divine, exactly what I needed after dealing with Jennifer by myself for an hour. I really was trying to play nice, but the woman tap-danced on my last nerve. Had Hunter not come home when he did, I would have completely lost it with her.

As I came down the hall from my bedroom, I heard the two of them talking. Curious about what was being said, I plastered myself against the wall and scooted closer.

My hand came up to cover my gasp as I heard Hunter offer to pay her rent. For a smart guy, he was an idiot. It wasn't my business, but it pissed me off.

I peeked my head around the corner.

"I'll write you a check," he said.

"Actually, cash would be better," she replied.

Oh! My! God!

Hunter went down the other hall to his office and I watched as Jennifer held Carina up and said to her, "Mama's getting paid, my little boo-boo bear. What should she buy? I knew coming back here was the right move."

I felt like a volcano ready to explode. What a schemer! I bet she wasn't even late on her rent.

Hunter came back and handed her a wad of cash. I had no idea how much, but it looked like a lot. If I said something, Hunter and I would end up fighting.

He'd accuse me of being jealous again.

It was his money to do with as he pleased, and it wasn't my place to tell him how to spend it. But for fuck's sake, how could he be so blind?

After dinner, Hunter went to his office to work while I had the pleasure of entertaining Jennifer. She sat on the couch while I chased after Princess Poops-a Lot.

Since Carina started crawling, life had changed. Everything was a new adventure to her. I swiped the television remote right before it went in her mouth, then she crawled to the potted ficus in the corner and pulled on the edge of the pot. I grabbed the plant and moved it to the balcony, where she wouldn't be able to tip it over.

The apartment was nowhere near babyproofed. I quickly realized we'd have to move everything down low to higher ground. Also... baby gates. They were going to be a necessity. *When did she get so fast?*

I chased after Carina, only to scoop her up right as she grabbed my flip-flop and began chewing on the toe.

And... teething toys. We definitely needed more of those.

"So...," Jennifer started. "How long do you plan on staying here?"

"What do you mean?" I asked, as I picked up all the shoes and put them on the entryway table.

"I mean, you're the nanny. Hunter needed you before, but now that I'm here, I'm not so sure you're needed anymore.

"Excuse me?" I set Carina on my hip.

"Eventually, I'll be taking care of Carina. I am her mother," she said, flashing me a smile.

"You know what? You're right." I plopped Carina on her lap. "Since you're her mother, you should be helping out more. And FYI... I don't plan on going anywhere."

"We'll see."

I stomped down the hall to Hunter's office. "Do you think you could come out and help me?"

He looked up from his computer. "Charli, you know I have to work. I need all this paperwork ready to present to my father."

"I understand, but Carina is getting into everything and it's exhausting."

Hunter's cheeks puffed up and deflated. "I don't mean to sound this way, but isn't that what I pay you for?"

Oh no he didn't!

I gritted my teeth. "Yes, but you don't pay me to babysit Miss Big Tits too."

He smirked. "Now, who's being dramatic? Miss Big Tits is a grown woman. She doesn't need you to babysit her."

"I beg to differ."

"I don't have time to fight with you. Please, just do as you're told."

If I didn't get away from him, I was liable to crawl over his desk and wrap my hands around his throat. "You got it, boss." I gave him a double thumbs-up followed by my middle fingers. *Childish?* Yep. *Did I care?* Not in the least.

"I saw that!" he yelled out as I left.

"You were supposed to," I called back.

I suggested Jennifer leave when Carina began to yawn. It was after nine o'clock and she'd worn out her welcome.

Jennifer planted sloppy kisses all over her daughter's face. "Good night, my little boo-boo bear. Mommy will see you tomorrow." She handed Carina back to me, scrunching up her nose. "I think she might need to be changed again."

I smiled. "I think you might be right. Something smells like shit."

Jennifer harrumphed as she walked out.

"Don't let the door hit you in the ass," I mumbled.

By the time Jennifer left, I was seething. I'd never met a more useless human being in my life.

My feelings toward her had nothing to do with jealousy. She wanted to do all the fun stuff with Carina, but none of the work. All she did tonight was take up space and annoy me.

After I put Carina to bed, I went back to Hunter's office. "Wanted to let you know your princess is asleep."

He nodded. "Did you, by chance, take any money from my wallet?"

I pulled back. "Are you accusing me of stealing?"

"Charli, stop. I'm not accusing you of anything. I thought I put cash in there yesterday morning, but when I went to pay for dinner, there was only a twenty-dollar bill. I just wondered if you took any for... I don't know... groceries or anything?"

"I don't touch your wallet. I only use the credit card you gave me, and you can easily track everything I've spent. Anything I buy for myself, I use my own money." I crossed my arms and jutted my chin out.

"You're getting defensive. It was only a question, not an accusation." He got up and came around his desk, wrapping me in his arms. "Thank you for handling things tonight."

I kept my arms stiff at my sides. "It's my job, remember?"

He ran his finger along the side of my face. "Don't be like that."

Squirming out of his arms, I took a step back. "We need to talk about Miss Big Tits."

Hunter scowled. "It was funny the first time, but her name is Jennifer."

"Is it? Because she told me it was Ginny."

He sighed. "What about Jennifer?"

"You need to put her on a schedule. She's totally disrupting our whole routine."

"We talked about this last night," he said, shoving his hands in his pockets.

I pointed at him. "You gave her money. I saw you."

He rocked back on his heels. "Not that it's your business, but I did. She was going to be evicted. She's trying to get on a positive path, and I support that."

"She's lying to you! I bet she took the money from your wallet too," I said, crossing my arms.

"That's a big accusation. You got anything to back it up?"

"You didn't have a problem accusing me."

"I didn't accuse you. I asked you a question. Big difference."

"Come to think of it, don't you think it's a coincidence that your watch went missing and now there's money gone from your wallet? Cuz I do!" Now that I was thinking about it, it made perfect sense.

"I think that you're totally out of line and you hate Jennifer so much that you'd say anything to get rid of her. I think that I've had a lot on my plate lately and this shit isn't helping."

"Well, let me throw one more thing on top of that shit pile... I want her gone!"

"That's not your decision to make. I'm doing what's best for Carina. Don't ask me to choose between you and my daughter because you'll lose every time."

I pointed to my chest. "I would never ask you to do that. I'm asking you to choose between me and Jennifer! She's like a cancer eating away at everything good."

319

"Don't be a bitch. Jennifer is part of Carina's life, which means she's part of my life. If you don't like it, I don't know what to tell you. No one is forcing you to be here."

"You're absolutely right." Taking deep breaths, I left his office and went to my room. I pulled my suitcase from under the bed and started emptying my drawers into it. This was utter bullshit. I furiously threw my clothes into the suitcase, and when it was full, I went to the bathroom and dumped all my toiletries into a duffel bag.

Hunter stood in the bathroom doorway with his hands pressed to both sides. "What are you doing?"

I ducked under his arm. "Leaving, exactly as you suggested."

He turned around and followed after me. "I didn't suggest you leave."

"The hell you didn't!" I zipped my suitcase and yanked it to the floor, then dragged it down the hallway.

"Charli, you're being irrational."

I whipped around. "And apparently, a bitch. I don't need this bullshit. I was here for you and Carina. I'll be damned if I'm going to watch you be an oblivious asshole. Last chance… Jennifer or me?"

"You're not being fair. It's an impossible choice. I have to do what's best for my daughter and you know it!"

"I understand." But I didn't understand at all. It was as if everything I thought we had was an illusion. Like I made it out to be more than it was. And maybe I did. I made the mistake of falling in love with Hunter Dorsey when I shouldn't have. It was supposed to be a job. Nothing more. "We both knew this was going to end; I'm doing both of us a favor."

Ask me to stay.

Tell me not to go.

Say you love me.

Every silent plea went unanswered as he stood there and stared at me.

I pulled his credit card from my purse and set it on the counter, along with the apartment and car keys.

Doubt crept in. *Was I being irrational? Was I being a bitch? Was this a total overreaction?* Maybe, but I didn't know what else to do.

Hunter took my head between his hands and kissed me. "You don't have to do this."

I almost melted into his arms, but if I didn't stand my ground, nothing would change. "Give me a reason not to."

Ask me to stay.

Tell me not to go.

Say you love me.

"Good luck, Charli. I hope all your dreams come true."

My voice caught in my throat. "You too. I hope everything works out."

I thought about going in and saying goodbye to Carina, but that would only make it harder to leave. Instead, I slowly walked to the door, giving him one last chance. Willing him, with all I had, to say the words that would change my mind.

Ask me to stay.

Tell me not to go.

Say you love me.

I opened the door and dragged my suitcase through. "Bye, Hunter.

"Bye, dollface."

I made it to the elevator, down to the lobby, and out to the parking garage to the old pickup truck I'd barely driven over the past few months. My heart broke with every step I took.

Of all the ways I imagined us ending, this wasn't it. I drove across town to the only place I wanted to be and knocked on the door.

When it opened, my brother looked at my suitcase.

I shrugged as the tears welled in my eyes and fell down my face. "I need a place to stay."

Chapter 49
Hunter

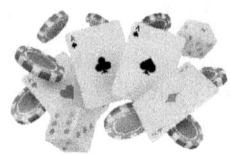

Tom walked into my office and threw a stack of papers on my desk. "You've got two thieves, not one."

I picked up the papers and scanned them. "What do you mean?"

"It's not only Leonard. His son is part of it too. Both of their names are all over this. Guess where the son works?"

As much as I wanted to know, I was more concerned with Charli. I hadn't heard a word from her since last night. The house was too quiet this morning when I woke Carina up to take her to Rose's. There was no fresh coffee. No witty banter. No kiss goodbye.

Just an empty, quiet apartment and my regret.

I should have asked her to stay.

I should have told her not to go.

I should have told her I loved her.

But I didn't do any of those things. I let her walk out the door.

"Have you talked to Charli?" I blurted.

Tom sighed. "She showed up at my place last night."

That was a relief. At least I knew where she was. "I didn't kick her out."

"I know. She told me what happened."

"She gave me an impossible choice." I didn't owe Tom shit, but I still felt the need to defend myself.

"If you say so." He sat in one of the plastic chairs. "Listen, it's not a secret that I never wanted her to work for you, and I definitely didn't want her to get involved with you, but you're not the same guy you used to be. I don't know if that's because of your daughter or Charli or some crazy epiphany, but I do know I'll always support my sister. I also know you were lucky to have her. You'll never find anyone as loyal, determined, or hardheaded as her. She's one of a kind."

Charli was all of those things and that's why I fell in love with her. "How is she?"

"Was up half the night crying. She was asleep on the couch when I left this morning."

I cringed. It killed me to know she cried. "I never wanted to hurt her."

"Yet, you did."

The guilt of that statement hit harder than I thought it would. "Yeah, I guess I did."

"She wanted me to find out if it was okay if she left the rest of her stuff at your place until she found an apartment."

"Of course, it's not going anywhere."

"Good. I'll let her know. Now, let's talk business. Do you want to know where the son works?"

I was still focused on Charli and didn't have a clue what he was talking about. "Whose son?"

"Leonard's son." Tom snapped his fingers at me. "Keep up."

"Right. Where does he work?"

"At the Bellagio. Looks like they've both been skimming from the company coffers. When we take Leonard down, it'll launch an investigation into the son, too."

I looked again at the papers Tom gave me. There was a corporate tree tracing back four levels and at the top were Leonard Moroski and Tobias

Moroski. "You're a genius, Tom. Thank you for doing this and thank you for not hacking into my life and destroying it."

"No promises on that yet. If Charli gives me the word, you're toast."

"Understood."

"As far as Leonard goes, I was happy to help. That guy is a total prick and—I can't even believe I'm saying this, but—I like you better. Even though you treated me and everyone else like shit, I think you're the right man for the job."

I swallowed the lump in my throat. "Thanks. When I get reinstated as CFO, I'm going to be better. It humbles me to say this, but I regret how I acted when I worked here before. This is where I want to be and I'm going to make things right."

Tom stood and pointed to the papers on my desk. "You're already making things right."

"It's a step in the right direction," I agreed.

"I can't say I understand why Charli fell in love with you, but you should think about making things right with her too."

His words didn't make sense. I was unlovable. I'd known it my whole life.

There was no way Charli was in love with me.

Was she?

Trent and I were already in my father's office when Leonard arrived. Trent casually sat opposite my father's desk while I leaned on the wall.

I'd been waiting for this for months and could barely contain my excitement, but it was imperative that Leonard not know about the bomb that was about to land on him.

"Have a seat, Leonard," my father instructed.

"What's going on?" he asked, pulling on his tie.

"It's an impromptu meeting." My father put his elbows on the desk and tapped his index fingers together. "We've been losing money for well over a year and, as I said in our staff meeting, I'm curious as to why that is. We've been running at near full capacity in the hotel and our casino floor has never been busier. The shows are packed, and our restaurant reservations are at a record level. I was wondering if, as CFO, you had any insight into why our profits are falling."

Leonard sat up taller. "I do have some thoughts."

"I'd love to hear them," my father said.

"In my opinion, we're overstaffed. That's why I cut my staff in the financial department. I was trying to do my part." My father leaned forward, encouraging him to continue. "Not only are we overstaffed, but we're paying them too much. Ask Hunter; he does the payroll. He can attest that what I'm saying is true."

All eyes turned toward me. I pushed off the wall and sat on the corner of my father's desk. "We do have a lot of staff; however, they are necessary to provide the services we offer. The wages we pay are generous but not overgenerous. Paying people well gives them an incentive to stay, and with less turnover, we can provide better services. It's one of the reasons people from all over the country come to Mystique. It's what keeps us at the top of the hospitality industry. Customers know our services are excellent and they'll be well taken care of. So, do I think cutting staff is the answer? No."

Leonard shook his head. "And this is why you're not the CFO anymore. Honestly, I don't even know why you're at this meeting."

"Oh, I think you'll find I have something very valuable to offer."

"Doubtful."

"I have a question," Trent said. "Didn't you work in Reno before coming to Las Vegas?"

"That's right."

"And why did you leave there?"

He waved Trent's question away. "It was time to move on. I don't understand what that has to do with Mystique's profits falling."

"Trust me, it's relevant," I said.

"You see, we've been doing some brainstorming, and we have some ideas." My father picked up the report Tom prepared and handed it over the desk to Leonard. "What do you know about this?"

Leonard took the papers and scanned them. A thin sheen of sweat broke out on his forehead. "What is this?"

"Oh, I think you know what it is," I answered.

"Actually, I don't." He set the papers back on my father's desk.

"Then I'm sure your attorney will be able to explain it." My father picked up his phone. "Send them in, please."

Within seconds, hotel security and the police—the real ones this time—entered the room.

Leonard jumped out of his chair. "What the hell is this?" he yelled.

The police officers stepped forward and wrenched Leonard's hands behind his back. "Leonard Moroski, you're under arrest for corporate embezzlement. You have the right to remain silent. Anything you say can and will be used against you in a court of law. You have the right to an attorney. If you cannot afford an attorney, one will be provided for you."

"This is complete bullshit! I'm going to sue your ass for false arrest and defamation! I'll sue you all!"

My father came around his desk and stood between Trent and me. "One more thing, Leonard. You're fired! Security will pack up your things and have them delivered." He nodded to the police, and they escorted Leonard Morosk-hole from the building.

"That felt good," Trent said.

"Really good," my father agreed. He turned to me and shook my hand. "The CFO job is yours. You've more than earned it."

Trent patted me on the back. "Welcome back, brother."

"Thank you. It feels good to be back."

My father smiled. "This is the way it was always supposed to be. It fills my heart to have both my sons here in their proper places."

I got my job back. I had my office back. And Leonard was going to prison.

I should have been the happiest guy in the world.

I got everything I wanted… except the girl.

Chapter 50
Charli

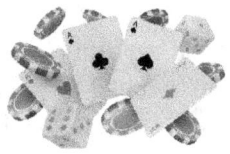

I shook the hand of the producer over his desk. "Welcome back, Charli."

"It's good to be back." I reauditioned and it went better than I could have hoped for. All the extra practice I'd done because of the personal training center Hunter built for me paid off. I was stronger and more confident than before my accident.

"We'll see you tomorrow."

"Thank you again. I won't let you down," I promised.

"I know you won't. I'm happy you're back."

I left the producer's office to find Jasmine waiting outside. When I came out, she held up her hands. "Well?"

I tried to suppress the smile from taking over my face. "I'm in."

Jasmine squealed and ran to me, wrapping me in her arms while jumping up and down. "The dynamic duo is back together again! I'm taking you to lunch."

We walked down the Strip arm in arm and ducked into one of the casinos for their world-famous burgers. I was thrilled that Oasis took me back, but it didn't pack the kind of punch I thought it would.

We scooted into opposite sides of the booth and the waitress dropped off two glasses of water. "This is so exciting!" Jasmine exclaimed.

I smiled as I pulled the wrapper off my straw, but it was weak at best. "Yep."

She tilted her head to the side. "Are you not excited to be coming back?"

I wrapped the paper around my finger. "No, I am. It's just… Hunter and I had a fight two days ago. I ended up packing my bags and leaving."

She covered my hands with hers. "Oh, honey! I'm so sorry. What happened?"

I told her the whole story about Jennifer and how she pretended to be someone else in the park. About how Hunter's watch went missing. About how she was always around yet barely tried to take care of Carina. About my ultimatum. When I was finished, I asked, "Am I wrong?"

"Sounds like she's a real piece of work. What does Hunter have to say about all this?"

I bowed my head. "He said no one was forcing me to stay. That was the straw that broke the camel's back. I thought I meant more to him, but I guess I was wrong. I think that's what kills me the most. I really fell for him."

Jasmine patted my hands. "I know you did, honey. If that man doesn't see what an amazing person you are, then he's not worth it."

"How come that doesn't make me feel any better?" I asked, twisting my lips to the side.

"Because he broke your heart."

Chapter 51
Hunter

When I got home from picking up Carina, Jennifer was waiting at my door. I don't know why it irritated me, but it did. I should have been in the best mood after moving back into my old office, even if it overlooked the dumpsters. It felt like a piece of my life had dropped back into its proper place.

Jennifer waved at me. "You're home late. I knocked, but Charli didn't answer. I've been out here waiting for like an hour."

"Charli's not home today." I left it vague. She didn't need to know that Charli moved out.

"Again? She wasn't here yesterday either. Sounds like you might need a new nanny."

I opened the door and sighed. I was going to need a new nanny. That was a fact I didn't want to think about. Some part of me was still hoping Charli would come back. "We're doing fine right now."

Jennifer walked in and dropped her large purse on the kitchen island. "I can help more if you need me to. All you have to do is ask," she singsonged.

"Did you get your rent paid?" Charli's words stuck in my head. *She's lying to you!* I didn't want to think it was true, but it was possible.

"Huh?"

"Your rent. Did you get it paid?"

"Oh yeah. My landlord was so happy. Thanks again for the help." Jennifer threw her arms over my shoulders, practically smothering my daughter, and kissed my cheek. "You're a lifesaver."

I gently untangled myself and handed her Carina. "I think she's wet. Can you change her for me?"

"Uh, yeah. Sure." She looked around for the diapers, like they would appear out of thin air.

"Diaper bag is on the chair."

Jennifer grabbed it and laid Carina on the rug, who rolled over and crawled toward the couch. Jennifer caught Carina and tried again. As she reached into the bag, Carina flipped over and snuck away on her hands and knees.

I watched this play out three times before I intervened. "Let me help you." I got all the supplies out and caught my daughter. "You're such a little speed demon now, aren't you?" I kissed her head and laid her down, then gave her a rattle to shake. Carina was so busy with her toy that she barely moved while I did the quick change.

"How did you do that?" Jennifer asked.

"I've watched Charli dozens of times. She's a real pro."

"Of course she is. When is she getting home? I was thinking she could make that chicken casserole she made last week. It was so good."

Jesus Christ! I was already mentally exhausted, and she'd only been here ten minutes. "Charli won't be home to make dinner and, really, it isn't part of her job, but the fridge is stocked; you're welcome to cook something."

She laughed. "I'm not much of a cook. I usually go for whatever is quick." Carina crawled over and sat at her feet and played with the straps

330

of her sandals. Jennifer pushed Carina's hand away, picking her up and placing her on her lap.

"Me neither." I went to the freezer and peered inside. "I have a frozen pizza."

"Hmm. Mario's down the street is better. Maybe we could order out."

I gritted my teeth and pulled the box from the freezer. "This is already paid for. It's frozen pizza or nothing."

"It's not like money is an issue for you." She laughed. "But if you want to go cheap on me, that's fine."

Calling me cheap after I gave her five grand for rent was insulting, but I held my tongue for the sake of my daughter. It was in Carina's best interest for her mother and me to get along. I preheated the oven and put the pizza on a tray, then leaned against the counter, watching her interact with my princess.

Jennifer held her up and spoke to her in a syrupy voice. "Did you miss your mama today? Can you say Mama?"

Carina kicked her legs. "No."

Jennifer frowned. "Say Mama."

"No!"

"I'm your mama!"

"No, no, no!"

I understood Jennifer's frustration, but I was oddly proud of my daughter for setting her boundaries. I stomped over and took Carina from her. "Hey, don't get upset with her; she's a baby. It's understandable that she'd be confused since you haven't been around."

"I've been around," she huffed. "I guess I'll have to spend more time with her. I can come over in the mornings and stay with her while you're at work. I mean, it would be better than having a stranger like Charli watch her. It doesn't seem like she's very dependable anyway."

Like hell I would let this woman stay in my apartment unsupervised. She could rob me blind or worse, take off with Carina, never to be seen again. "Charli has been dependable since day one. We won't need you to be here during the day."

"You can't keep me away from my child, Hunter. Kids need their moms."

I didn't disagree, but she should have thought about that when she dropped Carina at my front door. "No one is trying to keep you from her. I've been more than accommodating. You've gotten more visitation time than if you went through the court."

Her eyebrows raised. "Are you threatening to take me to court? Because we can go that route if you want to. You know, judges almost always rule in favor of the mother. I can take Carina away as fast as I gave her to you," she said with a snap of her fingers.

She poked at my one insecurity. The thought of not seeing my daughter every day had me backtracking. "I'm not threatening you; I'm only stating facts. I don't want to go through the court any more than you do. As long as we can keep it civil, I'm sure we can come to an agreement that works for both of us."

"Well, we already know we can be civil. We made Carina, didn't we? We were *very* civil that night." Her words were filled with innuendo. Yes, she had a pretty face and a banging body. Yes, we had sex. Yes, we were forever tied together by our daughter, but there was no spark, no chemistry. I felt nothing when I looked at her.

The only woman I wanted had walked out my door. She'd taken care of Carina, taken care of me and I took her for granted. She'd put up with my shit day after day without ever asking for a thing for herself. I would have given her everything, but I didn't give her the one thing she wanted most.

Me.

I should have asked her to stay.

I should have told her not to go.

I should have told her I loved her.

Now that she was gone, I realized what a fool I was for letting her leave.

Chapter 52
Charli

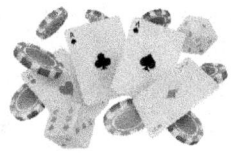

I had my first rehearsal with the cast of Dark Desires at Oasis. It felt good to be back in my element, soaring above the stage, feeling weightless and free. I put every ounce of energy I had into the routines. I lost myself in the music, contorting myself into unnatural positions and straining my muscles while making it look effortless. When I was twisted up in the silks, knowing one false move would send me crashing to the stage below, it was difficult to think about the things I was missing.

A hard body cocooning me in warmth while I slept.

Morning kisses and nighttime whispers.

Innocent giggles and toothless smiles.

If I thought too hard about it, I doubted my decision to walk away, even though I knew it was for the best. My time with Hunter was a fantasy. A pleasant interlude from the entire reason I came to Vegas. It was a welcome distraction.

But none of it was real.

The man I foolishly gave my heart to wasn't capable of loving me back. All the signs were there, but in true Charli fashion, I painted every red flag green. Just because I wanted something to be, didn't mean it was.

I couldn't even blame Hunter. He never made me promises.

It was my own fault for getting attached.

A sharp knock on the door broke me from my torturous thoughts. From my place on the couch, I turned to Tom who was making a sandwich in the kitchen. "Are you expecting company?"

He wiped his hands on a towel. "No. Are you?" I shook my head. "If that's Hunter, I'm going to be pissed. I don't want him here."

"It's not Hunter," I assured him. The man hadn't texted or called since I left. There was no way he'd come to Tom's apartment.

Tom opened the door to find Penny and Gia on the other side. They forced their way in. "Why didn't anyone tell us?" Penny asked. "I thought you were my friend, Tom."

My brother pushed up his glasses. "It wasn't my story to tell."

"I found out today that Carina has been staying with Rose during the day. I swear I'm going to kill my brother-in-law."

The girls were on fire, and I appreciated their unexpected support. I gave them a finger wave. "Hey, ladies."

They rushed to me, both giving me tight hugs. "What happened?" Penny asked. Gia was less subtle. "Do we need to rip his balls off?"

"I'm okay," I assured them.

Tom grabbed his sandwich from the kitchen. "I'm gonna go hang out in the other room," he said, hiking a thumb over his shoulder. He didn't do well with drama, and this was a bit much for him.

Gia sat down on the couch next to me. "Did he fire you? I swear, I thought that man had changed but he's the same old egotistical asshole."

As thankful as I was for their concern, I couldn't find it in myself to bad-mouth him. "It's not his fault. He didn't fire me or kick me out; I left on my own."

Penny sat on my other side. "Why? I thought things were going great."

"They were."

"Explain. You two seemed really into each other. What the hell happened?" Gia asked.

"Jennifer Johnson happened. Once she showed up, everything went downhill."

"You think he's into her?"

I wobbled my head back and forth. "I mean, she's pretty, so I wouldn't blame him if he was, but I don't think so. The woman was at the apartment every day and she drove me nuts. She didn't have the first clue how to take care of Carina, she treated me like her personal servant, and I think she was… is stealing from Hunter. He's so set on doing the right thing for his daughter that he's blind to all of it. I gave him an ultimatum: her or me."

"And he chose her," Penny concluded.

"In my eyes… yes. In his eyes, he chose his daughter. I'm not saying Jennifer can't be a part of Carina's life, but there has to be some boundaries. I don't trust her. I think her ulterior motive has more to do with bagging a millionaire than being a mother. I couldn't be a part of it any longer."

Gia tapped her fingers against her crimson lips. "Well, this complicates things. I came over here ready to castrate him. Do you think he still loves you?"

"I'm not sure he ever did," I said honestly. "I don't think he's built for love."

"The old Hunter, I'd agree… but he was different with you. Everyone saw it," Gia said.

"Everyone saw what they wanted to see, including me. I was the nanny, nothing more."

Penny put her hand on my shoulder. "I don't believe that. If it makes you feel any better, he's been completely miserable at work, growling at everyone."

"Him being miserable doesn't make me happy. I love Hunter and Carina. I miss them desperately, but I won't accept less than I deserve. He could have asked me to stay, but he didn't. He let me walk away. He didn't fight for me, and I want a man who thinks I'm worth fighting for. I don't think that's too much to ask."

335

Gia slumped. "Well, shit! You have a point. Trent followed me all the way back to Chicago. He drove through a snowstorm for me. That's how I knew he was the one."

"Brett didn't fight for me at first," Penny said. "I cried for days and took Tom to my sister's wedding instead. Then the big idiot showed up and made a huge spectacle of declaring his undying love for me. I enjoyed every minute of watching him squirm. It was pathetic, really, but he knew he'd messed up."

"See? That's what I'm talking about. I want that. I want the grand gesture."

"It could still happen. Maybe he needed you to leave to show him what he'd be missing."

"If he was missing me, he would have called or texted. It's been radio silence. It was a job and the job is over."

Penny wrapped her arms around me. "He might be too dumb to realize what a gem you are, but we're not. We're still going to drop in unannounced, go to lunch, and talk shit about the guys. You can never have too many girlfriends."

"I second that," Gia said, joining the hug.

"Thank you."

I may have lost Hunter, but I gained two great women in my life. That should have made me happy, yet I was afraid it would make losing him harder. A clean break would be easier. Less messy. Less reminders.

So, even though I could have used more friends, I had no intention of being theirs.

Chapter 53
Hunter

Every day without Charli was like a knife in my gut. I missed her sassy mouth, her gentle soul, and her loving heart. When she first moved into my apartment, she made me crazy, but now I craved her brand of chaos that breathed life into these four walls.

Jennifer still showed up like clockwork, her behavior becoming more erratic and annoying with each visit. It suffocated me. I was a prisoner in my own home. Once a place of solitude, my apartment was now more like a torture chamber.

I couldn't hide that Charli was no longer here. Too many days passed without her making an appearance.

Yesterday, Jennifer showed up with a suitcase, suggesting it would be easier if she moved in. *Fuck that!* The woman may have been Carina's mother, but the only thing we had in common was that we'd contributed DNA to create another human being. I felt nothing for her.

I wanted one day when she wasn't waiting for me when I got home from work.

Today wasn't that day.

She stood outside my door with a bag of groceries. "I brought dinner," she said, holding up the bag.

Finally, something useful. "Great."

She looked less put together than usual. Her hair was disheveled, like she'd been running her fingers through it all day and her lipstick was smeared, leaving a small streak on her chin. She spoke a million miles a minute, barely taking a breath. "It's nothing fancy, but I figured who needs fancy? Sometimes a girl needs comfort food. My mom always made me mac and cheese when I was a kid. We couldn't afford much but we always had mac and cheese. Nothing but the best for my little boo-boo bear."

I hated that nickname. It grated on my nerves like spreadsheets without headings. Princess Poops-a-Lot was funny, little boo-boo bear was annoying.

Even though Jennifer had been coming over for weeks, I still never got a straight answer about why she abandoned Carina. Every time I looked at my daughter, I couldn't imagine my life without her. Something didn't add up, but I'd yet to discover it.

Inside the apartment, I threw my keys and wallet on the island. I was at my wits' end with this woman. "You know, you don't have to be here every day. Maybe we could come up with a schedule."

Jennifer unloaded the groceries on the kitchen counter. "Don't be silly. I don't mind coming over, although you do have an empty bedroom. If I moved in it would be so much easier for you. I could watch Carina while you're at work like a mother should."

Again, with the moving in shit. The woman was either oblivious or delusional. I hadn't decided which yet. "Not happening."

She filled a pot with water and turned on the stove, then shook a spoon at me. "I'll change your mind. You like me; I can tell. We're family whether you admit it or not."

The fuck we were. Delusional. She was definitely delusional.

A knock on the door saved me from raining down reality on her bizarre parade. *Please let it be Charli.* She was the only one I wanted to see.

It wasn't Charli.

My brother stood on the other side of the door. I couldn't remember the last time he'd been here, but it had been years. "What the hell are you doing here?"

Trent pushed his way in. "I'm checking on you. Why didn't you tell me Charli was gone?"

I didn't owe him any explanations, but I was glad he was here. I'd been going stir-crazy keeping all this to myself. "I figured everyone would think I did something to her, and I didn't want to hear what a fuckup I was again."

He raised his eyebrow. "Did you fuck up?"

I grabbed the back of my neck and pulled on it. "I don't know. Maybe."

Jennifer pranced into the hallway. "Who's at the door?"

"Jennifer, this is my brother, Trent. Trent, meet Jennifer, Carina's mother."

Trent held out his hand, but Jennifer bypassed it, opting to inappropriately ambush him in a hug. "Oh, wow! I didn't know you had a brother!" Once she released him, she playfully swatted my shoulder. "You should have told me we were having company. I'm not sure we'll have enough for dinner."

"Oh, I'm not staying for dinner," Trent said.

"Are you suuurrre?" she asked, drawing out the word and gesturing wildly. "It's mac and cheeeeese."

"Sounds great, but I'll have to pass."

"Suit yourself," she said with a shrug, prancing back into the kitchen.

"That's Carina's mom?" Trent whispered. "Is she okay?"

I motioned for him to follow me to my office. Once inside, I locked the door. "She's driving me nuts! Every day it's the same shit. She just shows up here. It's getting weirder and weirder... *she's* getting weirder and weirder. She thinks we're going to be one big happy family. Yesterday she showed up with a suitcase."

"What the fucking fuck? You gotta get rid of her."

"How? Charli warned me this would happen. She told me to set boundaries, but did I listen? Nope. I thought she was being jealous."

339

"Did you kick Charli out?" he asked gruffly.

I ran my hands through my hair and tugged on the ends. "No. She wanted me to choose between her and Jennifer. She left when I told her I wouldn't do it. I thought I was doing what's best for Carina."

"And you think *that* is what's best for Carina?" He pointed toward the kitchen. "I hate to tell you this… but you fucked up big time. I've known the woman for two seconds and I can tell she's a loony toon."

"I know. I know. It's gotten worse. I've tried to drop hints, but she's not getting it. I don't know what to do. I don't want to take Carina's mom away from her."

Trent rested his hands on his hips and blew out his breath. "Is Jennifer worth losing Charli over?"

"I've already lost her."

"Do you want her back?"

"I'm miserable without her." That was the truth. Nothing was the same since Charli walked out of my life. "I shouldn't have let her leave. I should have asked her to stay. I should have told her I love her."

My brother smirked at me. "I knew it. You *are* in love with her. Feels like half of you is missing when she's not around?"

I nodded. "The better half."

"I won't disagree with that."

"Fuck! Why did it take me so long to figure this out?"

"Because we're men and we're too stubborn to admit when we're wrong."

"So what now?"

"You go in there and tell her she has to leave. Then you take her to court and do this the right way."

Fear coursed through me. "What if they take Carina away from me?"

"Don't worry about that. You have a whole group of people supporting you and Sam Steinburg is the best attorney in Vegas. She may get visitation, but everything is up for negotiation."

I nodded my head. "Okay… you're right. We'll tell the court everything. She gave Carina up once and she's a flight risk. We'll push for supervised visitation."

Trent put his hand on my shoulder. "Now you're thinking straight. This situation you have going on here isn't sustainable. You need to put an end to it."

Determined to do what was best for Carina and myself, I marched out of my office with Trent hot on my heels. In the kitchen, the pot of noodles boiled over while Carina banged on the tray of her high chair. "Da, da, da, da, da."

Jennifer was nowhere to be found.

"Where the hell is she? Did she leave?" Trent asked, as he turned off the stove.

Her oversized purse sat on the counter. "She's here somewhere. I'll check the bathroom." I rushed down the hall to where I bathed Carina and knocked on the closed door. "Jennifer?" When there was no answer, I knocked and twisted the knob. "Jennifer, unlock the door!" More silence followed. "I swear to god, if you make me kick down this door I'm going to be pissed."

Out of patience, I raised my foot and kicked the door. The flimsy lock gave way and the door flew open.

"Fuck!"

Jennifer was sprawled out on the floor, unconscious, with blood dripping from her nose. Lines of white powder covered the counter.

"Trent! Call 9-1-1!"

I'd been sitting in the emergency waiting room for the last hour. I performed CPR on Jennifer while we waited for the ambulance. When EMS arrived, they used a defibrillator on her to get a pulse. There was no telling the damage that was done, but thankfully she was alive.

I may not have liked her, but I wished her no ill will either.

However, the night's events made me question everything about Jennifer. All I knew about her was what the private investigator dug up. I didn't really *know* her.

All of Charli's accusations, which I thought were insane at the time, now seemed credible. I searched through my apartment's security cam footage from the last few weeks. Sure enough, Jennifer took my watch, money from my wallet, bottles of booze, pills from my cabinets, and even a picture of Carina I had on my refrigerator. I was positive the five grand I gave her never went to rent.

Trent and my father showed up at the emergency room with Sam. I stood and shook their hands. "Thank you for coming."

"There's nowhere else we'd be. We're family and we support each other," my father said.

Family.

It was a word I hated growing up, because I never felt like I was part of the family. I snubbed my nose at them every chance I got, but ever since Carina showed up, they'd been there for me. No matter how hard I pushed them away, they pulled me back in. I finally realized I was stronger with their support than I was on my own. And although my own mother didn't give a shit about me, I had people who did.

"Where's Carina?" I left her with Trent when I followed the ambulance.

"Mom and Gia are with her at your apartment. She's in good hands," Trent answered.

Mom.

That was another word I'd hated. I never saw Rose as my mom, but as a woman who was forced to care for me. That I was the son she never wanted. The truth was, I never gave her a chance. She did everything a mom was supposed to do and I practically spit in her face. I'd have been lost without her after Charli left. Rose never once hesitated to step up and help, even after I treated her like a pile of dog shit.

Amends.

I needed to make them. Not only with Rose, but my entire family. Carina deserved better from me.

"Did you bring the papers?" I asked Sam.

He nodded and handed the documents to me. "Everything is there. The conditions are clearly written. All she has to do is sign them."

"And the other arrangements?"

"It's taken care of," my father assured me.

Sam took off, but my father and brother stayed with me while I waited to see Jennifer. It was three more hours before I was allowed to see her.

When I walked in her room, she looked like a shell of herself. This was not the same woman who showed up unexpectedly at my door.

I sat in the chair next to her bed. "How do you feel?"

"Like shit." She looked away from me and stared off into space.

"We have some things to discuss. I won't have drugs around my daughter. You need help."

She slowly turned her head and glared at me. "You think I don't know that. It's why I brought Carina to you in the first place. I needed to work on myself. I wanted to be a good mother... I just fell off the wagon."

Finally, an honest answer about how Carina ended up on my doorstep. "You stole from me, you lied to me, and you put my daughter in danger. I don't take any of that lightly."

Her eyes welled with tears. "I'm sorry."

"I don't want your apologies. I want you to get your shit together. You're going to rehab." She started to balk, but I cut her off. "Once you finish the program, you'll submit to weekly drug testing. If you stay sober, you can start seeing Carina with supervised visitation. Until then, you won't be seeing her. You'll sign off on your parental rights and the conditions you need to meet to restore them."

Tears fell down Jennifer's cheeks. "I can't afford rehab."

"It's already been taken care of. You'll go directly from here to the facility. All the arrangements have been made."

"I have a life. A job, a dog, and an apartment. I can't up and leave."

"You can if you ever want to see your daughter again. All you have to do is sign the papers and follow the stipulations, otherwise I'll take you to court and have your parental rights permanently revoked. I'll bury you so deep in court fees, it'll take you years to dig out. No judge will grant custody to a drug addict." As much as I hated using money as a weapon, I did it for my daughter.

She crossed her arms and sobbed. "This isn't fair."

"What isn't fair is putting your daughter in danger. I don't want to take Carina away from you, but make no mistake, I'll stop at nothing to make sure she's safe." I shoved the papers and a pen in front of her. "All you have to do is sign and you'll have a chance to see her again."

Jennifer reluctantly took the pen and scribbled her name on the documents. "I'm going to do it. I'm going to get clean."

"I hope you do." I left her room and returned to the waiting area.

"Did she sign them?" my father asked.

"Yes." I hated what I did, but it was best for my daughter. "Not only was she using drugs, but she was stealing from me. The signs were there but I never saw them. I wanted Carina to have a mother so bad that I was blind to everything."

My father put his hand on my shoulder. "Don't be so hard on yourself. You, more than anyone, should know that blood doesn't make someone a mother… actions and love do."

He was talking about Rose, but I was thinking about Charli.

"If you want a mom for Carina," Trent said, "I know someone who'd be perfect for the job."

I ran my hand over the scruff on my chin. "Yeah, me too."

Trent slapped me on the back. "Then go get your girl."

That was exactly what I planned to do, and I hoped I wasn't too late.

Chapter 54
Charli

Every day that passed without hearing from Hunter made my heart sink further into my stomach. I put off looking for an apartment in the hope he would choose me over Jennifer, even though it was blatantly obvious he didn't.

Gia and Penny had tried to take me out for a girls' night, but I declined. Being around them would only remind me of what I lost. It was better to move forward instead of looking back. It hurt less.

Returning to Oasis and immersing myself in work was what was best for me. I spent endless hours in the gym and at the training center. Jasmine was right by my side.

"Are you ready?" She bounced on her toes as we stood backstage waiting.

"As ready as I'll ever be." This was my first performance since the accident. I was filled with anticipation, covered from head to toe in sequins and glitter. My muscles hummed and my heart beat erratically. I'd be lying to say that getting on the stage again didn't make me nervous, but I was ready. I'd been waiting months for this.

The stage went black, and I took my place at the bottom of the silks, wrapping the fabric around my leg. As soon as "Bring Me To Life" by Evanescence started, the spotlight flicked on, illuminating me. It was then that the audience disappeared... it was just me and the music and thirty feet of fabric. Nothing else mattered but being in the moment.

I began climbing, pulling myself up with my arms as I wrapped the fabric around my foot as an anchor. Up, up, up I went, and when I got to the top, I realized a tear was running down my cheek. The damn song was like a punch to the gut, the words about needing to feel something to live consumed me, because lately... I'd felt nothing.

Extending my legs above my head, I spun them like a helicopter, weaving the fabric between and around my legs and back like a harness. It was enough to support my weight, and I let go, suspending myself in the air as my arms and legs extended and my back arched. With one arm, I reached down and grabbed the silks, spinning them in tight circles, making my body twirl faster and faster until everything became a blur of light and sound.

With the silks wrapped tightly around my waist, I let go and let my body drop until I was jerked to a dramatic halt, cradled in the fabric. With a few twists and turns, I unwrapped the material from my waist and wove it around and around my legs, securing it tightly to my ankles with intricate layers. Although the silks weren't technically knotted, they would hold. With one twist of my shoulder, I began a free fall toward the stage as the fabric unraveled from my body. Like a shot of adrenaline coursing through my veins, I felt alive for the first time in days.

With every maneuver, every carefully choreographed spin of my legs or extension of my arms, I felt more and more like myself. My muscles burned, and my heart thumped wildly as I prepared for the final drop, wrapping the fabric between my legs and over my shoulders, securing it tight behind my bent knee. When the music hit its final crescendo, I straightened my leg, releasing the material and tumbling head over heels toward the floor with only one wrap around my waist to keep me from crashing.

Hanging upside down, I hooked the silks around my knee and slid to the bottom, where I swayed back and forth as the music ended, the strands of my long hair barely brushing the floor.

Applause thundered in the theater as the stage went black. I lowered myself to my feet and exited the stage, running into Jasmine's open arms. "You killed that, bitch! Hands down your best performance ever."

I hugged her tightly, not wanting to let go. "Thank you." Somewhere between climbing to the top of the silks and tumbling to the bottom, I made peace with the idea of living without Hunter. I'd always cherish our time together, but this is what I was meant to do. I remembered his parting words to me. *I hope all your dreams come true.* I believed he meant it, and I had no right to complain. I *was* living my dream. That was more than most people could say.

I made my way to the dressing room, accepting compliments and high fives from the other performers as I went. Although I would usually perform multiple times during a show, the producer thought it best I started with one routine on my first night back. I didn't argue. Performing in front of an audience was much different than in the training center. Hopefully, tonight I proved I was ready. I needed it.

Opening the door to our shared dressing room, I gasped. It was full of red roses. Not a single vase, but dozens of arrangements on every flat surface. My chest filled with apprehension; the flowers had to be from Hunter. I wasn't sure if they were a congratulations, a goodbye, or a second chance.

I cautiously entered the room, inhaling the overpowering scent. There on my vanity was a letter. I picked up the envelope and saw Hunter's perfect handwriting. *Dollface.*

Quickly opening the envelope, I pulled out the sheets of paper inside. Taking a deep breath, I unfolded them and read.

Dollface~

I'm writing this letter because I'm shit with words and when it comes to you, I've never said the right ones.

I knew from the moment I looked into your pretty blue eyes I was in trouble. You were too beautiful, too innocent, too good. I knew you'd have the power to destroy me.

I didn't want to let you into my life, yet you snuck into the cracks of my black heart and made a home there. You nurtured and healed and filled it with love. No matter how big of a jerk face I was, you still saw the good in me… until I pushed you away.

I realize now all the mistakes I made. I should have listened to your intuition. I should have known you had not only my best interest at heart, but Carina's too. You were right about everything, and I was a fool for doubting you.

I have missed the ever-loving fuck out of you. I should have told you not to leave. I should have asked you to stay. And most importantly, I should have told you I loved you.

You see, I thought I was doing the right thing by setting you free. You deserve to have all of your dreams come true. You deserve better than a bastard like me, but I'm a selfish prick, so I'm going to make you a proposal.

A job offer…

I need a woman who will stand by my side through the good and the bad. A woman who will call me on my bullshit and tell me when I'm being a complete asshole. A woman who will love me despite my faults, because I have many. A woman who has enough room in her heart for not only me, but my daughter as well. A woman who will love Carina like her own and teach her the true meaning of strength and beauty.

This job doesn't come with a paycheck but a promise.

I promise to take care of you and put no one else before my girls. I promise to support your dreams and help you fulfill your every fantasy. I will hold you up when you are weak and stand back when it's your time to shine. I will respect you, cherish you, and defend you. But most importantly, I promise to love you each and every day for as long as you will have me.

You make me a better man. Please come home because I am so lost without you.

~Hunter

The words blurred as tears poured down my face. It wasn't poetic, but it was everything I was so desperate to hear.

Although I was supposed to stay until the end of the show, I needed to see Hunter. I needed to look in his eyes to see if the words he wrote were true. My heart was starting to heal; I couldn't take the chance he would break it again.

Without changing my clothes, I put on my shoes then grabbed my purse and duffel bag. The door cracked open, and Jasmine squeezed through, shutting it behind her. She motioned to the flowers. "Where the hell did these come from?"

"Hunter."

"Wow! The man doesn't know the meaning of moderation, does he?"

I shook my head. "He tends to go a bit overboard. It's not the flowers that have me reeling though, it's this." I shoved the handwritten letter at her.

She quickly read it and looked up at me. "Do you believe him?"

"He has no reason to lie. I want to believe him, but I don't want to get hurt again."

Jasmine pouted her lips. "The only risks you'll regret are the ones you don't take. A man doesn't write shit like this unless he means it."

I bit the side of my fingernail. "It's reckless."

A smile spread across her face. "Then it sounds right up your alley."

"Cover for me, will ya?"

She grabbed my hands and gave them a tight squeeze. "Of course. Go get your man."

I threw open the dressing room door and almost collided with Hunter's hard chest. "Hi," he said, holding Carina on his hip, her eyes closed and her head resting on his shoulder. It was way past her bedtime.

Seeing them was a shock. I thought I'd have more time to think. I wasn't ready for him. "Hi."

"I saw your performance. It was as beautiful as you. You took my breath away, Charli."

"Thank you," I said, lowering my eyes at the unexpected compliment.

"Did you get my flowers?"

I chuckled. "Yeah, they're hard to miss."

"Did you read the letter?"

My eyes welled with tears. "I did."

He cupped my cheek with his free hand. "I love you, Charli. I've never said that to another woman before. No one has ever been worthy of my love. I'm not saying I'm worthy of yours, but I'd like the chance to prove that I can be."

My heart shattered again for an entirely different reason. "You are worthy of my love. You've had it for months. Walking away from the both of you was the hardest thing I've ever done."

"We miss you, Charli. So damn much. Come home with us and be a family."

Carina's eyes fluttered open. She reached out to me with her little hands. "Mama."

I smiled and more tears fell down my cheeks. "How can I say no to that?" Taking Carina from his arms, I hugged her to my chest and placed lipstick kisses all over her chubby face.

Hunter stuffed his hands in his pockets. "Does this mean you'll accept the position? Your boss is a dick, but the benefits are outstanding," he said, nodding to Carina.

I laughed. "I'm not worried about the boss. I know how to handle him."

"You certainly do." He held my face in both his hands and pressed his lips to mine. "I love you, Charlotte Bently. Let's go home."

Whoever said you can't have it all was wrong. I had a job performing, a man who loved me, and the start of a family. Life didn't get much better than that.

Epilogue
Hunter

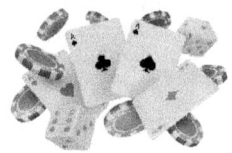

I stood in Trent's office, staring out the window that overlooked the casino. I used to be jealous of his view. I saw it as another thing Trent had that I didn't. A symbol of our father's love.

Now, I realized it was nothing but a piece of glass. It didn't mean shit.

Since working together to get rid of Leonard, the two of us were on better terms. We realized we could accomplish so much more when we weren't trying to rip each other's throats out. We'd spoken to the prosecutors for Leonard's embezzlement case. The evidence was solid, and it went deeper than Mystique. Seemed he and his son had been running this scam all over the country, never staying in one place more than a couple of years. Detectives were looking into their employment in Reno, Atlantic City, and New Orleans. Leonard and his piece-of-shit son were going to prison for a long time. I heard his wife filed for divorce. The guy lost everything because of greed, and he deserved whatever punishment was handed down.

Getting our money back was a different story. All of the Moroskis' assets had been seized. It could take years for the funds to be returned to us. Every casino involved wanted their piece of the pie and we'd be lucky if we recovered half of what he stole.

Trent entered his office with a scowl, closing the door behind him. "I told you I'd bring it tonight."

"Yeah, but I'm an impatient fuck. I couldn't wait."

He thrust the box into my hand. "Gia had it specially made. Don't forget to thank her."

"I won't." I opened the box and held up the piece of fabric. "It's perfect."

"You know Tom is going to have a fit about this," Trent said, sitting on the edge of his desk.

"Meh. He'll get over it. See you at six?"

He gave me a salute. "We'll be there."

I rushed home to Charli. She'd been back with me, where she belonged, for the last two months. I never knew true happiness before her.

It changed everything.

That wasn't exactly right... *she* changed everything.

Today, we were celebrating Carina's first birthday. Our apartment was decked out in balloons and streamers. Charli was in the kitchen, putting the last of the decorations on the cake.

I came up behind her, wrapping my arms around her waist. "Everything looks fantastic. You outdid yourself."

She turned her head to kiss me. "It's not every day that your princess turns one."

"Our princess," I corrected.

"It's too bad Jennifer is missing it."

"That was her choice, not ours." It only took Jennifer eleven days to check herself out of rehab and disappear. We hadn't heard from her since. I had no doubt that she would show up again one day. I wouldn't keep my daughter from knowing her, but Jennifer would have to prove herself before I'd let her anywhere near Carina.

"I know. I may not have liked the woman, but it still makes me sad that Carina won't have her mother here."

"She has you. You're the only mom she needs."

"You're too sweet."

They were words I never thought I'd hear out of a woman's mouth. I was a lot of things, but sweet wasn't one of them, except when it came to Charli and my daughter. They brought out the best in me. "Where is my baby girl?"

"She tired herself out crawling all over the apartment. I put her down for a nap about an hour ago."

"I'm going to wake her up."

Charli groaned. "Don't you know not to wake a sleeping baby?"

"It's her special day. I don't want her to miss it," I said as I walked down the hallway to the nursery. Carina was wide awake, chewing on her toes. "Today's the day, princess." I rubbed her round belly and tickled her.

After getting Carina cleaned up, I put her in the special dress and bloomers Charli had laid out on the dresser. Then I combed her soft, blond hair and put a pink barrette in to hold it back. She had grown so much in the past six months, and I dreaded the day she wouldn't need me anymore. But no matter how big she got, I'd always love and protect her. And although I was disappointed in Jennifer, I couldn't hate her. She gave me the best gift I was ever given. "Are you ready for your party?"

Carina patted my cheeks with her chubby hands. "Da, da, da, da, da."

At six o'clock on the dot, our guests began arriving: my dad and Rose, Trent and Gia, and Brett and Penny. We even invited Tom, who begrudgingly accepted the invitation. Although the guy was still skeptical of me, I was growing on him like a fungus. There was no way he was getting rid of me.

After cake and ice cream, where Carina smashed her fists into her own personal cake and shoved handfuls of the sticky goodness into her mouth, it was time for gifts. We all gathered around the living room as Charli and I sat on the floor with Carina, helping her pull the paper from the packages. She was more interested in the ribbons and boxes than the actual presents, but no one seemed to care. There were plenty of *ooohs* and *aaahs*, and

Rose took about a bazillion pictures. I couldn't have asked for a better grandma for my daughter.

There was no lack of love in the room for my princess. She'd won the hearts of her entire family and blood had nothing to do with it. There wasn't one of them who wouldn't do just about anything for Carina. She would grow up knowing she was loved and that was what I wanted most for her.

When the last gift had been opened, I reached behind the couch for one more. "What's that?" Charli asked.

"Seems like we almost forgot one." I put Carina on my lap and took the special gift Gia purchased for me out of the box. Pulling it over Carina's head, I pulled the shirt down over her dress. "It's perfect."

"Let me see," Charli insisted.

I set Carina on her feet and held her little hands as I helped her walk over to Charli, whose eyes began to mist. My daughter giggled the whole time and fell into Charli's waiting arms. Tears ran down her cheeks as she hugged Carina.

The shirt said, *Will you marry my daddy?*

I got on my knee and pulled the emerald-cut diamond ring from my pocket. "Charlotte Bently, you are the love of my life. You've done the impossible and turned me into a man people can tolerate." That earned a round of laughter from the room. "You've been the only mom Carina knows, and because of you, she's thriving. You opened your heart to us and turned this place into a home. There's only one thing missing, and that's this ring on your finger. Will you do us the honor of marrying me?"

Charli was a sobbing mess. She nodded her head frantically.

"I need to hear the words, Charli. Will you marry me?"

"Yes! A thousand times, yes!"

I slipped the ring on her finger and wrapped both of them in my arms. "Thank you, dollface, for making me the happiest man in the world."

Behind us, everyone clapped and hollered except for Tom. "Are you serious?" he groaned. "You're going to be my brother-in-law?"

"Must be your lucky day," I said with a smirk.

He frowned. "Don't think this lets you off the hook. If you hurt my sister, I won't hesitate to dox your ass and expose every questionable thing you've ever done in your life and that will only be the beginning of my retribution."

"Understood." I wasn't worried. Although I had no doubt that Tom would follow through with his threats, I wouldn't give him a reason. If Carina was my princess, then Charli was my queen. There wasn't a single thing I wouldn't do to make her happy.

Another Epilogue
Charli

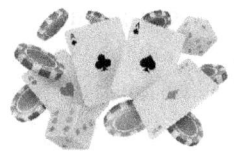

"She's going to break her neck."

I patted my husband on the back. "Relax, big guy. She's a natural."

Carina did back handsprings across the mat, sticking the landing like a pro. At eight years old, she was way ahead of the other girls in the class.

Our four-year-old, Harper, stood on her head and tried to somersault but landed on her bottom with a hard thud. She wanted to be like her big sister; however, I had a feeling gymnastics wouldn't be her thing.

Hunter held our youngest daughter, who had just turned two. "I wants to twy, Daddy," Madison said, wiggling out of his arms.

"You're too little, honey!" he yelled as she ran to me and grabbed my legs.

"Come on. Let's show Daddy how it's done," I encouraged her.

She squatted on the mat and put her arms out. I tucked her into a ball and helped her roll over. Madison stood with her hands in the air proudly. "Ta-da!"

He slow clapped. "Excellent job."

I rubbed my swollen belly as I got kicked in the kidney. "Somebody else wants to join in too."

"That's my boy," Hunter said, putting his hands on my stomach.

I shook my head. "We don't know that yet." Hunter and I decided not to find out the sex of our fourth and final child. He was hoping for a son, but I was convinced it was another daughter. My husband was severely outnumbered, but he didn't seem to care. He embraced being a girl dad.

I quit performing when we got pregnant with Harper. As Mrs. Hadley had warned me that day at the pool, the younger, prettier girls swept in and replaced Jasmine and me. I wasn't as heartbroken as I thought I would be. I'd lived my dream, and it was time to move on to the next stage in my life.

Hunter bought me an old warehouse and decked it out with all the best equipment. Jasmine and I started our own business, training the next generation of performers. The gym was an automatic success. Every parent, hoping their child would be the next star of Vegas, poured through our doors. It wasn't quite the same as being in the spotlight, but it let me continue doing what I loved and spend time with my family.

Shortly after Hunter proposed, we got married in Colorado, overlooking the mountains at sunset. We were surrounded by our friends and family who loved and supported us, even my brother, who still threatened Hunter at least once a month. Carina toddled down the aisle, throwing handfuls of flowers at the guests and was the cutest flower girl anyone had ever seen. Trent, who was Hunter's best man held her through the entire ceremony and even let her hold the rings.

When we returned to Vegas, Hunter and I bought a house close to his parents. Rose was a tremendous help with Carina, and later our other daughters. I seriously didn't know how we would have done it without her. Hunter made amends with Rose, and the first time he called her Mom, she burst into tears.

I learned that dreams and aspirations aren't stagnant things. They change over time, twisting and turning to become something beautiful. As I looked at my growing family, I knew I'd made the right choices, especially the reckless one to ignore everyone's warnings and take a nanny position from Hunter.

Who knew the day I showed up at Mystique looking for a job would lead to all of this? We might have had a bumpy start, but somewhere along the way… all my dreams came true.

What's next?
Technically Yours in Vegas

Read Tom's story, a friend-to-lovers, instant millionaire romance. No one can know Aurora's true identity... not even Tom. But in a city that never sleeps, secrets don't stay buried forever.

Want to know what happens at Hunter & Charli's wedding?
Get the **exclusive bonus scene** for free by signing up for my newsletter. This is the only place it's available!

https://www.subscribepage.com/
behaving_badly_in_vegas_bonus_scene

Get caught up with:
What Happens in Vegas (Trent & Gia)
Billionaire Bachelor in Vegas (Brett & Penny)

Thank you so much for choosing to read
Behaving Badly in Vegas. If you enjoyed the story, please leave a review on Amazon, Goodreads, or BookBub. They help so much!

Don't Want to Say Goodbye?

Check Out My Other Books:

Hearts Trilogy
Hearts on Fire
Shattered Hearts
Reviving My Heart

Wild Hearts Trilogy
Wild Hearts
Secrets of the Heart
Eternal Hearts

Forever Inked Novels
Tattooed Hearts: Tattooed Duet #1
Tattooed Souls: Tattooed Duet #2
Smoke and Mirrors
Regret and Redemption
Sin and Salvation

Vegas Love Series
What Happens in Vegas
Billionaire Bachelor in Vegas
Behaving Badly in Vegas
Technically Yours in Vegas

Acknowledgments

Thank you for choosing to read ***Behaving Badly in Vegas***. I loved telling the story of Hunter and Charli. This book has been brewing in my head for a long time. Hunter is a complicated character with a lot of layers. It was important to me to keep all his rough edges while still giving him redemption and a healthy dose of karma. I have plans for Tom too. Stay tuned for his story.

To my husband~ I could have never done this without your love and support. Thank you for affording me the opportunity to do what I really love. Not many people get the chance to retire from their job to pursue their passion. For that I will be forever grateful. Also, technology scares the crap out of me, and you've been a patient saint walking me through all my mishaps and frustrations. Thank you for believing in me!

To Linda and Heather~ You ladies are the best beta readers anyone could ask for! You've supported my journey and given me pep when mine was all gone. Your suggestions, critiques, and encouragement helped me in ways you'll never understand. Your constructive criticism improved this book so much and helped make it into something I'm proud of. I could never thank you enough for your help!

To my readers~ Thank you for supporting me in this journey. There are thousands of books that you could have chosen to read, and I am honored you chose mine. Please spread the word and leave a quick review on Amazon, Goodreads, or BookBub if you have enjoyed this book. Without you, writing would still be a dream.

About the Author

Sabrina Wagner writes sweet, sassy, sexy romance novels featuring stubborn men and the women who bring them to their knees. Her books will make you swoon, break your heart, and tickle your funny bone. They include found family, witty banter, and second chances.

Sabrina believes true friends should be treasured, a woman's strength is forged by the fire of affliction, and everyone deserves a happy ending. It's rare to find her without a book in her hand or a story spinning through her head. She's a hopeless romantic and knows all too well that life is full of twists and turns, but the bumpy road is what leads to our true destination.

Want to be the first to learn book news, updates and more?
Sign up for her Newsletter.
https://www.subscribepage.com/sabrinawagnernewsletter

www.ingramcontent.com/pod-product-compliance
Lightning Source LLC
Chambersburg PA
CBHW071204250626
47159CB00001B/201